Hot Single Docs: Meeting His Match

SUSAN CARLISLE

TINA BECKETT

WENDY S. MARCUS

D1494049

MILLS & BOON

Published in Great Britain 2018
by Mills & Boon, an imprint of HarperCollins*Publishers*
1 London Bridge Street, London, SE1 9GF

HOT SINGLE DOCS: MEETING HIS MATCH © 2018 Harlequin Books S.A.

NYC Angels: The Wallflower's Secret © 2013 Harlequin Books S.A
Special thanks and acknowledgement are given to Susan Carlisle for her contribution to the *NYC Angels* series.

NYC Angels: Flirting with Danger © 2013 Harlequin Books S.A
Special thanks and acknowledgement are given to Tina Beckett for her contribution to the *NYC Angels* series.

NYC Angels: Tempting Nurse Scarlet © 2013 Harlequin Books S.A
Special thanks and acknowledgement are given to Wendy S. Marcus for her contribution to the *NYC Angels* series

ISBN: 978-0-263-26810-2

09-0818

MIX
Paper from
responsible sources
FSC™ C007454

Susan C.. ixth gr...... .... Not allowed to watch TV until she'd brought the grade up, Susan filled her time with books. She turned her love of reading into a passion for writing, and now has over ten Medical Romances published through Mills & Boon. She writes about hot, sexy docs and the strong women who captivate them. Visit SusanCarlisle.com.

Born to a family that was always on the move, **Tina Beckett** learned to pack a suitcase almost before she knew how to tie her shoes. Fortunately she met a man who also loved to travel, and she snapped him right up. Married for over twenty years, Tina has three wonderful children and has lived in gorgeous places such as Portugal and Brazil.

Living where English reading material is difficult to find has its drawbacks, however. Tina had to come up with creative ways to satisfy her love for romance novels, so she picked up her pen and tried writing one. After her tenth book she realised she was hooked. She was officially a writer.

Tina loves to hear from readers. You can contact her through her website or 'friend' her on Facebook.

Wendy S. Marcus is an award-winning author of contemporary romance who lives in the beautiful Hudson Valley region of New York where she spends way too much time indoors on her computer. Writing. Really! Okay, more like…where she spends way too much time on Twitter and Facebook! To learn more about Wendy and the books she's managed to write, in spite of her social media addiction, visit WendySMarcus.com.

Hot Single Docs

COLLECTION

July 2018

August 2018

September 2018

October 2018

November 2018

December 2018

January 2019

February 2019

NYC ANGELS: THE WALLFLOWER'S SECRET

SUSAN CARLISLE

This one is for you, Drew. I love you.

CHAPTER ONE

PEDIATRIC NEUROSURGEON DR. Ryan O'Doherty's attention remained on the child lying in the ICU bed of Angel Mendez Children's Hospital in New York City as he spoke to the father. "I removed as much of the tumor as possible. I didn't get it all because I couldn't risk additional impairment."

This father wasn't the first person to hear those words and he wouldn't be the last. Ryan made a point not to gloss over the truth when speaking to parents. Despite the fact that Ryan knew he possessed more than competent skills, he'd done all he could for the child. He couldn't fix them all. Parents had to accept that.

"I understand. His mother and I will take him home and love him for as long as we can," the father said in a voice filled with tears.

The father had courage. He'd have to cling to it down the road.

The sharp, shrill sound of Ryan's phone filled the air. He tapped the screen, stopping the offending noise, and looked at the message. Human Resources. He'd forgotten all about being expected down there. What could possibly be so important in the paper-pusher department that he was needed so urgently?

He glanced at the father again. "The neurologist will

re-evaluate your son's case. I'll be here if needed," he said curtly. "Now, if you will excuse me…"

"Thanks for all you've done."

Ryan nodded. It was his job.

Ten minutes later, Ryan walked through the network of gray hallways on his way to the human resources department. Hospital leadership was notorious for putting HR departments in the basement of the oldest section of the hospital and in the furthest corner, if they could accomplish it. Angel's was no different. Ryan hadn't seen this particular region of the building since he'd become an official employee five years earlier.

He wasn't sure why he'd been summoned, but he'd received an email the day before, requesting his presence. When he'd called to say he was too busy to make the meeting, Matherson, the HR director, had stated it was mandatory that he attend. Ryan was sure the trip down would be a complete waste of his time. Whatever he was needed for, surely could be handled by email.

Despite technically being an employee, he still wasn't used to being called into someone's office. If there was something to be said he was typically the one doing the calling. Expected for a surgery consultation in just a few minutes, he needed to get this over with. He made the final turn in the hallway and pushed the faux woodgrain door open, entering the functional waiting area that would have been drab if not for the colorful framed pictures of children hanging on the wall.

Ryan headed straight to the middle-aged woman sitting behind the L-shaped reception desk. "Dr. O'Doherty here to see Mr. Matherson," he said with a smile he didn't feel. He'd learned long ago that it paid to mask your emotions.

"He's expecting you," the woman at the desk chirped, as if she'd said it hundreds of times.

Not bothering to sit, he stood over the receptionist as she picked up the phone and spoke into it, and looked around the room.

A young woman, maybe in her late twenties, sat facing the entrance in one of the three utilitarian chairs set against the office wall. She glanced up at him. Her large blue eyes reminded him of a summer afternoon, but held a sadness that contradicted their lovely color. With a single blink, the melancholy was replaced by an unwavering stare before she looked away.

"Dr. O'Doherty is here, Mr. Matherson." The receptionist listened a moment then glanced at the woman sitting in the chair.

Ryan followed the receptionist's look. The woman sat with her ankles crossed and her hands laced primly in her lap. There was little outstanding about her apart from those large eyes and a rope of hair that fell over her shoulder. She wore a business suit of light gray with a flimsy peach blouse beneath. A little too school-marmy for his tastes.

He could tell her clothes were of a fine quality. He snorted quietly. Must have been all those long-suffering shopping trips he'd made with his sisters that had given him that knowledge. He quirked a corner of his mouth. Should he be proud of that?

"Ms. Edwards, Mr. Matherson would like to see you and Dr. O'Doherty now."

Who was this Ms. Edwards and why would she have anything to do with him being here? Ryan's focus sharpened when she stood. The woman was tall, with a willowy frame that spoke of someone who took care of herself. Her gaze met his. The sadness he'd seen early in her eyes had been replaced by a resolute look. She held his gaze a moment before her attention turned to the HR man.

Mr. Matherson, a round bodied man with a balding head, had come round a corner. "Dr. O'Doherty and Ms. Edwards, please come back to my office."

Ryan stepped back and allowed her to go ahead of him. Her head reached his shoulder. Her wheat-colored hair was controlled by a braid. What was it called? He'd heard his sisters talk about them enough. Something foreign. A French braid, that was it. Even with the braid her hair went midway down her back. Did it touch her hips when free?

Ms. Edwards's eyes narrowed. Had she guessed his thoughts?

"Please come in and have a seat," Mr. Matherson instructed as he stepped around the desk facing the door and remained standing. Ms. Edwards took one of the burgundy vinyl chairs and Ryan sat in the other before Mr. Matherson settled in his seat.

"Dr. O'Doherty, this is Lucy Edwards, and she's just recently joined the Angel family."

Ryan offered his hand and a half-smile. "Ryan O'Doherty."

For a flicker of a second she hesitated before her small fingers slipped into his. Her grasp was firm, her hand soft and the touch brief. He liked the feel of her hand.

He gave Matherson an expectant look. They needed to get a move on with this meeting. His colleague was waiting on that consult. "So what brings us here?"

Matherson regarded Ryan as if he wasn't comfortable with others taking over his meetings. Clearing his throat, the HR man said, "Ms. Edwards is a family counselor. She comes with the highest credentials and praise from her last position. As I understand, she was the person the families regularly requested."

The woman beside him shifted uncomfortably. Pink touched her cheeks. She obviously didn't enjoy being the center of attention. That came as a surprise. In his experience, woman generally enjoyed being the main focus. What made this one different?

Matherson continued as if giving a great oratory to be remembered. "Angel's is setting up a new program called Coordinated Patient Care, where we're pairing a counselor with a doctor. Ms. Edwards is your partner. You'll be working with her on all your cases."

What was this? Another hospital bureaucratic feel-good project? Ryan leaned forward, piercing the rotund little man with a look. "Didn't we try something like this a couple of years ago and decide it didn't work?"

Matherson had the good grace to look contrite. "Similar, but this is a little different. You two are the beta test. If it works then we'll require other departments to follow suit."

"Is all this necessary? I'm sure Ms.…uh—"

"Edwards," the woman supplied.

He sensed more than saw her stiffen. "I'm sure Ms. Edwards and I could both use our time more wisely."

"Please don't speak for me." The woman who had been sitting stiffly beside him said, shifting direction. "Doctor, I can assure you that the closer the doctor-counselor relationship is, the better it is for the patient."

Her words were said in a soft Southern drawl laced with an edge of steel. So the woman had some backbone. Interesting.

He cocked a brow and smiled. "So-o-o." He dragged

out the word to match her drawl. "You believe that working closely with the doctor is important."

She rewarded him with a blush that added a brighter touch of pink to the ridge of her cheeks.

Matherson cleared his throat, but Ryan chose to ignore the man. He gifted her with a smile. The identical one he used when making an effort not to ruffle the nurses while at the same time trying to get his way.

"I didn't mean to imply that your job doesn't have merit, it's just that I don't think we need to personally discuss each patient. In fact, I don't discuss the same type of issues with my patients that you would be concerned with. You can make notes on their charts about any matters you think I should know about and I can read from there." Ryan stood. To his surprise, Ms. Edwards rose to face him.

"I can assure you, Doctor, our relationship will be strictly professional," she said through clenched teeth. She took a breath and continued, "Patients, as well as their families, need reassurance and comfort that you can't provide."

She couldn't have been more correct.

"That's my job and I do it well." She squared her shoulders, punctuating the statement.

"I'm sure that is true but I'm not going to waste my time in meetings when there is a perfectly good computer system we can use for correspondence. Now, if you'll both excuse me…"

"Dr. O'Doughty," Matherson said with a pointed look at Ryan, "I don't know if you fully understand what's being asked here. This is a trial program. The board's supporting it unanimously. Your *co-operation* would be noticed and to your advantage."

Ryan compressed his mouth. Matherson was mak-

ing a veiled reference to the fact that he hadn't been
offered the head of neurosurgery position and that his
co-operation would look good on his CV. By rights
the department head job should have been his. Instead,
they'd hired Alex Rodriguez.

Drawing his lips into a thin line, Ryan looked directly at Matherson for a long moment. The hospital
pencil-pusher did have the good grace to lower his eyes.
If going along with this ridiculous time-consuming co-
ordinated patient care idea would make him look good
on paper to the powers that be, then he'd make some
form of an effort. He'd at least give it lip service, but
based on his experience it would be a waste of time.
Shrugging a shoulder, he said, "Okay." He looked at
Ms. Edwards. "I guess we're a team, then."

Ms. Edwards angled her head, mistrust written all
over her face. Was she questioning his motives? Would
she let him get away with doing as little as possible?
Maybe there was more to this unassuming woman than
he'd originally supposed. If nothing else, it would be a
challenge to see if he could get her to smile. Find out
if he could make that sadness in her eyes disappear.

"So it's settled." Matherson sounded far more cheerful than Ryan felt. "Then I'll let you two get started."

Lucy glanced at the self-absorbed doctor walking half a
pace ahead of her up the hall. It had been hard enough
to leave her entire life behind to start a new job in an
unfamiliar city but being forced to work with a person
who resented her being foisted on him made it almost
impossible. Left no choice, she had to make this partnership work somehow.

Matherson, with the syrupy smile still on his face,
had inquired if the good doctor was going back up to

the neuro floor. When he said he was, Matherson had the nerve to ask him to show her the way. She'd been horribly embarrassed that Matherson had relegated this surgeon to a tour guide but didn't know a graceful way to say she'd find her own way.

As they left the HR department, Dr. O'Doherty held the door for her to go ahead of him. Someone had at least instilled manners in the self-absorbed man. She'd seen little else to impress her. That wasn't exactly true. She hadn't failed to notice his wide shoulders, piercing blue eyes and height. Even now his long legs were eating up the well-worn tile floor beneath them. Not often did she find a man that she couldn't meet almost eye to eye.

Gripping her purse, Lucy found herself tagging along behind him. With each step she became more irritated with his attitude. He walked as if he couldn't leave the HR or her quickly enough. Regardless, she appreciated him leading the way as they made one turn then another, past another bank of elevators. She had no idea where she was in the vast hospital.

That morning when she'd stood across the street in Central Park, facing the front entrance of Angel's, and had looked up, she hadn't begun to count the number of floors. The building spread across an entire block. To say she'd been intimidated would have been an understatement. Still, there had been something about the mixture of old and new architecture that had appealed to her. If nothing else, the bright yellow and red awning leading to the front door had made her think the place had warmth.

Being employed by a large hospital wasn't new to her. Most children's hospitals were attached to a larger teaching hospital that was affiliated with a big university. But compared to Angel's, those she'd worked in were dwarfs in size. She liked the nickname Angel's. Glancing at the man beside her, she decided he didn't act very angelic or hospitable.

Dr. O'Doherty finally stopped in front of a set of elevators and pushed the 'up' button.

Her job required her to read people. Dr. O'Doherty's rigid stance and unyielding demeanor said he wasn't pleased with having to answer to the HR department and now to her in a lesser way. She wasn't surprised. Typical surgeon. Highly typical neurosurgeon. Confident, in control and with minds closed to anyone's ideas but their own. Still, she had a job to do, and that meant co-operating with this guy. She had no choice but to make it work.

Clearing her throat, she said, "I understand this arrangement isn't really your idea of a good plan."

He moved to face her. "No, it isn't."

His displeasure didn't encourage her. If this was the way he acted over a simple request, she couldn't imagine his reaction to a serious issue. She was well acquainted with life-altering experiences. She wasn't going to waste her energy getting upset over anything as mundane as being partnered with the egotistical doctor.

"I'd like to make my end of it as painless as possible for both of us."

The elevator arrived, putting their conversation on hold. The doors opened and they stepped into an already crowded car. Dr. O'Doherty's solid frame brushed hers as they turned to face the front of the elevator. A prickle of awareness spread through her body.

On the ride upward, they stood close enough that the heat of his body warmed her down one side. It was the first time in months that the Arctic cold buried deep within her had melted even for a second. The numbness returned the moment the elevator doors opened and he moved away. She stepped out behind him, then paused.

He stopped and looked at her. "Something wrong?"

"No, I'm just always amazed at how completely different patients' areas are from the business parts of the hospital. These bright yellow walls are like coming into sunshine after being in gloom."

"I've never noticed."

She wasn't surprised.

"Can you get to your office from here?"

She glanced around, recognizing a framed picture of a child's artwork on the wall. "I know where I am now." He turned to leave and she asked, "So how're we going to handle this coordinated care plan, Dr. O'Doherty?"

Stopping, he turned back to her. "I'm going about it like I always have. Check the charts, Ms. Edwards."

"Mr. Matherson made it clear that wouldn't do. You might not like the idea but I expect you to do your part. Your patients are now mine also. I'm determined to give them the best care possible."

Dr. O'Doherty stepped a pace closer, leaned forward and pierced her with a penetrating blue stare. "And you don't think that's what I do?"

"I'm sure you're a more than capable surgeon, but there's always room for improvement where patient care outside the OR is concerned."

"Ms. Edwards, are you questioning my ability to be professional?"

She met his look squarely. "No, but I'll not let you dismiss me or my abilities either. I was approached by this hospital to do a job so someone must have thought I had something to offer the hospital and the neuro department in particular. I expect you to at least recognize that."

His attention remained on her long enough that her knees started to shake. Had she stepped over the line? With a huff, he said, "I do rounds at five. Promptly." With a curt turn he went down the hall as if he'd spent all the time he deemed necessary on her.

Lucy passed a number of patient rooms, rounded the large corner nurses' station and dodged a child in a wagon with a parent pulling it. Her heart tugged. Every small child she saw made her think of Emily. With relief, she finally reached the hall her office was on. Maybe going back to work in a children's hospital hadn't been one of her best ideas. But it had been the only job available when she'd needed to leave.

As bright, open and modern as the patients' floor was, in contrast her office was little more than a cubby hole. She shared the area with two other family counselors assigned to the neuro floor. Three desks were lined up side by side against a wall and if all three were working at the same time, they wouldn't be able to get to their desks without one of them stepping out into the hall. That didn't concern her. It was a fairly typical arrangement for support staff. She was happy to have her position and she'd work in whatever space provided.

Lucy checked her watch. There were a few hours before she had to meet Dr. O'Doherty for rounds. That gave her time to review his patient load and familiarize herself with each child's diagnosis. She'd make sure the doctor didn't have anything to complain about in regard to her work. It was her goal to make this partnership as stress-free as possible despite his opposition of the plan.

When she'd learned about this job she hadn't thought twice about taking it and had every intention of succeeding in it. She needed this position if she was going to survive and get her life back on track.

One of Lucy's officemates, a woman with pepper-colored hair and a generous smile, was coming in the door as Lucy was heading out. "Hey, how's it going?" Nancy asked.

"Fine."

"I heard you were teamed up with Dr. O'Doherty."

Lucy gave her a questioning look.

"Learned it from the hospital grapevine. Even from the basement news travels fast."

"I see." Lucy picked up her notepad.

"Ryan's such a cutie. We all love working with him. Kind of keeps to himself but he's a favorite among the nurses. More than one of them has a crush on him."

Lucy didn't know how to respond to that statement so she remained silent. She didn't see that ever becoming an issue for her.

"You know the kind of patients we see on this floor often break our hearts, but with Ryan around it sure makes it easier. That goes for the patients and us. He's a brilliant doctor. Not hard to look at either."

Lucy had to agree with the latter. Even so, he'd not made a great first impression as far as she was concerned. She had a new life to build and being a groupie of a doctor who already had a posse of female admirers didn't fall into her "need to do" list.

"Well, I'd better review some charts before rounds." Lucy gave her co-worker a wary smile and left the office.

She'd never been one for hospital gossip and actively stayed away from it when she could, but her office-mate's chatter had caught her interest. The more she knew about Dr. O'Doherty the better off she'd be.

She slipped into a vacant chair behind the nurses' station desk. Facing the state-of-the-art computer screen, she typed in her password and queried Dr. O'Doherty's in-house patients. A list containing five names came up. One by one she reviewed the patients' charts and made notes. She'd just finished scanning the last chart when a deep-throated laugh followed by the high-pitched giggle of a child came from down the hall.

"Dr. O'Doherty is at it again," the nurse standing beside her said with a smile.

Seconds later, he slow-galloped into view with a young girl on his back. His white lab coat had been discarded. The light blue knit shirt he wore stretched tautly across his broad chest. The man either had good genes or he worked out regularly. The child had a happy smile on her face and her arms were wrapped tightly around his neck. Her head was bound in white gauze.

He stopped at the nurses' station where Lucy and the nurse stood watching. "Ms. Edwards, I'd like you to meet Princess Michelle."

The girl giggled.

"She buttoned her shirt all by herself today and got to make a wish." He glanced back at the girl. "Princess Michelle," he said.

The girl giggled again.

"Can you tell Ms. Edwards what your wish was?" Ryan asked.

"I want a horsy ride," the girl said with a shy grin.

"Well, that sounds like a fine wish." Lucy smiled up at the child. "So how far are you going on this ride? Over the mountain? Across the river?"

The girl snickered and pointed. "End of hall."

"I see."

"This horse can't go too far away from the barn." He winked at the young nurse and she blinked and grinned.

The sting of pain Lucy experienced when she'd not

been included in the flirtatious action surprised her. It was a visual reminder he didn't consider her part of his circle. She was once again an outsider.

An easy lilt in his Brooklyn accent became more prominent as he continued to speak. "I'd better finish this princess's ride and get her home. It's almost supper time." He turned his head toward the girl, "What do you say to get the horse to go?"

"Giddy up," Michelle said with another round of giggles and off they went.

A smile covered her lips.

"Why, Ms. Edwards, is that a smile I see?" Dr. O'Doherty asked with a brow raised. "I wondered if it was possible."

To her amazement, she was smiling. Something that had happened rarely in the last few months. How had that exasperating man managed to make her smile? Maybe there was more to him than she had originally given him credit for. His bedside manner might not extend to her but apparently he cared about his patients.

The horse and rider set off down the passage then returned, and she waved. Her chest constricted. It wouldn't be long until Emily would be the same age as Michelle. Sadly, Lucy would never hear the sounds of Emily's childhood delight.

Half an hour later, Lucy asked one of the nurses which end of the hall Dr. O'Doherty usually started his rounds on. The nurse pointed to the right and Lucy headed in that direction. A group of six led by Dr. O'Doherty exited a patient's room as she approached. The crowd circled around him. Lucy stopped just outside the ring.

He looked over the head of a female intern wearing

a lab coat, with her head elevated in a worshipful manner, to glower at Lucy. "Everyone, this is Ms. Edwards."

The assemblage turned to inspect her. She shifted uneasily under the scrutiny.

"She's our newest family counselor. Please introduce yourself later. We have patients to see." His mouth tightened briefly but his words didn't falter. "Please see that she stays in the loop on all cases." His intense blue gaze pinned her again. "I'll have to get you up to speed later on the patient you missed."

She looked away.

Dr. O'Doherty made a few more comments as they moved down the hallway to the next patient, then the next, stopping in front of another door. He paused. His attention focused on her again. "This is Brian Banasiak. I removed a blood clot three days ago. This is one case I believe that it might be beneficial to have you involved in."

Might? Lucy wasn't sure she needed his seal of approval but she didn't say so. Neither was she certain how she felt about the left-handed compliment. In her last position she'd been considered the "go to" person when a family was having a difficult time coping with their child's illness or injury. Her role was seen as important in overall patient care.

Apparently Dr. O'Doherty viewed her work as a sideline to his godly power. She'd do her job effectively then maybe she could change the narrow-minded man's opinion.

"I understand his head trauma occurred during an auto accident," she said quietly. "I'm going to discuss the benefits of therapy at home with the parents. Also assistance with home schooling. These parents have a long road ahead of them. The adjustment of having gone from a perfectly normal child to one who needs help eating and dressing will be difficult at best to accept."

Dr. O'Doherty's look of surprise along with similar ones from the others made her want to pump her fist in elation. She'd managed to wow the man. Why it should matter she didn't know, but it felt good.

He pursed his lips and nodded as if he might be impressed. "Thank you, Ms. Edwards. You've obviously done your homework."

"The family clearly cares about their child and I gather are willing to do what it takes for Brian to recover. I'll be speaking with them first thing in the morning to determine any additional needs."

Dr. O'Doherty gave her a quick nod and with a rap of his knuckles on the door entered the room. Along with the rest of their group, Lucy moved to stand next to the boy's bed.

The parents of the boy came to stand across the bed from the group. Dr. O'Doherty paid them no attention.

"Brian, how're you feeling today?" Dr. O'Doherty asked.

The eight-year-old boy offered a weak smile. His entire head was swathed in white gauze. His eyes had dark circles under them and there was puffiness about his face that lingered from having surgery.

"Okay, I guess," the boy said with little enthusiasm.

"Well, from all I hear from your nurse, you're my star patient," Dr. O'Doherty stated. "So give me a high five."

That managed to get a slight smile out of the boy. He raised his small hand and met the doctor's larger one with a smack.

Dr. O'Doherty pulled his hand back. "Ow! See, you're already getting stronger."

Brian's smile broadened.

The doctor did have a way with kids.

"I'm going to take a look at your head. Maybe we can give you a smaller bandage."

"It's itchy." The boy wrinkled his nose.

"Yes. That means you're getting better. I'll see if we can't help with that problem."

As he removed the gauze, Lucy watched the parents' faces to gage their reactions. Death wasn't the only time people experienced grief. A major life trauma could bring on the emotion. Lucy knew that all too well. She'd run to get away from hers.

"Will he be able to ride a bike?" the boy's mother asked. "Do we have to worry about him falling?"

Dr. O'Doherty didn't look at the mother as he said, "Ms. Walters, my clinical nurse, can answer those questions for you." He continued to unwrap the bandage.

The mother looked like she'd been struck. She stepped back from the bed.

He continued to examine the surgical site then spoke to the floor nurse standing next to him. "I believe we can place a four-by-four bandage over this." He looked at the boy. "You'll look less like a pirate but it won't be so itchy."

That statement brought a real smile to the boy's face.

"I'll see you tomorrow," Dr. O'Doherty said, before turning to leave. He shook the big toe of the boy's foot as he moved toward the door

The mother followed him out into the hall. "Dr. O'Doherty, we were wondering what to expect next," the mother said, tears filling her eyes.

"My nurse will answer all your questions."

Lucy compressed her lips. Where had all the charm that had oozed from him seconds before gone?

"Will he ever be like he was?" The mother's eyes pleaded to know.

"I don't make those kinds of promises," Dr. O'Doherty clipped.

The mother looked stricken again.

This man had a sterling bedside manner where his patients were concerned but he sure lacked finesse with the parents. Why was he suddenly so cold?

Lucy stepped forward, not looking at Dr. O'Doherty for permission. She placed an arm around the woman's shoulders. "Mrs. Banasiak, I'm Lucy Edwards, the family counselor. I think I can help answer some of your questions."

The mother sagged in relief. She shot a look at Dr. O'Doherty and then said to Lucy, "Thank you, so much."

Dr. O'Doherty progressed on down the hall with his group in tow without a backward glance. Lucy hung back to speak to the parents further. The watery eyes and fragile smile of the mother touched Lucy's heart. These were the type of people who needed her. It felt good to be using her skills again.

Ryan paused in front of the last patient-to-be-seen door. Turning, he waited for the group to join him. Ms. Edwards was missing. Should he really be surprised? He discussed the patient, while his frustration grew. She could speak to the parents on her own time.

"We're glad you could join us," he said when she finally walked up.

Her eyes didn't meet his. The woman didn't like having the spotlight on her. By the way she dressed and spoke so softly, he guessed she spent most of her time in the shadows. "I needed to reassure the parents," she said quietly.

Pushing the door of the patient room open, he stepped in. "Hi, Lauren," he said to the ten-year-old sitting up in bed, watching TV. "I believe you'll be ready to go home tomorrow. How does that sound?"

The grandmother, who was the girl's caretaker, stepped to the bed. "That's wonderful. What do we need to do about getting her back in school when the time comes?"

A soft but strong voice beside him said, "I'll help with that."

"This is Lucy Edwards," he said to the grandmother. "She's my family counselor."

The only indication that Ms. Edwards didn't appreciate the word "*my*" was the slight tightening around her lips. That had been entirely the wrong thing to say. He didn't know how to repair the faux pas gracefully in front of a patient's family so he continued speaking to the grandmother. He'd apologize to Ms. Edwards later.

This quiet, gentle-voiced woman wasn't *his* anything. She wasn't even his type. He was used to dating freer-spirited women, who thought less and laughed more. Those who were loud and boisterous and were not interested in emotional attachments. Ms. Edwards had already demonstrated she was the touchy-feely type.

He left the room while the grandmother rattled off a list of questions for Ms. Edwards.

After answering a page, he returned to the nurses' station in search of Ms. Edwards. Not seeing her, he was forced to ask where her office was located. He'd never paid much attention to the family counselors. He knew they had a job to do and as far as he was concerned they did it. Rarely did he interact with one outside other than when they asked him a question or left a note on a chart.

He knocked lightly on the nondescript door with a small plate that showed he was in the correct place. The door was opened by a woman he recognized. "Hi, Ryan. What's up?"

"Hello, Nancy. I was trying to find Ms. Edwards."

"Yes-s-s." The word being drawn out came from inside. He'd found the right place. Ms. Edwards put far too many syllables in a word. He glanced around the woman in front of him. Ms. Edwards looked at him with wide, questioning eyes.

"I'll get out of your way. It's time to head home anyway," the older woman said. "Nice to see you, Ryan."

"You too." He smiled as she left and stepped into the doorway, holding the door open. "Do you mind if I come in a minute?"

The new counselor looked unsure but nodded her agreement.

He'd received warmer welcomes but guessed he couldn't blame her, considering their less than congenial start. She sat at the desk furthest away from the door. Her eyes resembled those of a startled animal as he pushed the door closed behind him. The look eased when he sat down in the chair furthest from her. Was she afraid of him? He conjured up one of his friendliest smiles.

She gave him an inquiring look.

"I just wanted to say I'm sorry for the comment about you being my family counselor. I misworded the statement. It won't happen again."

Her bearing softened. "Dr. O'Doherty—"

"Please call me Ryan. I'm a pretty casual guy generally." She looked unsure about the idea. "May I call you Lucy?"

She nodded slowly. "Uh, Ryan, I know you're not a fan of this coordinated patient care arrangement but I'd really like us to work together with as little conflict as possible."

He liked the way his name sounded when she said it. Kind of easygoing and warm. "I'll do my part but there have to be some ground rules."

She pursed her lips and her delicately shaped brows drew closer together. "And those would be?"

"I expect the people that work for me to be punctual and to stay with me as I make rounds. I don't wait."

"Dr. O'Doherty, I don't work for you. I work for the hospital, and ultimately for the patients. If I understood Mr. Matherson correctly, we do coordinated patient care. Which means we work together."

"My OR schedule, which the hospital dictates, means I don't have time to stand around waiting for you."

"And my job, which the hospital and the human heart dictate, is to care for the patient and the family during a difficult time. My job is to help the whole family. We…" She waved a hand around, broadly including him. "This hospital should care for the whole person. That's my job and I would appreciate you letting me do it."

He flinched. "My job is to be a surgeon, I fix the problem. I don't need to hand-hold patients or their families to do my job well."

"No, you don't, but it would be nice if you would at least try to on some level."

His body stiffened and he gave her a questioning look. "The parents of my patients need to hear the truth."

"I don't disagree with that. I just question the delivery."

"I thought that was why you were here?"

"It is, but parents like Brian's like to hear reassurances from the doctor."

She met his direct gaze for the first time for longer than a second. He stood. "Point taken."

"What time's your first case in the morning?"

"Seven. Why?"

"I like to be here when the child leaves the parents to go into surgery. It's when they need the most support. Many want to talk. They're scared. I'll walk them down to the waiting room."

He'd never given any thought to how difficult it was for parents to watch their child go into surgery. Didn't want to think about it. He opened the door.

"It's hard to let go," she said with wistfulness in her voice.

Did she know that from personal experience? Her eyes glazed over. Where had her thoughts gone? Thankfully she recovered, the hopeless expression disappearing, to be replaced by that of a trained professional again. That he was more than capable of dealing with.

"I guess it is." He closed the door between them. What was the woman with the sad, serious eyes hiding?

CHAPTER TWO

THAT EVENING LUCY arrived home later than she'd planned. To be at the hospital early for four mornings out of the week meant she had to stay late in the evenings to prepare. On top of that there was the time she spent getting to and from work. Accustomed to the freedom of driving a car, she found using the subway system restricting and oftentimes frustrating. Never good at reading maps, she had a tendency to take the wrong train far too often. This was one aspect of living in a huge city that she'd not thought through.

Her heavy-set, dark-haired landlord, who was standing outside the building, called, "Hello," as she started climbing the stairs to her studio apartment.

"Hi, Mr. Volpentesta," she returned with more enthusiasm than she'd had in a long time.

He presented her with a big, white, toothy smile.

Lucy made her way up to the third floor above the Italian bistro. She didn't mind the climb. It was good exercise and she'd always enjoyed being fit. Staying in shape and eating right were important to her. She sucked in a tight breath. That had been one of the many reasons she'd had no trouble carrying Emily.

Emily. The hurt throbbed deep. She had to get beyond the pain somehow.

Unlocking the door, she pushed it open and stepped into the studio apartment. A nice window allowed light into the space. A bed faced it and there was a small sitting area. In one back corner was a kitchenette, functional but tiny, and in the other corner was the bathroom, which included a tiny closet.

She'd managed to make the place homely with the few things she'd brought with her. When she had time she'd give it the care it deserved. It wasn't much by most people's standards but she enjoyed the multicultural, tree-lined neighborhood. She'd been lucky to find a place within her budget.

Alexis, her sister, didn't understand Lucy's need to move so far away and Lucy had no intention of ever sharing the real reason she'd left. It was her deepest shame. It had almost killed her but she'd had to get away. It was better for everyone that she leave, despite how much she missed her sister, and Emily. She wanted Alexis and her family to be happy. For her to hang around, wishing she was a part of their close-knit group, hadn't been healthy for any of them.

Dropping her purse on the table, which had obviously been confiscated from the bistro, she put the kettle on to heat water to make tea. Sweet iced tea was her drink of choice. No matter where she lived she took that small pleasure with her. Even in the cold early spring weather she couldn't give up that small part of her growing-up years. It was one of the passions she and her sister shared. She wouldn't go there. Spending her evening crying wasn't part of her plan.

Taking a deep breath, she moved to her bed, pulled off her business suit and replaced it with sweatpants and sweatshirt, then she tugged on slouchy socks.

The streetlight below her windows flickered on, washing the room in a warm glow that only added to her loneliness. She clicked on a lamp on her way back to the stove and after pouring the hot water over the tea bags and sugar she reached for a can of soup from the open cabinet.

She'd gone from carrying a baby and living in her sister's home, where love abounded, to a shabby room in an enormous impersonal city. She sank into one of the two chairs she had and put her face in her hands.

Stop it. Get a hold of yourself. You can survive this. You have to make your own life.

The next afternoon, she entered Daniel Hancock's room to find Ryan leaning back in a chair as if he made social visits to the teenage boy's room regularly. Ryan had removed a tumor from the sixteen-year-old's brain stem the week before.

"Ah, Ms. Edwards, just the person we were looking for," Ryan said, as if he was genuinely glad to see her, which created suspicion in her mind.

He'd made it clear the day before that he wasn't interested in her being involved in his cases unless he thought she was needed. Now he acted as if they were old friends and he was planning to ask her a favor. She was unsure how to read his attitude change. Up until this moment she would have characterized their relationship as two dogs circling each other, trying to decide how not to get in each other's way.

She'd play along. Approaching the end of the bed, she smiled at Daniel. "What can I do for you two gentlemen?"

"I was just telling Daniel that he can't return to

school right away. That he'll need to be home-schooled for a while until his site heals. Can you help to arrange that?"

"I'll see about it right away."

"Did you know that Daniel's the star of his high-school baseball team?"

"I had heard that." In fact, his future had begun to disappear when he hadn't been able to control his hand movements. Now, because of Ryan's skill, Daniel had a chance at his dream again. She could forgive some of Ryan's brashness for that alone. He might lack empathy at times but he had major surgical skills.

Ryan stood and, grinning, said to Daniel, "I hope to see you playing for the Yankees one day soon. I'll leave orders for the teacher to be cute and like baseball—how does that sound?"

Daniel gave him a weak smile but seemed pleased.

Ryan offered his hand to the teen. Lucy appreciated the way Ryan showed his respect for the young man by treating him as an equal. It was a way of giving Daniel a sense of control in a place where he felt he had none. Why hadn't Ryan given the same consideration to the mother the evening before?

She followed Ryan out of the room. "You know, Lucy, having you readily available may be a good thing after all."

"It isn't my job to be at your beck and call."

"Maybe not, but so far it's working out well." He grinned and walked off.

And she'd thought moving to New York was going to make her life easier. How long was this coordinated patient care agreement supposed to last?

Hours later all she wanted to do was go home and fall asleep. Instead, she was hunting down Ryan for a

signature on a couple of forms. She knew the vicinity of his office but she'd never been there. Punching
the automatic door-opener on the wall, she waited then
passed through a set of doors that led into a short hallway. Here she was no longer in the sunny land of the
patients' hall. Instead, it turned into the practical world
of business. She searched the uniformed name plates
until she found Ryan's beside the second door on the
right. It read: "Dr. Ryan O'Doherty, Associate of Neurosurgery".

She'd heard talk about Ryan not getting the department head job. Most of the nurses were surprised.
They'd all thought he would be a shoo-in. Apparently
popularity wasn't the deciding factor. If it had been
and the staff had voted, it would have been unanimous.
Even in the OR, where the pressure was greater and
personalities sometimes clashed, the staff all seemed
to appreciate Ryan's skill and winning ways. She just
wished some of those winning ways would spill over
when she had to deal with him.

His office door stood partially open. She knocked
and waited. No answer. The forms had to be signed tonight or first thing in the morning. Maybe she should
page him? No, she didn't want to do that. She'd just
leave the forms on his desk and text him, asking him
to sign them before he went into the OR. She rolled her
eyes. She was sure he'd be *real* glad to hear from her.

Apprehensive about entering Ryan's private space
without permission but thinking she had no choice, she
stepped into his office. His ever-present lab coat lay
across the back of his desk chair. He must have gone
for the day if he didn't have it on. On the other hand,
his office door was open.

She placed the papers on his desk and picked up a

pen lying there to write him a note. Maybe he would see them before she had a chance to text him.

Ryan stepped out of an adjacent doorway into the room.

She squealed, jumped. Her hand went over her heart before it settled with a thump. "Oh." Heaven help her, he wasn't wearing a shirt. She gulped. Coming into his office hadn't been a good idea.

Ryan's slacks hung low on his hips and his belt was undone. She couldn't take her eyes off his chest. An expanse of muscle covered in a light dusting of hair.

"What're you doing here?" he said brusquely. His tone stated clearly he wasn't pleased to see her. He stepped behind his desk and pulled out a drawer. Removing a shirt, he slipped it on and began to button it.

She followed his movements as he worked his way up the shirt. His long, tapered fingers moved swiftly. Ryan was a large man to be doing such delicate work as brain surgery. She'd heard he had a gentle touch with the scalpel.

What would it be like to be caressed by him? What kind of question was that? She shook her head. The last thing she needed to do was get moony-eyed over Ryan O'Doherty.

"Lucy, did you need something or did you just stop by to gape? Or maybe snoop?" His tone had turned teasing but still held an edge of distrust.

She straightened and moved away from the desk, trying to gather her poise as she went. "I do not snoop!"

His mouth quirked at one corner. "Then gape? Because you've yet to tell me why you're here."

"I need you to sign these forms so I can get Daniel's home schooling set up before he's discharged. These…" she pointed to the papers to prove she was telling the truth "…have to be in by tomorrow to make the deadline. That's if you still want him to have a cute teacher. They'll be all gone by tomorrow afternoon I was told," she said with the most insincere saccharine smile she could muster.

"Why, Ms. Edwards, you surprise me. I had no idea you had a sense of humor."

Ryan should've been livid at finding Lucy in his office without permission. This was his private domain and he wanted it to remain that way. The look of surprise on her face and the widening of her eyes when she'd seen his state of undress had defused his anger. She hadn't immediately turned away. Instead, her eyes had grown darker, her gaze fixed on his chest. It hadn't been one of her shy looks but one of bold appraisal. Pure male satisfaction had won out over his irritation. His ego officially skyrocketed.

She huffed, stepped over to the desk and picked up the papers. "If you would just sign these, I can get out of your way."

For some reason he was a little disappointed at the idea. This was the most entertaining time he'd spent with someone in a long time. Who would have thought he'd find the quiet, ordinary woman interesting? No, ordinary was the wrong word. There was nothing ordinary about Lucy.

Ryan picked up the forms and reviewed them. Setting them down again, he took the pen she'd dropped and signed a form. Out of the corner of his eye, he saw her looking around. He had learned quickly that she was observant, almost intuitive about people. What was she learning about him?

He glanced at her as he pulled the second form to

him. She studied his shelves filled with books intermingled with pictures and baseball memorabilia. Her gaze moved on to the opposite wall. There hung a framed picture of a Yankees baseball game in progress, which took up most of the space. Putting down the pen, he turned to sit on the edge of his desk. Lucy's consideration had traveled to the framed pictures on his desk.

Before he realized it, he'd said, "Those are my nieces and nephews." He pointed toward a picture with two dark-haired women in it. "My sisters." He rarely volunteered personal information to anyone. No wonder Lucy was so good at her job. Something about her made people want to tell her their secrets.

His gut clenched. He didn't want her to know his. "Is there anything else?" His words sounded more dismissive than he'd intended. He handed the forms to her.

All business again, she said, "I'll see that they are faxed before I go home."

He watched her leave his office. Why all of a sudden was he looking forward to coming to work the next day?

Ryan's running shoes made a rhythmic sound as he took the turn in the paved path on his way back to the hospital. He slowed when he saw Lucy sitting on a park bench. Her head was tipped back, her face held up to the sun. That golden rope of hair gleamed in the light. She'd removed her heavy cardigan and had her legs stretched out in front of her. He hadn't known her long but he suspected this was the most uninhibited she'd been in a long time.

She really was an attractive woman who seemed to want to blend in, go unnoticed. It hadn't worked where he was concerned. He'd noticed too much.

As he grew closer, he could see that her eyes were

closed. He wouldn't have disturbed her but just as he approached she shifted and sat up as if jolted awake.

"Hey," she said, drowsiness in her voice.

"Hey." He liked this off-guard Lucy. When she had her full faculties back in a second she'd close off fast. She acted as if she was wary of everyone and everything.

"Been running." She stated the obvious as he was standing there drenched in perspiration and wearing a sweatshirt and shorts.

"Yeah, one of the perks of working at Angel's is that the park is so close."

"I think so too. I already miss the lakes, forests and the spaciousness of the suburbs of Atlanta. Somehow knowing I can come to the park helps." She began to put on her sweater.

What had caused her to make such a drastic move? He couldn't ask that type of question if he wasn't prepared to share in return. "Have you had a chance to explore the park?"

She laughed. "It may not surprise you to hear that I'm afraid I might get lost. So I don't get out of sight of the hospital."

He smiled down at her. "Maybe I can give you a tour some time. We'll leave breadcrumbs if necessary."

"If I'm along, it'll be necessary."

"Well, I'll leave you to your sunning."

"I've got to go in too. I need to get some lunch before I meet you for clinic."

"I don't know if it's necessary for you to be at clinic today."

She stood and faced him with an unwavering look. "Why not? I thought we were past having this discussion."

He held up a hand. "It has nothing to do with me not

wanting you there. I'm only going to be seeing patients who were discharged before you arrived."

Her face relaxed. "I see. Just the same, I'd like to be there."

She started towards the hospital without a backward glance at him. He'd been dismissed, something he wasn't used to having happen from anyone other than his sisters.

Lucy entered the doctors' shared clinic building attached to the hospital. Ryan's day of the week to see patients was Wednesday. She looked around the waiting area of the clinic. It had large glass windows that provided a view of Central Park. Painted on the walls were murals with happy-faced animals. The orange furniture and light green carpet created a happy effect. Toy tables sat in an open space to the side. It was a place where children wouldn't be afraid to come.

She found Ryan waiting in the hall of the clinic. "I'm sorry, I'm late. No matter how much time I allow myself, I still eat it up having to backtrack everywhere I go." Lucy said as she caught her breath.

He smiled. "I'm starting to expect it."

"I'm getting better. I can get to work without getting off the subway and doubling back a station. I do get my exercise, though."

Ryan gave her body frank consideration. "I can see that you do."

Warmth washed over her. It felt wonderful to have a man look at her with interest. In the past few days they'd managed to develop a working relationship that was at least doable if not comfortable. On her part, she'd spent longer than normal getting to know Ryan's patients and their families. On his, he seemed to at least tolerate having her around.

"You know, I've been meaning to tell you that I like that Southern drawl."

The grin on his lips and the dimples it brought to his cheeks made him the sexiest man she'd ever seen.

"But you talk so slowly that I forget what you said at the beginning of the sentence by the time you get to the end of it."

She thrust her chin out and looked at him hard. "Are you making fun of me?"

The laugh lines around his eyes grew more prominent. "I would never do that."

Lucy couldn't help but return his teasing smile. Something she hadn't done in a long time. It felt good to have some humor in her life again.

A nurse came down the hall. "You first patient is in exam two, Dr. O'Doherty."

Ryan took the patient chart from the nurse and Lucy followed him. The man could turn on the charm when he chose. She'd have to watch out or he might use it against her.

Lucy joined him during each examination. All the patients were there for sixth-week post-op visits and would be released from Ryan's care after this clinical appointment. Neither he nor she would see them again unless the patients required additional surgery. Maybe that was why Ryan didn't invest more effort into getting to know the families. They weren't normally long-term patients for him.

"This is the last patient," Ryan told her as he pulled the chart out of the holder on the door. "Amanda Marcella. Three years old. "

He tapped lightly on the door then entered. Lucy

followed and he introduced her. "So, how's Amanda doing?" he asked the far-too-young mother.

"Okay, I guess."

Lucy cringed. If she had a child who was sick she wouldn't be treating the child's heath so nonchalantly.

The little girl had an external shunt located on the right side of her head. Ryan removed the bandages. He really had a tender way about him.

"This shunt isn't positioned correctly. The site needs to be checked and rebandaged. I'll show you how I want it done," he announced, engrossed in what he was doing.

"I don't like doing that sort of thing. My boyfriend has to do it," the mother said.

Ryan looked up. "This isn't something that you have a choice about. You have to take responsibility for your child."

He didn't wait for the mother to respond before he turned and left the room.

At the girl's stricken face, Lucy stepped toward her. "Do you have any one else who can help you?"

The girl shook her head slowly, her eyes filling with tears. "My parents kicked me out when I got pregnant with Amanda. I try to do what I can but I'm no good at being a nurse."

Ryan returned with a nurse in tow. She carried a disposable suture kit. "I'm going to put in a couple of stitches to secure the shunt. It'll still have to be bandaged and cleaned regularly." He looked at the mother to punctuate his point.

The mother's eyes grew larger and she screwed up her face with displeasure. Couldn't Ryan tell he was scaring the girl? If he did notice, why didn't he care?

"Why don't we wait outside while Dr. O'Doherty

is working?" Lucy suggested. The mother nodded and Lucy led her out into the hall.

"I know Dr. O'Doherty wants me to see about Amanda's head but I just can't. It makes me so sad to look at it."

Minutes later Ryan opened the door, letting them know that he was finished. Lucy and the mother returned to the room. Ryan looked at the mother and said, "The nurse will show you how to bandage the site. You'll need to bring Amanda back again next week. I'll expect to see that the wound has been cared for."

The girl mumbled, "Okay…" and took her whimpering child from the nurse.

Ryan left and Lucy gave the girl's shoulder a reassuring pat and joined him.

"I hate it when I perform surgery and the patient is improving but the parents won't take care of the child," Ryan said through clenched teeth, softly enough not to sound unprofessional. Lucy had no doubt that he wished he could say it loud enough that not only the mother could hear but everyone else as well.

"Can we go to an empty exam room and talk a sec?" Lucy asked.

He gave her a frustrated look but nodded his assent.

When they were in the room with the door closed behind them, she turned to him and said, "Ryan, you can't be so hard on that mother. She's little more than a child herself and terrified. She has no help at home and a sick child to care for."

"She has a duty to her child. She has to see that her child gets the care she needs."

"Her grief is so great she can't stand to look at her baby, it scares her," Lucy flung back. "Haven't you ever been in a spot where you thought you couldn't handle it?"

He went pale for a second but soon recovered. Still, she'd seen it. His reaction to the mother had been over the top—was his cool relationship with his patient's parents masking something more?

"What do you suggest?" he asked in a tight voice.

"I don't think forcing the girl to do the wound care is the answer. She needs help. Which I will see about getting her. Until then, if you would write an order for home health a couple of times a week, I think it would be best for her and the child."

She was shocked when a slight grin formed on his lips. "I'm starting to feel manipulated but I think you're right this time. I'll write the order." Taking the chart he held, he turned and left the room.

She'd eased one aspect of the girl's issues but she'd hit a nerve in Ryan's. Why?

The knock on her office door told her Ryan stood on the other side. Even the rap of his hand was distinctive. Her officemates had gone home long ago. She might have left sooner if she'd had more to go home to. Instead, she was busy trying to see what services were available to Amanda Marcella. Going to the door, she opened it.

"Hi, I was just wondering if you might have dinner with me tonight. Let me say thanks for helping out this afternoon and apologize for making you feel less than welcome on your first day." He grinned.

Ryan could slay dragons and carry off a princess' heart with that movement of his lips.

"Just doing my job. No thanks necessary. I appreciate the invitation but I think I'd better just go home." Why in the world wasn't she accepting an opportunity to go out with a good-looking, smart man? Because she could be one of those slayed by his grin. Because it couldn't go anywhere. But why did it have to?

"You don't think you can take a few minutes to keep a hard-working colleague company while he eats?" His grin widened.

She was starting to fall for his charm. "I guess I could for a few minutes. I am hungry. But do you mind if I pick the place?"

"Sure. Just so long as it's not a beans-and-sprouts place. I want meat and cheese and more meat."

Lucy smiled. Something she was doing more often when he was around. It felt good. "There's meat, along with great salads."

"Perfect. Let's go."

He stepped through the doorway and waited for her in the hall. For heaven's sake, what was she doing? She had no business going to dinner with Ryan O'Doherty. He was far too likeable. And he made her far too angry sometimes. She secured her scarf around her neck and pulled on her coat. Stepping into the hall, she pulled the door closed behind her and prepared to lock it.

Ryan was no longer there. It was late enough that most of the patients were in bed for the night. One lone mother spoke softly to her child and Lucy's heart constricted. She'd thought distance would ease her feelings about Emily but with each baby she saw there was a fresh stab of pain. Would it ever go away?

She looked around and found Ryan standing in front of the nurses' station, talking to one of the staff. The nurse was snickering. He looked in her direction and grinned.

His smile pushed the heartache away. She needed her mental faculties just to deal with him. The man had the ability to turn that charm on and off at will. All the nurses seemed to go calf-eyed whenever he walked down the hall. More than one had requested to care for his patients in order to have his attention for a few minutes.

That laughter and fun-loving attitude covered the seriousness of his job and the caring heart that she only glimpsed when he was dealing with the children. She'd seen him displeased and she was beginning to think few saw the emotional side of him. That he'd let it slip when she'd been around was something to ponder.

Ryan smiled and started toward her. The nurse saw Lucy and returned to her duties. When she reached Ryan he said, "I just got a page. I need to stop by the nursery for a few minutes to check on a child, if you don't mind."

No, she couldn't do that. It would kill her to see the babies. She would cry. "Um, why don't I just meet you in the lobby?"

"I would've thought you might want to meet the family, if they are there."

"I'll just wait and see if you are assigned the case."

He gave her a quizzical look. "Okay. I'll see you in the lobby as soon as I can."

Lucy breathed a sigh of relief as Ryan walked off. She just wasn't ready to face the nursery.

In the taxi, Ryan grinned when Lucy had to give the address of the restaurant for a second time. The cab driver didn't quite understand her sweet Southern drawl. He himself liked it, a lot. Her slower, softer accent was soothing. He especially liked it when she said his name.

Lucy had a way about her that relaxed him, and others as well. She wasn't authoritarian when she spoke but people listened to her. Plus her manner implied that everything would be all right given time. He'd seen it first hand when she talked to his patients' families. She'd given of herself. At one time, he'd done that more freely but now he had nothing left.

If he ever discovered he had something to give, he hoped someone like Lucy was around to share it with. But now wasn't the time. He'd never confided in anyone from work and he wouldn't be starting now, no matter how tempting it might be.

Lucy sat beside him in the back seat, staring out the window. He wasn't sure if she was avoiding looking at him or was just engrossed in the lights of the "city that never sleeps".

"Have you been to New York before?"

"Once, when I was a kid. With my parents. I don't remember much about it, though." The wistful tone in her voice made him think that it hadn't necessarily been a happy memory.

"I bet you never thought you'd be living here."

She glanced at him. "No, never," she said, before turning back to the window. "And with your accent, I'd guess you've never lived anywhere but here."

"Brooklyn boy, born and raised," he said proudly.

"So that's why you have the baseball picture in your office."

"Yeah. I'm a big Yankees fan. Do you keep up with baseball?"

"If you live in Atlanta you have to follow the Braves. My brother-in-law gets season tickets so I've gone to a few games."

"I have season tickets to the Yankees. Maybe you'd like to go to a game some time?" He shifted uncomfortably. What in the world was he doing, inviting her out to a game? That sounded too much like a date.

The taxi pulled up at the curb.

"Volpentesta's. That's some of the best pizza pie in the city. For someone who has been in the city no longer than you have, you sure know where to get a good meal."

Lucy smiled as she climbed out of the taxi. When she offered her share of the taxi fare he said, "It's on me. My idea for the pizza."

She didn't fight him, just waited on the brick sidewalk gone wavy with age. She tensed a second when he lightly touched the curve of her back but she eased just as quickly. As they came to the door of the restaurant, he reached around her to open it.

"Someone taught you good manners. That's the second time you've opened a door for me."

The dull pain that he carried in his chest sharpened for a second. "My father was very old school. He would say, 'Ryan, my boy, you treat a woman like you want your sisters to be treated. It's the O'Doherty way.'"

"Kind of got off track when you first met me, didn't you?"

"Hey, I showed you up to the floor."

"Yeah, but you would've liked to drop me down the elevator shaft."

"Was I that bad?"

She nodded.

"Then I'll try to make up for it over dinner, okay?"

She smiled. "I've really gotten over it, so don't let it worry you."

A man who was almost as round as he was tall approached them, his hands outstretched. He asked with a strong Italian accent, "Miss Lucy, how are you today?"

Her smiled reached her eyes. Ryan felt a hot stab of jealousy. What would it take to have her smile at him like that? He wasn't going to analyze that thought.

"Mr. Volpentesta, I'm doing fine. We would like a table."

"Anything for you, my dear."

Ryan gave her a quizzical look. The wait even on weeknights for a table at Volpentesta's was long and she'd just waltzed in without a reservation.

The restaurant was an authentic Italian bistro right down to the red checked cloths and the candle on the table. The room was dark enough to make for a pleasing ambiance but not so dim that he couldn't appreciate Lucy's incredibly expressive face.

She wore little make-up. On occasion he'd noticed that she'd applied a gloss to her lips that made them dewy looking. Her hair was always contained by a ribbon or clip or was braided. More than once he'd pictured what it might look like free. She was unique. He'd give her that.

It had been a long time since he'd found a woman so interesting. She reminded him of Irish coffee. Sweet, fresh cream on top with a stout bite beneath. What kind of magic was this woman conjuring over him?

"Come this way, my dear." Mr. Volpentesta led them to a table for two in a far corner of the room.

"How do you know him?" Ryan said close to her ear.

"I live upstairs." She turned and followed the man again.

"Good choice," he said, more to himself than her when they were given a cozy spot. What he'd had in mind had been more of a friendly meal than a lovers' evening. He looked around the room but not finding a better option he accepted his fate. He held her chair out and waited until Lucy was settled before he sat.

"Your father has left nothing out." She spread her napkin in her lap.

"He was a thorough man."

"Was?"

Left no choice, he said, "He died." He couldn't keep the heartache out of his voice.

At her stricken and pitying look, he wished he'd lied. She placed a hand on his forearm and gave him an earnest look. "I'm sorry."

Her touch and concern diminished his feeling of loss for a moment. For the first time he actually felt comforted by another human being. Why was it that this Southern belle touched more than just his arm? "I'm doing fine."

Mercifully, the waiter came to take their order and bought them a bottle of house wine. Ryan wasn't surprised when Lucy ordered a salad. When the waiter left he leaned forward and said, "Do you have any idea on how many levels of wrong it is to order a salad in a place like this?"

"I'm just not that hungry."

He gave her a speculative look. "If I were to guess, you haven't been eating like you should."

She shrugged and toyed with her silverware.

"Not going to comment on that one?"

"No," she said with less zeal than she had earlier, confirming he'd been correct.

He fished for something to keep the conversation going that wasn't too personal. He didn't think she'd answer more questions if they were. "So, did you grow up in Atlanta?" That wasn't as impersonal as he would've liked but he wanted to know more about her.

"Sort of, but mostly at a boarding school in north-east Georgia."

He cocked his head in question.

"My parents divorced. It was easier to send Alexis and me off than to take care of us."

His mother had died when he'd been young. Before his father had gotten too sick he'd been there to take care of Ryan and his sisters. They had never doubted that they were wanted and loved. "Alexis?"

"My twin sister."

"So you're a twin. Interesting. I bet you're close. My father said more than once that 'Family's everything. Without family you have nothing.'"

Clouds formed in her eyes. "I guess for some that's true," she said, sounding more resigned than wistful.

But not for her? "I shouldn't have said that." He took a swallow of his wine. The melancholy in her voice made him wish he'd not quoted his father.

"Alexis and I had each other. We were our own family…" She let the words trail off.

He had to find another subject. "You know, it turns out we're a better team than I anticipated."

"Even as slowly as I speak, I'm still worthwhile." She smirked.

Despite her making fun of him, he enjoyed her quick mind. "Truthfully, I like your accent. Makes me think of lazy, hot days and ice-cold drinks."

She blinked then her eyelids fluttered down. "Now you're embarrassing me." She looked at him. "You know something about me. How about telling me about you?"

"Brooklyn, and more Brooklyn. Med school NYU, intern Angel's, Angel's today."

"I see. The source of your clipped dialect, with a hint of Irish burr occasionally."

"Guilty. My father was second-generation Irish. My accent isn't anywhere near as strong as his was."

Was. He hated that word. Every time he said it, it just reaffirmed that his father was gone.

Their meals arrived. He inhaled the smell of the steaming pie. "This is going to taste wonderful." He glanced up as he bit into a slice of pizza. Lucy watched him. She looked down at her salad. "What?"

"Nothing."

"You were thinking something. Tell."

Her eyes slowly lifted. "I've never seen a man enjoy his food quite as much as you do."

He grinned around the warm pizza at his lips. "I told you I was hungry and this is darned good pizza. Thanks for bringing me here."

"You're welcome."

"You want to share?" He raised the slice in his hand. Somehow the word share took on an intimate connotation when it included her. "Come on, you should at least try your landlord's pie."

"I guess I could stand a bite."

He leaned over the table, holding the slice to her lips. She took a mouthful next to where he'd bitten. Somehow it made it far too familiar. As if their lips had touched. He was captivated by the change in her facial expression when it became one of ecstasy as she experienced the taste and texture of the morsel. His gaze remained glued to her lips when the tip of her tongue peeked out to caress the breadth of her full lips, seizing every particle of pleasure, leaving her pink mouth wet and glistening.

He shifted uncomfortably as his body reacted to the sight. Her utterly innocent look said she had no idea how incredibly erotic her actions were. Making her even more mesmerizing.

"Another?" He couldn't have stopped himself from

asking if he'd been offered a million dollars. He wanted her to repeat that sensual gesture. The downside was he wasn't sure he could leave the restaurant without embarrassing himself, or, worse, her.

"It was good, but, no, thanks."

Disappointed, he accepted her decision without pressing her to change her mind. With an effort he prevented his discomfort from showing. Based on her innocent appearance and just as enthralling was the fact she had no idea what she did to him.

He took another bite, hoping to clear his head, but it didn't help. She really was an enigma. In her slacks and sweater, she looked at if she had never experienced much of life, but he knew better.

They were finishing their meal over a discussion of the latest movies when Lucy's attention was drawn to something across the room. He turned to see what it was. A mother a few tables over was holding a baby of about six months old. What was it with her and babies? He still didn't understand her reaction to going to the nursery. He would've thought she'd have jumped at the chance to meet a new family.

"Something wrong?"

She looked at him with glassy eyes. "I was just missing my family."

He identified with missing loved ones. But those feelings could and should be managed. Dealing with a weepy woman was something he wasn't going to do. "I'm going to call it an evening. I've—we've, got an early morning. I'll walk you to your door."

"Go on. I'll be fine. I need to speak to Mr. Volpentesta anyway. I'll get the check."

"That won't happen. A gentleman pays the bill. It's the O'Doherty way."

* * *

Lucy climbed the stairs to her apartment. The place seemed less inviting after spending time with Ryan in the bustling restaurant. The solitude was stifling. She'd left everything that truly mattered in her life behind when she'd moved to New York. Maybe out of desperation she was hoping she and Ryan were becoming friends.

Their relationship had been rocky initially but they'd developed a mutual understanding in the last few days. He did what he needed to do and she tried not to get in his way. Up until today they'd shared nothing of their personal lives. Their work had forced them together but that hadn't made them friends. Maybe that was changing.

She unlocked and entered her apartment. Flipping on a lamp, she pulled the curtains closed, something she often forgot to do, not yet being used to living so close to others. She began to undress.

She'd enjoyed her meal with Ryan. It had been nice to eat with someone for a change. While living with Alexis and Sam, they'd eaten the evening meal together every night. It hadn't taken her long to miss that camaraderie, the feeling of being included.

Lucy had felt that same fellowship with Ryan tonight, but had he?

CHAPTER THREE

FRIDAY NIGHT, LUCY hadn't been home thirty minutes when her phone rang. The deep voice on the other end spoke so swiftly she didn't catch what he said. It sounded like Ryan but she wasn't sure.

"Ryan?"

"Yes. Lucy, we have a case coming in. You need to meet me in the emergency room."

"I'll be right there."

She dressed again quickly in jeans and a warm cream-colored pullover sweater. Wrapping a dark blue scarf around her neck and pulling on her coat, she headed out the door. After a subway ride and the usual couple of missed turns in the hospital, she found her way to the ER. At the nurses' desk, she asked what room Dr. O'Doherty was in.

"He's seeing a patient. Are you the parent?"

Lucy flinched. That question hit too close to home. That wasn't her job. "I'm the family counselor for Neurosurgery. Dr. O'Doherty is expecting me." She showed the clerk her badge.

"He's in exam room nineteen," the nurse said, indicating Lucy should go down the hall.

Lucy found the room and knocked on the door.

Pushing it open slightly, she stuck her head inside the dim room.

Ryan wore a heavy red sweater with a hint of a white T-shirt showing at the collar and dark jeans that fit his trim hips perfectly. His lab coat was nowhere in sight but, despite his dress, the air of authority around him said he belonged.

A young Hispanic boy of about six months lay on a pristine white sheet on top of a stretcher as if asleep. Lucy worked to make the golfball-size lump in her throat disappear. The boy was so close to Emily's age. This case was already hitting too close to home. The temptation to turn and run was great. The child's unnatural stillness indicated he'd been medicated. If anything like this happened to Emily…

Ryan lifted one of the boy's eyelids and directed a penlight into it. A couple stood nearby, the old man's arm circled the woman's shoulders, holding her close.

Taking a bracing lungful of air and letting it out slowly, Lucy slipped quietly into the room and stood nearby so not to interrupt Ryan's examination. She would get through this. See about the family then go home and regroup. That way she would have her emotions under control by morning.

An anxious-looking woman stood nearby, clutching a purse in a grip that could have strangled a living thing. Lucy's heart went out to her. Would she herself act the same way if it was Emily lying on the bed? She had to stop thinking in that context. This wasn't Emily and if it had been, she wasn't Lucy's to worry over.

In what must have been her nervousness, the woman broke into rapid Spanish. Ryan gave the mother a perplexed look. Apparently he had no idea what the woman was saying.

It was time for Lucy to brace herself and be the professional she was trained to be instead of the quiver-
ing mass of emotions she'd morphed into. She stepped
closer, lightly touching the mother on the arm to draw
her attention. In a low, even voice Lucy explained who
she was in Spanish. The woman visibly relaxed as Lucy
continued to speak. "I'm Lucy Edwards and I work with
Dr. O'Doherty. Your boy's in good hands. What's your
son's name?"

"Miguel."

"That's a nice name. Why don't you come over here
and sit?" With a shaking hand Lucy directed her toward a metal straight-backed chair near the wall. The
man followed them and stood close. She glanced to
where Ryan's wide shoulders still leaned over the child.
Taking a cleansing breath, she said, "As soon as Dr.
O'Doherty is through examining Miguel, he'll be able
to tell you more." The woman nodded, her eyes reflect-
ing all the fear she was feeling. "What's your relationship to Miguel?"

"His mother. No, I'm really his aunt."

The words bit into Lucy and a swirl of agony formed
in her stomach. Could things get any worse? Her hand
came to rest over the spot. *She was Emily's aunt, not
her mother.* Pressing her hand down, she hoped it would
ease the building torment but knew it couldn't. Would
she ever recover? Accept?

"His mother ran off and left him with me."

She'd run off and left Emily. But it had been different. Her sister was Emily's mother. Why wasn't there
another chair for her to sit on? She had to grasp her emotions to hold them in check. She'd break down later and
let the tears flow. Something she'd sworn never to do

again. Lucy almost missed what the woman was saying as she reminded herself to breathe.

"Miguel's mother didn't understand his illness. It scared her. This…" the woman placed a hand on the forearm of the man standing beside her "…is my father. Miguel and I live with him."

With fortitude Lucy would never have thought she possessed, she managed to continue consoling the woman and her father. Maybe if she focused on their needs instead of her own, the anguish would diminish. She continued to tell herself that lie.

Having finished his examination, Ryan approached them. Lucy looked up to find his eyes on her. He nodded with what she read as his appreciation and respect but his brows crowded together seconds too long. Was the agony she felt written on her face? She tried to school her appearance not to show her feelings. The question in Ryan's eyes was replaced by a grave look.

"Ms. Edwards, may I speak with you a moment?"

She nodded then told the woman and her father she'd be right back. Ryan waited for her outside the door. When she stood close enough that he wouldn't be overheard by others in the ER, he said, "This child needs surgery."

"I understand."

"I won't lie. This will be a tough one."

"Then you need to explain it to them. Reassure them."

"I'm not going to do that." Ryan didn't think getting run over by a sixteen-wheeler truck could have knocked the wind out of him more completely. He couldn't and wouldn't provide the care Lucy was pushing him toward.

"They're scared. They need the reassurance that you can give them."

"Lucy, I do surgery. Not feelings. That's your department," he said, his voice rising. "You do your job."

She flinched but didn't move. "I am doing my job by seeing that you do yours. I'll translate. All you have to do is explain what's going to happen. Parents need to know their doctor cares."

He had cared. That was the problem. He knew the hurt it caused. He knew pain so great that if he let it out of the box it would groan, snarl and devour him.

"No. You handle it." He turned to walk away.

She grabbed his arm. "Look, someone has to tell this family something right away. I'm not the doctor. I don't have the medical knowledge. You're an excellent surgeon, just let them know that. Give them some hope. That's all you have to do." They stared at each other for a long moment before she said quietly, "I'd hate to tell Mr. Matherson that you refused to co-operate on the coordinated care project."

"The hell you will," he bellowed, and shook his arm out of her grasp.

Lucy's head jerked around toward the ER desk. His gaze followed. The staff behind the desk and in the hall had stopped in place to look at them with astonishment, curiosity and anticipation on their faces.

Great. If this got back to Matherson or, worse, Rodriguez...

He looked at Lucy. "Okay. But I do it my way," he growled.

Lucy nodded. At least she didn't smirk. If she had, he didn't know how he would've reacted. He'd talk to the parents but he'd leave feelings out of it. He'd survived his father's death and illness on his own and others could handle their problems. He offered his medical skills to his patients, performed surgery to the best of his ability but he couldn't get involved outside his work in the OR.

They re-entered the room.

The family remained seated and he stood over them as he spoke. Lucy translated. "As I understand it, Dr. Matthews, your son's neurologist, has explained that the child has experienced a *grand mal* seizure. The drugs that he has been taking are no longer working effectively. The seizures your son is having now will only get worse as time goes on. Your son—"

"Miguel," Lucy offered.

That was just like Lucy to make it personal. Something he didn't want. Ryan glared at her then turned back to the mother. "Miguel's going to need surgery to slow these down. At first Dr. Matthews thought the surgery might need to be done right away. I believe that Miguel needs to stay in the hospital and be monitored for a few days. But he will need surgery. Even after that the seizures will continue, but they shouldn't be as severe."

The mother was openly crying by the time he'd finished. All he wanted was to get out of there. Nothing he could say or do would make it better for them. He wasn't going to try. No matter how hard Lucy pushed.

He looked at her. "I need to make some arrangements and a couple of calls. I'll have to see about setting up a surgery time and date. Right now, I want him to remain sedated and rest. Dr. Matthews has already started the admission process."

"I'll see that they understand." She mouthed, "Thank you."

That wasn't going to smooth over how he felt about being forced to talk to the parents. His stomach was one big mess of knots. He left without a backward glance.

Thirty minutes later and still seething from the earlier ordeal, Ryan stalked to the family counselors' office. For a person who couldn't have told anyone where it was at the beginning of the week, he was actually visiting it for the third time. Lucy had made him go through the wringer and he intended to make it clear he would not allow it to happen again.

It was late enough that the floor was quiet and the lights had been turned down in the hallway. A light glowed beneath the office door. He rapped on the door with enough force that the nurse at the end of the hall looked up from where she was charting.

There was movement in the room and the door remained closed. Lucy must be in there. He'd raised his hand to knock again when the door opened.

"Yes?" She met his gaze. "Is something wrong?"

"As a matter of fact, there is. I will not be blackmailed."

Both their heads tuned toward the shushing sound coming from down the hall. The nurse had her finger held across her lips.

"Let's go into your office." He gave her a nudge. Her uncertain look brought his anger down a notch. He hadn't intended to scare her. "Please, Lucy."

She backed into the room but didn't meet his eyes. He entered and closed the door, and Lucy moved as far back in the room as the tiny space would allow. She didn't sit, so neither did he.

He shoved his hands into his pockets. "Just what was that all about down there in the ER? Why the big push to get me to be so concerned about the family's feelings? You went too far tonight, Lucy." He stepped a pace closer as he spoke.

She stood her ground. "Because the least they deserved was to have their doctor's, and especially their surgeon's, concern. They want to hear the good and the bad from *you*. They want to feel they can trust you with their loved one's life. To do that they have to know you. They have to have a relationship with you, even if it is only a surface one. They're putting the most precious thing in their lives into your hands and that takes real courage.

"Do you have any idea what it is like to hand your child over to someone? To trust them to give them the care and attention that you would?"

Her large, dramatic eyes glistened. Was she going to cry?

"Are you so insensitive that you can't have any compassion for the parents of your patients? It's a good thing you're not a thoracic surgeon because I don't think you'd even recognize a heart if you saw one."

Ryan recoiled as if he'd been slapped. He'd come here with the intention of getting an apology and instead he was getting a dressing down. Where was all this venom coming from?

She turned to her desk, putting her back to him. "I've had enough for today. I'm headed home. We can talk about this tomorrow."

"No, we can't." He used his OR hand-me-an-instrument voice. "We're going to talk about it now. I don't think that entire tirade was to do with me or what happened in the ER tonight."

She pulled out the desk drawer and brought out her purse. "Look, Ryan, I'm too tired to hash this out tonight. I'd just like to go home."

"We're not going anywhere until you explain to me—"

"You can't keep me here."

"I can." He moved so that he leaned against the door. "But I'd prefer not to." Her luminous eyes pleaded with him and his heart caught. The part he'd thought had died with his father. Lucy was pulling him, kicking and screaming, back to life.

"Something is wrong. Don't tell me you're just upset about the boy because I won't buy it. Even with your tender heart, you wouldn't be this upset."

"Not only a brain surgeon but a psychiatrist too. My, you must've been a genius in med school to be as young as you are and pull off two degrees."

"Not a genius but I do pride myself on being perceptive. Or at least I used to be." That had been until Alex Rodriguez had been brought in to take the department head position that Ryan had been so sure was his. "Anyway, we're not talking about me."

She pulled her coat and scarf off the back of her chair. "I'm sorry if I hurt your feelings but it needed to be said. Now, if you'll excuse me...?" She stepped toward him as if hoping to intimidate him into letting her pass.

He shook his head. "Not until you explain."

She dropped into a desk chair. He took the chair closest, propping his elbows on his knees and facing her.

"Sharing wasn't outlined in the co-ordinated patient care manual. Can't you just let it go?"

"You owe me an explanation for your attack." That at least got a contrite look from her. Was he losing his mind? He didn't confide in people and he didn't get involved in another person's personal life.

"You're going to make me say it?"

He nodded.

"Miguel's mother isn't really his mother."

"Miguel?" His brows dipped. He was completely lost.

"Your newest patient." Her voice had a tone of impatience and a touch of disappointment.

He was catching up. What did Miguel have to do with her problem? "Oh, yes, Miguel Rivera."

"His mother is really his aunt."

She wasn't usually this vague. His puzzled look must have indicated he had no idea of the significance of that statement.

"I carried a baby for my sister and her husband. I had in vitro fertilization," she said quietly.

Being a surrogate for her sister had been Lucy's ultimate pleasure. Handing over the baby she'd carried her greatest pain. In order to survive emotionally, she'd left. Emily was her sister's baby, not her own. No matter how much her heart screamed differently.

She stood and said in a flat voice, "Now can I go?"

Ryan's eyes widened. He blinked and shifted slightly, as if he was formulating his words carefully. "Of all the things I might have thought you'd say, that wasn't one of them."

To voice the words had been painful, but there was something freeing about having said them. She couldn't believe she'd told Ryan of all people. He'd more than once proved he couldn't connect on an emotional level. If she had been going to confess to someone, he wouldn't have been her choice. She'd only shared her pain because he'd caught her in a weak moment and he'd insisted.

Still, being new to town and working long hours, he was the closest person to a friend she had. He was the only soul other than Mr. Volpentesta that she saw regularly. That thought was so sad she didn't take time to analyze it for fear she would start crying. Here she was revealing her deepest pain to someone who hadn't wanted her even taking up his time just a few days earlier.

Ryan stood. "I've heard of women being surrogates, but I've never known anyone that has done it."

She'd obviously shocked him. For some reason she felt the need to make him understand. "My twin sister Alexis and her husband Sam tried to conceive for years. When Alexis asked me if I would carry their baby, I couldn't turn her down. Didn't want to…" The words trailed off. *If I'd known…*

His eyes widened as if he suddenly saw the picture clearly. "So when Miguel's mother said she was really his aunt, it hit too close to home?"

She nodded. "It almost killed me to give Emily up." She looked at her hands clasped around her purse.

"Emily?"

"My ba—uh…niece."

He placed a large hand on her shoulder. The heat from him seeped into her, easing some of the ache. As if he'd realized what he was doing, he let his hand fall away.

"That must have been hard."

Ryan sounded sincere but a little unsure. Her head spun. Was this the same doctor she'd had a heated confrontation with just an hour earlier about being compassionate? She'd never seen this side of him with the families. Maybe what happened tonight had knocked some of that crustiness off. She looked into his gorgeous blue eyes that compelled her to continue.

"My head said she didn't belong to me, but my heart said differently. I made the fatal mistake of starting to think of her as mine." She'd shared all she could. Her nerves were raw.

"You didn't want to give her up."

She couldn't have been more surprised. He understood. "That's why I took this job, to get away. Had to figure out how to get my life back. I'd like to go home now."

He opened the door. "Put on your coat. I'm going to see you home."

Ryan delayed until he was sure Lucy had made it safely inside her apartment. She'd insisted that he not walk up with her so instead he'd had the taxi wait until he saw her light come on.

He was on an emotional overload. If it had been a warmer day, he'd be sweating. He'd felt more and cared more than he'd wanted to in the last twelve hours. Taken a double shot. All of a sudden he'd been forced to support a family and had later become Lucy's confessor.

He'd been more in touch with others' emotions than he had been since his father's death. His father's debilitating disease had not only taken him but had slowly taken Ryan's soul as well. He couldn't let himself be pulled into that eddy again. He would be back to going round and round. If he didn't feel, didn't care, then it didn't hurt. Supporting someone emotionally was beyond his ability any more.

Today he'd stepped too close to the edge. At Lucy's pronouncement and the troubled look in her eyes, he'd almost gone over that edge. Only through fist-clenching control had he not taken Lucy in his arms.

They'd both stepped over the professional line today. After the emotional flood Lucy had experienced, would she be able to handle her job? She was supposed to be there to support and care for Miguel's family. Could she maintain that openness that made her so effective?

Lucy was worming her way into his life so effort-lessly that she would begin to expect something he couldn't give to both her and his patients. She'd want everything and he had nothing. He had to step back a pace. Keep their relationship professional only. It was up to him to make it happen.

The problem came down to whether he had the strength to remain distant when he looked into those stunning jeweled blue eyes misted over with unhap-piness.

Lucy hadn't heard from Ryan over the weekend. She'd not really expected to but she'd hoped he would at least call and check on her. It had felt good to share her bur-den with him. Just talking about Emily had made it eas-ier. There had been a time she couldn't have uttered the words. Now at least she could think about Emily without crying. If Ryan hadn't insisted she talk, she might still be stymied by the pain. It wasn't gone but it had eased.

On Monday she didn't see Ryan until evening rounds and there was no opportunity to talk to him outside of giving reports on the patients.

They were just finishing up when Ryan announced to the group, "Miguel Rivera's surgery is scheduled for tomorrow first thing."

"I helped walk the mother through the insurance process and found them a place to stay while Miguel's in ICU," Lucy reported.

Ryan gave her a curt nod that held none of his usual humor. It was as if they were strangers again who knew nothing about each other and never intended to. He laughed and joked with the other staff members but hadn't even spoken to her directly. This was worse than his reaction to her on the day they'd met. She hadn't expected them to be best friends but she hadn't anticipated being thoroughly ignored either.

She didn't make it a habit of confiding in anyone other than her sister, and now that was gone she had no one. It disturbed her that the single time she'd stepped out beyond her safety zone she'd been treated like she didn't exist.

Maybe she should give him the benefit of the doubt. Was he worried about Miguel's surgery? Ryan had already proved that he was the kind of guy that compartmentalized. Still, she'd come to expect a certain attitude from him and she missed his easy grin.

Miguel's surgery was an all-day affair. Lucy came to the hospital early so that she'd be available if the family needed her. She had to work harder than usual to keep her emotions in check. Miguel reminded her so much of Emily that she had to call on her professional persona and do what she'd been trained to do. During the day, between seeing to her other cases, she checked in with the family. She happened to be sitting with them when Ryan came in after surgery to speak to the family.

The dark blue scrubs he wore brought out his vivid eyes. He hesitated a second when he saw her. He looked tired, the lines around his mouth a little more evident. After giving her a brief nod, he turned his focus on the mother and grandfather waiting anxiously to hear what he had to say.

"You will translate?" Ryan asked, again without looking at her.

"Yes."

Ryan didn't go down to the mother's eye level, but instead stood away from her. She looked up at him from where she sat. Disappointment filled Lucy. She'd hoped that what had happened the other night would make a difference in his rapport with families.

"Miguel's doing well. He came through surgery fine but it will not be an easy recovery. He'll be in ICU for a few days. If all goes well he'll go out to the children's ward after that. The first few days we have to be very careful."

"Thank you," the mother gushed, jumping up to wrap her arms around his waist.

Ryan looked shocked but patted the woman's shoulder. "You're welcome."

Lucy might have found it comical if it hadn't been for Ryan ignoring her.

He pushed away from the woman, shook the man's hand and left without a backward glance. Lucy understood this time wasn't about her but she still couldn't help the disappointment she felt that Ryan hadn't said something to her.

She'd planned to stay late in order to go into ICU with Miguel's family for the first time. The boy's nurse spoke enough Spanish to answer simple questions, allowing Lucy to leave without worrying about the family being on their own. She followed behind the Riveras as they left the unit. Ryan was sitting behind the unit desk. He looked up briefly and met her gaze before his eyes returned to what he was doing. A prickle along her spine said that he had watched her walk out the doors.

Where was the guy she'd thought might be a friend? She'd had enough of the cold-shoulder treatment. She was going to find out.

Ryan had just finished rounds for the evening. He'd done them later than usual. His clinical staff always knew that it would be a late night after he'd had a big surgery and made plans accordingly. Today was one of those days. He'd had his clinical nurse notify Lucy.

She was waiting along with everyone else in the hall, looking efficient and fresh despite the late hour. It had been a long day for her also. She'd been there every step of the way with the Rivera family. Ryan had been impressed with how well she seemed to be holding up under what had to be a difficult situation for her. To his discontent, he'd found himself worrying about her. Wondering how she was doing. That was a road he didn't want to travel.

When she'd visited ICU with the family he had been aware of every move she'd made. She'd looked tired, but every bit as committed to the family as he'd hoped she would be. A couple of times she'd looked in his direction with questioning eyes that had also held disappointment. It had been far more difficult not to engage with her than he'd anticipated. Still, he thought it was for the best.

He made every effort to make it through rounds as efficiently as possible. Lucy spoke to each of the families before she left the patient's room. The families had smiles on their faces when the door closed behind him and his group. She'd turned out to be a real asset. Without a word, she turned toward her office with determined steps.

Having finished on the floor, he headed to his office for a quick wash up before checking on Miguel. There would be no going home for him tonight.

There was a knock on his office door. A nurse coming to get him this late at night wouldn't be good news. "Come in," he called.

Lucy stalked forward, stopping in front of his desk.

"There's a problem?" By the determined look on her face there must be. He had a nagging idea he knew exactly what was bothering her.

"Yes, I'd like to discuss something with you."

Discuss? Lucy didn't look like she was in a discussing mood. He'd never heard her sound so forceful, even more so than she'd been a few nights earlier. She'd shared her heartache with him the other night. That had scared him. He didn't want to know anything else. "Lucy, it's been a long day and I'm not really up for some major discussion if it'll wait."

"It won't," she snapped.

Apparently she was on a mission. "Then you can have a seat while I finish cleaning up."

"I'll stand." She pulled her sweater tighter around her chest.

"As you wish."

Her lips tightened. What would it be like to kiss those full lips into a smile of pleasure? Make her forget why she was here? Hadn't he promised himself that he wouldn't allow those thoughts? What he needed to do was find some nurse and take her out on a date. Have a good time.

He'd managed to keep Lucy at a distance for the last couple of days but he still couldn't get the sad look she had when she'd told him about Emily out of his mind. He even remembered the child's name. He was already far too involved.

After toweling off, he rubbed a hand over his more than five o'clock shadow and decided to shave. Stalling all he could in the hope that Lucy would leave. Five minutes later he stepped out into his office again.

Lucy still remained rooted in the same spot she'd been in when he'd left her. Her brows were drawn together and her mouth had eased but remained in a thin line. She pulled the ever-present cardigan tighter around her and crossed her arms. Her look said she might boil over at any minute.

"So what's the problem? I know this can't be about Miguel. He was doing fine when I called to check on him a few minutes ago."

"No, this is about us."

"I wasn't aware there was an 'us'."

Before that moment he couldn't have imagined her standing any straighter or looking more out of sorts, but he'd underestimated her. The blue in her eyes went diamond sharp. If she'd had the capability, he was sure she would've sliced him up into small pieces. He moved behind his desk and faced her.

"There isn't an *us*. Not the kind you're insinuating." Her southern drawl had lost its gentleness, taking on an edge that showed she had a strength she kept hidden. She took a deep breath that made him curl his fingers into fists to keep from touching her.

"What I'm trying to say is that I don't appreciate the cold-shoulder treatment that you've been giving me the last couple of days. I shared something incredibly personal. Painful. At your request. Then you start acting like you don't know me."

There was no volcano in any part of the world that could've looked more furious and spat more sparks than the woman standing in front of him. But he couldn't let that sway him. "So, because you told me your life story I'm supposed to be your best friend?"

Lucy jerked back as if she'd been physically slapped.

For the first time in her life she thought about striking another person in anger. She clenched her teeth.

Hitting him was the least of what she'd like to do. Run him over with a car, set him on fire, pull his fingernails out with pliers. *Ooh, the man!*

She was through being the peacemaker, the one who bent over to make everyone happy. "Look, you egotistical, arrogant man, I don't expect you to be my best friend but what I do expect is for you to be civil.

"The staff has noticed how you treat me. I've been asked what I did to make you mad. For some reason, not obvious to me, you're well liked. Your attitude towards me makes my job more difficult because the staff assumes I have done something wrong. I'm the new kid on the block so they'll side with you." She stopped long enough to take a breath.

When he opened his mouth to speak she held up a hand, stalling him. "What I want—no, demand—is that you show me the professional respect that I deserve. I will never make the mistake of believing that I'm anything other than a colleague you are forced to work with. Until we are told differently, I will do my job in the most professional manner possible and I expect the same from you."

He took a step toward her. "Are you finished?" he said between clenched teeth.

She hesitated. "No. Actually, I'm not." Her voice rose, which she almost never allowed to happen. "Fear not, I'll never confide anything of a personal nature again to you."

With that said, she turned and stalked out the door. Her hands shook and her knuckles had turned white where they were balled beside her. The clacking of her heels on the tile hallway matched the beat of her racing heart.

Boy, that had felt good. Liberating. She'd had no

idea how much pain and anguish she'd kept bottled up. Maybe Ryan didn't deserve the full blast of the emotions she'd kept in check over the last few months. Heck, yeah, he did. He'd been a real jerk. The release had been freeing. She'd been stupid to ever think they could be friends.

It had been empowering. To let go for once. To fight for herself.

She would've dealt with her feelings about him backing away from her in private, but when it came into the patient care area she'd had to draw a line. Then she'd had to say something. She smiled. She'd lectured, more like.

Heading for her office, she passed a nurse who said, "Hi, Lucy." She gave her a bright smile. The nurse gave her a funny look but returned Lucy's smile. She was relieved to find her office empty. She didn't want to discuss what had just happened with anyone while she was still feeling mad. If she did, the other person would be so surprised to know she had just told off the wonderful, charming, friend-to-all-the-nurses-and-patients Dr. Ryan O'Doherty. Haw!

That was, everyone but her.

Was she jealous because he didn't treat her the same? No, that couldn't be. Maybe it was. He had at least made it known that he appreciated her contributions in the last week. She had just read him wrongly. He didn't like her. She could deal with that. What really annoyed her was that she liked him.

The light on her computer blinked, indicating she had a message. Tapping a key with more force than necessary, her email inbox opened. She scanned it. The message was from Mr. Matherson in HR. He requested that she and Ryan attend Jack Carter's going-away party together as a sign that the co-ordinated patient care program was working.

"Great. Just great." She was starting to agree with Ryan's negative view of this program.

A new message came up. The address indicated it was from Ryan. She clicked. His terse message read: *"Assume you received same email. Will pick you up at seven."*

CHAPTER FOUR

RYAN STEPPED ONTO the landing of the third floor above Volpentesta's Restaurant and studied the glossily painted doors. Lucy's response to his email had been "*Third floor, red door.*" That had been the sum total of their personal communication since she had stalked out of his office.

During rounds she'd made it a point not to stand near him. To make the Siberian, dead-of-winter, glacial temperature between them worse, she seemed even sunnier and happier to see the patients and the other staff members than usual. None of that sunshine fell on him.

If she'd had a question about a patient she'd turned to his clinical nurse for answers. Even when Miguel had had a high fever while still in ICU and Ryan had had a real concern that the boy might require another trip to surgery, it hadn't been him Lucy had turned to for information in order to reassure the parents.

He'd been concerned about her reaction to Miguel's downturn but he wouldn't let himself ask her about it. He wasn't going to that place he'd been during his father's illness. But, still, he cared.

Lucy couldn't have made it clearer that she had no use for him if she'd shouted it over the intercom. It had been the longest week of his life.

Wasn't that the way he'd wanted it? Yeah, but living in exile hadn't turned out to be as easy as he'd thought.

For heaven's sake, he did brain surgery for a living, on children no less, and the quiet, unassuming woman had rattled his world. He suspected this would be the least agreeable date he'd ever been on. With resigned steps he approached her door and paused for a second before knocking. He'd not been this nervous since he'd done his first solo surgery. This woman wouldn't intimidate him, he refused to allow it.

Taking a deep breath and letting it out slowly, he tapped on the door. It opened with a suddenness that startled him.

"I'm ready," Lucy said in a snippy voice.

Her anger hadn't cooled. Instead of making him mad, she'd managed to make him feel guilty. He didn't like that feeling at all.

Lucy stepped out into the landing and pulled the door closed behind her. Her coat was already on and buttoned. A scarf in shades of pink orbited her neck. There was a faint smell of wildflowers about her.

Recovering from the shock of her sudden appearance, he found his breath caught in a stranglehold with the realization that Lucy's hair was down. He'd never seen it anything less than under control. Tonight it hung in honey-gold ringlets around her face and down her back. Way down her back. He'd imagined, more than once, what the mass would look like set free but none of his ideas had come near the reality. Her hair was outstanding, glorious, mesmerizing. If he could only touch…

He lifted a hand. She jerked back as if burnt.

That hurt. Could the little boy caught with his hand in a cookie jar have felt any more humiliated? Disappointed? "After you," he mumbled as he moved back to let her precede him.

He watched in fascination as her wheat-colored mane bounced across her back as she went down the stairs. Her hair stood out in contrast against the chocolate color of her coat. He'd always thought of himself as a leg man but in this case that might not be accurate. What would it be like to have that curtain of gorgeous hair hanging above him while her eyes twinkled at him and her mouth lowered to his? He groaned low in his chest.

She glanced back at him. The unwelcoming look on her face said *Don't you dare* before it continued down. The woman couldn't possibly know his thoughts, could she?

He had to get control of his libido or the night would be even more difficult than he'd originally assumed. Lucy was already angry with him and lusting after her wouldn't make her happier. Grateful for the cold blast of wind that met him straight on when he stepped out of the building, he squared his shoulders. He could do this. If he had to, he'd walk outside when the need to touch her became too strong. Maybe they could get away with putting in an appearance then leaving.

Lucy turned and looked at him as if asking what came next.

"This way." He stepped toward the restaurant valet attendant, resisting the urge to cup her elbow. She walked beside him but not so close that they touched. He handed the parking slip to the attendant.

Her eyes went wide. "You're driving? I thought we'd take a taxi."

"Not tonight."

When the attendant pulled the low, two-seater sports car in front of them Ryan had the pleasure of watching as Lucy's mouth form an O. He grinned. She liked his car. Lucy allowed his touch as he helped her into the car. A ringlet of her heavenly hair curled along his arm. He took his chance and touched it briefly. *So soft.*

Closing her door, he walked around the vehicle, bracing himself to be confined in a small space with a woman snapping mad at him. Could her anger and his lust coexist without turning to fireworks before they made it to the Ritz?

Lucy looked away from the stop-and-go traffic as they worked their way up Fifth Avenue. She studied Ryan's profile by the glow of the city lights. The luminous yellows, greens, oranges and blues flashed across his straight nose and firm jaw. By anyone's definition Ryan was handsome. When he smiled, breathtakingly so. But being attractive was only surface deep. Where it really counted, he'd let her down. He'd pushed her away. She didn't like someone playing tug of war with her emotions.

Ryan glanced at her and she quickly looked away.

"Everything okay?"

"You mean besides us being forced to attend this party together?"

"You do know it wasn't my idea." His words were as flat as a table.

She sighed. "I know." Silence filled the space between them as if they were strangers.

Minutes later Ryan said, "I had no idea you had so much hair. You always keep it up or in a braid."

"Too much. I grow it for Locks for Life."

"What's that?"

"I give my hair to make wigs for cancer patients."

Had he mumbled "What a shame"?

"Does your twin have the same kind of hair?"

"No. We're not identical."

"It's beautiful, you know."

Warmth that had nothing to do with the car heater blanketed her, but she wasn't going to be pulled in by him again. She no longer trusted him but she couldn't deny it felt good to receive a compliment from such a virile man. "Thank you, but you do know that you don't have to pay me compliments. I'm not your date who needs to be charmed. This is a business party."

"I'm sorry if giving you sincere praise and making conversation disturbs you."

"Let's just get through this evening with as little personal conversation as possible."

"I'm not promising that."

They had stopped at the next light before she spoke again. "I didn't think anyone who lived in the city drove."

"I don't drive often but I like to when I can. You know, this could almost be considered a personal topic." The smile in his voice shone through clearly.

Lucy huffed. The man was making fun of her. Typical male. Have it out and move on as if nothing had happened. That didn't work for her. She was still upset with him.

Getting through the party was going to be a challenge, with Ryan's charm swirling around and his talent for exasperating her. The evening could go one of two ways. She could blow up at him again or fall at his feet. The latter she couldn't let happen. Compounding the problem was that if she'd noticed how handsome he was on a daily basis it didn't come close to how fine he looked tonight.

His jet-black tux fit his shoulders to perfection. A tall

man, his formal dress had seemed to make him tower over her as he'd helped her into the car. The stark white of his shirt accented his dark skin. The entire package screamed man of power. His haircut didn't completely control the thickness of his locks. Was it soft or bristly to the touch? Those thoughts were better left in a drawer. She gulped and held her purse in a death grip as she resisted the urge to touch him.

She made a resolution. Her goal was threefold: get through the party; return home; and prepare herself to be professional again on Monday. The other day Ryan had made it clear he wasn't interested in discussing anything close to being deeply personal. She'd be glad to honor that.

There was no doubt in her mind that she wouldn't have been his date if it hadn't been necessary to keep in the good graces of the hospital. She just hated the tension that hung between them. It was a strain to always be on guard. At one time she'd thought they might be friends. Could have been if he'd not treated her as if she'd done something wrong by showing her feelings.

Ryan pulled the car skillfully to the curb in front of the brass doors of the Ritz. The attendant opened her door but Ryan was there to help her out. He offered his hand and she placed hers in it but let go as soon as she was on the sidewalk. She liked his touch too much. He opened the door of the hotel for her like the gentleman he'd been taught to be. The O'Doherty way didn't extend to friendship apparently.

Only by hanging onto her anger did she manage not to step closer to him and breathe in his scent. He smelled of tropical islands and salt breezes. It would've been heavenly to be escorted by such a dazzling man if he'd wanted to be with her. But he didn't.

She was relieved Ryan didn't offer his arm but instead followed a half a pace behind her as they entered the hotel. Close enough for her to feel protected by his large body but not overpowered. The zing she'd experienced when she'd touched his hand as he helped her out of the car still lingered. She could only imagine the extent of her reaction if she'd held his arm.

They walked across the marble-tiled hotel lobby towards the ornate circular staircase. She glanced back at Ryan. His attention was on Dr. Rodriguez, who was pacing nearby while talking on his phone.

When Ryan met her look his lips were tightly compressed. He cupped her elbow and they continued forward. "I'd like us to get through this evening as civilly as possible," he said as they climbed the stairs. His relaxed attitude had been replaced by one of a man on a mission. "This is important to my career and yours as well, I'd guess."

She looked at him. It hadn't been a good idea to look into his beautiful persuasive eyes. After swallowing hard, she said, "I don't see a problem. I'll play my part."

His brows took a downward turn as if he wasn't completely pleased with her response. "Then there shouldn't be an issue."

"Agreed."

As couples passed them on the stairs, Ryan moved closer to her to accommodate them. "Smile. You look like I'm escorting you to the guillotine." She gave him a wry smile.

"See, that isn't so hard." His breath whispered across her cheek.

A shiver shot through her. Being drawn in by his charisma wasn't part of the plan. She had a part to play that couldn't include falling for him.

Reaching the top of the stairs, they walked through the double doors into a room filled with people mingling. Attending this function with Ryan had not been her choice but she was still grateful to have him there. In a twisted bit of irony he was her anchor in a sea of unknown people. "I'd like to check my coat."

"Sure. While you're doing that I'll get us some champagne."

She didn't usually drink, or at least hadn't in a long time. While she'd been carrying Emily it had been off limits. At that time, everything in her life had revolved around the pregnancy. Now her life rotated around trying to get past it. Lucy handed her coat to the girl behind the counter and slipped the check ticket into her sequin-trimmed handbag. Fanning her scarf out, she adjusted it across her shoulders.

She'd had to shop on the fly after receiving the emails from Matherson, then Ryan. The second-hand consignment store a block away had saved the day. With pure relief, she'd found her dress. The instant she'd tried it on she'd known it was the one.

The salmon shade was the perfect color for her. It added life to her cheeks that hadn't been there for ages. The front dipped a little too low but it showed off her breasts to their best advantage. Two straps crisscrossed her back and the silky fabric fit snugly around the bodice and hips to drop into a cloud of folds. The dress bolstered her confidence, which she desperately needed tonight. She pushed her hair over one shoulder and licked her lips. Having done all she could to brace herself, she went in search of Ryan.

She spotted him leaning on an elbow at a high cocktail table. A champagne flute sat in front of him and the other he held by his fingertips. He was like James

Bond, dashing and just as dangerous. She'd have to remind herself constantly of how disenchanted she was with him or he'd sweep her off her feet before she knew what had happened.

Ryan watched a group of people standing across the room before his head turned and his focus rested on Lucy. He blinked then straightened to his full height. He stared. Lucy's heart fluttered. He took a long draw on the liquid from the glass he still held before he set the flute down. With long strides he came to meet her.

He stopped in front of her and leaned in intimately close. "You may get angry, and I know this will step over into the personal area, but, damn, you're beautiful."

Heat flooded her neck and face. Grateful for the low lighting, she smiled. "Thank you. I think I'll let you get away with it this time."

He laughed. The deep, rough sound flowed over her.

It was dangerous to be out with him. They'd been together less than an hour and she was already having difficulty keeping up her guard. To have someone tell her she was beautiful and look at her as if she belonged to him, as Ryan was doing now, was all she'd ever wanted. To belong. Be accepted. To have a little niche in the world that was hers alone. Like her sister had.

Ryan's pleasure remained on his face and her stomach did a loop the loop. That smile was for her.

"Come on, have some champagne. Then we'll make the rounds and do our duty." He led her back to the table where he'd stood and handed her a flute.

She glanced at the floor, forcing her emotions under control. How could he look at her like that while the words out of his mouth said he'd like to be as far from her as possible? She took the champagne. Maybe the liquid courage would help with the confusion she felt.

"Just try a sip or two. It'll help calm your nerves." Ryan raised his glass to his lips.

"How do you know my nerves need calming?"

"Your hands are trembling."

Great. After days of making her feel like a wall ornament he passed without notice, now he was paying attention to her. She did need to settle her nerves.

She sipped the gold liquid and enjoyed the bubbles playing a melody in her mouth before she replaced the flute on the table. Clasping her hands to appear calm, she said, "The email invitation implied that we should sign a pledge card to help raise money for the clinic in Harlem."

Ryan grinned. "Yeah. It didn't take Jack long to get on board, with Nina doing the convincing."

"I'd like to take care of that before I forget."

"Good idea. I think that's being done at a table over there." He pointed to the other side of the room.

"You lead," Ryan told her. Lucy turned and stared in the direction he'd suggested. Ryan placed a hand at her back and shock waves rippled through him. He'd touched bare skin. He jerked his hand away as if he'd been branded. One more surprise and he would be dragging her out of here to someplace private. She looked like sin and smelled like spring.

Lucy didn't slow down as she worked her way through and around the people standing in groups, talking. He drew in a breath and followed her. He'd have sworn he'd been sucker-punched when she'd walked towards him. The simply but functionally dressed family counselor had transformed into a sultry siren of sensuality. Nothing about her indicated she'd once carried a baby.

He didn't care if she thought it was being too personal to say she was beautiful. He couldn't help himself. He'd not been the only one staring at Lucy. And he didn't like it. Suddenly he wanted her all to himself. That wasn't a realistic wish.

Lucy and he had just broken out into an open area and were headed towards the pledge table when his name was called.

"Ryan O'Doherty. I had hoped to see you here."

He turned to find Alex Rodriguez standing behind him. "Alex," he said, more tartly that he should have.

Lucy waited patiently beside him. He guessed she wasn't missing a single nuance of his and Alex's interaction.

"We need to have a quick talk. Be in my office tomorrow morning before your first case." Alex's veiled dictate didn't go over Ryan's head.

The only answer he could give was, "Sure, I'll be there at six-thirty. I'd like to speak to you also."

They stared at each other like two alpha wolves deciding how they were going to share the same space. Ryan knew Alex had already won. He was the head of the neuro department now.

"Good," Alex said, and looked at Lucy.

"Have you met Ms. Edwards?" Ryan asked Alex.

"I have. Glad to have you working with us, Ms. Edwards."

"Thank you."

"Dr. Woods." Ryan waved at the blonde woman walking past.

She stopped. "Hello, Ryan." She smiled but when her gaze fell on Alex it dimmed.

Had Alex crossed swords with her also? "Layla," Ryan continued, "I'm sorry I wasn't here when the announcement was made that you're going to be the new pediatric head. Congratulations."

"Thanks, Ryan."

He looked at Lucy. "Have you met Lucy Edwards, the new neuro family counselor, and Dr. Alex Rodriguez, our new neuro head?"

"Hello, Lucy." Layla offered her hand to Lucy then turned to Alex, hesitating before she took the hand Alex extended. "Alex."

She gave his name a hard edge and their handshake was almost over before it had begun. Did they have some history? Interesting. Maybe Ryan wasn't the only one that Alex had rubbed up the wrong way.

"Hello, Layla," Alex said, his tone almost as cutting as hers.

"You two already met?" Ryan asked, looking from one to the other.

"Yes," Alex answered, but his attention remained on Layla. "How're you?

"Fine. And you?"

"Well."

If there was an iceberg between Lucy and himself, it was nothing compared to the frigid fog gusting off the two people in front of him.

"Is your husband here with you?" Alex asked, glancing around the room.

Even in the dim light Ryan could see Layla blanch. "No, we're divorced."

"I'm sorry to hear that," Alex said, but his response lacked a ring of sincerity. "If you'll excuse me, I see someone I need to speak to." He nodded curtly to the group and was gone.

"Lucy and I are on our way to sign pledge cards. Would you like to join us?" Ryan asked Layla.

"Thank you, but I've already stopped by. I need to speak to Jack a second so I'll see you around," Layla answered, not looking at him. Instead, her gaze rested on Alex's back as he moved across the room.

"Then we'll see you later." Ryan put his hand at Lucy's waist. A thrill went through him when she didn't move away.

"Nice to meet you, Dr. Woods." Lucy said. When Layla was out of earshot, Lucy whispered, "What was that all about?"

"I don't know but I'd say there's some history between them. And not the good kind."

"I'd say she isn't the only one that feels that way." She looked meaningfully at him. "I know you wanted the department head job."

"I did. Do." Once again she had him telling her things he should keep to himself.

"I would've thought you would've been the logical choice."

"Me too." He'd put in his time, paid his dues and had been confident he'd be the committee's pick.

"Do you have any idea why they didn't?"

"Yeah. Bad day for an interview."

She looked at him keenly. "How's that?"

"Who's getting personal now?"

She sneered at him. "This has to do with the hospital. It's not personal."

"Seems personal to me." He'd have to tell her or she wouldn't give up. "My father passed away the week before the interview. I left straight after the interview to attend his funeral. My mind hadn't been on impressing the committee."

His father's illness and death had not only destroyed Ryan emotionally but it had also damaged his career.

The timing of his bid for a leadership position couldn't have been scheduled on a worse date. He'd make sure when the next opportunity arose that he'd done everything he could to sway the decision in his direction. He was determined to make his father proud. That was why he'd agreed to be a part of the co-ordinated patient care program. Why he had brought the woman next to him to this party.

Lucy put her hand on his arm. "Ryan, I'm sorry. That seems so unfair." She looked at him with deep compassion.

Were her feelings always on display? "And that's life."

"That's a little more cynical sounding than I believe you are."

This conversation had already touched areas he wasn't interested in exploring. He gave her a twisted smile. "Come on, let's see about those cards and then get something to eat. Maybe have a dance," Ryan suggested.

Lucy wasn't too sure about the dance part. That would require Ryan to touch her and if he did so she was afraid she might make a fool of herself. "I'll go for the food. I'm not dancing with you. This is no date."

She glanced at him. Had Ryan said, "You want to bet?"

Minutes later they were making their way towards the hors d'oeuvres tables despite being stopped a number of times by greetings from people Ryan knew. He was flawless in his manners and introduced her every time. The charming O'Doherty way.

Ryan seemed to be popular with women and men alike. He was always ready with a witty remark and a quick smile. Why couldn't she and Ryan have that kind of relationship? Oh, no. She was letting him do it to her again. He'd made it perfectly clear how he felt and she'd do well to remember that.

"Why don't we sit down for a while and enjoy this without juggling the plates?" Ryan suggested, heading toward an empty table.

They lapsed into silence as they ate. Lucy's animosity had dwindled but she still wasn't at ease with him, afraid she'd share too much or, worse, sound needy. Her heart went out to him about his father. He'd obviously cared intensely for the man. And to have lost the department head job must've hit Ryan hard as well. For as little as she had shared with him on a personal level tonight, she'd managed to learn a great deal about Ryan.

While taking small bites, she looked around the room at the upper-level staff of a world-renowned children's hospital. In spite of dealing with life and death on a daily basis, they were still humans with problems of their own. She glanced at Ryan. He too had issues, even though he worked to hide them behind that facade of humor and charm. She couldn't point a finger. She also hid her pain.

Her gaze settled on a group that included Dr. Woods. She kept glancing toward the entrance, where Dr. Rodriguez had his arm around a pretty woman's waist and was leading her out the door. Dr. Woods shrugged a shoulder and turned to speak to the man beside her. Something about the way she'd been watching Dr. Rodriguez intently was in direct contrast to the nonchalant way she was acting. Lucy's belief was that Dr. Woods' look implied she wasn't pleased to see Dr. Rodriguez leave with a woman.

Their issues weren't Lucy's concern. She had enough

of her own, starting with the man sitting beside her. "How much longer do you think we need to stay?" she asked.

"Why?" Ryan popped another canapé into his mouth. "You in a hurry to get away from me?"

"I thought it was the other way around."

"Why would you think that?" His face took on a perplexed look. "I thought we were having a pretty good time."

"Well, you made it more than clear that you weren't interested in spending any more personal time with me than necessary." She nudged her half-empty plate to the center of the table and stood. "If you're not ready to go, I don't mind taking a taxi."

He stood. "We can go. We've done our duty. I'd just hoped to get one dance with you."

"This isn't a date. It's work," she said over her shoulder as she made her way to the coat-check counter. "Dancing comes under the heading of personal."

She claimed her coat. Ryan took it from her and held it while she slipped it on. He stood so close that his body warmed her back. She stepped forward on the pretense of putting her scarf on in order just to catch her breath.

As Ryan and Lucy descended the stairs she said, "By the way, I understand about the department job but that doesn't explain way you don't like Dr. Rodriguez. There's something more going on there."

"More?" He did not want to talk about this.

"Yeah. I thought you were supposed to be Mr. Happy-Go-Lucky and you were…what would be the word?…strident, harsh, displeased…" She stopped on the step and looked up at him as if trying to pull the right expression out of the air. "You don't care for the man. Why?"

"It's personal."

"Right. You're going to play that card."

"Why not? You've been throwing the word around all night."

They'd reached the bottom of the stairs when Lucy said, "Closing off when you might have to share more than a joke. Typical."

"Look, I'm sorry if you think I have no concern for your vulnerabilities, but I've done nothing wrong. I'm not your confessor. You spilled, I listened, and now we move on." He couldn't let her know that he admired what she'd done. If he did, she might use him as her confessor again. He desired her supple body and itched to caress her hair, but he wanted nothing to do with being involved in her life.

If Lucy could have produced steam, he didn't doubt it would be coming out of her ears right now. "Of all the contemptuous, uncaring things you could have said. You're nothing like people think you are."

"How many of us really are?"

"That's a pretty pessimistic way to look at life.'

They continued across the lobby. "It might be, but you can't deny that it's the truth. We all hide things from others." He should know. Most of his life he guarded closely.

"Yes, we do."

"But for some reason you think I should tell all. Is that little family counselor who wants to make it all better working after hours tonight?" Goading her was starting to be fun. At least, if she was mad at him he'd be less temped to explore his fascination with her. She was so beautiful with her hair cascading around her shoulders. Her eyes glittering with anger only heightened that beauty.

"Oh, you…you… You've managed to make it personal!"

That did it. He'd heard that word one too many times. As they passed a small alcove he took her waist and pulled her in. "I'm going to show you *personal*."

Combing his fingers into her hair, he brought his mouth down to hers. It wasn't a gentle kiss. He wanted to consume her. Wanted to get her out of his system, out of his life. The world slowed to nothing but Lucy and the moment. He'd not felt so free in a long time.

She jerked away and he immediately regretted the loss of her lips. He wanted more. The evening had certainly turned out far more positively than he'd anticipated.

Lucy's eyes were wide as she gazed at him blankly. She blinked and in that second she found reality again. With a quick look around, she checked to see if anyone had seen them. Relief flooded her features when no one was visible.

Her eyes flashed at him as she hissed, "You had no business doing that!"

"It wasn't business, it was personal."

She clenched her mouth shout, glared at him before she swung around and stalked away.

He caught up with her before she made it out of the main entrance. "The valet service is out the other door."

"I'm getting a taxi."

His fingers circled her arm. She stopped and looked pointedly at his hand. He released her. "Come on, Lucy. I apologize. It won't happen again. I brought you and I'm going to see you home."

* * *

Lucy said nothing as they rode back to her apartment. He glanced at her while they stopped in traffic. There was a pensive look on her face and her fingers touched her bottom lip. He grinned. So she wasn't as unaffected by his kiss as she acted.

Good, then maybe he'd get to kiss her again. One taste hadn't been enough.

When he entered her street she said, "Just pull up in front of the restaurant. It's not necessary to park. I can get in on my own." She raised a hand. "I know that goes against your raisin' but I've had enough tonight."

He hadn't had enough and he didn't think she had either but he wouldn't argue the point. Stopping by the curb in front of her apartment, he let Lucy out as she'd requested. "See you tomorrow, Lucy."

"Tomorrow," she said, as if she was parroting him instead of really thinking about what she was saying. She bit her lower lip.

His male ego took flight. Yes, there would be more kisses.

CHAPTER FIVE

Lucy stared off into what little space there was in her office.

Ryan had kissed her. Had kissed her good. He'd kissed her like no one else ever had. Her lips tingled from the memory. She stuck the tip of her tongue out and licked the center of her bottom lip. Could she still taste him? With an effort she stopped herself from moaning.

"Lucy, you okay?"

"What?" She looked around.

"I've called your name twice. Something bothering you?" Nancy asked.

"Oh, no, I'm fine. Just thinking."

"How's it going with Ryan?"

Lucy's heart revved up. Her body temperature rose. Beyond a shadow of a doubt her face had gone beet red. "We're fine."

Nancy looked at her longer than Lucy found comfortable. "You aren't falling for the silver-tongued devil, are you?"

"No. We're just co-workers." Lucy tried to sound as convincing as possible, tried to convince herself that his kiss had meant nothing.

"I see," Nancy said, but disbelief ricocheted around

the room. She smiled knowingly at Lucy before she picked up papers off her desk. "Hey, it's Saturday night. Why don't you come to O'Malley's Pub for a drink before you head home? Everyone will be there. I'll introduce you around. Should have done it already."

Lucy wavered only a second between going home to spend the evening alone or getting to know other staff members better. "I think I'd like that. Thanks."

"Great. What time is Ryan usually through with rounds?"

"Today it should be about six."

"Perfect. I'll meet you here."

"I'll be ready." Maybe going out with a group and having some fun would get her mind off Ryan O'Doherty. Still she couldn't help but have a fluttery feeling in her middle at the thought of seeing him again.

"So, Alex, what can I help you with?" Ryan asked as he took a seat in one of the two chairs in front of Alex Rodriguez's desk.

"Ryan, I thought I should speak to you privately about a couple of matters that came up during the patients' review meeting yesterday," Alex said, leaning back in his chair.

Ryan looked at him expectantly.

"I heard that you and Ms. Edwards had a public shouting match in the ER the other evening." Alex's voice made it clear he wasn't pleased.

Ryan had let Lucy push him too far. His emotions had gotten away from him. Something he rarely, if ever, allowed to happen. Now he was being criticized because of it.

"Things like that reflect poorly on my department and you professionally," Alex finished with a note of reprimand. In a very unsubtle way Alex was making it clear he wouldn't tolerate it happening again.

"Ms. Edwards and I did have a heated discussion about a patient. We've worked out our differences."

"Good. That's what I wanted to hear. Do I need to speak with Ms. Edwards?"

Ryan shifted in his chair. He couldn't have Lucy telling Alex what they'd been arguing about. "That won't be necessary."

Alex nodded. "Now for the other issue. I understand that the Rivera kid's progress hasn't gone as expected."

The hair on the back of Ryan's neck stood at attention as he shifted into fighting mode. What was this guy getting at? With his background he didn't have any room to talk. Or accuse.

"*Miguel*—" Ryan stressed the boy's name "—is doing quite well now. He did have a setback in ICU but he didn't require additional surgery. His recovery has been slower than I originally estimated but he's coming along fine nonetheless. Why? Is there a problem?"

"All I'm doing is asking the question that was put to me. I'm not accusing you of anything. In order to have a solid, top-notch neuro department, I need to know what's going on. It's my job to protect my staff but also make modifications when necessary in patient care."

Ryan wasn't sure how he was supposed to respond to those statements. He glared at Alex. He didn't appreciate the implication that he couldn't manage the case or manage his job in general. He needed to get a handle on his ire if he didn't want to create a problem. Like it or not, Alex was his superior. Antagonizing him wouldn't be to his own advantage. "What exactly are you insinuating?"

"I'm not insinuating anything. I'm just voicing a concern."

"Just for the record, you should know that I've done my homework. I know about you and your malpractice case."

Alex leaned forward. The only visible sign that Ryan had hit a sore spot was the tic in Alex's jaw.

Ryan received a small amount of perverse pleasure from the other man's reaction. "I haven't shared this information with anyone else. I'll admit that I wanted your job but not if I had to act underhandedly to get it. I wanted it based on my merit and skill. The committee voted for you. You're a talented doctor and no matter how much I'd like to have your position; I can't fault your skills as a surgeon."

"I appreciate that," Alex said. "Thank you for clearing the air. It'll be my job to see that you are left alone to care for your patients. You can count on me standing behind you. If there's a problem regarding administration then we'll discuss it behind closed doors." Alex stood and offered his hand.

"Agreed." Ryan shook the other man's hand. He was pleased with the tentative plan he and Alex had established to stay out of each other's way based on mutual respect. Ryan still wanted the position of head of Neuro and one day he would have it.

Long hours later he found Lucy sitting in the surgery waiting room with the family of his most recent surgery patient. He'd stopped being surprised at the consideration she gave to parents.

Lucy looked up at him from under half-lowered eyelids as he finished speaking to the family. She really was a lovely woman. Her hair was pulled back, making him wish he could take it down and feel its silkiness one more time.

That evening, she showed up for rounds, adding information as necessary. He was hyper-conscious of every move she made. She held a clipboard against her chest like a breastplate, as if preparing to go to war for her patients. The free tentacle of hair she pushed at impatiently when she spoke intrigued him. Her lips captivated him the most. The urge to create an excuse to see her in his office was so tempting. Only because he respected her enough not to make her feel cheap or self-conscious had he not let his baser instincts run wild.

The woman had gotten to him. First it had been her gentle ways, then her strong backbone as she'd told him off, then her sexy looks and tasty lips last night.

"I think Miguel might be well enough to go home early next week. Ms. Edwards, will everything be in place on your end for that to happen?" he asked. Did the others notice her cute, shy ways? What was he going to be doing next, spouting poetry? He had the hots for the leggy family counselor and if he wasn't careful it was going to show.

"I have everything lined up. All it needs is your signature on the orders."

"Good. I'll take care of that. I understand there was some concern that the family might have difficulty getting him back here for the post-surgery check-ups."

"There's a group called Care Ride that helps patients with transportation to and from appointments. They either send a car or see that the family has a subway pass for X number of times. I've already signed up Miguel's family and they have been approved."

"Excellent." Ryan smiled at her. "Then I think we'll

send the young man home the better for his visit to
Angel's."

The group standing around him chuckled and he
winked at her.

Lucy's heart leaped and did a somersault. He'd included
her. A warm feeling washed over her. She was starting
to belong somewhere, even if it was just at her job. She
was a part of Ryan's team.

Twenty minutes later, with purse in hand, she was
on her way to meet Nancy in the lobby. Her co-worker
needed to deliver some paperwork to a different department so they had decided to meet downstairs. Lucy
circled by the nurses' station on her way out. Ryan sat
behind the desk.

He rolled the chair back when he saw her and smiled.
"Hi."

She tingled all over at the sight of him. It happened
so often around Ryan she'd begun to think of it as her
body's normal reaction. She'd given up fighting it and
settled for not letting it be on display.

"It's more like bye. See you next week." She kept
walking.

He stood and met her at the end of the long nurses'
desk. "Hey." He scanned the area as if looking to see
if anyone was paying attention to them. His blue gaze
met hers. "How about we have some Volpentesta's pizza
together tonight?"

She wasn't sure she could handle being alone with
him again after last night. He was well aware of her
loneliness and vulnerabilities. Would he take advantage of that? Could she trust him? She certainly couldn't
rely on herself to stop him if he kissed her. Wanting to
belong so badly, would she recognize it if Ryan didn't

feel the same? Could she survive if he treated her like he had before? She was a basket of nerves.

With a sense of relief she said, "I've got plans."

His look of surprise, then disappointment, made her heart flip. Ryan didn't get turned down.

"I want someone to be interested in eating with me for me, not for the pizza my landlord makes."

"That has nothing to do with it. I… I—"

"I'm kidding Ryan. You're not the only one who can make a joke."

He looked around again before his gaze came back to bore into hers. This time the crystal blue held a sauna-warm intensity. "I thought I proved last night that I like you. You taste better than any pizza I've ever had." His voice had softened.

Heat filled her and she looked away.

"What're you doing tonight?"

"Hey, Lucy, I thought you were going to meet me in the lobby?" Nancy said as she approached them.

"I was on my way. Sorry you had to come back up."

Nancy looked from her to Ryan and grinned. "Ryan, we're on our way to O'Malley's for a drink. Want to join us?"

Only with supreme self-control did Lucy suppress a groan. No way would she ever relax with Ryan in the group. It was all she could do not to act like she had a schoolgirl crush around him as it was. She certainly didn't want anyone else to notice. Nancy was already too suspicious for Lucy's liking.

"Sure. I've got a couple of other things to see about here. I'll meet you there." Ryan grinned at Lucy.

"Great. We'll save you a seat," Nancy said.

O'Malley's Pub was loud and busy when Nancy and Lucy arrived. Lucy was grateful for all the noise because it made it more difficult for Nancy to quiz her about Ryan. The questions had been free flowing since she and Nancy had left the hospital and during the short walk to the bar.

Nancy waved at a group in the corner. Lucy followed her as she weaved her way through the mass of people to the table. They settled in and Nancy introduced her to everyone. Some of them Lucy recognized, but others were completely new to her.

"We need to save a seat for Ryan," Nancy announced.

Those that heard Nancy turned to look at her in surprise. "Dr. O'Doherty? He never comes out with us. What gives?"

As popular as Ryan was with the staff, Lucy was surprised he'd not spent more time socializing with them. As she thought about the man, in he walked. Had she been watching for him? Even across the crowded room he'd managed to zero in on her. He smiled and headed her way.

Ryan had changed from his ever-present scrubs into worn jeans and a light blue sweater. The collar of his button-up shirt showed above the neckline. As he approached, women turned to watch him. Her insides trembled.

"Room for another?" he asked, standing between her and Nancy.

"Sure." Nancy scooted over and Lucy did also. Ryan squeezed between them on the wooden bench. The tight space meant Ryan's firm body was sandwiched against hers from hip to thigh. His heat branded her along the length of her leg. She squirmed, trying to put as much room between them as possible.

He looked at her, which brought his face much too close for her comfort, and whispered, "If you continue to wiggle like that, I might think you're issuing an invitation."

She sucked in a breath and jerked her head around to look at him.

He grinned.

The waitress circled by them and took their order.

"I'll get this round," Ryan said, smiling at Nancy then her, "just for asking me along." His look said he knew Lucy would have never invited him.

The conversation flowed around the table. She mostly listened. Ryan told a story and everyone laughed. He really was fun. Despite all his story-telling and jokes, he rarely shared anything personal about himself. What little she'd learned he'd been forced to tell her in order not to appear rude. Even his story tonight was about someone else.

Was he hiding something or was he just so closed off he couldn't share?

At one point, he leaned forward to hear what someone was saying farther down the table and Lucy had a wonderful view of his broad shoulders and back. The muscles across his back rippled beneath his sweater as he reached for a basket of peanuts. His hair brushed against the top of his collar and there was a line around the back of his head where his surgical cap had been tied. It looked like he'd tried to get rid of 'cap hair' by running his fingers through it, leaving it with a mussed look that had a boyish appeal.

Lucy folded her hands tightly in her lap, stopping if not completely relieving the desire to touch those irresistible locks.

He leaned back and looked at her. "Is something wrong?"

People were always asking her that when she thought

about him. She was going to have to work on not showing her emotions so much. In answer to his question,
yeah, she was beginning to feel too much. She didn't
trust herself. Didn't trust him.

"I'm fine. Just tired, I guess."

"We've both had a long day. Come on, I'll see you
home."

"That's not necessary. I've learned to manage on my
own. I wasn't late but once this week."

He leaned closer. "My, that is an improvement. Still,
I'd like to see you get home safely."

She wouldn't have thought it possible but Ryan
moved further into her personal space. Somehow it
seemed safer to take her chances on her own.

Glancing away from his compelling look, she found
the others at the table watching them. Did they think
he was going to kiss her, like she was afraid he would?
"Uh, sure."

He stood, stepping over the heavy bench, and waited
for her to do the same.

"I'm going to see Lucy home. She isn't feeling well."

There were mummers of concern around the table.
Lucy smiled at them weakly.

She couldn't refute Ryan's statement because it
would make her look silly. Waving a hand, she murmured, "Goodnight."

The table quickly returned to their discussions. Ryan
led the way, taking her hand. He used his big physique
as a wedge through the crowd of people and pulled her
along behind him. They picked their coats off a peg by
the door and put them on. Soon they were out on the
sidewalk, standing in the cool, windy night air. Ryan
let go of her hand and she felt the loss immediately. She
hefted her purse strap over her shoulder then stuffed

her hands into her pockets in an effort to contain the warmth he'd left behind.

Lucy faced him. "You know that they all think something is going on between us."

"Isn't there?" He cocked his head to the side and gave her a slight grin.

"Not that I know of." She started down the sidewalk. He fell in beside her. "A week ago you treated me like I had the plague. You weren't even speaking to me. Why would I think anything has changed?"

"Maybe because I kissed you and you kissed me back."

"You think just one kiss is going to make a difference?"

He stopped and she did too. "I'm shocked that the tender-hearted, make-everyone-feel-better woman is really a skeptic at heart."

"You can't turn a cute phrase every time you don't like the subject matter."

He grinned. "I'm pretty sure I can."

"I wished I could stay mad…" she muttered.

"I heard that."

They fell into silence by mutual agreement as they walked. All the lights in Manhattan had been switched on. Lucy missed being able to see the stars in the sky but there was also something intriguing about living in a techno show. "I'm always amazed at all the lights and sounds here," she breathed.

"Yeah, it's pretty fascinating. And noisy. You should see the lights from my place. I think you'd be impressed."

"You sure that isn't some come-on line, like 'Would you like to see my etchings?'"

His deep-throated laugh made her think of hot fudge

over a brownie. Sinfully wonderful. He really had a magnificent, heartfelt laugh. She needed more laughter in her life. Ryan being the source both flabbergasted and unnerved her.

"Well, it could be but actually it's the truth."

They walked slowly down the street, occasionally dodging people. "So is that how the great Dr. O'Doherty lures women into his wolf's lair, by saying come look at my view?"

"I don't invite just anyone to my home." His voice had turned serious.

"Really? Why?"

"Because I like my privacy."

When the wind picked up and a light drizzle began to fall he said, "I'll get us a cab."

"No, I can get home from here. I'll take the subway."

"Okay."

"Okay?"

"Yeah, okay. I'll ride with you."

Lucy didn't try to argue. She'd figured out it wasn't worth the trouble. They found the subway entrance and used their passes to go through the turnstile. The station was crowded with the evening after-work foot traffic. As they waited, they were pushed closer and closer together.

Was everyone and everything conspiring to keep her shoved against Ryan? No matter where they went it seemed like his body was in contact with hers. She loved the warmth and security he provided but it was hard on her already edgy nerves. Maybe she should've agreed to the taxi. At least it would have allowed a foot of space between them.

When the train came, Ryan pulled her back against

him, wrapped an arm around her waist and held her close as the car unloaded.

"Let's go." He nudged her forward as the last person stepped off the train. He moved her in and down the car to stand next to a pole. All the seats were taken. "You're going to have to learn to be aggressive if you ride at this time of day," he whispered next to her ear.

He made the words sound far more suggestive than they should have been. They had her thinking of firelight, him, the floor. She shook her head. That was no place for her mind to wander. She searched for a handhold on the bar to steady herself for when the train launched out of the station. None were available.

"Brace yourself against me," Ryan said from behind her.

"I'll manage."

"Yes, and fall. Maybe hurt yourself or someone else." He widened his stance and again wrapped his solid arm around her. "Remember I offered a taxi."

"I think you're just using this crowd as an excuse."

"Excuse for what? To hold you? Come to think of it, it *is* working to my favor."

"Ryan, don't tease me. I don't need this."

She tried to pull away but he tightened his embrace fractionally before the beep sounded to notify everyone that the doors were closing.

"I'm not teasing. Give me a chance to make it up to you."

She sure wanted to. Would he treat her just the same again? This time she was afraid she'd have more invested. It could hurt worse.

They rode in the same intimately close position until they reached her stop. Since when had a ride on a dirty, hot, packed subway car become sexually exciting? Even with a crowd of people around them her world had narrowed down to just Ryan and the effect he had on her body.

"Isn't this your stop?" His breath brushed her ear.

"Uh?"

"You get off next."

"Oh, yeah."

"Where has your mind been?" His chuckle was low and suggestive.

Darn the man. He knew exactly what he was doing to her. The cold damp of the outside was a blast to her hyper-sensitive system. A welcome relief from the heat. It woke her from the blissful Ryan-filled trance and jerked her back to reality. She stepped away from him, putting as much distance between them as she could. Her body had reached overload and she needed to regain her perspective. He didn't leave her side or touch her as they walked the block to her apartment. She stopped at the foot of the stairs and faced him.

"Thanks for seeing me home, even if it wasn't necessary."

"My pleasure. I enjoyed it." He had a wicked look in his eye.

"I'll see you next week."

"You're not going to invite me up?"

"No."

"That hurts."

"I don't know what's going on here. What I do know is that you're playing at something. After tonight at the bar, all the tongues will wag about us. I need as little emotional upheaval in my life as possible. I have no interest in becoming part of the O'Doherty harem."

"The woman speaks her mind. For starters, I don't have a harem. Nice idea, but I work too many hours to keep a group of women happy. Second, you've been doing too much thinking. Why don't we just try being friends again? I don't have to take calls tomorrow so how about I show you around New York? Is there any place that you've never been but would like to go?"

"I thought we were friends—"

He put up his hands as if to warn her off. "Okay, I'll say it. I'm sorry. I messed up. Tomorrow will be no strings attached. No expectations, just two people enjoying a day off. How about that?"

She took so long to answer that his uncertainty that she would say yes started to show.

"Okay, then I'd like to see the Statue of Liberty." When she'd visited New York as a child her parents had been planning to take her and Alexis out to see it, but instead they'd gotten into a huge fight and that part of the trip had been forgotten. It would be nice to see the statue and share it with someone instead of going by herself.

"Perfect. I love the old girl. How about we sleep in and I pick you up around eleven?" He made it sound like he was issuing an order in ICU. As if Lucy would dare defy one of his directives. "Wear your fun clothes and something warm. It's cold on the ferry over to the island this time of year. See you tomorrow." He turned and raised a hand for the taxi that was passing by.

Had she just been sucked into the vortex that was Ryan O'Doherty?

Ryan couldn't remember looking forward to a day off more. At least, not since the time his father had surprised him with tickets to a Yankees game when he'd been a kid. It had been more than he could do to concentrate on his schoolwork that week, with thoughts of going to the big game. Thankfully he didn't have a week to contemplate spending the day with Lucy.

He'd asked her to his house. He took his solitude seriously and didn't share outside his family. He dated—after all he was a red-blooded man and had needs. He'd had his share of women but had never let them get too close. For some reason, Lucy had slipped under that barrier. He wanted her to see his place, wanted to share his home, his special view with her.

Most of his days off he spent with his sisters and their kids. In fact, they'd been shocked then pleased when he had told them he was taking Lucy out to the statue. There were far more questions than he was willing to answer about Lucy but they accepted for the time being what few he gave. He knew they weren't done. They worried about him and he didn't like that.

Ryan knocked on Lucy's apartment door right at eleven. There was a scuffle of movement before she opened the door. "I'm not quite ready. I'll only be a minute."

"Mind if I come in?" he asked.

Lucy paused longer than he would've liked to give her answer.

"I guess." She opened the door wider and he followed her into the small but neat apartment. The first thing that struck him was the lack of personal items. Even as a bachelor he had family pictures around his home. It was very telling. There was nothing there to indicate she had any family that she cared about, and he knew differently.

She wore jeans that fit her slim figure perfectly, not leaving a single curve untouched. Lean and fit, she looked lovely. He wished the bulky cream-colored sweater didn't hide her luscious breasts. He had told her to dress warmly so he only had himself to blame. She'd pulled her hair up and through the back of a baseball hat and braided it. She looked like a woman-child instead of the competent, mature woman he knew her to be.

After slipping her arms in to a pea jacket and looping a bright pink scarf around her neck that hung below the hem of the coat, she said, "I'm ready."

"Great. I think we've got a perfect day to visit. The sun's shining and the wind isn't up too high. We need to hustle to make the ferry. I managed to get us tickets on the one o'clock. We were lucky. They take reservations and there were only two left. Otherwise we might have had a long wait."

At Battery Park, Ryan paid the cab driver and grabbed Lucy's hand. "We better run for it." He loped so she could keep up with his longer stride. As they raced across the park to where the ferry was docked, he glanced back to check on Lucy. Her bright smile and rosy face made him grin like a foolish kid. She looked happy.

"I've not run like that in a long time," Lucy said, panting as they stood in line to go through security.

"Neither have I. It felt good."

Lucy looked up at him. "It did, didn't it?"

He wrapped his arm around her shoulders and gave her a quick hug. "We'll run back after we see Liberty if you like."

She grinned. "I think I'd be just as happy with a walk."

He laughed.

They made it past security and Ryan fished their tickets out of his pocket as the powerful engines of the ferry started to boil.

"Where did you get those? Do you have an 'in' with the port authorities?"

He waved the papers in his hand. "The internet is a wonderful thing."

They walked aboard and found a spot on top. Out in the open they could get a three-hundred-and-sixty-degree view of the city, the bay and New Jersey.

"It's amazing," Lucy said as she stood beside him and looked towards the statue.

"I love this city."

"You've never wanted to live anywhere else?" She looked at him as if his next words would be committed to memory.

"No. How about you? Anyplace special you'd like to live?'

"Not really. Other than my sister's I've not had a place to call home in a long time."

Her words drifted away on the wind as they crossed the harbor. He might have had it rough with his mother dying so young but his dad had always made sure that Ryan had a home. Just as he'd made sure his sisters had known they had one when his father had gotten sick. He didn't know what he would do without his family...

Lucy shuddered. He wrapped his arm around her waist and pulled her close. She didn't resist but relaxed against him. Ryan liked the feel of her next to him. "Having fun yet?" he asked as they closed in on Liberty Island.

"Yes. More than I thought I would."

He studied her a moment. "What exactly does that mean? You didn't think it would be fun to spend the day with me?"

"I wasn't sure."

"You could damage a man's ego."

"I think you have enough of one that it can take a hit."

He squeezed her tighter in retaliation. When she giggled he let her go. "Did you really think you wouldn't have a good time with me?"

"I'm not going to get the cold shoulder again after we share something personal, am I?"

"Funny, very funny. Coming from a woman I couldn't get a smile out of a week ago."

The ferry docked and they followed the other passengers down the gangplank. They spent the next two hours exploring the grounds of the statue and listening to a park ranger tell the history of the lady.

"Can we climb to the top?" Lucy asked.

"They're doing repairs. I'm sorry, it's closed. We'll come back when it opens."

"Oh, I had hoped to look out of her."

She had the sweetest pout on her face. He leaned down and gave her a quick kiss, unable to resist her pucker.

Lucy put her hand to her lips. "Why did you do that?"

"Because you look so sad."

"Oh."

He looked up at the top of the statue. If he didn't focus on something else he was afraid he'd kiss her again. She looked so adorable in her confusion. "My father brought my sisters and me here when we were kids. It was an experience to remember. Every year my father let us take turns picking some place in the city that we would like to go. This was mine. I wasn't nearly as happy with one of my sister's picks."

"What was that?"

"She wanted to go to the Met."

Lucy's laughter made him feel good deep down inside. "You don't like art?"

"I do. But as a twelve-year-old it was a punishment." She giggled some more.

"Dad's rule was that we were to go as a family. I went but I wasn't happy about it."

"Those memories must be fun to share now." Her voice had taken on a melancholy sound.

He took her hand and gave it a gentle squeeze. "The holidays are something when we all get together. Loud and lots of fun." He stopped abruptly. His father wouldn't be here this year. That's the first time he'd allowed a thought like that to enter his mind.

This time Lucy returned his comfort. "You'll miss him."

She'd known without asking what was bothering him. He recognized her counseling voice and found it comforting. "I will." This was supposed to be a fun day for them both, and he wasn't going to let sad memories overshadow the day. "Hey, you interested in seeing Ellis Island?"

"Sure. If we have time."

"Then come on. I'll show you the name of the first O'Doherty to come to America. We can look and see if any of your family members came through too."

Lucy wasn't as confident that they would find any of her family noted as being on Ellis Island as Ryan was. Edwards was such a common name that if they did, there would be hundreds or thousands. It didn't matter. She was having such a good time that she'd go along with any idea he had.

Ryan's view of family was so different from hers. Her family life was so fractured that she could hardly remember the last time they'd all been in the same room. Could they do that now and be civil? No one had tried to get them together in a long time. Maybe it was time someone did. Yeah, right, she couldn't even face her sister.

She and Ryan stood atop the ferry taking them from Liberty Island over to Ellis Island. No other tourist braved the chilly air. The wind was cold but Ryan wrapped his arm around her shoulder and she burrowed into his warmth. He gave her a history lesson on the two islands and the museum over the roar of the engines. After he finished one story, she looked up at him and said, "You're a great tour guide but…"

Ryan raised a brow as if she'd dared to question his skills.

"Sometimes you talk so fast I only understand the first and last words." She grinned at him.

"Let me see if this is slow enough for you." His lips brushed hers, teased and tasted.

She was falling for the guy. Falling hard.

Was it that he'd offered her the first real happiness she'd had in months or was she just so desperate to be noticed for who she was that she'd fall for anybody who gave her attention? She'd always been the youngest, had stood in Alexis's shadow as the quieter one, had been the baby carrier, and now she wanted to be the one who stood out.

Ryan made her feel special. She was going to go with that feeling, revel in it, experience it, grasp it and hold it tight for as long as she could.

CHAPTER SIX

LUCY HELD RYAN'S hand as they exited the boat and entered the Ellis Island National Monument. The warehouse-type building had housed immigrants who had funneled through on their way to gaining freedom and new citizenship. Still hand in hand, Ryan showed her around the different levels, wandering past black and white pictures of people who had stayed on the island.

She probably should have removed her hand but didn't want to. His friendly but secure clasp gave her a feeling of belonging. What would it mean to truly belong to Ryan O'Doherty?

"I often wonder what it must have been like to leave everything you know and love behind and pick up and move somewhere else," Ryan commented as they looked at a picture of a man holding a child in his arms. "I don't know if I could do that."

Hadn't she done that very same thing? Just not on as grand a scale as leaving the country where she had been born. In many ways, she was no different. She was struggling to find her place in the world.

"They had to work to rebuild their lives."

She was doing that also. The job was there but she floundered with the other aspects. Today had been the first day that she'd felt like her old self in a long time. She liked it.

"Let's go have a look at that book." Ryan directed her toward the center of the large building. He stopped before a glass case. Inside lay an old register with names written in faded ink.

"Come on." He grabbed her hand and gently pulled her towards a computer screen on a wall nearby. He sounded as excited as a kid wanting to show off a toy. "All you do is type your last name in and see what comes up."

"You do yours first." She didn't know much about her family tree. That hadn't been a priority when her parents had been together. Certainly hadn't been mentioned after their divorce. Even her grandparents had deserted her.

"All right." Ryan tapped the keys.

A list came up on the screen of all the O'Dohertys who had passed through Ellis Island.

"See, this is my grandfather." Ryan pointed with his index finger. "He was just a baby then. These are his siblings. All nine of them." He ran his fingertip down the list of names. "I can't imagine having nine children," he said in wonder.

"That does seem excessive." Her heart caught. She'd given birth to a child.

"A couple sounds like plenty to me," he said off-handedly.

Pain filled her. She'd already had a baby. "That sounds about right," she said dryly.

"I'm sorry. I shouldn't have said that."

She shrugged. "It's okay. I have to learn to live with it. Move on. It's a fact and I can't change it."

He gave her a quick hug. "I think you're doing a great job." He kissed the top of her head and let her go.

She appreciated his show of support. If she wasn't careful she could get too used to it. "Tell me about this grandfather or great-grandfather who picked up and moved his whole family."

"Well, he was pretty much like everybody else who came through here. He was Irish and wanted a better life. Settled in Brooklyn, worked hard but had little other than family. And family is everything."

"And your dad and mom?"

He looked away as if he wouldn't answer then he turned back to her. "Mom was the local girl who married the big Irish policeman who came into the café where she worked. Mother used to say she fell in love with his Irish brogue and the rest of him just came with it."

"So that's where you get the hint of an inflection intermingled with your Brooklyn clip."

He chuckled. "That's a nice way of putting it. Mostly the Brooklyn has taken over but every once in a while the Irish really shows through."

"How old were you when your mother died?"

"Thirteen."

She didn't miss the hitch of pain in the word. "Your sisters?"

"My sisters were a number of years younger. Dad became both parents."

"That must have been tough, on all of you."

"It was, but I think it was toughest on Dad. He'd lost the love of his life. He wasn't only the breadwinner but he had to be the stable factor in our lives when his was crumbling."

"Crumbling?"

He hesitated as if he didn't want to say more. "He got sick. He developed motor neuron disease."

"You had said he'd died but not that he'd died so slowly. That must have been horrible for him. You and your sisters." She grasped one of his biceps and squeezed, hoping to relay her sympathy.

As if he'd gone off into the past, he continued, "I saw him struggle to keep his job for as long as he could. Then be forced to give up one more thing he loved."

He needed to talk. She knew not only from her experience as a counselor but because she'd been in the same place when her parents had divorced and again when she'd left Alexis and Emily. Ryan and she had both known loss.

"I had to watch this rock of a man slowly die. He had to be put into a nursing home. I thought it might kill him to go but I was the one it almost killed. I hated it that he needed to be there."

Ryan was pouring out his pain like water that had been dammed and needed a place to go. How long had he been keeping all this pain to himself? No wonder he'd isolated himself from the families of his patients. She felt troubled. She'd pushed him to be more open.

"You carried the responsibility, didn't you? For everything. Him, your sisters. For holding things together."

He looked at her as if amazed. As if for the first time he recognized that someone understood.

"Yeah. I visited him as often as I could. Took care of my sisters."

Ryan's reaction to what she'd told him about Emily suddenly made sense. He'd supported others' emotions for so long that he didn't want to carry hers. She hadn't once heard anyone at the hospital talk about his father having just died. She bet he'd never let on to anyone what he was going through. He'd just shared a part of himself that few saw. She was honored to be one of those people.

"You're a good man, Ryan O'Doherty." She would have hugged him but she didn't think he would appreciate that much pity. He was also a proud man.

"Are you through?" a man with a wife and couple of kids standing nearby asked.

"Yes," Ryan said, stepping away from the computer.

He took her hand again and she gave his a squeeze. She didn't want him to close himself off like he'd done before.

As they walked toward the entrance, Ryan said, "We didn't look up your family name." He turned as if to go back.

She tugged on his hand. "We'll do it next time." Would there be a next time? It would be nice if there was. She was enjoying her day with Ryan.

They boarded the ferry that would take them back to Manhattan and found a spot inside, out of the late afternoon wind.

"Are you hungry?"

Lucy found to her surprise she was, in more ways than one. "I'm getting that way."

"If we have another hot chocolate, will that hold you over for an hour or so?"

"I think I can survive that long."

"Do you like Chinese?"

"I do."

"Then Chinese it is." He pulled out his phone and made a call before he left to order their hot drinks.

They said little as they sipped their hot chocolate. Lucy was surprised how quickly she'd become comfortable in Ryan's presence. They had bonded in a way she'd never expected they would or could. After their first meeting she would have said it was impossible for them to find common ground.

"Look here," Ryan said.

"What's wrong?"

He leaned over and kissed her, his tongue lightly brushing her upper lip. It was quick and warm and, oh, so short.

When he pulled away she said, "Why did you do that? You could have told me and I would have used a napkin."

His blue eyes danced with mischief. "If I'd done that I wouldn't have gotten that last extra sweet taste of chocolate."

"No, I guess you wouldn't have."

She was having fun. She looked into the eyes of the big, sensitive, caring and highly intelligent man beside her with the devilish sense of humor and knew she'd lost her ability to be rational about him. She had real feelings for the guy. It was an intoxicating while at the same time disturbing reality. Would there be more heartache in her future?

Ryan licked his lips as if getting every last drop of chocolate from them and grinned at her. "You have any more to share?"

"I do not." She looked so indignant that he laughed. She grinned at him.

He couldn't believe that he'd told Lucy so much about his father. He'd never confided to anyone outside his family and for the most part he'd not even done that. His father had been an intensely proud man and Ryan had been gifted with that same propensity, good or bad. It was an issue of pride for Ryan that he could handle his own problems. He'd never shared his innermost feelings with anyone before but Lucy made him feel secure enough to do so.

Why had he? He should feel naked and vulnerable now that she knew so much about him. Instead, relief had washed over him at being able to tell someone about the burden of loss and pain he carried. He found it rather liberating.

"Hey, I've been meaning to ask you where you learned to speak Spanish so well. I don't think of Georgia as the go-to place."

"I learned it from my father's Mexican housekeeper at his home in LA. Alexis and I spent a lot of time with her. I just picked it up."

He pulled her to him and smiled down at her. "And it came in handy a few times."

"Just a few?" She smiled shyly back at him.

He wanted to kiss her, not a quick peck or a teasing brush but a real kiss right there in front of everybody. He brought her against him. His lips met her soft warm ones that tasted faintly of chocolate.

She grabbed his coat and pulled, going up on her toes. Her acceptance fed his desire. He requested admission with the end of his tongue, and she granted it. Entering, he found a heated cavern of pleasure. This was a kiss.

"Hey, buddy. Get a room," someone called.

Lucy jerked away, but she still had handfuls of his coat. Her eyes were large and awestruck, her lips cherry red from his kiss.

"Was that a friendly kiss?"

He laughed. "The friendliest. Come on…" He took her hand.

"Where are we going?"

"My place."

"I'm going to see those lights?"

"Yes."

"Ryan, I don't think—"

"I said fun and no pressure, remember? I keep my word."

"That would be the O'Doherty way."

"Yes, it would."

Lucy was still reeling from Ryan's kiss as she followed him out of the subway into the early evening air.

They had shared a real kiss. The kiss of a man who wanted a woman. Was she stepping into water over her head? If she was, would she sink so far under Ryan's spell that she'd never come up?

They were in an area of small privately owned stores. People milled on the sidewalks in front of the stores. She'd never been to Brooklyn but she'd not expected to find the small-community feel within a large metropolis. Ryan's stride changed, became more leisurely, as if he'd returned home.

"I live about a half a mile from here. Would you like to walk or should I call for a taxi?"

"Walking would be nice. I'd like to see where you grew up."

As they strolled hand in hand Ryan spoke to a shop owner, introduced her to a former high school teacher and her husband. Others waved or called out to him. It was a community proud of their home-grown boy done well.

"You love living here, don't you?"

"What's not to love? And I've known nothing else."

"Never thought of moving on up? The super-neuro-surgeon who outgrew his roots?"

"No, here suits me just fine."

And it did. What was it like to be that secure in those around you that you knew you belonged?

They walked down a small hill that had a line of new-looking condos that had not been constructed to look so modern that they didn't blend with the rest of the buildings along the waterfront. At the one closest to the East River, Ryan stopped in front of a door stained a dark color. He fished in his pocket and pulled out keys.

"You live here?" Lucy made no effort to hide her amazement. "What a beautiful spot." Across the East River was Lower Manhattan with all its enormous buildings, including those around Wall Street.

"Come on in," Ryan said as he opened the door. "Our Chinese should be here soon. We'll eat out on the deck."

He led her straight through the living room, stopping long enough to flip on a light in the kitchen before they went out a glass door to a deck. It ran the length of the condo out the back and had a privacy fence separating him from his neighbor. There was a small table with two chairs and an oversized and wide lounge that faced the city.

"I think we timed it just right for dinner and a show."

She put her hands on her hips and gave him a skeptical look. "So you're sticking with that story?"

"I am."

"We eat and then the light show begins."

The doorbell buzzed. "That will be our supper."

While Ryan was gone, Lucy looked across the river, watching the shadows begin to fall across the buildings and the orange of the western sky become the backdrop. Ryan had a lovely place to live.

He returned with two paper bags filled with wonderful-smelling food. "I thought we'd have a picnic. Eat out of the boxes. Share." Going back inside, he brought out two glasses and a bottle of wine. With minimal effort he opened the bottle and poured them both drinks. He then pulled boxes and other items out of the sacks and placed them on the table. "Have a seat."

She pulled out a chair and sat. "Is there a fork?"

"Fork! There are no forks with Chinese food." He grinned at her as he picked up chopsticks covered in paper and handed them to her with a flair of a magician. "Have any experience?"

"A little."

"I'll help you." He opened a box of rice, pushed it toward her and opened another for himself. A larger container with chicken and broccoli he placed between them. He stripped the paper off the chopsticks and manipulated them like a pro between his lean fingers. She shouldn't have been surprised. The dexterity he used to do delicate brain surgery would lend itself to using chopsticks to eat.

She followed suit with the chopsticks but her ability was much more hit and miss than his. Ryan laughed when she must have looked like a snapping turtle going after a morsel before it fell back into the box.

"You're going to starve at that rate and I'm going to look like a poor host. Let me help." He scooted closer and offered her a bite on the end of his chopsticks.

She continued to make efforts of her own while he filled in between them. Over one offering she looked up and found him looking at her intently. It was heady to be the center of his attention. One who loved those he cared about so totally. She could be overwhelmed by his magnetism with little effort on his part.

Ryan looked away, breaking the moment, and dropped his chopsticks into an empty container. He stood and put out his hand. "Come on, we're going to miss the show."

She put her palm against his and stood. He led her to the lounger. Letting go of her hand, he settled into the chair and stretched out his long legs. "Join me." He patted the space next to him.

The lounge should have been large enough for two but with Ryan's size it seemed far too small. "There's not enough room for both of us. I'll just pull a chair over here."

"I'll make room." He scooted over as if he planned to give her plenty of room. "The show's much better from here."

She sat alongside him. They touched from shoulder to foot. She pulled her coat closer around her. He picked up a blanket from beside the chair and spread it over their legs. "Lift your head." She did so and he slid an arm behind her neck, resting his hand on her shoulder. He tucked her closer. "Relax."

"I am relaxed."

"No, you're not. You're as tight as a guitar string."

She shifted and found a more comfortable position.

"You know, if you keep that up this may not remain just a light show between friends."

She stiffened. What had she been thinking to agree to this?

Ryan chuckled. "I'm kidding. I'm not going to do anything that you don't want me to."

Hadn't he kept his word so far? The problem was, she wanted him to do plenty. Settling next to him and clasping her hands in her lap, she looked at the horizon. The lights of the city began to flicker on. "Oh, this is amazing. I just saw the lights on the top of the Chrysler Building come on."

"It's beautiful." He fingered the tail of her braid, which was lying against her arm.

"Thanks for sharing this with me. It's everything you said it was."

"You're welcome."

They continued to watch until the kaleidoscope of colors from the buildings reflected off the water. Could anything be more wonderful than being in Ryan's arms and watching the sun set to a beautiful light show?

"Wow, this view is something. You must be in demand as a date for this alone."

"So you think my sex appeal is location-related?" He spoke so close to her ear that his warm breath brushed her skin.

She kept her focus on the lights of the city. "I think you're fishing for a compliment."

"Maybe. I thought I told you that I don't bring people home."

"By people, do you mean women?"

"Yes. Women. You're the only woman who has ever shared my view."

She sat up and twisted around so she could look down at him. "Why?"

His fingers played with the end of her braid, which now fell over one breast. His look met hers. "Because," he said, his voice low, "you're the only one I've ever wanted to share it with." Wrapping a hand around the mass of hair, he tugged gently, bringing her down to him. His hand cupped her head as he guided her mouth to his. His breath brushed her lips. "I'm going to kiss you. It won't be a friendly kiss. If you don't want this, you need to tell me to stop now."

"The O'Doherty way? A gentleman always." Her lips touched his.

He pulled her head closer, slanting his mouth and taking the kiss deeper. His tongue found the seam of her lips and demanded entrance. When she didn't immediately open he pulled back and placed small searching kisses along her bottom lip. He shifted her until she lay along him. Her body followed the contours of his.

Did heaven feel like this?

When the bill of her cap hit him in the forehead she reached up and pulled it off.

He ran his hand down her braid. "I love your hair. You have no idea how many times I've wanted to touch it."

She reached to remove the band. What little light there was spilled out from the kitchen.

"No, don't. I want to be the one who sets it free." His voice had gone low and gruff, creating tingles inside her.

Gently he removed the band from the end. He drew a finger between the sections of the braid, slowly releasing them as if he were opening a present he'd been eager to see for weeks. His sure, precise movements told of his skill as a surgeon. What she did to her hair every day he turned into a sensual experience.

"I know of no one who has hair as beautiful as yours." He fanned his fingers out and ran them over her head, finishing the job. The waves fell about her shoulders and flowed around them. Filling his hands, Ryan watched in fascination as it spilled between his fingers. He brought a long lock to his cheek, sliding it across his skin.

His mouth returned to hers and this time when he asked, she opened. His tongue entered, savored, sipped and swirled, while his hands burrowed into her hair to hold her head.

She squirmed.

"Easy, honey. We have all night if you wish." His tone was low and soothing but the tension in his body and the ridge below her hip said he was just as aroused as she was.

Her hands traveled up his chest and wrapped around his neck. Her mouth came down to his, then tugged on his bottom lip before she pressed her mouth firmly against his, letting him know just how much she desired him.

His hands spread her hair out along her back and moved to her waist. He ran a hand under her coat and lightly grazed the inch of bare skin separating her shirt from her pants.

She shivered.

He released her mouth and kissed his way across her cheek to nuzzle behind her ear. His hands glided over the hyper-sensitive skin of her back.

She moaned.

"You like that, do you?" He nuzzled her again while his hands pushed her shirt upwards. He released her bra, his fingertips grazing the under-curve of her breast.

She flinched at the shock of sensation that rocketed through her. His fingertips were prickling heat and softest torture as they trailed over her skin.

"Lift up, honey."

"We can't do this here?"

"Why not?" He hushed her opposition by bringing his mouth to hers and giving her another mind-altering kiss. "Are you cold?"

If he continued to kiss her like that, she'd do anything he wanted. She arched her back, allowing him to push her coat away. The movement brought her center into intimate contact with his rigid manhood.

Ryan O'Doherty wanted her. *Her.*

"Put your hands on my shoulders."

She did so and he stripped her shirt and bra away. Before she could lower her arms his mouth found a nipple. His lips dropped away with infinite slowness. His actions and the cold air touching her sensitive tip caused her to shudder.

His low chuckle was one of pure male satisfaction.

She hadn't recovered from the honeyed moment before Ryan showed the same mind-blowing attention to the other breast. His hands skimmed her waist then flowed leisurely upwards until his hands cupped both breasts. He lifted, and weighed them.

They'd changed while she'd carried Emily. Would he mind?

"Perfection," he murmured, before he kissed the tip of each one again.

Not recovered from his devotion, she sucked in a swift breath when his hands skimmed downwards and dipped below the waist of her jeans while he left kisses across her breasts. She whimpered.

"More?"

"Mmm." She sounded entirely too sensual even to her own ears. Ryan was making her feel more than she'd ever felt before and he'd done little more than kiss her.

She brought her hands down to his chest. He shifted so they lay facing each other and continued to fondle her breasts as if he found them extremely fascinating. She was grateful he couldn't see them well. They weren't as firm or high as they had been before Emily.

Her hand slid down to the edge of his sweater to play with the hem.

"You can touch me," Ryan said before he nipped at her earlobe. "In fact, I wish you would," he said as he found her mouth again.

She accepted his invitation and slid her hands under his pullover. It was warm there but his T-shirt still created a barrier. Touching skin was her goal.

Ryan must have heard her groan of frustration because he let go of her and pulled his jacket off and then his sweater. Jerked his shirt from his waistband. "I might lose my mind before you get up the nerve."

"I don't want to do anything wrong."

He leaned back so that he could look at her face. "This isn't your first time, is it?"

"No, but it's been a long time. I wasn't the girl with the most boyfriends."

A soft smile of satisfaction came to his lips. "I'm surprised there weren't hundreds." She gave him her best "I don't believe that" look, which he answered with another kiss.

"Honey, the only thing you can do wrong is not do." His lips went to her collarbone and moved lower.

She ran her hand under his shirt and upwards until he was forced to remove it too. "That's better," she said as she wrapped her arms around his neck and pulled him to her. "Cold?"

"No. How about you?"

"Mmm. No."

Ryan went willingly towards her. The touch of her breasts against his bare chest almost ended any further foreplay. Her hair dropped around them like a silk curtain.

He had to have her. Soon.

Her hands fluttered over his skin, creating tiny points

of pleasure as they went, but he wanted more. That shyness that he'd seen earlier had returned. It intrigued him that someone so sure of herself in some areas was so completely insecure in others. Cupping Lucy's bottom, he brought her snugly against his manhood, letting her know clearly what she was doing to him.

Lucy flexed in answer, making his heartbeat rise, his blood pound in his head. Her lips found his chest as if she'd discovered the perfect playground. Her cheek rested just far enough above his torso for her to rub against his chest hair. Her warm breath blew gently against his skin, driving his desire higher. The fascination and pleasure she found in him was like balm to his damaged heart.

Ryan stroked along the waistband of her jeans. Each time he dipped beneath he was rewarded with a hitch in her breathing. He brushed her hair away from her face so that he could watch as she explored him. When he went to unfasten her jeans she grabbed his wrist.

"What's wrong, honey? All I want to do is touch you."

"I've…uh…had a baby. Things have been…stretched, moved around."

He kissed her, showing her just how sexy he found her. "I'd be surprised if they hadn't been." He kissed her again. "Come on. I think it's time we go in."

At her stricken look, he grinned. "I said nothing about being done. We're just going to try a little experiment."

"I don't think I'm ready for that."

"I'm positive you are." He climbed out of the chair and stood. Grateful for the cool air circling him, he ached for want of her.

She reached for her shirt and he snatched it way.

"You're not going to need that. Wrap up in the blanket. I'll get our clothes."

Taking her hand, he opened the deck door, led her through and kicked it closed behind them. He had no intention of letting her go. With that rabbit-in-the-headlights look in her eyes, he was afraid she might run. He kept her hand firmly in his as they climbed the metal stairs with the cable-wire handrails to his bedroom.

CHAPTER SEVEN

LUCY'S BREATH CAUGHT. Ryan's bedroom had a large picture window that shared the same view as the deck. His bed faced the scene. He turned on a small lamp sitting atop a dresser. It gave off just enough light to see well but not so bright as to be harsh.

Ryan led her to the bed. He let go of her hand and rested his hands on each of her shoulders. He gently pushed down until she sat on the edge. He backed away, just out of touching distance. Despite still being wrapped in the blanket, she felt more undressed than he was. She wanted him close, close enough that she could run her fingers over his muscled chest before she lost her nerve. Lifting a hand, she reached out. Capturing it, he gently squeezed her fingers and backed up a pace. He grinned. "I've created a monster."

"Ryan—" She started to stand.

"Just listen a minute."

She sank to the edge of the bed.

"In this room there will be no barriers. Be it clothes, emotions or thoughts. We can do and say anything without it leaving these walls."

"O'Doherty law," she murmured.

"Yes."

The more he spoke the less she could control her

hands. They shook. She clutched the blanket, hoping he wouldn't see.

Ryan removed his socks and shoes, dropping them on the floor. His hands went to his jeans, flipping the button from the hole. She couldn't look away, her concentration on the movement of his fingers. The only sound in the room was their breathing.

He pushed his pants down to the floor and stepped out of them. The evidence of his desire tented his boxers as he stood in front of her. The heat between her legs, banked when they'd come in the house, flowed again. This time it grew stronger. Ryan looked like a god standing before a display of multicolored lights. She was speechless.

"You're scaring me, Lucy. But I love it."

She blinked. "There's that ego."

"Yeah, and the way you're looking at me only makes it and other parts grow."

Unable to help herself, she stared at his manhood, which stood tall and proud between them. She promptly blushed when her gaze met his pleased one.

Completely confident, he came toward her. Why shouldn't he be? She drew in a shallow breath. He was stunning. The total cliché Irish package—dark skin, expansive shoulders, thick hair and a grin to die for. The mind-boggling thing was that he was hers for the taking.

He stood so close, all bare and beautiful. She didn't know where to look, finally focusing on a spot on the wall. He reached out a hand. She placed hers in his.

He tugged her to him, giving her a kiss that started a fire in her. "Now you go stand where I did."

"What?" Her heart fluttered in her chest. She drew the blanket tighter.

"You heard me. It's your turn. I'm going to watch."

She shook her head. "I can't."

"I think you can. I went first so it's only fair that you go."

She dragged the blanket with her and turned to find him sitting on the bed where she had been.

"Let it go."

She shook her head. "I've never stripped before."

"Look at me, Lucy." His words were said so softly yet with such force that he left her no doubt he'd accept nothing less than her compliance. Her gaze found his.

"I want to make love to you. All of you. Your mind, body and soul. I want a strong, self-assured woman in my bed and I know you are that woman. Let the blanket go."

She fought a war in her mind. Part of her wanted to let the blanket fall but the insecure side screamed not to. Ryan's expression never wavered. He believed in her. Did she believe in herself?

Taking a deep breath as if preparing to jump off a cliff into water, she let go. Unable to stop herself, her arms covered her breasts.

"Put your arms down. I want to admire you."

Her confidence level wrenched upwards. Ryan wanted to admire, not just see.

"You are a goddess. Your hair is gorgeous. The way it falls over your breasts and flirts with your waist. I want to feel it all around me. Caress all the places it touches."

She bit her bottom lip.

"Now your socks and shoes."

Lucy bent to do his bidding. Her breasts hung before her and she knew without looking that his focus centered on them. In a fit of courage she pulled her hair away so that he had a clear view.

When her gaze met his again, his held a pained look. His eyes were hooded and his lips tight, as if he was working to restrain himself. Still she hesitated at the snap of her jeans. What if he didn't like what he saw?

"Lucy."

He wasn't asking, he was demanding that she meet him halfway. She flipped the button and unzipped her jeans. With a shimmy, they fell to the floor. Ryan's look flicked downwards but quickly returned to hold hers. She stepped out of her pants and stood before him in her pink panties.

"All or nothing, Lucy, your choice. This can start here or you can run and hide."

The last words made her loop her thumbs in her panties and shove them down.

She didn't miss his gasp in the silent room.

"Perfect. Completely perfect in every way. Come here."

She gradually moved toward him. His eyes held her mesmerized. He hadn't touched her but his gaze spoke of admiration, desire as it stroked each part of her body.

Ryan widened his legs and she walked between them until her knees touched the bed. He placed his hands on her waist. They trembled slightly. That encouraged her. It was empowering to know she affected this strong, highly intelligent man so.

He pressed his lips to her belly.

A quiver ran though her.

"You're a beautiful woman. Every silky inch of you." His lips slipped upward in a caress that made her skin tingle. "All glorious woman," he murmured against her ribs before his mouth moved down the curve of her hip. "Perfection."

He liked what he saw.

Lucy's hand cupped the back of his head and held it there. For the first time in a long time she felt like a complete woman, whole again. This man before her had just given her a precious gift.

Ryan leaned back on the bed and pulled her on top of him. "I want you, Lucy. Now. I don't think I can wait any longer." His lips found hers and his kiss was hot and demanding.

She shifted, settling more intimately against his hard body, and deepened the kiss in answer.

Minutes later he rolled, taking her with him so that she was beneath him. "Let go a sec." She did. He stood, found his pants and pulled a packet from a pocket.

"You were so sure of me you had a condom in your pocket?"

"Just a man with a dream."

Ryan lifted her against him. Carrying her to the top of the bed, he sat her down and pulled the covers back then eased her under the sheets. He came down beside her and she watched as he sheathed himself.

"We'll go slower next time, I promise. But right now I've got to have you."

He entered her. When she tensed he stopped and eased away but returned and went deeper with each movement. Lucy spiraled higher, higher until there was nothing but bliss.

Ryan was but one thrust behind.

Could she be in love? Yes, she already was.

Lucy woke to the sun shining and sounds of a steady heartbeat beneath her ear as her cheek rested on Ryan's chest. He lay on his back, one hand thrown across the huge bed and the other curling over her bare hip beneath the sheet. She wadded a corner of the material in her hand and pulled it up to cover her breasts.

He'd proved more than once during the night that he didn't find her post-baby body less than fascinating. In fact, he'd taken time to express with words as well as actions that he appreciated her body and found her desirable. No dip or crevice had been overlooked. He'd spent an inordinate amount of time along the insides of her thighs. She warmed deep within from the memory.

From where her head rested in the arch of his shoulder, she watched as she skimmed her palm over the soft mat of hair covering the center of his chest, seeing the individual strands dance. Lifting her hand a fraction of an inch higher, she let her hand just tickle the ends of each curly hair. She found all of him irresistible. Too much so.

Was this the beginning of something truly wonderful or was she headed for heartache all over again? She wanted what Alexis had but could she trust herself enough to know if this was real? Could her heart stand devastation again?

She sighed heavily.

"Hey, what was that for? You could make a guy feel insecure, sounding like that."

She placed her lips on his chest and turned to look up at him. "First thing in the morning and you're already fishing for a compliment."

"I don't have to fish. I know how good I am by the way you put all those extra syllables in my name as you climax."

She buried her face in his shoulder. A smile of pure satisfaction crossed her lips. The man knew how to make her feel wanted and special. She stroked his hair.

"And I found out when that Irish in your speech makes an appearance."

"Great." He kissed the top of her head. "I have a 'tell'?"

"Oh, I could tell all right." She giggled as her hand traveled lower.

"Lucy." That soft Irish burr became stronger, circling her name like a caress. "You want to hear more?"

"I think I just might."

A long satisfying hour later, Ryan asked, "Is there anything special you'd like to do today? I have to check in at the hospital but I'm all yours after that."

"I don't know…"

"How about I make breakfast then take you to the St. Regis Hotel for afternoon tea."

"You like tea? I think of you more of a baseball and hotdog guy."

"I am, but the season hasn't started yet. I've heard my sister talking about going to tea and how much she enjoyed it. I just thought you might like it as well."

"So you like froufrou? Amazing."

"Froufrou?" He curled up his nose.

"You know—tea, violin music, garden parties."

"Hell, no!"

She laughed at the appalled look on his face.

"Really, tea at the St. Regis sounds wonderful. I'd just like to be dressed appropriately. So while you're at the hospital I'll go home and change."

"Sounds good."

Ryan dropped Lucy off at her place and went to the hospital to check on his patients. He stopped in his office long enough to make reservations at the St. Regis Hotel. He already missed Lucy and it had only been a few hours since he'd seen her. She had an effect on him like no other woman had ever had. Snatching his sports jacket off the coat rack in his office, he went out the door with a smile on his face. A decision about where their affair might go didn't have to be made today. They'd just enjoy being together and see where that led.

He climbed the steps to Lucy's apartment two at a time, unable to wait to kiss her again. He'd made fun of his brothers-in-law and rolled his eyes when they'd acted like this about his sisters. He hoped they never found out that he was walking around with a syrupy smile on his face. If they did, he'd pay for all the times he'd laughed at them.

At his knock on Lucy's door, someone opened it. *Was he at the correct door?*

He'd expected a simple but elegantly dressed woman whose hair was in place and a shy smile of greeting. Maybe a slight blush from heated memories of their night together. Instead, the woman in front of him had hair that stood out in wild disarray around her face and shoulders as if she been tugging on it then running her fingers through it. Her mouth was pinched in a hard line and her eyes were red-rimmed. She wore baggy sweats and an old hoodie.

What had happened to the happy, smiling Lucy he'd left a few hours ago? She'd even volunteered a good-bye kiss without him asking. A delicious kiss at that.

"Lucy, honey, what's happened?"

"They're here in town!"

"Who?" Aliens, terrorists, the IRS? From the look of alarm in her eyes, he could only think the worst.

"Alexis, Sam and Emily."

He cocked his head to the side. "Alexis. Your sister?"

He made no effort to keep the astonishment out of his voice. Was that what this was all about?

She nodded.

"That's great. I'd love to meet them."

"It isn't great," she all but shouted before she turned to pace the room. Grasping her hair, she pulled it back and let it go to fall in wild array around her face again. The woman who kept tight control over her hair and didn't raise her voice had made an abrupt change.

He stepped into the apartment and shut the door behind him. As she came by him the second time, he caught her hand and pulled her into a hug. She stood inflexible in his arms for a moment before she wrapped her arms around his waist. He held her. It wasn't until her shoulders shook and spots on his chest felt damp through his shirt that he realized she was crying. "Honey, you're not making sense. You're going to have to tell me what's going on if you expect me to help."

"I don't expect you to help."

That hurt on a level he didn't want to explore. At a loss how to respond, he said, "I'd like to." To his surprise, he meant it. He placed his hands on her shoulders and pushed her away until he could see her face. She wore the classical look of panic. Taking her hand, he led her to the bed.

"Let's sit down and you tell me what has you in such a state."

She dropped to her bed. He took a spot beside her, close enough to touch her but not so close it was difficult to read her facial expressions.

"Look, Ryan, I don't want to go into it. I'm sorry about not going to tea, but I'd just like to be left alone."

"I'm not leaving you like this."

She made a movement to get up, but he grabbed her hand and held her in place. "Talk to me, Lucy."

It took so long for her to answer he was afraid she might not.

"Alexis wants to see me."

"Of course she wants to see you, you're her sister."

She buried her face in her hands. "I'll just have to tell her I'm too busy at work to meet them. I've only been here a few weeks and I can't get away." She spoke as if he wasn't there any longer.

"What? Why? I would think you'd be glad to see her. Especially Emily."

She flinched at the baby's name.

"I know it'll be hard but you don't want to live with regret in your life. If you really think about it, you want to." He stood and looked down at the top of her head. "Of course you're going to see her. They're your family. They came all this way."

Lucy jumped up and went to stand at the window. "If I see Alexis, she'll know."

"Know what? I realize you had a hard time giving up Emily but this has to go beyond that. You're an intelligent woman. You knew all along that was the plan."

She twisted away from the view of the top of a tree outside to look at him. Her face was contorted with pain. "You don't get it," she spat. "It's not just about Emily. It's about me." She poked at her chest a couple of times. "How I feel. About how I shouldn't feel."

He stepped toward her into her personal space in an effort to intimidate her into expressing her true feelings. If she got mad enough, maybe the truth would come out. "Then tell me how you feel."

She looked down at the floor. "I'm jealous of what she has. Her happiness. Her perfect little family. There's no place for me. I'm miserable when I'm around them. In the way. And worse than that, I hate myself for feeling that way." She spat out the words. "The best thing for them and me is to stay away from each other."

Ryan jerked back, his heart constricting. She couldn't mean that. Family was everything. No matter how hard you had to work at it, you stayed together, cared for each other, did what had to be done. "Lucy, you don't mean that. I took care of my sisters, my father as he slowly died, and I would do it all over again if I had to. That's what a family does."

Her head jerked up. She leaned towards him and looked him in the eye. "I'm not you."

"You're more like me than you think," he said quietly. Had he misread her? His family was the center of his life. How could he be interested in someone who didn't understand the value of family? He took a deep breath, getting control of his own emotions.

"Lucy," he said in a quiet, soothing voice, hoping his even tone would make her speak and think more rationally. "You cared enough to carry a baby for her. You put your life on hold, took a risk to your body. Those are not signs of someone who doesn't care. She's your twin. That bond will always be there. Even if you want to hide from her."

As if a bubble had been popped she deflated before his eyes. All the fight fizzled out of her. He enveloped her in a hug. She hung on as if he were her lifeline.

"Honey, you need to see your sister. Work through these feelings."

Her fingers dug in, then relaxed on his back. He could feel her struggle within herself.

"Go with me," Lucy said against his chest.

He'd never planned to become her emotional support but having her in his arms made him want to be there for her. He'd been the emotional rock for his family through the last ten years while his father had been dying. He'd had enough.

That had been until Lucy had come into his life, demanding he care again. To his astonishment, he wanted to be that rock of support for Lucy. He didn't know how she'd done it but there it was. He wanted her to be happy. She needed to see her sister if she was ever to let go and find contentment.

"I don't know. I think you need to see her alone. Work though this without me getting in the way."

"But if you came with me as moral support?"

He looked into her pale face and pleading eyes. "Your family doesn't even know me, honey. Under these circumstances, I don't think that would be the best time to meet."

"But you said you wanted to meet my sister."

That had been before he'd realized the emotional strain Lucy was under. He was just coming to grips with his feelings for her. He wasn't ready to make the commitment of meeting her family.

She gave him a pointed look as if this was going to be the make-or-break moment in their relationship. If he became her emotional support this time, would she expect him to always be there for her? Could he do that?

"I understand." She stepped back. Smoothing her hair and squaring her shoulders, she looked at him with her large eyes peppered with bone-deep pain.

Guilt washed over him. "Okay." Even to his own ears he didn't sound enthusiastic.

Relief filled Lucy. Having Ryan with her when she faced Alexis would help strengthen her. The shame formed a lump in her stomach, making her want to double over in pain. Admitting to Ryan her feelings about Emily had been difficult enough, but to have to confess her pathetic feelings of jealousy had been far worse.

How could she explain to Alexis she was envious of her? Her own sister? That it hurt to be around her and her family. She wanted to be a part of that unit but she wasn't. That she had seen her sister's resentment. If you really loved someone, you shouldn't be jealous of them. You should want the best for them. Be happy for them, but...

Lucy wrapped her arms around Ryan's neck and hugged him. "Thank you. I really appreciate it." This was one thing she didn't want to do alone.

He gave her a quick kiss. "You're welcome, honey." He sounded sincere but there was still an unsure look in his eyes. "So when do we see them?"

"They're staying in an apartment near Times Square. Sam's company keeps it for employee travel. Alexis wanted to come here but I told her it was too small and they didn't need to be hauling Emily up three flights. They want me to come to dinner this evening."

"Okay. You call and let your sister know that you're coming and make sure it's all right for me to come along."

"I'm really sorry I've dumped my personal problems on you."

"Stop saying you're sorry. We'll get through this."

A stricken look crossed his face for a second but soon changed to a gentle smile. He'd said *we*. Was she asking too much of him? Was this too personal, too involved for him?

Ryan held her hand while she spoke to her sister. Afterwards, his hands went to her shoulders. He turned her round and nudged her towards the bathroom. "Now go and get yourself together."

Ryan's deep voice speaking to a person at the St. Regis was the last thing she heard before stepping under the shower. Through still unsure how she'd handle seeing Emily or Alexis again, she felt reassured that Ryan would be there with her. Twenty minutes later she came out of the bathroom dressed in a robe with her wet hair twisted in a towel on top of her head.

Ryan sat on her small sofa, making it look very inadequate for his large size. One ankle was propped on the other knee. He'd removed his jacket, leaving it hung over the top of a chair at the table. Amazingly, he seemed right at home in the small apartment.

He had the phone to his ear. From the questions he was asking, he was speaking to someone at the hospital. His dedication to his job was one of the many facets of his personality she admired. Caring for his patients was his top priority. That compassion extended to her.

Looking up, he gave her a smile of encouragement. She made an effort to return it but she didn't think she pulled it off when his brows dipped in concern. The self-conscious feeling when he watched her intensified while she gathered her underwear. She wasn't used to that kind of scrutiny from anybody, particularly from a devastatingly sexy man.

She stepped into her tiny closet and pushed clothes around on the rack, unable to make up her mind about what to wear. A long arm reached past her. She squeaked.

Ryan pulled a hanger supporting an aqua-colored sweater dress off the pole. "I like you in this one." He hung it on the hook on the closet door. "You wore it the third day you came to work."

"You noticed?" She'd had no idea he'd observed her that closely.

"Yeah, I noticed a lot of things about you." Ryan reached an arm around her waist and pulled her back to his front. His fingers splayed over her robe to cover her stomach.

She rested against him, enjoying the warmth and strength of him that seeped through her. He kissed her neck. She shivered.

He moved upwards and found that spot behind her ear. The one he'd discovered the night before. He kissed it. "You're so tense. Honey, you've got to ease up on yourself or you're going to make yourself sick. I know just what to do to relieve that stress." The hand on her stomach pressed her back against him even more, leaving her in no doubt what he meant. He continued to nibble at her ear.

Her head fell against his shoulder. He slipped a hand beneath her robe and cupped a breast. She panted softly as his fingers teased, working their magic. His hand slid downwards as he pushed the robe open, leaving a trail of heat along her skin. Pulling at the belt of her robe, he gained access to her bare body. His hand inched further down. His index finger flirted with her opening then retreated. She moaned. Warm heat pooled in her.

"Lucy?"

"Mmm?"

He whispered against her ear. "What do you want?"

"More." She felt his smile against her skin.

His finger slipped in to find her core. She went up on tiptoe and leaned back against him.

"How do you feel?"

"Good."

"How good?" His finger moved again.

"Oh, so good."

Ryan watched as Lucy nibbled at her bottom lip. Her unease had increased as they'd waited for the elevator that would take them up to Alexis's floor. Letting go of his hand, she pushed at her hair. It wasn't necessary because she'd swirled and curled it, pulling the mass into a messy knot at the back of her neck. "How're you feeling?" he asked.

"I was better earlier."

She still sounded more stressed than he would have liked. She was going to scare her sister if she didn't lighten up some.

"Do we need to find a closet?" he asked.

He laughed at her stricken look. "We can't have sex every time I'm upset."

"I don't know. I'm available."

She gave a real smile for the first time since he'd left her at her apartment that morning. "Thanks for the offer. I'll keep that in mind."

He'd watched the movement of her lips and had immediately wanted to find somewhere private. Getting enough of her was becoming a problem.

As they rode up in the elevator, her frantic look became more pronounced. She fumbled with her purse, dropping it. Picking it up, Ryan handed it back to her. "Honey, take a deep breath."

She did so.

Where had the woman gone who had marched into his office and told him off in no uncertain terms?

"Now, give me your hand." He held out his hand palm up and gave her his most reassuring grin.

The door of the elevator slid open and they stepped

into the hall. Lucy's grip tightened as they neared the door of her sister's apartment, as if she was drawing strength from him. Standing in front of the door, she tried to pull her hand from his. She was going to run.

He brought her close, kissing her until she melted against him. "You can do this." He gave her another quick peck.

She nodded and squared her shoulders. Ryan knocked on the door.

CHAPTER EIGHT

Lucy was still under Ryan's spell until the door opened and Alexis rushed out, wrapping Lucy in a bear hug.

"Oh, Lucy, it's so good to see you. I've missed you." Alexis sounded as if she was choked up with happiness.

Shame washed over Lucy as she stiffened in her twin's embrace. Afraid Alexis would pick up on the slightest vibe, she returned the hug. She didn't want her sister to know, wouldn't let her know. She couldn't hurt her sister.

Alexis released her and looked at Ryan.

Lucy gathered her thoughts enough to say, "Alexis, this is Ryan O'Doherty. A…uh…friend of mine."

Ryan smiled his killer smile. "Hi, Alexis. It's nice to meet you. I knew you weren't identical twins but I still see the family resemblance in the eyes." The O'Doherty charm was flowing.

Alexis grinned.

Lucy appreciated him picking up the introduction. It gave her time to gather herself.

"Y'all come in." Alexis turned and opened the door wider.

Ryan's large warm hand rested on Lucy's back, a reassuring reminder that he was there for her. He had her back figuratively and literally.

"Your sister has a nice drawl but it isn't as sweet as yours," he whispered into her ear before closing the door behind them. As they entered the living area, a smiling Sam was carrying little Emily to meet them. Lucy froze. Ryan almost stumbled into her. Gracefully, he recovered and stood beside her. His hand brushed up then down her back, letting her know that he was aware of her response.

"Lucy, we're so glad to see you. We thought if you were too busy to come see us we'd just come see you."

"Hi, uh…Sam." She faltered with his name, her attention so completely focused on Emily.

"I'm Ryan O'Doherty."

She barely registered Ryan speaking. The two men shook hands.

Only because she'd lost the warmth of Ryan's hand did her gaze break away from the baby. She had grown so much and become more beautiful since she'd seen her.

Sam pulled her into a one-armed hug and she returned it quickly. She never wanted to see that unsure look on Alexis's face again.

Alexis's attention turned to Ryan. "So, are you the doctor who keeps Lucy so busy that she doesn't have time to call us?" She moved to stand beside Sam.

Ryan glanced at Lucy and winked. "We've been busy." His look suggested something different than hospital business.

Lucy couldn't help but give him a small smile. His wink always made her feel as if she belonged. He was trying so hard to ease her out of her worries but the intense jealousy stuck like chewed gum. Her attention turned back to the little cherub in Sam's arms. She itched to reach for Emily and pull her close to inhale her baby fresh smell. But she couldn't. It would be too hard to let her go. She stepped away to put some space between her and the child.

"This is Emily," Sam proudly said to Ryan. "Our baby girl."

For the first time the deep searing pain she normally felt when Sam made that statement wasn't as strong. Thankfully the ache was easing. Becoming what it should be. Although everything in her still begged to reach out and take Emily, but she dared not do it.

"Come on in and have a seat." Alexis directed them to the living area. Two sofas faced each other with a low table between them. "Let me take your coats. We thought we'd just have dinner catered in. It would be so much easier than going out with Emily. That way we can really talk." She placed the coats over a chair near the door.

"That sounds nice." Lucy forced out the polite comment as she took a seat on the sofa.

How had she let her feelings get so out of control that she had to make an effort to have a conversation with her sister? She didn't like it but didn't know what to do about it. It was as if she and Alexis were old friends trying to find common ground again.

They'd been everything to each other before Emily had come along. Alexis marrying Sam had changed things between them but that had been nothing compared to how they'd been after Emily had arrived. They'd once shared everything but now Lucy hid a crippling ugly secret.

Ryan sat beside her, not too close but near enough that his leg lightly touched her knee. The small contact fortified her.

"Before I settle down for a talk, I need to get Emily a bottle. Hope you like Italian, Ryan. It's Lucy's favorite."

"I shouldn't be surprised. She lives above an Italian restaurant."

Alexis looked at Lucy. "Really? I didn't know that."

"Yeah, I haven't had a chance to tell you," Lucy said.

"Well, you'll have to tell me all about it over dinner. It should be here soon," Alexis said, before going into the other room.

The doorbell rang. "That'll be our food," Sam said. "Hey, Lucy, would you hold Emily while I get that?" He handed the child to her without waiting for a reply.

Could she touch Emily and not break down? She cradled the soft, cuddly baby to her chest with trembling arms.

Sam left them.

She nuzzled Emily's neck, pulling her close.

"She's a cutie," Ryan said. "You're an exceptional person Lucy Edwards."

Her heart lightened. He thought she was special. She hadn't realized how much she'd needed to hear that. Ryan being the one who believed she was incredible made it twice as nice.

Ryan offered his finger to Emily and she clutched it with a chubby hand.

Lucy glanced at Ryan. He watched her intently with a mixture of concern and amazement on his handsome face. Was he judging her reactions?

"How're you doing?" he asked quietly.

"I'm making it." She turned to Emily so that she could see the child's face. Alexis's features were showcased there, not her own. Something shifted inside her, allowing her heart to let go. She no longer felt like a spurned mother but an aunt. Still, her envy for what

Alexis had still festered. She wanted her own child, a husband, family. To belong. To never be pushed out again.

"I'm proud of you." Ryan gave her a quick kiss on the temple.

Alexis returned. "I see that Emily's enjoying getting to know her auntie again. Hasn't she grown?"

She gave them all a bright smile and took Emily from Lucy, who let the baby go with less reluctance than she'd expected. Mercifully, Alexis was so caught up in Emily that she didn't notice how uncomfortable Lucy was. At least she'd been able to cover it well. Without Ryan's reassuring presence, she would have broken down and spilled her horrible secret.

"She *has* grown. Is she a good baby?" Lucy managed to ask, clasping her hands together.

"The best." Alexis sat, adjusted Emily and put a bottle in her mouth.

When Ryan's large hand covered hers, Lucy held on tight.

Ryan was impressed with how well Lucy was handling what he'd come to realize was an extremely difficult situation for her. She was making all the right noises and had even held Emily without breaking into pieces. He was proud of her. She was trying, but the strain showed in the tension around her lips and her rigid posture.

He'd been emotionally empty after his father had died and had kept it together only because his sisters had needed him. He never thought he'd willingly be anyone's emotional crutch again. Then along had come Lucy with her big blue eyes and quiet ways, and here he was doing everything in his power to support her, encourage her.

She could've done it without him. He'd seen her

spunk and determination when she'd told him off. It had made him feel like he was important to her when she'd asked him to come along here. She believed she needed him.

Sam brought the food to the table and came back to join them.

"Here. You finish with Emily," Alexis said, offering the baby to her husband, "and I'll take care of the food. Lucy, come help me and we can talk."

Lucy hesitated a second before she scooted away from Ryan to go to the dining table.

Lucy had given the impression she was shy when they'd met but in reality she had a backbone as sturdy as the Brooklyn Bridge and the sweetest way of showing a man that he mattered. She didn't give half. She gave all.

He glanced away from where Sam was settling in a chair with his daughter to the women moving around the table. As always his attention rested on the gutsy blonde woman. Lucy would be a fierce warrior and protector of anyone she loved. That's why she cared so deeply for Alexis and for Emily. It was who she was. She expected to receive the same in return. Would accept nothing less. Could he give it? He had no choice but to try, unable to imagine her not being in his life.

"Lucy's a special person," Sam said.

Ryan looked at him. Was that a warning? "Yes, she is. Very special." He glanced in Lucy's direction a number of times to check on her. The tension in her face had eased. He was sure that having something to focus her mind on helped.

Alexis obviously doted on Lucy. They shared some facial features but that was where the resemblance ended. Where Lucy was tall and unassuming, Alexis was petit and feisty. He liked Alexis but Lucy's gentle, easy way suited him much better. Even Sam had shown his affection for Lucy in his hug when they had arrived and his smiles in her direction. She had a family who obviously cared for her so why did she feel like she was on the outside?

"Okay, guys, food's on the table," called Alexis.

They gathered around the small table. He let his leg touch Lucy's. Just a reminder that he believed in her.

She gave him a weak smile.

Alexis spent most of the meal tending to Emily, who sat in a seat on the floor beside her mother. Sam watched the mother and child with a look of adoration on his face. Ryan now understood why Lucy felt like an outsider. Alexis and Sam probably had no idea of how they shut others out. Lucy would never tell them. She watched them also as if she couldn't pull her eyes away.

"Lucy, how do you like that great big old hospital you are working in now?" Sam asked.

"It's fine."

"She stays lost half the time," Ryan remarked smiling at her. "I've threatened to send a search party out for her a number of times."

Lucy grinned but it didn't reach her eyes.

"Sam, you interested in baseball?" Ryan asked, trying to steer the discussion away from her. Her face showed obvious relief when the conversation turned into a heated discussion about who would win the baseball pennant that fall.

During a lull, Ryan looked at Lucy. Her attention was on her plate as she pushed her food around. She had eaten little.

Alexis must have noticed also because she asked, "Lucy, are you feeling okay?"

"Oh, yeah. I'm fine." Lucy sounded artificially bright.

Just then Emily demanded Alexis's attention and she let the subject drop.

Sam, watching his wife and child, said, "Lucy, thank you so much for giving us this."

If Ryan hadn't been so in tune with Lucy he might have missed her barely perceptible flinch. That was the last thing she needed to hear. Emily was a gift she'd given her sister out of love and the Lucy he knew didn't want them to feel indebted. Being reminded of what she'd done made her feel uncomfortable. He found her hand under the table and gave it a reassuring squeeze. She gripped it back as if it were a lifeline.

"This little one has fallen asleep. It's time for bed," Alexis said. "Lucy, would you like to help me?"

"Sure," Lucy said, with little eagerness. Before she left the table she looked at him. He smiled encouragingly.

Ryan liked Alexis and Sam but couldn't they see how hard this was on Lucy? If Alexis wasn't so caught up in being a new mother she would notice Lucy was less than excited about being here. Lucy put on the same determined face he'd seen her wear when she was fighting for a patient as she followed Alexis and a drowsy Emily into another room.

He'd never been prouder of anyone. She was fighting an emotional battle like a champion. Heaven help him. He'd fallen in love.

It was a wonderful, scary and totally bewildering feeling. Yet somehow so right.

Lucy stood motionless in the doorway of the bedroom. Alexis would be destroyed if she ever found out her twin wanted to run.

Why couldn't she handle this better? Her job was to

help people through tough situations and she couldn't even be rational about her own problems. Known for her calming and forthright encouragement with patients' families, she was completely irrational where her own issues were concerned. She was such a fraud.

"Would you mind taking her dress off while I get her nightclothes together?" Alexis asked over her shoulder as she laid Emily in a crib. "I had no idea it took so much stuff to travel with someone so small."

Lucy took a breath. Just knowing Ryan was close had gotten her this far. She stepped to the bed and began to undress Emily. The sleepy-eyed baby looked up at her with complete trust. Unable to stop herself, Lucy leaned down and gave Emily a kiss on her forehead.

She wanted what Alexis had. Not this child, but her own. A family.

Alexis's bright sunny world was in complete contrast to the dark, lonely one Lucy lived in. Jealousy was a nasty emotion and Lucy wanted it to go away.

"I hate to wake a sleeping baby to change her clothes but I wanted her to look cute when you got here." Alexis came up beside Lucy, who gave the job of dressing Emily over to her.

Minutes later, as Alexis finished tucking Emily into her crib, Sam entered and came to stand beside the crib. Lucy stepped back, giving him room. He kissed Emily then, putting an arm around Alexis's shoulders, he kissed her temple. Together they looked down at their sleeping child. It was a poignant family moment.

A moment that Lucy wasn't a part of. She and Alexis had only had each other for so long, and now Alexis had her own family. Lucy had been pushed out.

Panic, fiery and foul, bubbled in her. Disgust rose in her throat. She had to get out of here. If she didn't she might burst. *I can't let her know.* It might cut that thin thread of a relationship she still had with her sister.

With blurry eyes, she rushed out of the room. Ryan met her, his forehead wrinkled, and his look penetrated her. Why couldn't she hide anything from him? "We have to go," she said tightly, reaching for her coat. "I have to go."

"You can't just leave," he whispered. "It'll hurt your sister's feelings." He took hold of her shoulders, stopping her frantic movements.

"If I stay I'll hurt her more," she responded in quiet desperation.

Alexis and Sam joined them.

Lucy kept her back to them as she gathered her and Ryan's coat from the chair. "We have to go. Ryan's been paged. He has a patient he needs to check on."

"Can't you stay, Lucy?" Alexis said. The disappointment in her voice grabbed at Lucy's heart.

"I have to go with him. We're part of a special program. We have to see all the patients at the same time. Co-ordinated patient care." She needed to slow down. Her words were running together.

"Surely you don't have to make every visit," Alexis insisted. "We haven't really gotten to talk. I wanted us to have a real visit."

"This is a patient in the ER." Lucy slid her arm inside the sleeve of her coat as Ryan held it. She glanced at Alexis and came undone. The disappointment in her sister's eyes made her heart clench. She was hurting Alexis, and she couldn't stop herself. Her feelings were a huge monster rising up to consume her.

"Oh, well, I guess I understand." Alexis didn't sound as if she did. "We'll see you tomorrow, won't we?"

Ryan shrugged into his jacket and joined Lucy at

the door. She looked at him and the worry in his eyes said he was only going along with her lies in order not to upset her sister further. The thin line of his lips said clearly he wasn't pleased.

As Lucy opened the door she said, "I'll have to see how it goes at work. I'll give you a call." She reached out and managed to give Alexis as brief and soothing a hug as she could manage.

Ryan waited until they were out of the apartment and in the dim light of the street before he asked, "Lucy, what happened?"

"I just couldn't stay there any longer."

She started down the street at a quick pace. Even with his long strides he had to work to keep up with her. "Come on, Lucy. Talk to me. I thought you were doing great."

Releasing a huff of indignation loud enough to draw the attention of others passing by, she said, "No, I wasn't. That…" she waved a hand in the direction they'd come from "…was my sister. She defended me. Took care of me. Supported and encouraged me all our lives. And me, I can't even be happy for her." The last few words came out almost as a sob.

Ryan grabbed her arm, stopping her in the middle of the sidewalk. "Lucy, listen."

She jerked her arm away and continued walking. "I don't want to talk about it any more."

He followed a few steps behind her, letting her work off her anger and frustration. When she'd cooled down he'd hail them a cab. Three blocks later she paused at the cross streets. She looked up at the buildings as if searching for a landmark, then at the street signs, before her head went down and her shoulders slumped. She had no idea which direction to turn. His heart broke for her. She was lost, both emotionally and physically.

The innate need to protect and support this proud woman who gave to and cared for others so wholeheartedly welled up in him. She'd given her sister the supreme gift of a child but couldn't see that because of the all-consuming dislike she felt for herself for desiring the same things out of life. Being around her had forced him to open up emotionally again. In that way, she'd even given him a gift.

He needed her. He didn't know how it had happened but it had.

Catching up to her, he pulled her securely against him and wrapped his arms around her. She didn't struggle. He held her a minute then raised a hand to get the attention of a passing cab driver. She said nothing as they waited for the yellow car to pull to the curb. "Come on, honey. It's time to go home."

Lucy used a determined voice to correct Ryan when he gave his address to the cab driver. "No, I want to go home." She told the driver her street. He looked at Ryan for confirmation. Ryan nodded.

She allowed him to hold her close, appreciating his strength. How could he possibly stand to be around someone who resented her own sister's happiness? She didn't like herself and she couldn't comprehend how he could either. Ryan was far too fine a man to have anything to do with a person who didn't have the capacity to love unconditionally.

The drive to her apartment was too short because she didn't want to lose the feel of being in Ryan's arms but too long because all she wanted to do was crawl into bed, curl up in a ball and pretend she didn't exist. As the driver pulled onto her street she said, "Ryan, keep the cab. I'll be fine going up myself."

"I'm coming with you." The tic in his jaw and the tone of his voice said he wouldn't be dismissed that easily.

Their feet made clomping noises as they climbed the worn wooden stairs to her floor. Ryan's hand rested at the slope of her back. She was exhausted in mind, body and particularly spirit. When she was unsuccessful at putting her key into the door lock the second time, Ryan took it from her and opened the door. He followed her in and closed the door behind him.

She went to her bed and sank down on it. He came toward her and she looked up. Why didn't he go home? "I'd like to be alone."

"Lucy…" He sounded so unsure. "Don't push me away. I want to help. But I don't know how."

"You did what you could by being there with me tonight. There's nothing more you can do."

"But you've got to work this through. Go back and talk to your sister. If not now, call her in the morning."

"I can't."

Ryan paced to the window and back. "No, that's not true. It's that you won't." He sounded disgusted.

She jumped up, faced him. "How can you say that? I did what you wanted. I went to see Alexis. Did you see what happened? I couldn't handle it."

Ryan's look didn't waver as he leaned toward her. "No, I didn't see that. What I saw was you trying despite your fear. You made the effort. You care about your sister. Emily. Even Sam. Everyone. And they care about you. You may not see it but I do. In fact, you wouldn't be this upset if you didn't care."

"I can't tell her how I feel. She wouldn't understand.

How can I explain what I don't understand?" She buried her face in her hands. "I'm just too ashamed."

He let out an exasperated breath. "Doing brain surgery is easier than getting through to you."

She glared at him. "You making a joke isn't going to make this one go away, Ryan. You can't make this all better for me. I've decided to stay out of my sister's life. It's for the best."

"This isn't the real you. Where's that woman who told me off and made it clear I wasn't her date at a party? The one so intriguing to me that I couldn't stay away from her? The one who made me want to get involved no matter how hard I tried not to? The one willing to fight for her patients?"

She sat on the edge of the bed again and looked up at him. "I don't know. Maybe she never really existed. I'm such a phony anyway. I tell families all the time what they need to do or how to act, and I can't even get my own life straight. I'm a mess.

"Ryan, you're a good guy. You cared for your father, your sisters and now I come along and you're stepping in to support me. I can't do that to you. I think I just need time alone to figure out my life. I don't want to ruin yours."

Ryan stepped back as if she had slapped him, hard. "Lucy, you're wrong. Way wrong. I swore never to carry the emotional needs of others ever again after my father died. I promised myself I'd never completely open up to my patients or anyone else again and then you came along. I want to be here for you. You're making a choice to be miserable. Your sister loves you. I care for you, and you won't accept either."

She raised her chin "You think Alexis is going to love me after I tell her how I feel?"

"I do. She showed how much she cares just by coming all this way to see you. I saw it when her eyes lit up when she opened the door. She's concerned for how you are doing. That's a plus in your life. Don't throw it away. Sometimes we just have to do some hard things because we love someone. Some really difficult things. Talk to her. Work through this."

"That's right, Mr. Bottle-Up-All-Your-Feelings wants me to bare my soul to my sister and hurt her more."

Ryan stalked toward her stepping into her personal space. "What do you want me to bare? That my father was the strongest man I've ever known and that I watched him slowly disappear? That I sat by his bed every minute I wasn't at school or working? That I saw fear in his eyes that I knew had to match mine? That I became responsible for my sisters during the worst time in our lives? Is that what you want me to share? Is that enough sharing for you? Enough to let you know I care deeply? That I do care about you?"

"Ryan, I just can't do this now. I don't know what to think."

Shaking his head, he looked at her. "You're a bright, sensitive, caring person, Lucy. Don't push Alexis away. And don't push me away."

"My sister was the one steady thing in my life. How can I feel this way towards her?"

Ryan sat on the bed beside her and put an arm around her shoulders. "I want to be the constant person in your life now. I know this isn't the perfect time, heck, it's probably the worst time in the history of mankind to tell you I love you. But there it is. I do. I'm here for you."

Her heart raced. She stared at him in disbelief. How could he? She was a mess. She didn't even love herself right now. "Please don't." She moved away from him and knew she'd regret it for the rest of her life but she had to.

He took her hand. "I understand you better than you think. I know how tough caring can be. What it's like to wish the person you love more than anyone else in the world would die quickly for their sake while at the same time wanting to hang onto them for as long as you can. I know what it is like to wish for something you can't have. Lucy, I'm offering you something you can have."

"No, Ryan, I can't let you love me."

He let go of her hand and stared down at her as if defeated. His beautiful blue eyes held shadows that she'd put there. "You don't get a choice in that," he said slowly.

She crossed her arms over her chest. "You don't get it. I don't know how to love. To really love. I've failed my sister. I'm failing you now. How can you love this messed-up, screwed-up me?" He just looked at her with a mixture of astonishment and sadness in his eyes. She studied his face, wanting with all her heart to give him what he asked for. But she couldn't.

He leaned over and kissed her cheek. "Goodbye, Lucy."

His kisses the night before had been all fire and passion, but the simple caress of his lips on her cheek held a devastating finality that filled her with a grief bone deep.

Apart from when Ryan had followed his father's casket down the aisle of the church, walking down the stairs and away from Lucy was the longest journey of Ryan's existence. For once in his life he'd opened his heart to someone and she'd shoved it back at him.

Lucy wasn't who he'd thought she was. He wanted the woman who'd shown such spunk when he'd made her mad. The one who'd had the fortitude to carry a child for her sister, the strength to move away from everything she knew to one of the largest cities in the world and to share her pain with him. Why couldn't he make her see that she had what it took to talk to her sister?

He pushed the door to his condo open. Dumping his wallet and keys on the bar in the kitchen, he climbed the stairs to his room. He stopped in the doorway and looked at the bed.

That morning Lucy had insisted, "We can't leave it undone. I make my bed every morning."

"And I have a housekeeper who comes in twice a week."

When she started shaking out the sheet, he'd taken the other side to help.

As he'd tucked a corner she'd said, "Hey, you can't just wad that up and put it under there." She circled the bed, reaching down to pull the material out.

"Don't tell me how I'm supposed to make a bed," he'd said, sounding as indignant as possible before he'd grabbed her and rolled her onto the bed. She'd giggled. He'd shared her mirth. He hadn't laughed so freely since before his father had become sick. Had almost forgotten how good it felt to be alive. Happily alive.

He'd kissed her and that was all it had taken. They'd not taken time to remove their clothes and she hadn't seemed to mind. In fact, his desperate need for her had seemed to fuel her own. She'd crawled on top and had taken over their lovemaking.

That's what it had been. Him loving her. He'd not recognized it then but it was clear now. So much so that it hurt to look at the bed, to remember. His body ached from the mere thought of her.

Walking to the dark brown chair that faced the window, he plopped down, put his legs across the matching footstool and crossed his ankles. The lights of the city had lost some of their luster. Scooting his butt forward, he braced his head against the back of the chair and closed his eyes. He wouldn't be sleeping in his bed tonight.

Lucy curled under her sheets still fully clothed and pulled her legs to her chest, becoming a ball. She buried her head in a pillow and let the tears flow. It had been horrible when she'd left Alexis and Emily behind and moved to New York. But nothing compared to giving up Ryan.

She'd hurt him. He'd said he loved her and she'd thrown it back in his face. She was unworthy of his love. She missed Ryan's arms being around her, his strong, calming presence. It had taken him no time to become embedded in her life.

She'd slept next to Ryan for only one night but she already missed his warm body pressed against hers. What did he see in her? She was a mess. Here she was supposed to be helping others and she couldn't even handle her own life.

How had her world spun so out of control? How could she ever face him at work again? Maybe she should speak to Mr. Matherson and see if she could be reassigned to another neurosurgeon. No, she couldn't do that. It might damage Ryan's career if she did. She couldn't hurt him like that. She'd just have to endure and be the professional she was known to be. But could she stand the pain of seeing him daily?

CHAPTER NINE

"THE PATIENT'S DOING as expected," Ryan informed the assembly around him in the hallway of the neurosurgery floor midmorning. The group didn't include Lucy. She'd excused herself as soon as they had come out of the patient's room. He had to make an effort not to watch her walk away. They'd not spoken since he'd left her apartment three days earlier.

It was up to Lucy to make the first move. She was the one who'd pushed him away. She'd never said she loved him. Despite being distraught about her issues with her sister, she'd sounded very clear-headed where he was concerned. Learning to live with her decision was going to be difficult. Even harder was accepting it. Compounding the issue was having to continue to work together.

She'd taken care of her responsibilities, making meticulous notes on patient charts. His clinical nurse questioned him a couple of times about an issue that Lucy had noted but which she hadn't directly spoken to him about. In fact, she refused to look at him. She was living by the letter of the law regarding their co-operative patient care but there was no spirit of partnership in her actions any more.

He grieved for her. Only by sheer iron will did he

not go in search of her or ask about her. She'd made her feelings clear. How could they have been so in sync and now have an ocean-wide chasm between them? He missed the peaceful, quiet way she'd had about her. How she'd made his hectic, often stressful life easier just by being near.

Helping her was impossible. She had to work out her issues on her own. He'd offered her love and his support and she'd pushed them away. He was paying dearly for it.

The worst was the physical ache. His body craved her, making his nights almost longer than his sanity could tolerate.

Having a few minutes before starting his weekly paperwork, he headed across the street and into Central Park. He needed to get out, away. Clear his head. As large as the hospital was, it still closed in on him, knowing that Lucy was so near but still so untouchable.

He strolled around a bend on the paved walkway and there sat his nemesis and love of his heart. She looked out over the lake, her face held up to the sun and her lunch spread out on the bench beside her. His body went on full alert. Every fiber of his being wanted to reach out and snatch her to him. Thankfully, his pride held him in check.

Her eyes opened, widened. Had she heard him or just sensed someone was near? She looked as if she was debating whether or not to ignore him. She squared her shoulders and looked directly at him.

"Hello, Ryan," she said. The sounds of the city were hushed by the foliage of the trees and bushes. The few voices he could make out were in the distance. It would have been a perfect opportunity to take her in his arms for a kiss. But if he did that he would want more. A little of Lucy would never be enough. He wanted it all and he wanted her to want it all too.

A thin smile came to his lips. She was tough. He'd give her that. Far tougher than he was. But, then, she didn't care about him as he cared for her. She had never once said she loved him. Forcing a foot forward, he came to stand in front of her. "Lucy." His traitorous body hummed, being near her. She'd crushed his heart and still he wanted her so desperately it was almost a living thing, crawling to be released. "Could I speak to you a minute?"

"I thought we'd said all that needed to be said." Her flinch gave him a second of satisfaction before it turned to guilt. It shouldn't be this way between them. "I'm sorry. That was uncalled for."

Lucy looked around as if checking to see if anyone was paying attention to them. Apparently finding they weren't, she said, "I understand. I've hurt you, and for that I'm sorry."

The North Pole would become a heated swimming pool before he let her know how badly she'd hurt him. "It didn't work out. We're both adults. We know the score."

She blinked then looked away.

He'd sounded harsh, he knew. But he couldn't continue to do his job, live his life if he didn't start getting a handle on his emotions where she was concerned. The first step was making clear to her that he was moving on.

"Ryan, about Miguel Rivera. His mother called. She's upset because she's having difficulty getting Miguel into a program designed for children with epilepsy this summer. It's too expensive for her to pay for and she wanted to know if you would consider recommending he attend. She believes he would qualify for a scholarship on your recommendation."

"Have you checked this camp out?"

"I have. I think it would be very beneficial for Miguel."

Ryan shouldn't have bothered to ask the question. Lucy was thorough, if nothing else. She looked at him, really looked at him, for the first time in days. Those beseeching eyes would have him doing anything. How he still wanted her! "Then I trust your judgment. See that the paperwork gets to my desk. If they don't get the scholarship, let me know. I'll pay for him to attend."

She sucked in a breath.

"Don't act so surprised. You're not the only one who can be philanthropic. Put the paperwork on my desk, and I'll sign it this afternoon."

"Thank you, Ryan."

"Is that all?"

"I'd really like to say one more thing."

Ryan shifted his weight from one foot to the other, waiting. Something about the hesitant way she said the words made him think he wasn't going to like what came next.

"I'm only saying this because I care about you."

His mouth quirked and took on a dubious line. Lucy had the good grace to look contrite.

"I'd like you to think about why you have such a difficult time talking to families—"

"I'm not going to discuss—"

"Ryan, you need to hear me out. You've retreated behind the pain and sorrow of your father's illness and death for so long that you can't bring yourself to be near anyone else in the same pain. You'd be a better doctor, even a happier person, if you would try, just

try to see that and be a little more open with your patients' families."

He glared down at her. She'd thrown what they'd
had together away and now she wanted to give him
personal advice?

Before she could say more or he could respond, a
nurse from the floor approached them. "Hi," she said
with a smile.

As she passed Ryan asked, "Are you headed back
in?"

"Yes," the nurse said, surprise in her tone.

"Mind if I walk with you?"

She gave him a brilliant smile. "Sure."

"Enjoy your lunch, Lucy." He turned and fell into
step with the pretty nurse, whose eager, encouraging
eyes made him wish that he could see that same look
coming from Lucy.

Lucy had cried so much in the last few days that she
didn't think she could ever cry again. She was wrong.
As she watched Ryan walk away and heard the cute
nurse's laugh, she was afraid another sobbing session
was coming on. She wadded up her meal and shoved
it into her sack.

Her days and nights had started to run together. She
hadn't really slept since the night she had lain curled
in Ryan's arms. Going through the motions was the
only way she could describe her efforts at work. She'd
managed to do what needed to be done for her patients
but little else.

Most of her energy had gone into making sure her
and Ryan's paths didn't cross. Working in such a large
hospital had helped. It hadn't worked today, though.
She'd been completely surprised to see him in the park.

Also the fact that Ryan spent so much time in the OR had helped.

She wasn't proud of the fact she'd checked the schedule each morning and planned her visits to the patients' rooms when she knew there was the least chance of running into him. Even though she made every effort not to see him, her body turned against her whenever she did. Heat rose in her every time she saw him.

Her life had gone from barely tolerable when she'd left Alexis's home to impossible. The only shining moments had been those spent with Ryan. Now even those were gone. Knowing she'd made the right choice didn't make it any easier to live without him. Seeing him daily at the hospital was a constant painful reminder of how much she cared.

She didn't have to look at him to know when his gaze was on her. She felt it. Hot, heavy and beckoning. When she glanced at him he made sure to be looking elsewhere. His sunny, ready smile had become almost non-existent. The nurses were making comments about how much he'd changed, speculating on the cause.

He wasn't happy and neither was she, but she didn't know how to change it. Even if she wanted to, would Ryan forgive her for all the things she'd said to him? Based on the ease with which he'd left her to walk with the nurse, she'd say she'd lost her chance.

Her efforts to dodge Ryan were working better than those she used to keep Alexis at bay. Where Ryan was silently accepting, Alexis was overt and demanding. There were twice-daily calls asking when they might get together. Lucy had ignored the first day's worth. The second day she'd actually spoken to Alexis but only long enough to say she was too busy to meet her.

She had to get control of her life. Did she want to

continually live like this? She'd shocked herself when she'd stood up to Ryan. Even more so when she'd undressed in front of him and all of Lower Manhattan. She should be able to talk to her sister. Ryan was lost to her but maybe her sister wasn't. She had to try. Nothing could be worse than what she had now.

She called Alexis as soon as she was out of bed the next morning.

"Alexis, can we get together tomorrow? I'm taking the afternoon off."

"That sounds wonderful. We're leaving the day after tomorrow and I've hardly seen you. I'll meet you at the hospital if you want."

Lucy couldn't risk her sister running into Ryan. "I'll come to your place. Take you out for lunch."

"I'm looking forward to it. I've missed you, Luce."

"Me, too," Lucy whispered, after Alexis had hung up.

Lucy pushed away the strands of her hair that had escaped from the tight bun she'd worn the last few days. Just thinking about how much Ryan loved her hair made her feel self-conscious. Having it down reminded her of how he'd played with it as she'd explored his body. If she kept tight control of her hair, maybe she could govern her memories as well. She shuddered. Those moments were events she shouldn't dwell on.

She raised her hand in the air to hail a cab. It surprised her how acclimatized to living in New York City she'd become in just a few weeks. Where she'd been intimidated by the large bustling city when she'd first arrived, now she could throw up an arm and hail a cab with ease.

Even the subway system was starting to feel familiar

to her and her on-time rate was improving because she wasn't lost all the time. She was starting to think of the city as home. Where she'd been a meek and mild person unsure of what to do and where to go, she'd become much more confident. That was empowering.

How often had she told her patient families that when they got out on the other side of the tough times they would find a bright spot? It was no different for her. She had lived her life not in the shadow of Alexis but with her leading the way all the time. Now she was her own person, having to fight her own battles. She was a stronger person for making the move to New York.

She could face Alexis. Would tell her the truth. With new resolve Lucy stepped out of the taxi and entered Alexis's building, making her way up to the correct floor. Could things between them be worse than they already had been? She loved Alexis and Alexis loved her. They would get through this. Wasn't it the same with Ryan? She wasn't so sure. Could she forgive him if he'd treated her as badly as she'd treated him?

She rapped her knuckles firmly against Alexis's door. Squaring her shoulders and lifting her chin to cover the jitters that felt like a flock of birds taking off in her belly, Lucy waited.

Too soon for her nerves the door opened and Alexis stood there. The warm smile of welcome Lucy had received days earlier had disappeared. Alexis pierced her with a look.

"Come in and tell me what's going on."

Lucy should have known she couldn't hide from her sister long. Nothing got by her. She knew Lucy too well.

Alexis closed the door behind Lucy, reminding her of bars closing on a jail cell. She wouldn't be released until Alexis got want she wanted. That suited Lucy just fine. She was ready to bare her heart. Would do what it took to get back what she'd lost.

Alexis headed toward a sofa, leaving Lucy to follow. "Emily's napping and Sam's at the office at a meeting. We have time to talk. Really talk," Alexis said, sitting on the sofa.

Lucy had always received a hug from Alexis when they hadn't seen each other in a while. It was telling that she hadn't offered one this time. Lucy would have to call on her new-found determination to get through this. She followed Alexis to the living room, taking the sofa opposite hers.

"What happened to you the other night? I know what you told me but I also know you well enough to know when you're lying. Something's going on and I want to know what it is."

Alexis had never been one to dance around what she wanted to know. Lucy had to tell the truth. Alexis deserved to hear the whole dreadful story.

She focused on the tip of her black dress boot, unable to make eye contact with Alexis. "I had to leave Atlanta."

"Had to leave? Why?" Patience was never Alexis's strong suit. Lucy had always been the one to wait and listen.

"Because I was too close to Emily. It was too hard. I thought you were starting to resent me."

Alexis's mouth fell open as she leaned forward. "I don't understand."

She didn't imagine that Alexis did. Alexis's thoughts had never wavered away from the fact she was going to have a baby to think about how it was affecting her sister. Lucy looked at Alexis, seeing her in a different light for the first time ever. Lucy had always revered Alexis, thinking she could do no wrong.

Now she recognized that Alexis had been so focused on her own needs that she'd had no idea of what Lucy had been going through. Lucy didn't love Alexis any less, she just recognized that Alexis's concern had more to do with her having a family than with Lucy's welfare. It was not a criticism. It was a reminder that Lucy had to build a life of her own. Move on.

"Alexis, we talked of Emily being yours. You made all the doctor's appointments. I knew in my head that she belonged to you and Sam, but as she grew and my body changed, it became harder to think of myself as just an incubator. As hard as I tried not to, I felt the baby belonging to me more and more."

Alexis's sharp intake of breath made Lucy flinch but she had to go on.

"Do you remember that day you came home and Sam had his hand on my belly? He was feeling her kick for the first time. I saw the look on your face. You resented me. I knew then I was going to have to do something drastic after the baby was born. I started applying for jobs then. My post partum emotions didn't help. You and Sam and Emily became this tight little unit that didn't include me."

"Luce, we didn't—"

Lucy held up a hand. "Let me finish or I might not be able to. I know my feelings were irrational. But I couldn't make them go way. The problem was I was jealous. Jealous of you with Emily. Jealous of you having Sam. Jealous that I had no family of my own."

"You had us. I'm your family."

Lucy looked away. "No, my own husband, child. The jealousy was eating me up inside. I had to get away.

When the job offer up here came I snatched it. My excuse was that I was feeling too attached to Emily when it was really that I was jealous of what you had. The longer I stayed at your house the more those awful feelings grew. I was disgusted with myself.

"I'm jealous of your happiness! You found it and I haven't. You and I were a team. It had always been us against the world. Then Sam came along. You still included me, things weren't that different, but Emily changed everything. You had your little family and I had nothing."

She looked up to find tears rolling down Alexis's face. They matched the ones on her own cheeks.

"I'm so ashamed, Alexis. If you love someone you should want them to have all the happiness in the world, not be jealous of them. I had no intention of seeing you the other day. Only because Ryan agreed to come with me did I show up. I just couldn't face you." She caught Alexis's gaze and said with all the sincerity she could muster, "I'm so sorry. For it all. Please forgive me. I love you, Emily and Sam."

Alexis's stricken look tore at Lucy's heart. Her sister was just as hurt as Lucy had feared she would be. Seconds later, Alexis popped up and came around the coffee table that stood between them. She sat next to Lucy and pulled her into a tight hug. "Aw, honey, I wish you'd said something. Sam and I love you. We want you to be happy too, not for us to be happy at your expense."

It felt good to have Alexis's understanding, concern and touch. "I don't want you to feel guilty. I've carried enough of that for both of us. Please forgive me." Lucy gave her a pleading look.

Alexis let go of Lucy enough that they could look at each other. "There's nothing to forgive. I had no idea what a toll carrying Emily was having on you. Sam and I had no idea. You gave us no hint. You should've said something."

"I couldn't. As jealous as I was, I still couldn't ruin your happiness."

Alexis took both of Lucy's hands in hers and looked at her with gloomy eyes. "Luce, I'm so sorry. We should've been more sensitive to your feelings."

"I don't want you or Sam to feel bad. As hard as coming here the other night was for me, it also made me face my fears and feelings. I'm stronger for it. I'm moving on, learning to cope, and I don't want anything to ever stand between us again."

Alexis wrapped Lucy in another hug, which she accepted and returned with every fiber of her being. She hung on until she and Alexis had moved from crying to laughing. With that came a sense of wellbeing that hadn't been there in the last few months, except for those precious moments in Ryan's arms.

"Enough of the crying. I'm going to call Sam and see when he'll be home. He can watch Emily while you and I go out and have a good old-fashioned girls' evening out," Alexis declared, in that childhood one-twin-is-more-dominant-than-the-other voice.

"I'd really like that," Lucy said, not hiding the emotion that crept into her voice. "I've missed you."

Alexis gave her a hug. "And I you. Do you know of any good places to do some shopping in this big city?"

"I think Macy's would cover everything we might need and more."

"Then Macy's it is."

A cry from the adjoining room announced that Emily was awake.

"Do you mind if I get her?" Lucy asked.

"I would love for you to."

Lucy reached into the crib and brought the warm child to her chest. Emily gave a whimper and quieted. Lucy inhaled the sweet smell of her. "Hi, sweetheart. It's your Aunt Lucy."

Hours later, with shopping bags in her hand and a smile on her face, Lucy asked, "Would you like to see where I live? It isn't much."

"I'd love to," Alexis responded, with more eagerness than the tiny apartment warranted.

"Come on, I'll show you how a real New Yorker travels." Lucy headed down the steps into the subway station. Half an hour later she and Alexis were strolling along the narrow, bumpy sidewalk of her tree-lined street.

"What a nice area to live in. If I had to live in a city this large, I'd like to live somewhere like this. It feels like a real neighborhood," Alexis commented.

"It is, but it doesn't have the view of the city that Ryan has from Brooklyn." He'd been on Lucy's mind all day, especially after she'd begun to adjust to being a doting aunt and loyal sister. She missed him with all her heart. If they couldn't return to what they'd had, she wanted them to at least be friends. No, that wasn't true. They couldn't go back to being friends. She wanted Ryan to be more than that. There had to be some way to make up for what she'd said to him.

"And you know about his view how?" Alexis put a suggestive tone in her voice. "I've been wanting to ask but was afraid to because of all the other emotions we've been drowning in today. But you opened the gate so I'm asking. What's going on with you two?"

Lucy touched Alexis's arm. "You can ask me anything. I'll never again close you out. Ever."

"I love you, Lucy."

"And I love you. Here's my apartment."

A short time later Lucy and Alexis were sitting at the table, having glasses of iced tea, when Alexis asked, "Now, tell me about Ryan. How do you know about his view exactly?" Her look was pointed enough to make Lucy squirm and blush simultaneously.

"I've seen it."

"You have? I knew there was something going on between you two." Alexis's seemed pleased with herself. She waited as if she expected Lucy to say more.

Under her watchful eyes, Lucy played with the moisture on the side of her glass.

"You really care about him, don't you?"

"Yeah. Too much. And I messed up big time."

"What happened?" Alexis put her glass down and leaned toward Lucy.

"Oh, Alexis, he told me he loved me."

Alexis squealed. "That's wonderful."

"I said he couldn't. I pushed him away."

Alexis's eyes widen in disbelief. "Why did you do that?"

"He told me right after we left your place. I was already upset. I didn't think he could or should love anyone who was jealous of her own sister."

Alexis huffed and reached across the table, taking one of Lucy's hands in her own. "Isn't that just like a man? To pick the worst possible moment, when we're not thinking straight, to say something like I love you for the first time."

"I've hurt him so badly. He won't have anything to do with me now."

"Honey, all you have to do is tell him that you love him too."

"What if he's changed his mind?"

Alexis snorted. "He'd be crazy if he did."

"We barely speak."

"I don't think you're giving him or yourself enough credit. He doesn't strike me as a man who gives up on someone he loves."

Could she convince Ryan of her love? "I don't know…"

"Lucy, you've changed. You're more self-sufficient. More confident. Almost outspoken. You do it the same way you came to talk to me. Make Ryan listen. If he doesn't, it's his loss."

Lucy's greatest fear was that it would be her loss too.

Ryan clicked a computer key, making the screen go black. Matherson's email requested that he and Lucy meet with him to discuss the co-ordinated patient care project. He and Lucy hadn't had a real conversation other than that short one in the park in over a week. She'd not even shown up for evening rounds the day before. He hadn't wanted to wonder where she was or, worse, worry about her. He'd done both.

She'd started to treat New York more like home but she could still easily get lost. As tender-hearted as she was, she could even be guided wrongly by someone in the subway. He loved her and was intensely concerned. Nothing between them had diminished since the night she'd pushed him out of her life. The separation made his ache for her bottomless. He wanted her not to matter but regardless of what he did he couldn't get her out of his mind and heart.

He hated to admit to the mountain-sized relief he'd

felt when she'd slipped into the clinic examination room that afternoon during Miguel Rivera's post-surgery check-up. Doing a double-take, he'd looked at her again. She'd cut her hair. It was loose and flowing, touching the top of her shoulders. His heart had skipped. She'd looked gorgeous. As much as he loved her hair, this version was every bit as breathtaking as the other.

Lucy had replaced her rather drab clothes with a straight skirt, a blouse of light blue and a multicolored sweater that showed off her breasts to their best advantage. Was she trying to kill him? He was confused. What was happening here?

Miguel's mother's face lit up when she saw Lucy. After she'd spoken to the mother, she looked at him and gave him a shy smile.

She kept the sucker punches coming. She hadn't met his look straight on in days, much less smiled at him. He didn't know what had happened to make her change her reaction to him but he wouldn't complain. Still, he couldn't let her super-sexy smile fool him into believing that she wanted anything more than a stable working relationship. He wouldn't let her stomp on his heart again. Heck, she was still stomping on it. His sense of self-preservation refused to let her know what she was doing to him.

What she'd said to him in the park about him letting his father's illness control his life had made him mad. He'd stewed over it. Where did she get off, telling him something like that? When his temper had cooled he'd realized that she might be right.

Ryan cleared his throat and said flatly, "Will you translate?"

Her smile faded. "Yes." Her professional armor slid into place.

He smiled at the mother. "Please tell her that Miguel's doing well. And that she's been doing a fine job in caring for the wound."

He waited while Lucy relayed his remark.

Miguel's mother smiled at Ryan. *"Gracias."*

It did feel good to have a parent look at him with something more than disappointment. With his examination completed he said, "Please bring Miguel in to see me again in six weeks. I hope you are taking care of yourself also." Lucy repeated his request in Spanish with a slight smile on her face. While she was doing so, he picked up Miguel. "He's a handsome boy." Ryan smiled at the mother again.

The mother said something to Lucy and giggled, before taking Miguel and heading towards the door. Lucy responded with a grin. He raised his chin in question.

"She said you're handsome also. I agreed," she said, so softly he wasn't sure he'd heard it.

"You got Matherson's email?"

Her smile slipped. "I did."

"I'll see you there, then."

"Sure." She looked at him as if she wanted to say more. When she didn't, he left. If he stayed any longer he was afraid he might do something he'd regret. Like take her in his arms and beg her to reconsider. Tell her he'd do anything to work things out between them.

CHAPTER TEN

LUCY CONTINUED DOWN the corridor, paying special attention to the signs directing her to the HR department. The enormous hospital still intimidated her when she got off her beaten path. She'd not returned to the HR department since the day she and Ryan had met. She didn't remember much about how she'd gotten there and certainly recalled little from Ryan's guided trip other than his displeasure.

She'd checked her emails in the hope he'd offer to walk down with her, but after their few terse words during Miguel's clinic visit she'd not been surprised when there had been none. She'd hurt him so deeply that his gentleman's manners were slipping where she was concerned.

He remained polite, which was the O'Doherty way, but there was a ten-foot-high, eight-foot-thick wall around him with no door for her to beat on. He still charmed the nurses and the children but there was a look in his eyes that she couldn't quite put a name to, or didn't want to. She'd give anything to see him grin at her.

With relief and only one double back, she pushed the HR door open to find Ryan already there. He reclined in a chair, his white lab coat unbuttoned. His tie looked as if he'd tugged on it in irritation and his hair was in disarray. He glanced at the clock on the wall. She smiled to herself. He knew she had a hard time finding her way around the hospital. It served him right to have to wait since he'd not offered to walk down with her.

He looked tired. There had been a number of new cases in the last few days but his weariness seemed to come from deeper inside. His eyes lacked that twinkle she'd grown accustomed to and loved. Had she been the cause of that luster disappearing? If she'd thought he would allow it, she would have taken him in her arms.

Was he sleeping as poorly as she was? Even though she and Alexis had cleared the air, her life still had a gaping hole. What she missed sat in front of her, but he might as well be a hundred miles away. Ryan had never looked less approachable.

Ryan glanced at her and she gave him a hesitant smile. He didn't return it. Would he ever forgive her?

She glanced to where the receptionist should be sitting and saw no one then looked at Ryan. "Where's the receptionist? Does Matherson know you're here?"

"No one was around when I got here. I knew you would probably be late so I was waiting before I looked for Matherson."

He stood. His somewhat unruly locks looked even more so, as if he'd been running his hands through it regularly. She wished she could. The thought did her no good. Only made her want what she couldn't have.

Ryan straightened his lab coat then stepped toward her. Her breath caught. Was he going to touch her? Instead, he stepped past her. Sorrow filled her.

"Come on, let's get this over with," Ryan grumbled. "I still have work to do and it's been a long week."

He didn't look at her after that statement. Had what

had happened between them affected his week? They had started down the short hall in the direction of Matherson's office when he stepped out of it.

"Good. Here you are," he said, all smiles. "Sorry you had to wait. My receptionist left early."

The man sounded far too cheerful for her liking. By the curl to Ryan's lip, he wasn't too impressed either. Maybe Matherson wouldn't drag this meeting out. As soon as she got this over with she was going home to a hot bath. She glanced at Ryan. Maybe a good cleansing cry as well.

"Come in. Have a seat," Matherson said as he took his chair behind the desk that was too large for the room.

Ryan stood to the side, letting her enter the office ahead of him. It was the closest they had been in days. As she passed, she caught a hint of the scent that was Ryan's alone. With great effort she managed not to step closer to him, though her body vibrated with the need to.

She was relieved when she sat as her knees had begun to wobble. Ryan waited until she settled into her chair before he took his. The chairs were situated so close that when he placed his arm on the rest, it came within an inch of hers. She moved her arm and clasped her hands in her lap, fearing the powerful urge she had to touch him.

"So," Matherson began, leaning back in his chair, "how's the co-operative patient care working out between you two?" He ended the question with a sappy smile.

Ryan shifted slightly in his chair at Matherson's use of the words "you two".

"Fine," she and Ryan said at the same time, not looking at each other.

"That's all you have to report?" Matherson looked back and forth between them, his brow contracting "Could you be more specific, Dr. O'Doherty?"

"I think it has gone pretty much as I expected. I thought little of the idea to begin with and still do. The only difference between how I handled patient care before and what I do now is that I have to call Ms. Edwards before I meet the patient. Which does take time."

She glanced at Ryan then scooted forward in her chair, gaining Matherson's attention. "He had to wait a couple of times for me. I'm new to the hospital and had to learn my way around. The same for the city. I don't believe that lessens my effectiveness."

"So you believe the project has merit?" Matherson asked.

"I do." She glanced at Ryan again and found him looking straight ahead. "I assisted in the patient's and the family's emotional needs. Something that surgeons often don't address. I thought from the total patient care aspect it has value," Lucy volunteered. "I was involved early on in easing family into the reality they were facing."

Ryan snorted. His manners had disappeared. She and Matherson looked at him. "Yes, but I'm not sure that the hand-holding is necessary when the patient is in the ER."

She swung to face Ryan. One of her knees bumping his hard thigh sent a shock wave through her before she pulled it away. "Really, Dr. O'Doherty? You seemed to appreciate my hand-holding just fine when you needed a translator." She couldn't keep the edge out of her voice.

Ryan didn't look at her but at Matherson. "I concede that. Ms. Edwards was of value then."

Ooh, the man! Lucy waited until Ryan and Matherson were both looking at her. Through clenched teeth she said, "Are you implying that what I do isn't as important as being the all-powerful, all-knowing surgeon?"

"What I'm saying is that we don't have to be joined at the hip," he said through a taut jaw.

She flinched at his choice of words. Was he baiting her? Reminding herself to remain professional, she responded, "You're right." She turned to Matherson. "We shouldn't have been required to attend Jack Carter's party together."

"So that didn't go well?" Matherson sat forward as if he was enjoying their exchange.

"There are parts that are better left not discussed," she murmured.

Someone called from the outer office. "Anyone here?"

"If you will excuse me a minute, I'll be right back." Matherson said, coming around the desk and heading out the door.

"So, do you have something particular in mind?" Ryan leaned toward her.

Two could play this game. "Yes, as a matter of fact I do."

"Then why not just say it? I'm sure Mr. Matherson would be interested. You've had no trouble speaking your mind before."

He was right. Since she'd moved to New York, no, met him, she'd taken to speaking up for herself. But this wasn't the time. The discussion was too personal.

Too heart-wrenching. "Ryan, please don't do this here," she whispered.

"Why not? I admit I kissed you. And what's more, you liked it."

"Please, Matherson can hear you," she whispered in desperation.

"You don't think I show my feelings enough," he said, standing and pulling her up out of the chair. "How about this for showing some emotion?"

His mouth came down on hers hard and heavy as if he wanted to brand her and consume her at the same time. Nothing in her life had felt more wonderful. She curved a hand around his neck, savoring the moment she'd thought never to have again. With a soft moan of bliss she leaned in and soaked in the feel of him. Her world turned, funneled into a tornado and Ryan was the eye. Nothing mattered but the feel of his lips on hers.

The loud clearing of a throat from the doorway broke them apart. Matherson stood there, a look of shock on his face.

Blood rushed up her neck. The stricken and surprised look on Matherson's face had to match hers. She glanced at Ryan. He was grinning like he'd just made the winning home run in the bottom of the ninth at a Yankees game.

What had just happened? She'd been kissing the surgeon she'd been assigned to work with in front of the head of the HR department! It hadn't been just any kiss. It had been an open-mouthed, moaning kiss. Could she feel more mortified? She'd learned to stand up for herself in the last few weeks but Ryan's—and admittedly her own—kiss had been far out of her comfort zone when done in front of an audience.

She couldn't meet Matherson's gaze, and she sure

wasn't going to look at Ryan. Appalled at their actions, she still wanted to step back into Ryan's arms and have his generous lips find hers again. She desired more than a kiss. Her body shook with the need to draw him to her. "I have to go."

Her knee hit the chair leg in her fervor to leave the room. Not sure how she did it, she made her way out of the office and the department. Wishing for her old sensible shoes back, she walked as fast as her new heels would allow. At the first bank of elevators she pushed the button for the eighth floor. Getting in the first door that opened, she rode up. Not until they opened again did she realize it was the eighth floor of a different wing of the hospital.

She wanted to stomp on the floor and scream *Ryan, Ryan, Ryan*. Instead, she took her frustration out on the down call button and punched it with the end of her finger. Why had he done it? Why had he kissed her in front of Matherson? She'd never been more embarrassed in her life. Did he mean anything by it other than to kiss her into submission? Regardless, it had been heaven to have his mouth on hers again.

Ryan lounged against the wall outside Lucy's office door. He crossed his hands over his chest and prepared to wait. This time he didn't mind doing so. The taste of Lucy lingered on his lips. She'd returned his kiss. Held nothing back, even in front of Matherson. Maybe there was hope after all.

When she turned the corner of the hall a few minutes later, he suppressed a smile. The Lucy that had stood up to him was back. He'd seen some evidence of it in Matherson's office but by the look on her face now, he knew he was in for it. The best part was that he was looking forward to the fight and hopefully the making up. The last week had been one of pure misery.

As she stalked toward him he said, "You got lost again."

He smiled when she mumbled, "Darned elevators." She stopped beside him and shoved her key in the door. "I don't need you making fun of me. You've hardly spoken to me in a week." She turned to face him. "Then you pulled that stunt in front of Matherson."

Lucy flung her hair back as she turned to fiddle with the key. "How could you?"

Her wildflower scent touched his nostrils. He wanted to bury his nose in that warm, silky spot on her neck that he knew so well and inhale all of her. Pushing down a groan, he leaned towards her. "If you don't talk sweeter to me, I just might do it again right here."

She jerked her head up to look down the hall toward the nurses' station. "Don't," she muttered.

"Why, Lucy? Because you're afraid you might like it? I thought you were the one who believes in sharing feelings."

She pushed the office door open and entered. He followed, not giving her a chance to close the door on him.

"You might not lose your job, but I could."

"No, you won't. I told Matherson I'd be glad to continue working with you. That I thought he made a much better matchmaker than HR director."

"You said that?" she squeaked.

He shut the office door behind him. For once he appreciated an automatic lock. "Okay, maybe I left that last part off."

She turned to face him, hands on her hips. "If we continue to work together you can't kiss me every time I voice my opinion."

"Yes, I can." He grinned, stepping a pace closer, grateful the office was small.

"Huh?"

"I think you love me."

She blinked. Then a smile formed on her lips. "Pretty sure of yourself, aren't you, Dr. O'Doherty?"

He moved closer until her breasts touched his chest. "Kiss me again, Lucy."

She placed her hands on his shoulders and looked into his dark blue eyes as she touched her lips to his. Heaven. He opened for her and she slipped her tongue in to meet his. He greeted and encouraged it. Her hands moved to wrap around his neck as he became master of the kiss, drawing her to him and heating her so that she melted against him.

Divine minutes later he pulled away and looked into her face as he combed his fingers through her hair. "You cut it." He groaned with disappointment.

"It was time and I needed to make a statement I'd changed."

His other hand went to her waist. "You did that with your wardrobe alone."

"You noticed? The way you've been giving me the cold shoulder, I thought you might not have."

He trailed his fingers over her hip. "Oh, I noticed and so did the male interns. I might have spoken a little harshly to one after I caught him watching you walk away."

"So, I'm not the only one who has jealousy issues." She cupped his face. "I'm sorry I hurt you. I just couldn't get things straight in my head. I was so eaten up with envy and confused about my life that I couldn't think straight."

"Have you got it figured out?"

"You were right." Her hands ran over his shoulders to stop at his biceps as she looked into his eyes. "Alexis had no idea. She and I had a long talk. I discovered I've being using her as a security blanket all my life. I needed to find my own identity."

"Do you still want what Alexis has?"

"No."

His heart fell, taking his hope with it. She didn't want a family any more. Which meant that even if she loved him, which she hadn't said she did, it would never work between them. He wanted children. He wasn't staying around to have his heart trampled twice.

He took a step back and let his hands fall to his sides. "I understand. I just came by to apologize for embarrassing you. I won't let it happen again."

"Ryan." She caught his hand as he turned. "I don't think you do understand."

He looked at their hands then up at her face.

"I don't want what Alexis has. I want more. A husband of my own and lots and lots of children."

His heart fluttered and started to live again. "And who do you plan to have father these children?" he asked, moving close again.

"I was hoping you might consider the job," she said with a flicker of shy lashes that he found alluring. "I love you, Ryan O'Doherty. With all my heart. Do you maybe still care for me?"

He swept her up into his arms again, holding her as tight as he dared. Joy surged through him. She wrapped her arms around his neck, holding him just as tightly.

"I love you," she said over and over.

He moved so that he could see her face. It was killing him to have to ask but he had to know. "You're sure that you're not just replacing Alexis with me?"

She cupped his cheek again. "I'm not. For the first time in my life I'm an individual. I could survive on my own. But I don't want to. I want you."

Ryan hugged her close. Minutes went by before he let her slide down him. His lips hovered close to hers. "I love you, too. Never stopped and never will."

Long, wonderful, contented and soul-filling hours later, Ryan rolled over in his bed to look at Lucy naked beside him. She'd come a long way, not once trying to conceal herself or prevent him from looking until he'd had his fill. Not even an argument when he'd wanted to make love to her with the lights on.

Unable to resist, he dipped down to kiss her rosy lips before he asked, "When do you think Alexis and Sam will visit again?"

Her brow wrinkled in confusion. "I don't know. Why?"

Leaning over her, he kissed away the crease. "I thought we might invite them to a wedding if they could come back soon."

"And if they can't come back soon?" She trailed fingers over his chest.

"Then they may miss it," he growled as her fingers traveled lower.

Her gaze left her fingers to come up and meet his. "Are you asking me to marry you?"

He grinned. "Lucy Edwards, I promise to give you that family you dream of. You'll always be a part of me, never alone again. You are my life. I love you. Will you marry me?"

Those blue eyes she loved expressed that love so clearly. She wrapped her arms around Ryan's neck and pulled him closer. Precious minutes later her lips released his. "Oh, yes, I'll marry you. Whenever you say."

She put her head down on his chest and listened to the steady beat of his heart. The one that held her in it. "I've been thinking."

"I'm not sure I like that idea.'

Lucy gave him a nip with her teeth. "Not funny." She rose so that she could see his eyes. "I was just thinking about how much I admire how close you and your family are. And how far apart mine has been for so long. I'd like to invite my parents to the wedding. It's time someone reached out and tried to build some kind of connection. Maybe a wedding is a good place to begin."

He covered her body with his and his mouth rumbled against hers. "I think that's a great idea. Now, how about we practice that having a family of our own idea?"

"You have to ask?" She gave him a quick kiss. "You make me happy, Ryan. Something I've not been in a long time."

"I aim to please."

"The O'Doherty way," she whispered, as his mouth took hers in a kiss warm with promises of tomorrows to come.

* * * * *

NYC ANGELS: FLIRTING WITH DANGER

TINA BECKETT

To my dear husband, who has held my hand
when I needed it held and has smiled at my
insanely ridiculous desire to own a chicken, and
who promised that someday I would have one.
I'm holding you to that promise, honey!

CHAPTER ONE

NOTHING COULD CONCEAL her shame.

Not this time. Still, Chloe Jenkins yanked the belt of her beige trench coat tighter, until she was sure it would cut her in two—much like her heart had been. What had seemed sexy a half-hour ago now seemed unbearably pathetic and sleazy. The New York City subway station was jammed with bodies, even at this hour, and she shoved wet hanks of hair from her eyes, glad to finally be out of the rain.

What was she supposed to do now?

Hurling your wedding rings at your cheating bastard of a husband with the words "Consider this our divorce!" may have seemed like the perfect exit line—the only way to escape with a shred of dignity—but charging out of that hotel room had left her with few options. She was in a huge city where she knew no one.

Except...

The air shuddered from her lungs. There had to be some other way.

She could always go home to Connecticut.

And face her brother? Her family? They'd known the truth all along, but she'd been too much of a naïve sap to listen.

The doors opened and she stepped into the train,

careful to keep her bare toes far from the nearest occupant.

She could head to a car rental facility. She had her purse and her wallet, thank heavens.

But she'd foolishly left her shoes behind in the room, and it was illegal to drive like this, even if they'd lease her a car. And if the tie on her coat came loose, she'd be totally exposed.

Her face burned hotter. Okay, maybe she wouldn't be totally exposed, but the peek-a-boo black negligee and sheer panties left little to the imagination.

Even for her ex, who—when she emerged from beneath the cocoon of covers, fury spilling from every pore—had allowed his eyes to crawl over her body, a spark of interest finally coming to life in the drunken depths.

God. Why had she even bothered to try?

Because she didn't believe in giving up. At least, she hadn't before now.

The train suddenly slowed as it came to its next stop, and she lost her balance for a few frightening seconds, scrabbling to regain her handhold while keeping her coat from coming open.

Someone bumped into her from behind as they tried to exit, the hard shove sending her reeling a second time. She bit her lip and tasted blood.

"Sorry." Hands came out to steady her, but Chloe flinched away, terrified someone would find out what she'd tried to do. She checked with the tip of her tongue the damage her teeth had caused. Not exactly the way she'd planned to spend the night.

You're right, baby, she does *look frigid.*

Travis's current paramour had clung to his arm and

giggled at the sight of Chloe under the covers, the duvet pulled up to her chin.

What had been meant as a last-ditch effort to save her marriage had turned into a guillotine instead, one that had nicked her, even as she'd released the cord and let it drop—cleaving what had been one into two and setting her free.

Travis hadn't even blinked in the face of her rage. Probably too full of whiskey to care. He'd suggested she stick around…implied she might even want to join in the fun. Her fist had balled up tight, ready to deliver the mean right hook her brother had once taught her, before she stopped herself, realizing it would do no good.

It was over.

A wave of nausea washed up her throat.

She could call her brother and…do what exactly? It was almost midnight, and Jason was a couple of hundred miles away. Besides, he'd ask all kinds of questions. Was she really ready to publicly admit that Travis had wanted the family's money? He certainly hadn't wanted her. Not really. No matter how charming he'd been during their courtship. No, he'd wanted a leg up in the financial investment industry, which he'd gotten…and more.

God. She'd saved herself for him. And for what? Love sure hadn't been any sweeter on the other side of the marriage bed.

She tried to think.

If she called Jason right now, he was liable to go all big-brotherly on her. She didn't need defending. She needed to get away. For a while, anyway. To plan her next move—at least the one beyond filing for an actual divorce, which she planned to do first thing Monday morning.

So, until then she could just get a room at another hotel.

In her nightgown? Strains of "Pretty Woman" began playing in her head. Yeah. She knew exactly what they'd think she was with plastered hair, thigh-high coat, and no shoes. No respectable hotel would let her through the doors.

And the unrespectable ones…

That was no better solution than the first option. Her eyes went to the tangled colors on the map posted above the doors of the subway train.

As much as she hated the idea, her thoughts circled back to the one person she knew in New York: Brad Davis. She knew where he worked—the Angel Mendez Children's Hospital—but she had no idea what part of town that was in, or where her brother's old friend lived. Or even what subway line she should be on right now. She knew how to find Brad, though. Social media was good for at least one thing.

Bracing her feet against the sway of the train and digging out her smartphone, she took a deep breath and pulled up her friends list.

Brad paced the living room of his high-rise apartment, half irritated, half intrigued. It was Friday night, and he'd just sent his date home with a smiled apology and a smoothly worded explanation about family coming into town unexpectedly.

Which wasn't a total lie. Chloe *was* practically family. In fact, he'd spent more of his teenage years at Chloe and Jason's house than he had at his own. And despite being known more for his biker jacket, spiked wrist cuff and well-practiced sneer than for his social graces, his best friend's folks had made it clear he was welcome any time. Had made sure he'd known they cared about him, even as he'd wondered if his own parents knew he existed.

And Chloe…

His mind sifted through images of the past, each overlapping the other until it formed a collage of memories, full of pink cheeks and adolescent banter.

No one had been more shocked than he, six years ago, to learn she was getting married, or to arrive at the wedding and realize what a gorgeous young woman she'd grown up to be. Asking her to dance had been the ultimate mistake. As they'd taken one quick spin around the dance floor, the hem of her lacy white gown swishing in time with their slow movements, he'd suddenly realized she was no longer the gawky kid who had tagged along after him and her brother. The glint of a hairpin imprisoning a long graceful curl had made his palms itch. What would happen if he reached up and…

His arms had instinctively tightened to resist the temptation, the act pulling her fully against him. His body had reacted, his pulse rate climbing dangerously. A soft gasp had left her throat, and the fingers that had been politely resting on his shoulder curled into the fabric of his suit jacket.

He'd looked down just as her eyes came up. Raw awareness had shimmered between them, and her teeth had sunk deep into her bottom lip—the lip he hadn't been able to stop staring at. The world around him had faded away, and the self-destructive tendencies he'd thought long gone had swooped down, nearly consuming him.

As if recognizing danger, Chloe's husband had suddenly appeared beside them, his hand outstretched, a warning frown between his brows. He'd spirited her away, a mysterious ethereal creature with huge blue eyes and slender curves. The memory of her body pressed to his had stayed with him long into the night.

Nope. No thinking about curves, racing pulses or anything else. She was his best friend's sister. Sweet. Innocent.

Married.

Nothing like the women he dated—sophisticated women who knew exactly what the words "no strings" meant and would play by his set of rules. Women who were the opposite of Chloe Jenkins.

So what was she doing, wandering the streets of New York at midnight? By herself? She'd said there'd been a hitch in her hotel reservations. Why not just choose another place, then? Or drive home to Connecticut, if it came down to it?

He'd only seen her once since her wedding day, and she'd never attempted to contact him. Until tonight.

He should have said no. Should have reminded himself of that crazy dance and told her to steer clear of him—or told her he had company, with just enough emphasis to let her know exactly what that meant.

But there'd been something about her voice on the phone. A shaky uncertainty, as if she'd *expected* him to flat-out refuse to let her come up—something he would never do to Chloe, even if Jason weren't his best friend. Even if seeing her again messed with his head and brought up thoughts better left buried.

The buzzer to his apartment rang, and he punched the button on the keypad that would release the lock on the main entry downstairs.

Doubly glad he'd sent Katrina on her way, he opened the door and waited for the elevator to arrive on the fifteenth floor.

In less than a minute the doors whirred open, and whereas his date's four-inch heels had clacked purposefully across the space, Chloe stepped onto the cream marble floor with the grace of a dancer, not the slightest sound coming from her pale, high-arched feet.

And yep. There it was. The buzzing in his skull that signaled danger.

He blinked and looked closer, realizing what he'd first thought were some kind of flesh-colored shoes were actually nothing of the kind. Pink tipped nails glittered in the hallway light. Even as he stared, she curled her toes under her feet as if trying to hide them. His head cleared in an instant.

What the hell was going on?

Had she been robbed? Assaulted?

His gaze traveled up her slim calves and over her knees and lingered on the hem of her raincoat, a white-knuckled fist keeping the edges together.

Concern erased all traces of irritation. "Chloe, are you okay?"

"Y-yes."

He finally met her eyes and found them bright. Too bright—the blue depths teeming with some terrible emotion.

One glance at the twin mascara tracks running down her delicate face, the swollen bottom lip, and he knew.

Chloe was in trouble. Big trouble.

CHAPTER TWO

CHLOE PERCHED ON the edge of an overstuffed leather couch and took another sip of her whiskey—her second glass—wincing as it hit the sore spot on her lip.

Sitting on the matching ottoman across from her, Brad's eyes glittered with the same dangerous undertones they'd held fifteen minutes ago in the hallway when he'd gently touched the corner of her mouth and asked, "Where is the bastard?"

It had taken her a moment to realize he thought Travis had hit her.

He had. Just not with his fists.

There was no way she could explain the bitter humiliation that clogged her throat, that made her want to crawl away and hide from the world. Not to a man like Brad, who'd gone through girlfriends in droves back in high school. Girls who had been drawn to the same rough-edged smile she'd once been, only hers had been a childish infatuation that had eventually faded away, like a temporary tattoo.

Until the night of her wedding. When a single touch had brought it all roaring back. She'd been mortified at her reaction. Terrified that he'd see the truth in her eyes. Travis had rescued her just in time.

Rescued. That was one way to put it. Especially since

her Prince Charming had turned out to be the villain of the story.

She continued to sip her drink, welcoming the fiery warmth that bloomed in her stomach.

"Let me take your coat, at least." Brad's low voice broke through her inner turmoil.

"No!" Her hand went to the tie, fiddling with it. "I—I'm still cold."

What was she going to do? If she stayed the night, he was going to figure out she didn't have much on under the coat. She could crash on Brad's couch, huddled under a blanket—but the image of herself in the hotel bedroom doing much the same thing caused something between a laugh and a cry to exit her throat.

"Okay." He sat straight up, elbows coming off his knees. "Ready to tell me what happened?"

Her glance flickered to Brad's onyx-tiled fireplace. "I already explained. My hotel was overbooked. There were...people staying in the room."

And she could only imagine what those "people" were now doing.

Unless Travis had already passed out, as he tended to do on the nights he'd had too much to drink. Her wedding night had been a disaster. As had the nights that had followed. When her girlfriends had giggled about how many times in a row they'd done you-know-what on their honeymoons, she'd laughed right along with them, all the while wondering if there really was something wrong with her.

Travis's frustration had grown as her response to him had become more and more mechanical—as she'd forced herself to participate. As a result, he'd started working longer hours. To save for their future, he'd said. She'd had no idea her parents had been one of his biggest clients until she'd found some paperwork on his desk—along with some hefty fees they'd paid Travis for managing their investment accounts.

Despite the warning signs, she'd never suspected anything was off until she came home sick from her night shift at the hospital to hear terrible shrieking noises coming from the bedroom. She'd raced back to find him naked—flat on his back—another woman straddling his hips. He'd pleaded for forgiveness, promised it was a mistake, said it would never happen again.

Stay? Or leave?

She'd decided to fight for her marriage. For eight long months. Tonight had been the *pièce de résistance* in her campaign to rekindle the spark he'd once felt toward her. She'd seduce him.

Only Travis hadn't needed seducing.

He just needed someone other than her.

Her eyes closed, and she took a longer pull on her drink. So much for her two weeks' worth of vacation.

"Hey." The murmured word dragged her back to the surface, even though she just wanted to keep sinking into the mire, never to resurface. "Do you want me to call Jason?"

Her lids parted, and she struggled to focus on the handsome face across from her. "Please don't. He'll just worry."

"He should worry." He nodded toward her feet. "Where are your shoes, Chloe?"

She gnawed the inside of her cheek. Why hadn't she come up with a plausible explanation for that?

Because there wasn't one. Other than the truth, which she wasn't ready to voice.

Why had she ever thought she could "vamp" anyone? Especially her husband, whose rough-and-tumble approach to lovemaking did nothing but leave her feeling sore and inadequate. She was pretty sure the woman in her bed hadn't been crying out in pain, so the problem wasn't with her husband, evidently.

Frigid. The word echoed in her head, the mean nastiness of it making the hair rise on the nape of her neck.

She lifted the glass and found it empty. Held it out.

"I don't think…" Brad began.

Only to stop when she whispered, "Please."

Getting up, he went over to the bar, retrieved a cut-glass decanter of amber liquid and poured some in her glass, the *lug-lug* from the bottle strangely satisfying.

She noticed he didn't refill his own tumbler, just took up his post again and watched her. Her shoulder hitched in an awkward shrug. "If you were in the middle of doing something, don't let me stop you."

She giggled as she said the last word, and her eyes widened. "Sorry. It's been a while." And she'd never been much of a drinker. It was amazing how it dulled the pain, though.

Something she could get used to.

He ignored her comment and said, "Shoes?"

Oh, that's right. He wanted to know what she'd done with her stupid shoes.

"I left them behind, along with all my other little shackles." That rock in her ring hadn't been so little. But then again, her daddy's investment money had probably paid for it, too. Something about that thought made her laugh again.

Brad's hand covered hers, his fingers as warm as fire. Just like the alcohol sloshing around inside her. But when she tried to lift the glass to her lips, it wouldn't move. Because Brad was physically holding her arm in place.

"Hey." She tried to tug free of his grip.

"I think you've had enough for tonight."

"Oh, no. Not nearly enough." Her head felt like some kind of weird flower that when deprived of drink began to wilt…wilt…wilt…until someone watered it again. She snapped it back upright when her forehead touched Brad's muscular arm and tried to burrow into it, a strange lethargy taking hold of her.

Gentle fingers prised hers loose from the glass and set the drink on the wooden floor beside the ottoman. Just as she started to wilt again she felt arms at her back, beneath her knees, and she levitated just like she'd seen in those horror movies when a demon possessed someone's body. But when she tried to hold her arms out to float higher, she found them trapped against her sides.

And while this demon growled in a low, deep voice just like the ones in the films, the tone didn't sound angry. Instead, the soft words circled the air above her face. She pulled them into her lungs, knowing somehow this being was powerful enough to keep all the other demons at bay. Including Travis. Her breath exited again on a sigh, along with the will to do anything but snuggle close and slip away into oblivion.

Brad pushed open the door to his bedroom, thankful he and Katrina had not spent time on the king-sized mattress like he'd planned. Instead, he set Chloe on top of the brown silk coverlet, not quite sure what to do with her. The guest bedroom hadn't been used in ages and he didn't think the bed even had a sheet on under the tan striped spread.

He gazed down at her, something inside him softening as memories from their childhood washed over him. The three of them bobbing in the pool in Jason's parents' backyard, tossing a young Chloe high into the air and hearing her happy scream as she hit the water and sank—then spluttered back to the surface ready for more.

How embarrassed he'd been when his friend's folks had to come to the police station to pick him up when, at eighteen years of age and fed up with life, he'd careened around a dangerous curve on his motorcycle, intent on putting an end to his pain, only to have the damn bike slide out from under him on the unpaved road before he'd hit full speed. When he'd opened his eyes—still very much alive—all he'd been able to think of was that his parents had been right about him: he screwed up everything.

Chloe's parents had dragged him home with them that night. He could still see the wide-eyed stare Chloe had given him when he'd walked through the front door, road rash burning up one of his cheeks and the side of his right arm. The way she'd covered her mouth with both hands in horror.

That look had convinced him that checking out really would hurt someone—even if his parents had sniffed in disgust and simply sent his chopper off to the nearest repair shop without a word. They'd tended to show their displeasure in an entirely different way—a locked door was a powerful weapon.

Yes, he and Chloe Jenkins had been through a lot together.

But never in his wildest dreams had he pictured her in his bed. Well, maybe he had. But he'd damned himself from here to eternity for wanting to peel off her wedding dress and have her innocence all to himself.

Shaking off the thought, he started to pull one corner of the bedspread around her, but her coat was still wet. He really didn't want her to sleep in it—especially as she'd begun shaking the second she'd entered the apartment, despite the fact that late spring in New York tended toward warm and humid. Her continued shivering was the only reason he'd handed her the glass of whiskey in the first place.

He couldn't do anything about her damp hair—the loose strands a charming melding of blond and red—but he could slip her coat off and at least let her sleep in dry clothes.

His fingers went to the knot at her waist, and he frowned at how tightly she'd cinched the thing. If he'd had any doubts about leaving her in it, that quashed them. He worked at the tie until one loop loosened then slid free. Taking a deep breath, he parted the edges of the coat. The air whistled right back out of his lungs at the sight that met his tired eyes.

Holy hell.

A black negligee—opaque lace on top with a floaty skirt made of some kind of see-through fabric—was all she had on…well, other than the tiniest pair of panties known to mankind. Panties that were clearly visible. Clearly sheer.

He swallowed hard, torn between the desire to devour her with his eyes and wrap the coat tightly back around her. His body was having a tough time knowing which of his mixed signals to obey, although he might as well finish what he'd started and take the coat the rest of the way off, so she could at least sleep in comfort.

Unlike him, who'd probably have this image seared onto the backs of his eyelids for the rest of his life.

He slid the coat off her, turning her body to the side as he pulled it out from under her. What in God's name had Chloe been thinking, walking around downtown New York like this?

She was the cautious one. The one who'd balked at riding on the back of his motorcycle, even after he'd tamed some of his wilder urges.

And yet here she was. In his apartment, like a sexy flasher from one of those secretary fantasies. She sure as hell hadn't come here to seduce *him* with the get-up.

Then who?

He remembered the smeared mascara. The haunted look in her eyes.

It suddenly became clear in a rush. Jason's random comments about his brother-in-law took on new meaning. How he'd said Chloe never complained but Jason was convinced something was wrong with their marriage and had been for a long time. Travis always seemed to be off somewhere or other on business, leaving Chloe at home alone.

Brad pulled the covers over her, hiding her from his own prying eyes—something that he was now thoroughly ashamed of.

He could almost bet Travis was in a hotel room somewhere in New York. And that Chloe's shoes were there as well. He could easily guess why she'd come to town and what she must have found once she'd arrived. His fingers tightened around the coat in his hands until his knuckles ached as he stared down at her long lashes, the dark circles under her eyes…the slight swelling on her lip.

Damn that man. He'd hurt Chloe.

If it was the last thing Brad did, he was going to make Travis Maroni pay for his sins.

CHAPTER THREE

"I GOT A CALL this morning. He's looking for her."

Jason's worried voice met him as soon as Brad answered his cellphone. He looked up from the case notes of Angel's newest prenatal patient, a thirty-five-year-old woman whose ultrasound scan had revealed a fetal heart defect. The baby was fine *in utero*, but would die within minutes once out of that safe environment if something wasn't done.

To top it all off, he'd arrived at his office that morning to find a snarky resignation letter from Katrina, his date from the previous evening. She'd evidently not been as blasé about being shooed from his apartment as she'd seemed to be at the time.

Which meant his unit was now short-staffed.

That's what he got for getting involved with a colleague. Never again.

"Brad, you still there?"

"Yeah, yeah. Sorry. Just trying to think." That was another thing. There was no way he was going to let Chloe head home before he knew exactly what was going on between her and that scumbag husband of hers. "She wasn't in good shape last night, Jason, which is why I called. I figured you'd be worried."

"I'm glad you did. We had no idea she was even

headed to New York. Dad is fit to be tied. Travis swears it's all a big misunderstanding, that Chloe took off after an argument, but he's not fooling anyone. If he weren't my sister's husband…"

Brad's thoughts exactly. "Is he still in New York?"

"No, he's home. Said he was surprised not to find Chloe here. Claims to be worried as hell."

There was no way Brad would have ever left New York without searching every inch of it first. For the man just to drive home without even trying to locate her was unthinkable. What if she'd been mugged…or worse?

"Did you tell him she was at my place?"

"I'm not telling him anything." There was a pause over the line. "Is she okay? Physically, I mean?"

"She seemed to be. She was still asleep when I left this morning." Should he tell Jason about the split lip or what she'd been wearing when she'd shown up at the apartment? He'd laid a pair of exercise sweats and a black T-shirt across the end of his bed. He figured she could pull the laces around the waist tight enough to keep the pants from sliding below the swell of her hips. Which brought his mind right back to those soft curves that were everything a man could want.

Except she was Chloe.

And it was best to keep her racy attire between the two of them—no need for Jason to know. He didn't want to embarrass her any more than necessary.

An idea formed. "Is she still working at the community hospital there in Hartford?" Chloe had graduated from nursing school about the same time he had graduated from med school. She'd even specialized in pediatrics, if he remembered right.

"Yes, why?"

"Can you call them and explain the situation? Ask them to give her some time off?"

"I think she's got some vacation time coming, but I'll check to make sure. Dad invested quite a bit of money in one of their service projects a year or two ago." A chuckle came over the phone. "Chloe just about blew a gasket when she heard, asked him if he was trying to buy a permanent position for her."

Brad could imagine that quite well. He'd been on the receiving end of that outrage a time or two—like when he'd caught her holding hands with a boy on the swing at her parents' house. The glare he'd given the kid had sent him scrambling for the sidewalk. But when he'd tried to give Chloe a stern warning, she'd sniffed and claimed there was nothing to worry about. She'd decided to wait until she got married to "do it."

Did people even do that nowadays?

Evidently they did, because when he'd laughed in her face, she'd flushed scarlet and then balled her fingers into a tight fist before punching him in the chest. Right on top of the fading bruise from his motorcycle accident. It had stung, but it had also gotten her point across: her virginity was no joking matter.

Something his mind had also toyed with the night of her wedding. Had she really saved herself? Only to wind up with a jerk like Travis?

His hand went to the spot and rubbed it as if he could still feel where she'd walloped him. And, really, he could. A circular Celtic symbol—the tree of life at its center—was inked on the very spot his road rash had once covered, starting at his chest and wrapping around the top of his left shoulder. A reminder to always choose life.

Thankfully his polo shirts now covered up that little

bit of history. Some of his patients might not understand what the tattoo had come to symbolize.

He shook himself back to the present and Jason's phone call. "I've just had a nurse quit on me. I don't know if Chloe will go for it, but maybe she'd be interested in filling the spot for a while. At least until she can sort through whatever happened with Travis. Or until I can talk the nurse into coming back."

Why was the thought of calling Katrina suddenly distasteful?

"That's a great idea. Maybe she's finally ready to unload the bastard."

"Maybe." Brad scrubbed a hand across his jaw, his eyes going back to the notes on his desk. "I'll let you know what she says. She can stay at the apartment until she decides what she wants to do. It's not easy to get a short-term lease nowadays."

And just why had he offered that? He wasn't exactly celibate, neither did he have any plans to become so. He gave an internal shrug. She was an adult. Surely they could work out some kind of arrangement. After all, it wasn't a permanent thing. Probably a week or two at the most. She might not even go for it—he was beginning to hope she wouldn't, in fact.

But deep down inside something whispered that he was telling the biggest lie of his life. Because he did want her to stay. Wanted to somehow keep her safe from whoever had hurt her.

And if she turned him down and walked away?

He might just have to coax her to change her mind.

"You want me to what?"

Chloe stared across the table at Brad. He was offering her a job? She toyed with the tie on the sweats he'd loaned her and tried to keep her face from flaming in renewed embarrassment. When she'd awoken coatless on a huge king-sized bed with no memory of how she'd gotten there, she'd thought for a panicked second she might have slept with him. His warm masculine scent permeated the space, from the pillow where she'd laid her head to the clothes currently enveloping her body.

But there'd been no sign that he'd slept in the bed, neither was there that familiar morning-after ache—an unpleasant side effect of sex with her husband.

But still. His offer had come out of nowhere.

Brad glanced up from the plate of takeout Yakisoba, brows raised. "One of the nurses in the prenatal unit quit unexpectedly. I wondered if you might want to fill in until we can find a permanent replacement."

"Why?"

"Why not?" He studied her from across the table. "Unless you're anxious to get home."

Dammit. The fire licked along her cheeks again. She had no intention of going home—not that the monstrosity she and Travis had lived in had ever really been home. She'd already contacted a lawyer in Connecticut and started the ball rolling on her divorce. No, you weren't supposed to make any major changes during a crisis, but she'd already decided to leave if her swan dive into the deep end of the seduction pool didn't work.

Swan dive. Right.

Instead of a smooth, clean entry into the water, she'd landed with a belly flop that had been deafening, knocking the wind from her lungs and leaving her clawing her way to the surface.

Well, she was there now, taking her first breath of freedom after six long, suffocating years. She was never submerging herself like that ever again.

Not for anyone.

"I was actually thinking of relocating," she said slowly, the idea taking root and sprouting its first leaf. She could do this.

Unless her father was behind Brad's offer, just like she suspected him of being behind her promotion at the hospital. "Wait, did Daddy call and ask you to hire me?"

Brad's eyes narrowed for a second or two. "Do you think I'm lying to you, Chloe?"

It wouldn't be the first time she'd been lied to. "No, but…"

"But what?"

She licked her lips. "I don't want you doing this because you feel sorry for me." As much as she wanted to, she couldn't seem to hold his gaze, fiddling with her chopsticks instead. "I'm filing for divorce."

"I'm glad."

The low voice caused her head to come up. Some knowing glimmer in the depths of Brad's eyes caused her to bristle. As if he'd expected this outcome all along. "You and Jason never gave him a chance."

"No. But you did."

Yes, and now her brother and Brad were free to gloat about her stupidity behind her back. Wouldn't she, if she were in their place?

Instead, his hand covered hers, the warmth seeping through her icy skin. "Whatever else you might think, I wanted it to work out. Wanted you to be happy."

Just as Jason had. He'd kissed her cheek at the rehearsal dinner and whispered that very thing. "Be happy, little sis."

She swallowed the wave of emotion. Brad had always been there for her, even though he'd never been loud and showy about it. He had always been one of the first people on the scene when something had happened—whether it had been when her sickly appendix had needed to come out, or standing beside her as she'd cried over the grave of Treehouse, her dog.

And later he and Jason had accompanied her on her first official post PADI certification dive off the New Jersey coast, and they'd later explored several local shipwreck sites. She blinked away memories of those muscular legs propelling him through the water with ease, of his fingers gripping hers as he'd tugged her away from areas he'd felt were too dangerous. He'd had no idea that he'd been the most dangerous thing in the ocean. At least to her equilibrium.

Despite those awkward moments, she'd always been able to count on him. Maybe it was time she returned the favor. If he really was in a bind, shouldn't she be willing to lend a hand?

"Thank you." She sighed. "About the position. I would imagine there'd be plenty of nurses ready to jump at the chance to work at Angel's." She loved the hospital's nickname, loved how it seemed to fit, as if the hospital served as the guardian angel of sick children everywhere.

Brad sat back in his chair. "There are, but it'll take time to put out a call for applications and then wade through them all."

"What about an apartment? There's no way I can commute from Hartford." Neither would she want to.

"I thought you might consider staying here. I have an extra bedroom. I'm sure we could stay out of each other's hair."

She bit her lip. Speaking of bedrooms, she'd noticed there was no way to lock the door of his room. Oh, there was a keyhole, but no key to secure it that she could see. The same held true for the bathroom. When she'd looked at the other doors—with the exception of the front door—she'd found the same thing. No keys for any of them. He lived alone, so he probably didn't think anything of it, but if she stayed here she wanted to be able to at least lock the bathroom.

His voice broke through. "What are you thinking?"

She scrambled around for an answer and finally just blurted it out. "Where are your keys?"

"Keys?"

"For all your doors."

His face went utterly still for a second or two then he shrugged. "There's no one else living here, so I haven't felt the need to mess with them."

Just as she'd thought. "But you do have them somewhere, right?"

"I do." There was something strange about the way he answered her, but she couldn't put her finger on it so she tried a different tack.

"Well, what about your life? I don't want to disrupt whatever you've got going on by staying here." She stopped again when his frown deepened. "Are you... um, seeing someone?"

The lines between his brows eased, and one corner of his mouth quirked up. "Not at the moment."

"Oh."

"Even if that situation changes, the apartment has thick walls."

Heat swept up her neck and threatened to shoot from her ears. In other words, she wouldn't hear anything that went on. Maybe not, but her imagination would fill in the blanks. "Are you sure you want me staying—"

"I wouldn't have offered if I didn't mean it."

His brows went up. "Unless you don't think you can handle it."

The battle cry from their younger years hung in the air between them. The only time she hadn't risen to one of those challenges had been when he'd rolled up next to her on his motorcycle, fresh from getting his medical license, and had dared her to take a victory lap around town with him. The thought of being pressed tight against his back, her inner thighs gripping his, had made something dangerous shimmy through her abdomen—the exact sensation she'd experienced when they'd danced at her wedding. It had brought a wariness that was even stronger than her fear of motorcycles.

She'd gulped before chickening out—blaming it on his long-forgotten accident in high school.

And now? Was she still chicken?

With those light green eyes watching her every move, trying to ferret out any exposed weakness? She'd vowed to give herself a brand-new start. To do that—and to survive her time with Brad—she needed to live by a whole new set of rules. His. And if he could throw down the gauntlet, she would just pick it up and twirl it over her head.

Dropping her chopsticks onto her plate, she leaned forward, all too aware that she was dressed in the man's clothes and was about to agree to live in his home. But that was small potatoes. She'd survived the horror of knowing he'd seen her body in all its questionable glory last night—and he'd evidently been unmoved by the sight. So they were good to go.

"As long as I can have a key to my bedroom and the bathroom, I think I can handle it all right," she said sweetly. "But…can you?"

CHAPTER FOUR

THE JEANS FIT PERFECTLY.

Of course they would. Brad could probably tell a woman's clothing size with a single glance. And the smoky-green belted top did make the blue of her eyes stand out. She couldn't remember the last time Travis had bought her an article of clothing.

Not that she'd wanted him to. She assumed men didn't like doing that sort of thing, unless it was buying slinky lingerie.

Well, in reality, Brad had had no choice. It wasn't like she could go shopping in the get-up she'd arrived in—which she'd stuffed in a plastic bag and thrown right in the trash. The fewer reminders she had of that night the better. Even so, answering the door and finding Brad's doorman standing there with a wrapped package in his hand had been a surprise. Swallowing her pride and accepting his offer hadn't been easy.

But at least it meant she could go out and shop for her own clothing…including hospital gear. Brad said scrubs were the order of the day, the funkier the better. And true to his word he'd produced two shiny new keys, one for her bedroom and one for the bathroom, so she could at least dress and bathe in private.

A spark of excitement zipped through her. Brand-new scrubs were fitting for a brand-new life. This was the perfect opportunity to start over. The lawyer she'd spoken with had assured her she'd only need to face Travis one more time…across the courtroom when the divorce was finalized.

Although there was a certain amount of guilt swirling around inside of her over her failed marriage, she felt more relief than anything. No more worrying about showing enough enthusiasm in bed or fearing the slightest twitch of discomfort would bring about one of Travis's long-suffering sighs.

She checked out the view from behind in the full-length mirror in Brad's bedroom, carefully avoiding glancing at the expanse of reflective glass mounted on the ceiling over that huge bed. Somehow she didn't think he used it for shaving.

Chloe shuddered. At least her ex had never suggested putting mirrors in their bedroom. Her eyes tracked to the bed again, the image of Brad's muscular frame sweeping through her mind, the tattoo across his shoulder bunching with each movement.

Her mouth went dry. She closed her eyes and tried to remember exactly what that tattoo looked like. It had been some kind of jagged circle enclosing a tree. As a teenager, her eyes had gone to it again and again as he'd sprawled out on a lounge chair by her parents' pool. Even then he'd cut a powerful figure. No wonder she'd had a crush on him.

But as gorgeous as he was, there'd been a raw, untamed quality to him that had frightened her at times. Travis had been smooth and refined…steady and safe in comparison, which had been what she'd thought she wanted.

She gave a pained laugh. Boy, were appearances deceptive. Travis had been anything but safe.

At least now she was free.

Digging in her handbag, she located her phone and sent Brad a text thanking him for the clothes and letting him know she was headed out to go shopping for some new things. He'd promised to take her to the hospital tomorrow to show her the prenatal wing and introduce her to the staff.

Just as she got ready to head to the lobby and ask the doorman to hail a cab, the phone rang. She stared at it, wondering if she should answer it or let the machine pick up. But maybe Brad had gotten her text and was calling her to firm up times for dinner or something.

She lifted the receiver from its cradle. "Hello?"

There was a pause then a woman's voice came through. "Who is this?"

Uh-oh. That was *not* a happy tone.

"Chloe Jenkins. I'm a...friend of Brad's." It was true, right? "He's not here right now, though. Can I take a message?"

"This is Katrina. I wanted to see if he got the note I left him."

Note? Brad hadn't mentioned anything about one. But why would he? Those mirrors came back to her thoughts. Of course. This was probably one of Brad's "women."

"I...um. I'm not sure." How was this for awkward? "I can leave him a message and let him know you called."

"Don't bother." If anything, the woman's voice had grown even colder. "He's got my number. If he wants me, he can call me."

Chloe gulped. If he wanted her? Did she mean as in beneath the mirrors?

Oh, lordy. This could get really weird if a parade of women started trekking through at all hours of the night.

The sound of the dial tone in her ear told her the lady in question hadn't even bothered to say goodbye before hanging up. But, then, why would she? This Katrina person didn't even know who she was.

She dropped the phone back onto its stand, making a mental note not to pick it up again. Ever. Otherwise someone could get the wrong idea about why *she* was staying here. She had no intention of becoming part of Brad's female entourage.

Actually, the woman's call had come at the perfect time because she needed to remind herself of her reasons for being there. It was to get away from Travis, not to dive head first back into the dating pool.

Although from Travis's cutting remarks about her prowess in the bedroom she might not need to worry about that for a long time to come. She certainly didn't want to relive any of those awful moments, especially with a stranger.

She'd have to eventually, though. She didn't want to go through life alone. She wanted children. A family. It's why she'd gotten married in the first place, to have what her parents had. A love that endured for decades.

Maybe she could talk to someone about her difficulties in that area. She certainly couldn't talk to Jason, not only because he'd always despised Travis but because of the ick factor involved. And the few girlfriends she had couldn't really give her a man's point of view— other than claiming Travis was a jerk who was terrible in bed. But was he? Other women seemed to like his moves just fine, judging from the bimbo who'd been hanging all over him at the hotel. So the problem had to be with her.

But how to fix it…

She glanced at the phone, remembering Katrina's irked voice. Brad had been with lots of women. And Katrina's attitude indicated that they didn't mind the instant replays. They *wanted* to be with him. Were peeved when they couldn't be.

What better person to pinpoint where she'd gone wrong with Travis and give her some pointers on how to act in any future relationships. It wouldn't be strange, right? The two of them had been friends since childhood. He had no idea she'd had a crush on him during their teenage years. And his experience with the female sex could give her insights that a stranger might be too embarrassed to be honest about. Brad could always be counted on to tell it like it was. No sugar coating involved with that man.

She took a deep breath and let it out. That settled it, then. She'd broach the subject somehow and see how he reacted. If he acted like it was no big deal, she'd pick his brain and try to figure out exactly what a man wanted from a woman.

Because, whatever it was, she didn't have it…and she had no idea where to get it.

Brad stood in the observation room above the surgical suite and watched as the surgeon prepped his patient for a hysterotomy. It was the same procedure his fetal heart patient would have to undergo in a month or two, except this particular fetal surgery was being done to close a neural tube defect and avoid a woman giving birth to a child with physical deficits. Few open fetal surgeries were done each year because of the risks to the baby, but Angel's was considered one of the best facilities in the country. People came to them from all over the U.S.

He shifted to the right to get a better view as the skilled fingers of the surgeon reached the uterus and prepared to open it.

Cade Coleman, the newest member of Angel's surgical staff, had been called in to perform the delicate procedure, and while Brad could acknowledge the man's expertise, he and the surgeon had already butted heads during the few weeks he'd been at the hospital.

Including the timing of the current surgery.

Brad didn't know exactly how Coleman had been appointed second in command without even a trial period, but the man evidently had some pull with Angel's resident neurosurgeon, Alex Rodriguez, although Brad couldn't imagine anyone forcing Alex's hand on anything. There'd been rumors of a secret meeting between the two, which Brad had initially shrugged off as gossip. But something had gone down because Alex hadn't quite been able to meet Brad's eyes when he'd told him the news.

Hell, could life get any more complicated? First Chloe showed up on his doorstep, her wounded eyes revealing far more than she knew. Then Katrina wigged out on him just as the prenatal wing was heading into its busiest season. Throw a hard-headed surgeon into the mix and Brad had his hands full.

Perfect.

Using the controls to zoom in on the surgical site, he watched the monitor as Cade reached into Melanie Roberts's womb with gloved fingers and gently drew the fetus into view. A boy. Melanie probably already knew that, though, through the wonders of ultrasound. The same test that had revealed the defect.

Turning the baby to expose the bubble-like forma-
tion on his lower spine, Coleman's magnifying goggles
zeroed in on the problem—the tiny camera mounted
on his headgear giving Brad the same clear view. The
defect was about an inch long, close to the base of the
spine, but despite the location, the open portion of
the back could still cause problems with the child's
lower limbs if not corrected. At twenty-one weeks, the
fetus's kick reflex was still strong and healthy, the perfect time to operate, according to Coleman.

As if feeling Brad's eyes on him, Cade glanced toward the huge bank of windows to his right. The mag-
nified view of the operating room on a second monitor
only made the furrows visible above the surgeon's goggles seem that much deeper. No doubt it rankled to
have to answer to someone else when he'd run his own
department in LA. But if you moved hospitals, you
couldn't expect to start at the top. And if the man had
any illusions about replacing Brad, he had another think
coming. If either of them left, it would be Coleman.

Brad looked up from the monitor and gave the other
man a slight nod to indicate he'd seen the problem and
agreed with whatever Cade saw fit to do. The surgeon
turned back to his tiny patient and Brad's thoughts went
back to Chloe.

Hell, he'd talked to Jason again that morning and almost the first thing out of his friend's mouth had been
a stern reminder that Chloe was still his little sister. As
if Brad didn't know that.

What did Jason expect him to do? Make a move on
her? Impossible.

Unbidden, his brain played back the sight he'd uncov-
ered when he'd taken off Chloe's coat. His reaction had
been anything but brotherly. Neither had his reaction

to seeing her stroll through the apartment in his sweat pants the next morning. But he was practically a family member—kind of like a first cousin, right?—and he'd better remember it. Chloe was fragile right now. Vulnerable. He, more than anyone, should remember what it was like to be rejected by those who were supposed to love you unconditionally—but who, instead, were completely indifferent to your efforts to please them.

Just like Travis had been with Chloe's efforts? Something inside him said yes, that's exactly what had happened. She'd gone there dressed in an outfit that should have had the man salivating like a hungry hyena. It had certainly gotten a reaction out of *him*. Instead, Travis had done or said something that had cut her to the quick.

Something that had caused her to flee into the night.

Brad didn't want to be that man. Didn't want to hurt someone who'd once meant a lot to him.

Someone who still did. Sweet innocent, idealistic Chloe.

One wrong move on his part and he could hurt her even more. Especially if he couldn't keep himself in check. If anything could keep him on the straight and narrow, that realization should.

At least, he hoped it would.

CHAPTER FIVE

HE HAD TO BE KIDDING.

Resting on Brad's bent thigh was a dark shiny helmet that matched the one currently on his head, the visor flipped up so he could see her. And he was seated— booted foot casually propped up on the left pedal—on top of a motorcycle. One that looked eerily familiar. When he'd said he'd meet her in the parking garage this morning, she'd assumed he'd be pulling up next to her in a Beamer, not on a Harley.

He could have stepped right out of one of her old photos from days gone by. She'd thought that with all his success his old mode of transportation would have been one of the first things to go. Evidently some things never changed. Was that really his old motorcycle? The one he'd had his accident on? A shiver of fear went through her.

"I—I can't ride on that."

His mouth quirked, and he held out the helmet. "I'll be careful. Promise." The black leather jacket he wore—along with a second one draped on the seat behind him—said otherwise. The pair screamed danger with a capital D.

Gripping the strap of her purse as if it alone could save her, she said, "Don't you have a car, like normal doctors?"

"Since when have I ever done things that others deem 'normal'?"

Was he referring to his parents? They'd always disapproved of Brad's motorcycle riding, although she'd never heard them say anything outright. But she'd overheard Jason talking to their mom and dad once about how Brad felt more at home at their house than at his own. Jason had said he could see why. Brad's folks were a matched set—snooty, looking down their noses at anything that didn't meet with their approval. Their own son was high on that list, evidently, since they looked right through him, instead of at him.

Chloe hesitated. Yes, Brad knew she was afraid of motorcycles, especially after she'd seen the damage done by his accident. But did she really want him to put her in the same category as his parents…thinking she was too good to be seen riding on one?

His gaze slid across her cheeks. Touched lower. "I'll take good care of you, Chloe. I give you my word." He balanced the helmet on his leg again then reached out his hand, palm up.

She licked her lips, then, as if hypnotized, she put her fingers in his and let him tug her a few steps closer until his knee touched the side of her thigh. Another shiver went through her, this one having nothing to do with fear but something even worse.

Could she really ride on that thing, behind him? She'd balked once before. Not just because of her fear but because of how unpredictable her reactions to him were. And the feeling that she'd be betraying Travis if she let her guard down, even for a second.

Knowing what she did now, that naïve sentiment was laughable.

Travis was no longer a part of her life, and he never

would be again. So shouldn't she get out and see exactly what she'd been missing?

But…on a motorcycle?

Why the hell not?

Lifting her chin, she grabbed the helmet from his leg, turned it round and jammed it on her head. The sense of claustrophobia was immediate, as was the urge to claw the thing back off again.

It's supposed to cradle your head, dummy, how else is it going to protect you?

Maybe he noticed her panic because Brad put down the kickstand and hauled the bike back onto it, before swinging his leg over the seat and standing in front of her. Placing his hands on her shoulders and turning her to face him, he took hold of the straps on either side of the helmet and fastened them, adjusting the fit, his warm fingers grazing her throat repeatedly. He pushed her visor up and tilted her head so he could peer in at her. "How does it feel?"

Oh, baby. Did he mean the helmet or his touch?

Don't be ridiculous. Of course he's talking about the helmet.

"Tight. Hot."

His Adam's apple dipped, and he stared at her for a moment, before answering. "It's supposed to be snug."

His voice was a little rougher than it had been a moment ago. Had she said something stupid? Or maybe he was having second thoughts about riding with her. "Are you sure this is a good idea?"

He gave a low laugh. "I thought so up until a few seconds ago."

"How long will it take to reach the hospital?"

"Depending on traffic, about fifteen minutes."

"Okay. Let's get this over with."

He nodded, handing her the second jacket and waiting until she'd zipped it up. His warm scent clung to the leather, and it was all she could do not to close her eyes and breathe it deep into her lungs. The fact that it was there, surrounding her, gave her a dose of courage that had been sorely missing a few seconds ago. He'd promised to take care of her, and Brad had never gone back on a promise that she knew of.

Getting back on the motorcycle, Brad pushed it forward and eased up the kickstand. "There are footrests just behind mine. So climb up and hang on."

Tightening her resolve, she walked the couple of steps it took to reach him then steadied herself by putting a hand on his shoulder. Pretending she was mounting a horse, she swung her leg over the back of the seat, trying to sit as far back as possible—which proved *im*-possible. The thing was angled so that she slid forward until her tummy was pancaked against his back.

This was going to be the longest fifteen minutes of her life.

"Can you hear me?" The low voice in her ear made her jerk, until she realized it was coming through her helmet. Brad must have some kind of built-in walkie-talkie system that let him communicate with whoever was on the back.

He'd ridden double like this before. Often enough to buy special helmets. Why did the thought make a warning hiss go off in her head?

"Chloe?"

She forced her lips to move. "I can hear you."

"There should be a mike below the strap. Swing it up to the front."

Finding a hard plastic object coming off the side of

the helmet, she adjusted it so that it was in front of her mouth. "Better?"

"Yep." He rolled the motorcycle forward a few feet and Chloe scrambled to put her hands on his waist. "When we start moving, you're going to want to hang on tighter than that, okay?"

Tighter than she already was? She felt like her fingers were digging into the firm muscles of his sides as it was. "Got it."

Feeling around for the footrests, she planted her feet on them, just as Brad turned a key and the motorcycle rumbled to life beneath her. With the helmet on, it wasn't nearly as loud as she'd expected it to be.

"Okay. When the garage door opens, we'll be on our way. Keep your feet up, even at stops, and lean into the turns."

"Check." She couldn't stop a little giggle. She knew he had to instruct her on how to ride, but she'd never dreamed that three days after her disastrous trip to Travis's hotel room she'd be on her way to a new job and the start of a new life. Even the shuddery fear she felt about riding with Brad couldn't erase her elation. This was the right decision. She felt it in her bones.

The garage door to the apartment building slid up, and Brad revved the engine and rolled through them at a reasonable speed. Nothing like the showy skids and hot-dogging he'd once done to impress the high-school girls. Still, her heart jumped into her throat as he turned left and entered the morning snarl of traffic—the sounds of car engines and buses periodically rupturing the bubble of silence created by her helmet.

On the first real turn she instinctively wrapped her arms around Brad's waist, realizing he was right. She needed to hold on and try to lean when he did. The best way to do that was to be physically connected to him, in much the same way as she'd moved with the horse she'd had years ago. Her hips slid forward even more, pressing intimately against him, her thighs squeezing his in order to maintain her balance. Every inch of her was aware of every inch of him. At first she put it down to basic survival instinct, but that weird tingle down low had nothing to do with survival.

Then Brad turned another corner, wiping away every thought except hanging on, probably much tighter than necessary.

During the first few minutes she was too afraid to move, but once she got used to the vibration from the engine beneath her and the easy way Brad handled the big bike, she began to loosen up a bit and enjoy the ride.

They stopped for a red light. Brad's feet hit the ground to keep them stable, and Chloe drew in a deep breath, noticing the claustrophobia she'd felt earlier was almost gone.

"You okay back there?"

"So far, so good. It's not as bad as I thought it would be." It wasn't quite a lie.

A soft laugh came through. "And I never thought I'd see the day when Chloe Jenkins would agree to ride on my bike."

A reference to her refusal years ago? She smiled, her heart lightening for the first time. "The times are a-changin'."

"Hmm. Want to learn to ride one?"

Her stomach did a back flip. "Yeah, well, the times aren't changing that much. I think I'm going to stick with being a passenger. A bad one."

He reached back to squeeze her leg. "You're doing great."

The light turned green, and Brad revved the engine enough to take off. Her arms instinctively wrapped around him once again, the fingers of her left hand gripping her other one in a vise. It was better than having her palms splayed across his rock-hard abs—a position that seemed far too intimate. Sure, they'd horsed around when they'd been younger and had done plenty of touching. But this was different, although Brad didn't seem affected by it at all.

Despite the concern he'd shown on the night of her arrival, he'd soon reverted to type, viewing the world through a lens of amused cynicism.

Although traffic was bumper to bumper, they were moving at a fairly steady pace and before she knew it they'd cleared Central Park, where green gave way to a pristine white building. Even from her perch Chloe could see the hospital off to their left. "Is there underground parking?"

"There is for our patients. There are a couple of lots near the hospital where we can park, which is what I do on the days I drive to work."

"Isn't that expensive?" Chloe had assumed everyone parked on hospital grounds. But things in New York City were evidently different than they were in Connecticut.

"Staff gets a discount." There was a pause as Brad pulled into a lot across the street from the hospital. "I sometimes take the subway to work, but I didn't think you'd be too anxious to get back on it."

She blinked. "How did you know I rode the subway?"

"My doorman said you had that shell-shocked look of first-time riders."

Little did he know that the shock had been from

something very different. Although the fact that Brad had ridden to work just for her touched her. "Thank you. But I'll be okay. Let me at least help with the parking costs."

A suited valet came forward, eyes wide as he looked from them to the bike. He quickly found his professionalism, reaching out a hand to help Chloe off. Her legs were shaking, much to her chagrin, but she smiled at the man anyway. When she glanced at Brad, she noticed his frown, even through the shaded visor. He put down the kickstand and yanked off his helmet, taking the keys from the ignition.

When she fumbled around for the catch to her own helmet, both men moved forward, but the valet stopped almost immediately when Brad handed him the key and held up his hospital ID. "We'll be here until around seven."

The valet nodded, glancing one last time at Chloe before handing Brad a ticket.

Once the man had started the motorcycle and driven into the lot, Brad turned back to her and unsnapped her helmet. She squinched her nose. "I don't even want to think about what my hair looks like. I'm not going to make a very good first impression."

Before she had a chance to do anything about it, warm fingers were brushing damp locks from her forehead and her cheeks and restoring order to her side part. "You could never make a bad impression, Chloe."

That's what he thought. He'd never had her in bed.

Her brows tightened. That was all behind her now. It was time to move on, and she intended to do just that. Maybe she'd even flirt with the first attractive man who came across her path.

Her glance went to Brad and then skipped away.

Yikes! Just the thought of flirting with him sent a zing of panic shooting through her chest. Along with a dangerous sense of anticipation that left her breathless. Yep, dangerous was a good word for what she was feeling.

She'd promised herself she'd ask him some pointed questions about men and how their minds worked, but could she really go through with it? Especially after the way she'd felt on the back of his bike?

Maybe she'd test out her theory with the *second* attractive man who came across her path. Just in case. Until she could finally work up the courage to look Brad in the eye and demand he tell her everything he knew.

CHAPTER SIX

"Chloe, this is Layla Woods, head of our general pediatric department."

The slender blonde standing just inside the hospital lobby held out her hand with a friendly smile. "Nice to meet you. Brad says you're joining his team on the fourth floor."

Chloe wasn't sure how to answer that question. Brad had made it pretty clear he was still looking for someone to take the previous nurse's place. Besides, she'd be going back to her old job at the end of her vacation. "I'm helping out. Temporarily."

She took a moment to glance around. Not only was the lobby big, with glossy marble floors and brightly painted walls, it was also refreshingly cool. Chloe welcomed the chilly air blowing across her heated body. Part of the warmth was due to the city streets, but some of it was also from riding behind her new boss. The crowded subway was sounding better and better.

A red-wigged Raggedy Ann stood a few feet away, cheerfully directing patients and visitors to different wings of the hospital. Well, that was different. But she liked the upbeat, bustling atmosphere of the entryway. Almost a reflection of the city itself.

"Well, it's good to have you," Layla said, bringing

her attention back. "I'm new to Angel's too, so if you have any questions, holler. It's probably something I've already asked."

Brad's phone went off, and he glanced down at the readout with a frown. "I need to get this, sorry. As Layla said, we're up on the fourth floor, if you want to make your way there. They're expecting you."

The other woman tutted at him. "You can't just abandon her. I'll show her around and then take her up myself."

"Thanks. I appreciate it." He punched a button on his phone. "See you in a few."

"Okay."

Standing next to Layla, Chloe suddenly felt big and clunky, even though she was only an inch or two taller than the other woman. But where the pediatrician was made up of subtle curves and well-defined angles, Chloe's hips and boobs were definitely rounder. In shoe terms, Layla was a graceful strappy sandal, while Chloe was a sensible pump.

She sighed. No wonder Travis had gone looking elsewhere.

"You ready?" Another wide smile accompanied the question, and Chloe relaxed. There was nothing snooty or haughty about Layla. Just kindness that shone through her eyes. Along with a strange tinge of sadness.

Everyone had their own problems, she supposed.

The hospital was huge, and Layla's tour took a little longer than expected. When Chloe glanced down at her watch, hoping she wasn't going to get in trouble for being late, the other woman touched her hand. "It's okay. I'm sure Brad's let them know that you're with me."

Chloe nodded and peeked inside the washroom door

that Layla had pushed open. "Are you from New York?" she asked.

"Texas. You?"

"Connecticut."

"That's closer to home, at least."

Too close. Chloe gave a pained laugh, horrified to feel the prick of tears. "You know, right now I wish home *was* in Texas."

Layla pulled her into the restroom, peering beneath the stall doors to make sure they were empty. "Are you okay?"

Shaking her head in exasperation at herself, she said, "Not really. But I will be."

One gentle squeeze to the arm later Chloe found words tumbling from her mouth that she had never dreamed of telling anyone. Certainly not her brother or Brad. But something about the other woman—maybe the wise eyes that seemed to see everything—drew the festering poison from her inner wounds like a healing salve. She finished her story with, "I'm filing for divorce."

Layla gave her a quick hug. "It seems we're alike in more ways than one. Remind me to tell you about it some time." She sighed and shook her head. "But for now I think we need to get you upstairs."

When Chloe peeked at her watch again, she was horrified to see an hour had passed since Brad had left her. "I'm so sorry. I'm sure you have other things to do."

"I'm glad I was here when you came in. I haven't…" Her words trailed off. "Well, that's for another day. If you want to, we can get together for drinks some time. O'Malley's is just round the corner. It's a regular haunt for those of us at Angel's."

"Thank you. That sounds great." Maybe starting over

wouldn't be as hard as she'd feared. If the job worked out, Brad might consider keeping her on. Surely Layla or someone could point her in the direction of a reasonably priced apartment. Or someone in need of a roommate.

Because Brad wasn't going to want her to live with him for ever. And she shouldn't want that either. Not after all that weirdness she'd felt on the back of his motorcycle.

If that feeling grew…

She rolled her eyes as they made their way to the elevator.

She would just ask him those questions she'd thought about earlier and then get out of his life. And sooner was looking a whole lot better than later.

It made his blood boil.

Maybe that old expression was true after all, because where there'd been one irritated bubble floating around a moment ago, there was now a steady stream of them rolling up and down the veins of his arms. Filling his chest. Gathering in his skull.

He scowled at the nurses' desk, where Cade Coleman stood talking to none other than Chloe. *His* Chloe.

Okay, she wasn't his. But she was under his care— which was something he never thought he'd say about a woman. And there was something about the way she looked at Cade from beneath her lashes. The ready smile that curved her lips. The color blooming along her cheeks.

His eyes narrowed when she took a strand of hair and twirled it round her index finger.

He'd been on the receiving end of plenty of hair twirls. It usually meant one thing.

Surely she didn't find the guy attractive.

Well, she sure as hell hadn't looked at *him* that way.

As for Coleman, what was he doing, making a move on one of his nurses? One who had only been here for three days.

Whatever it was, he was going to nip it in the bud because Jason would be crawling all over him if he let someone take advantage of Chloe.

"Is there a problem here?"

Chloe's glance went to his, and she jerked upright, the lock of hair falling from her fingers to join the rest of the glossy strands. "I was just…just…" If her cheeks had been pink before, they were flaming now.

What was going on?

Cade, whose elbow had been resting on the counter, casually raised a brow. "No problem. We just hadn't been formally introduced yet."

An oversight Brad hadn't even attempted to rectify. There was something about the surgeon that made his hackles rise. In all honesty, it was probably because they were both stubborn and opinionated and used to being in charge. Tensions had been high ever since he'd joined the team, but Brad had figured as long as they each stuck to his own job and didn't get in the way of the other, they'd be able to coexist peacefully. Not if Chloe's well-being was at stake, however.

"Chloe?"

She shrugged, her hands clasped on top of the desk. "Like he said, we were just getting to know each other."

Brad's jaw tightened further. Definitely no hair-twirling going on when she spoke to him. But there was a whole lot of guilt in her eyes.

What the hell was she playing at?

Before he could say anything further, Cade rapped his knuckles lightly on the desk, making Chloe jump. "Well, now that we've become a little better acquainted, I'll let you get back to it. I have a few patients to see. I'll talk to you later."

With a brusque nod in Brad's direction he headed for the elevators across from the nurses' station.

"So?" His attention went back to Chloe.

"Can we please talk about this later?"

His brows went up. "If I knew what the hell 'this' was, I'd feel a whole lot better."

"It's nothing. I just don't know how to…" She shook her head and looked away.

Sliding his fingers under her chin, he coaxed her gaze back to his. "You don't know how to what?"

She licked her lips. "Flirt."

The word was so low he wasn't sure he'd heard it correctly. "I'm sorry, did you say flirt?"

The word set his teeth on edge. And sent his thoughts racing.

Tugging from his grip, she wrapped her arms around her waist, eyes flashing. "I know it must seem stupid to you, but it was one of the reasons…"

One of the other nurses came to the station and settled into a chair, smiling at both of them, obviously unaware of the tense undercurrents.

But at least that angry bubbling sensation inside Brad's chest had eased. Chloe wasn't really interested in Cade. At least, he didn't think she was.

"When does your shift end?"

Ginny, the other nurse, spoke up. "I've been trying to get her to leave for the last half-hour."

"You're already off duty?"

"I feel funny just…leaving."

The pause before "leaving" was telling. She didn't want anyone to know where she was staying. Kind of hard since the address she'd given to Human Resources was his. For the second time in a week he wondered if housing Chloe was a good idea. But he was already committed to this course, and Jason was counting on him.

Tread carefully, bud. If she wanted to keep their living arrangements secret, then he'd better honor that decision.

"I have one other patient to see, and then I'm off as well."

Chloe nodded. "I'll see you later, then."

"Sounds good."

Walking away from the station, he tried to get his head screwed back on straight. But it was tough, because Chloe and Cade weren't his only worries right now. Katrina hadn't quite dropped out of the picture, like he'd hoped she would. She'd not only called and spoken to Chloe, she'd left an angry message on his voice mail. She'd also stopped in at the hospital and had been none too pleased—according to Ginny—to find they'd already replaced her.

It reaffirmed his decision to keep personal and business relationships in two separate compartments. Which made things with Chloe even more complicated. Because the contents of those particular compartments were oozing from minuscule cracks, mingling with each other.

Unlike Katrina, who'd begun on the business end of the spectrum and moved over to the personal, Chloe was the opposite. And if he wasn't careful he'd mess things up not only with her but with her whole family. That was the last thing he wanted to do. He cared about the Jenkins clan. And he and Jason went even further back.

They were the one steady thing in his life. The only relationship he hadn't somehow screwed up.

Yet.

CHAPTER SEVEN

"How are you feeling today?"

Chloe checked Melanie Roberts's IV drip. About six months pregnant, with pink cheeks and a glowing complexion, she seemed the picture of health. Looks could be deceiving, though, because hidden deep within her there'd been a serious problem that had needed to be fixed.

Just like Chloe.

With Melanie's unborn baby afflicted with spina bifida, Cade had been forced to operate on her a few days ago and all had gone well, according to reports. She'd need to stay in the hospital for a few more days to make sure she didn't go into premature labor, and then she'd have to continue on meds to keep her uterus from reacting to the trauma of surgery. Bed rest for the next couple of months. But so far so good. Although they wouldn't know for sure until after she delivered, the baby's prognosis for a normal life was excellent.

Melanie glanced at the IV. "Are you sure the pain medication isn't going to hurt the baby?"

Putting her hand on the woman's shoulder, she gave her a smile. "I'm sure your doctor is being extremely careful. Have you seen him today?"

"Dr. Coleman came in to check on me. And my regular obstetrician is supposed to come by this afternoon."

Chloe busied herself with fluffing pillows and tucking blankets to hide the warmth in her cheeks as Cade's name was mentioned. She'd thought Brad would burst a blood vessel when he'd seen her at the desk yesterday with the surgeon. It had been then that she'd realized that instead of charming Cade with her attempts at flirting she'd been making a fool of herself. Again. When Brad had got her to confess, his brows had drawn together. She'd thought he was going to say something more, but then Ginny had come back to the nurses' station and conversation had fizzled before dying completely.

He'd met her after work, but instead of riding home on his motorcycle he'd put her in a cab and said he'd see her at the apartment. He hadn't. Because as soon as she'd arrived, she'd gone straight to the guest room. Brad hadn't knocked on the door, although she'd known he'd arrived as well. A half-hour later, though, she'd heard the front door open and close. He'd gone out and stayed out until the wee hours of the morning.

Had he been with the nurse who'd called her the other day? It was none of her business if he had. Still, a tiny bloom of hurt had come to life.

She forced her attention back to her patient. "Did you ask Dr. Coleman about your medication?"

"He said it was fine, that the baby shouldn't be affected. It's just that…" she twisted the blankets "…it's just been such a shock. I took the prenatal vitamins just like I was told to. Weren't they supposed to prevent this?"

"Sometimes these things happen, no matter what you do."

Like her impending divorce? If she'd tried harder, done more of what she knew Travis liked in bed, could she have prevented him from getting it elsewhere?

That had been the problem. She had tried. But being coerced to perform had meant she had never been given the chance to try new things of her own free will. To give to him spontaneously from a heart full of love. Instead, his overtures had been more like a boss issuing orders: *No, not there…here. Harder. Keep going.* There had been no cuddling, no slow build-up of passion. It had been all or nothing with Travis. And even when she'd given it her all, she'd gotten little or nothing in return.

She shook herself out of the memories as she finished up with the patient and went back into the hallway. She was free of that now. Free of treating sex like a duty that she dreaded. Which was why she'd been shocked at the tingling she'd felt sitting behind Brad on the bike. You'd think she'd never respond to another man again. Especially not this soon.

Maybe it was just her hormones urging her to procreate. But she'd never felt the need to have kids with Travis. And he'd never pressed that issue either. Another thing to be glad of.

But she did want children eventually, which meant, unless she wanted to embark on that particular journey alone, she'd have to wade into the dating pool again, the sooner the better.

Only this time she wasn't committing until she was sure she wasn't going to wind right back up where she'd been for the last six years. She wanted someone she shared common ground with. Maybe even someone in the medical field.

Brad's image came to mind, and she pushed it back

down. No. He wasn't a better choice than Travis had been. He skipped from woman to woman without a care in the world. Only where Travis had merely broken her pride, if she was honest with herself, Brad could break something much deeper.

No, she needed someone steady and even-tempered. Someone who wasn't cocky or arrogant. Someone who didn't spin out on his motorcycle and nearly kill himself.

Someone... She wrinkled her nose when the word "boring" twirled around in her skull, dancing out of reach every time she tried to grab it and kick it to the curb.

Cade wasn't boring. But he also wasn't someone she could see herself being seriously interested in. It had been fun to try to kid around with him, at least until Brad had made her feel like an idiot.

Why did he even care?

The elevator doors swished open and the man himself exited. Her legs tensed, ready to pivot and hurry away in the other direction. Then their eyes met and it was too late. He made his way over to her.

"How's your day going?"

"Pretty well. I just finished checking on Melanie Roberts. She asked whether the pain meds could affect the baby."

"Did you ask Dr. Coleman about it?"

Strange, the way he always referred to the surgeon by his last name. Almost as if he didn't like the man. "I haven't seen him today. But if I do, I will." She bit her lip. "Would you mind talking to her in the meantime? I think it would put her mind at ease."

"Sure." He glanced at the nurses' desk and then back at her.

"Did you stay in last night?"

She decided to play dumb, as if she hadn't noticed he'd stayed out half the night. "I don't know what you mean."

"Did you eat dinner?"

Jerking her eyes away from his, she lifted her chin. "I did. I went out."

She had technically gone round the corner to grab a burger, but she knew her words could be easily misconstrued. Knew she'd phrased them that way on purpose. But something about the way he'd left her alone had stung, and she was desperate for him not to find out how much. He hadn't been home, so there's no way he'd know she'd eaten by herself. Just like she had in the later stages of her marriage.

"Oh?" His fingers scrubbed the side of his jaw. "Have a good time?"

"I did." She decided to do a little probing of her own. "How about you? Do anything interesting?"

"Not really. Took a ride. Saw the city lights."

Sure he had. She noticed he didn't mention whether he'd taken that ride alone or not. "I'm sure they were pretty." She could only hope the sarcastic edge she'd given her words had been lost on him.

"They were. I'd have invited you to come along, but I know my bike makes you nervous. Didn't think I should push my luck by asking you to do it again."

Was that why he'd sent her home in a cab? He thought she was chicken? She was, but not for the reasons he thought.

"I think you might be surprised."

One of his brows went up. The left one. Why had Chloe never noticed those permanent little lines above it that came from repeating the gesture over the years?

"So you've decided you like motorcycles now?"

Definitely not. But she'd felt safe tucked up against his back. Among other things. But that was something she was never going to admit.

"Let's just say it was tolerable."

"Just what every man wants to hear."

The smile that had started to form on her lips slunk away. No, it probably wasn't what men wanted to hear. Even if it was true.

She had to remind herself that Brad wasn't Travis. "Sorry."

"I think you'd like it better if we weren't in traffic. Riding down an open highway is like nothing in this world." He reached up to tuck her hair behind her ear, the way he'd done when she'd been a teenager—after he'd tugged it playfully, that was. Heat swept over her. Her body hadn't forgotten the sensation, even if her mind had. His fingers scraped deliciously across her cheek as they withdrew, only to pause before retracing their steps.

He murmured, "I'll have to take you some time."

"Take me?" Chloe swallowed, her insides tightening in response to his touch.

"On my bike."

Her face went red hot. Oh, Lord. Why was she suddenly ascribing all kinds of motives to his words?

Because she could still remember what it was like to have her arms around his waist, hear his low, gruff voice piped directly in her ear, feel the vibrations from the engine rumbling through her entire body...

Yeah, she'd be up for that again, despite all her lectures to herself to the contrary. "I'd like that."

"Would you?" Was it her imagination or had his eyes darkened? "How about one day this weekend?"

"I work Saturday, but I'm off on Sunday." She

couldn't believe she was actually considering going. A thought hit her. "You weren't thinking of going home to Connecticut, were you?" That was the last place she wanted to be right now.

"No. I was thinking about heading upstate and spending the day."

"At your parents' house?" The last she'd heard, they'd moved away to somewhere in New York State. The relationship between him and his parents had always been strained, to say the least, but maybe that had changed over the years.

His hand dropped back to his side. "No."

That one word told her the way nothing else could that she'd been wrong. Brad's feelings towards them hadn't changed. Although from what Jason had told her about them, she couldn't blame him.

"So what's upstate, then?"

"Nothing. It's just not the city." He paused for a minute. "It feels good to get away sometimes."

That was surprising as well. Not that he needed to get away but that he wanted her to go with him. She was sure he had plenty of women clamoring for the chance to be his traveling companion. Yet he'd chosen her.

She gave an internal eye roll. This was getting ridiculous.

First you think he's saying he wants to have sex with you on his bike—which is probably physically impossible. Then you delude yourself into thinking he wants to spend time with you in a romantic setting. Grow up, Chloe!

He was only offering to take her because he had to. He felt responsible for her, the way he had as a teenager when he'd made sure she'd got home safely. Just what she wanted. To be a burden.

She sighed. "You don't have to take care of me, you know. I've lived a lot of years on my own."

"And you shouldn't have. Travis should have…" His voice trailed away. "Let's just say I want to show you what you've been missing."

Her mind took off running in another dangerous direction. What she'd been missing?

As if realizing how his words had come across, he clarified, "I was talking about New York."

"Oh." She seemed to deflate all at once. Of course he'd been talking about the state itself. What else would he have been talking about? Sex? Again?

She needed to realize once and for all that Brad didn't see her that way. And it was unlikely that would ever change.

CHAPTER EIGHT

"I WANT YOU to be careful around Dr. Coleman."

Reclining on a blanket in the park, half-asleep in the warmth of the sun, Chloe wasn't sure she'd heard Brad correctly. She half sat up, resting her weight on her elbows. "I beg your pardon?"

"You talked about learning how to…flirt." It seemed like he'd had to push that word out between clenched teeth. "He's not the man to try that with."

A quick flutter of something went through her, similar to the one she'd felt on the trip over. Brad had been right. Riding through the countryside on his motorcycle had been nothing like riding in city traffic. It had been exhilarating.

"And why is that?"

He lifted his wineglass to his lips and observed her for a second. "I don't want to see you get hurt again. And I think he's capable of doing just that."

Chloe disagreed, but didn't say anything. "So who would be a safer choice? You?"

"No."

The abrupt word took her aback. "Really? Why not?" The words were out before she could stop them. Did she really want to know the answer?

"I don't flirt."

Wow. "Ever?"

"Not the harmless stuff you're talking about. When I'm interested in a woman, she knows it. And she knows exactly where I want it to lead."

A shiver went over her as she pictured those mirrors in his room. She assumed he wasn't talking about marriage.

What would it be like to have a man like Brad put the moves on her? The closest she'd ever gotten had been at her wedding. And she'd just about convinced herself that those events had been fabricated by an overactive imagination. "So you can't be friendly with a woman unless you plan on sleeping with her?"

"'Can't' is not the word I'd choose." Brad set his empty wineglass next to the box of food. "Let's just say I'm not interested in wasting time playing games."

Playing games? Stung, she snapped, "Forget I said anything. I think I'll take my chances with Cade."

He dragged a hand through his hair. "Dammit, Chloe. Haven't you heard a thing I've said?"

"Yes. I heard you say you don't flirt, so I'm back to where I started."

His eyes narrowed. "You want to play games? Fine. Tell me what you have in mind."

In all honesty, she wanted to know why she wasn't worth his time. Did she want to wind up in bed with him—which was what he'd implied would happen if he showed his interest? No. But just for once she wanted to know what it would be like to have someone as dangerous as Brad pursue her with the intention of capturing her.

She shrugged. "I just don't want to make a fool out of myself, that's all."

"With Coleman?"

"With anyone."

"Okay, you've got a captive audience. So give it your best shot."

"Right now?"

A slow smile curved his lips, and he leaned forward and drew his thumb along her cheekbone. "Right here, Chloe. Right now."

Liquid heat ignited along the trail he'd left on her skin, and she could scarcely believe what she was hearing. Was he serious? She kept perfectly still as his touch continued to assault her senses, afraid that if she reacted she'd scare him off. She didn't know exactly why he was willing to make an exception, but she was going to grab it with both hands. Because if she didn't, she'd be back where she'd been when this had started: alone, with no hope of that ever changing.

"So where do you want to start?" What the hell had possessed him to agree to be her flirt buddy? Oh, he knew exactly what it was. Her veiled threat to involve Coleman. And the idea that Coleman would want her to be an altogether different kind of buddy.

His thoughts darkened. He'd told her the truth. He wasn't into the light-hearted back-and-forth quips that seemed to go on for weeks while he waited for some vague green light that allowed him to move to the next stage. No, when he wanted sex, he chose a woman who was just as interested in getting to the point as he was. He had no desire to climb on the emotional roller-coaster that went along with relationships. Or to be trapped in a box with no way out.

Sex was sex and nothing more.

He instinctively knew the act meant much more to Chloe, though. It was the reason she'd saved that part of herself for marriage. And look what she'd gotten in exchange. Heartache and a man who'd had no qualms about taking what she'd offered and then tossing it aside when he was done.

Isn't that what you do with women?

No. It was the reason he didn't play around with innocents like Chloe. And why he didn't want Coleman to either. She wasn't a love 'em and leave 'em type of woman.

She'd stuck with Travis for six years, even though Jason said things had been bad for quite a while. For crying out loud, she hadn't even been willing to get on the back of his motorcycle after he'd passed the last of his medical exams because she'd been afraid Travis might get the wrong idea. Oh, she hadn't said it, but he'd seen the truth in her face. In the way the glow had faded from those beautiful baby blues.

So why was he allowing her to push him into doing this? He was not the right person for this particular job. He wasn't accustomed to holding back when he wanted something.

And if he decided he wanted Chloe?

Not a chance. He was a big boy. He could do this with his eyes closed.

He propped himself on an elbow next to her and raised his brows. "So, let's say we're out on a date, and you wanted to let me know you're interested. What would you do?" The image of her in that negligee passed briefly behind his eyelids. He chased it away with a muttered oath. She shrugged, staring down at the blanket.

He tilted her chin, forcing her to look at him. "This was your idea. Having second thoughts?"

"I don't want you to make fun of me."

"I've never felt less like laughing in my life." On the contrary, a sick sense of anticipation was building inside him that he couldn't will away as easily as he would have liked.

This girl was his best friend's sister, for God's sake.

"How will I know if I'm even doing it right?"

"I think I'll be able to tell." If the way his body had responded to having her behind him on the motorcycle was any indication, he wasn't totally immune to her, despite his assertions to the contrary.

She moistened her lips, the soft bottom one glistening. "I think I'd rather just ask you questions and have you answer them."

Even easier. "Okay. Fire away."

"So…" Her voice dropped almost to a whisper and she hesitated for a second or two. "If you were here on a picnic with one of your dates, what would she do to hold your interest?"

One of his dates? He'd probably be sliding her panties down her thighs right about now.

Why did this game suddenly seem a little too dangerous?

And why was he all too eager to keep playing?

"Well…" He thought for a moment, trying to come up with something halfway chaste. "She might turn towards me so we were facing each other."

There. See? Easy. He'd give her a couple of quick tips and they'd be on their way home.

Instead of nodding her head and continuing with her questions, Chloe shifted to the side until she was resting on one elbow just like he was. The position made the dip of her waist and the curve of her hip stand out in sharp relief. He couldn't stop his eyes from following the line.

"Kind of like this?" she asked.

"Exactly like that."

"Okay. What else?"

His body quickened. Hell, she'd wanted to know if it was working. A little too well, and she wasn't even trying. And if she did?

Things could get out of hand. He should put a stop to this now, before she realized what she was doing to him. He was curious, though, to see how far she was willing to carry this little charade. He decided to push her. Maybe he could even scare her back into her shell.

"Well, she might sweep the hair off my forehead as she listens to me talk." His voice seemed to be affected by the tightening of his throat, coming out a little rougher than he intended. That could work to his benefit, though.

Chloe seemed totally oblivious, however. She reached out and did as he suggested, sliding her fingers deep into his hair, lingering when she should have withdrawn. "You used to tug my hair all the time when I was a kid, remember?" At his nod, she ran her fingers through it again. "Yours is softer than I thought it would be."

"Is it?" The tight sensation in his throat began to spread, reaching his chest, crawling along his abdomen and beyond. And she seemed to have no idea. Not good.

"This is really helping," she murmured. "Thank you for agreeing."

Yes. Thank you. His mind wasn't nearly as happy as the rest of him was. It was currently kicking his ass from here to across the sea.

"Tell me what else I would do."

As if he were a puppet—and he knew exactly what was pulling the strings, and it wasn't his head—he kept digging a deeper hole. "Well, *I* might move a little closer." He proceeded to do exactly that, sliding to within a few inches of where she lay. "Then I might stroke the side of her face, down her neck until I reached her shoulder." His hand followed the route in time with his words.

As he touched her shoulder—he wasn't even sure he'd applied any pressure to it at all—she lay back on the blanket, her eyes staring up at him. Waiting to see what was next on the agenda.

God help him, the words just seemed to keep coming. "Then…I might kiss her. Like this."

With that, his head began its fatal descent, until his lips touched hers.

CHAPTER NINE

A BUTTERFLY'S WINGS.

That's what Brad's lips felt like as they brushed across hers once, twice, three times. The sensation was intoxicatingly gentle, barely there at all. She'd never been kissed like this in her life.

She wanted to open her mouth, to drag him closer and really feel his mouth against hers, but she was too busy reveling in this luscious new world—one she'd never known existed.

Until this very moment.

A strange sound came up from her throat, a cross between a whimper and a groan. A quiet plea for more? Whatever it was, it changed the dynamic between them. His whole body came to a complete standstill for several seconds before coming back to life. He went down on his forearms, her breasts flattening as he settled over her. Warm hands moved to either side of her face and held it still.

That was when she realized that not only had she moaned against his mouth, she was straining upwards as well, hoping to increase the pressure. Brad seemed determined to keep to the original pace, his weight physically keeping her from speeding things up.

And that torturous, traitorous kiss…

Not plundering. Not invading. Just a sweet, steady touch designed to drive her insane.

His name wound around in her brain, seeking an exit that didn't exist.

Brad left her mouth, his lips brushing along her jaw in a long, slow journey that made her shiver with longing, made her insides coil tight in anticipation.

Oh, Lord, what was happening to her? The world was moving too fast and too slow, she was too hot…too cold.

Nothing was the way she'd expected it to be. The way it had always been.

"This is what I'd do." Warm breath slid along her ear carrying words she strained to catch. "I'd kiss her. Until she couldn't breathe. Couldn't think."

She was already there. So there.

But before she had a chance to respond he was gone, cranking his body upright and dragging a hand through his hair, while she lay stunned, her breath coming in short, desperate spurts.

He gave a hard laugh, his eyes staring down into hers, pupils as black as she'd ever seen them. "See? That's why I don't do flirting. It doesn't take much."

Her sluggish brain struggled to process the words.

It didn't take much to what? Turn her into a churning cauldron of need?

Oh, God. Was that what that was? He'd sensed what was happening with her—had been forced to back off before she reached for him with greedy hands? Before the light flirting she'd asked for suddenly turned to something much more serious?

He'd done exactly what *she'd* set out to do to Travis in that hotel room in New York City: seduce her.

And, unlike her failure with her ex, Brad had succeeded far too well. All it had taken had been one small touch.

* * *

Armed with a fresh cup of coffee, Chloe made her way across the street. She needed to get away for a little while and the tall shade trees of Central Park had beckoned her from the fourth-floor hospital windows all morning long. It was already warm but temperatures hadn't yet rocketed enough to cause the horse-drawn carriages to stop operating, though they might later on.

She sat on one of the benches that lined the street and gave a sigh of relief. Maybe the constant drone of city sounds would help drown out the cacophony in her head. Her fingers went to her lips as the events of this past weekend swept over her again. Unlike her thoughts, no amount of noise was going to erase the sensation of Brad's mouth on hers. Something that had followed her into her dreams, disrupting her sleep and making her feel edgy and irritable.

She hadn't seen Brad since their arrival at the hospital that morning, and for that she was glad. So much for not letting things get awkward. That kiss had shot that plan to hell.

Not only was there no more flirting going on, there wasn't much talking either. Well, except for shop talk. They could chat about patients and treatments until the wee hours of the morning and never hit on anything more personal than the glucose counts of such and such a patient.

Cade Coleman, on the other hand, had drifted in and out of the nurses' station today without a care in the world, giving her a friendly wink from time to time. Hopefully Brad wouldn't catch him and think she was practicing on the surgeon again. There was already some kind of growing tension between the men, and she didn't want to do anything to make the situation worse.

Taking a sip of coffee, she leaned back against the bench, taking in the constant flow of cars. This world was so different from the one she'd left behind in Connecticut. Everything was bigger. The buildings. The traffic jams and construction. Even Central Park itself had seemed to stretch on for ever when she'd looked down on it from the upper floors of the hospital.

Instead of making her long for the familiarity of her county hospital, the movement and activity here seemed to energize her, making her feel alive in a way she hadn't felt for a very long time. Maybe some of that was due to being free of Travis. But she wondered if it wasn't the city itself.

Her cellphone went off. Glancing at the readout, she saw it was the hospital.

"Chloe Jenkins here."

"Where are you?"

Brad's voice. Impersonal. Brusque. Just like it had been ever since they'd come back from the picnic.

"Central Park. Why?"

"We've got a TTTS. Can you get back here?"

TTTS... Her brain flashed through the acronym. Twin to twin transfusion syndrome.

"Stage?" she asked.

"Three."

Not good.

Although fairly rare, TTTS was restricted to identical twins who shared a placenta. One fetus's blood was shunted to the other, endangering not only the donor twin but also the recipient, if it progressed past a certain point. "On my way."

Dumping her empty paper cup into a nearby trash can, she stayed on the phone as she hurried to the corner to wait for the light to change. A million questions came into her mind. "Did her OB/GYN do an amnio reduction on the recipient twin?"

Brad's voice came back through. "Yes, but the problem is still progressing. Coleman wants to do a laser ablation."

Wow. If Cade wanted to destroy the blood vessels linking the two babies, things had to be serious. "When?"

"They're trying to schedule it immediately, which is why I need you back here. The nurses' station will be short-staffed otherwise."

She would have liked the opportunity to watch the procedure—as Angel's was one of the few hospitals in the U.S. that offered it—but she was here to help however she could.

The light changed, and she jogged across the crosswalk. "I should be there in about five minutes."

"Okay. See you when you get here."

Had she imagined the relief in Brad's voice? Of course she had.

As the doors of the hospital swished open a couple of minutes later, and the rush of cool air from the interior hit her, she smiled at the ordered chaos that met her eyes. A pink-haired clown—whose eight-foot height could only be the result of stilts—was busy swaying to some kind of rap music, his real smile almost as wide as the one painted on his face. His reflection gleamed in the mirrors and the polished floors. About ten delighted children had gathered around him, clapping in time to the beat.

It was easy to forget she worked in a children's hospital as the tiny patients on the fourth floor were still cocooned in their mothers, dependent on skilled doctors for their very lives. But here on the ground floor everyone was equal, doctors and patients alike.

A wave from across the foyer caught her attention. Layla, holding the hand of a young cancer patient, who, despite the patchy hair and pale delicate skin, was laughing. Layla put an arm protectively around her small charge as she smiled at Chloe, making an imaginary phone with her free hand and holding it up to her ear. *"Call me,"* she mouthed.

Chloe smiled back and gave her a thumbs-up. It was good to have a friend. Especially now.

The elevator gave a soft ping as it arrived on the fourth floor, but as soon as she stepped out she saw Ginny at the nurses' station, along with two other nurses. Where was the shortage Brad had talked about?

Maybe they hadn't gone to prepare yet. Although they didn't normally pull nurses from the floor to assist. That job fell to the surgical nurses.

Brad appeared round the corner with Cade, the two of them in deep conversation.

Well, at least they were being civil to one another. They both spotted her at the same time, Brad frowning while Cade called out a greeting. "I understand you're going to observe the procedure."

She was? Her eyes went to Brad for confirmation as they drew near. "We don't get very many of these and I thought you might be interested." His voice had softened a bit.

How on earth had he guessed something like that? And why lie about his reason for wanting her to come back? Had he thought she wouldn't show if he told her?

Cade said his goodbyes, saying he needed to go scrub for the upcoming surgery.

Brad glanced down at her with a raised brow. "When

I couldn't find you, I thought something might have happened." Before she could ask what he meant, he continued, "Something like Travis showing up."

Ah, that explained it. Even so, she couldn't stop the little jump in her stomach that he'd cared enough to keep track of where she was—had been afraid she might need to be rescued.

She did. But only from herself, evidently.

"Are you really going to let me observe?"

"If you want to." He nodded in the direction Cade had gone. "I had to give him a reason for calling you out of the blue."

The jump in her stomach turned into a pogo stick, bouncing between happiness with Brad and irritation with herself.

"I'd love to watch."

"Okay. I'd planned on observing as well, so I'll take you up. We can grab some coffee on the way." He started toward the elevators. "I hope I didn't disturb anything by calling you."

"Nope. Just sitting across the street on a bench."

He nodded. "I've been known to do that myself from time to time."

He had? Something in her wondered if he might have sat on the same bench she had. The thought caused that crazy pogo stick to land squarely on the happiness side of the equation.

"I've already had coffee," she said. "I probably shouldn't have another cup."

"We'll go straight up, then."

The ride in the elevator seemed to take for ever this time. Chloe strained to find something to talk about. "How's the mother handling the news?"

He scrubbed a hand along his jaw. "She'd already

armed herself with information, so she knew this was a possibility."

"No, I mean how's she *handling* it?"

His hand fell to his side and he smiled. "You always were a softie."

"Yeah? Well, someone has to be."

"Mom is hanging in there. I think her husband is more scared than she is." He tweaked her hair. "And I always knew your soft outer layer hid a will of iron."

If only he knew. That iron core she'd once possessed was now pitted with rust and corrosion. One more hard kick and it would fall apart completely. Which was why she had to be careful with Brad. That kiss had taken its toll on her.

Was still taking its toll.

Brad would never knowingly hurt her, though. Not if he could help it.

But what if he couldn't? What if she, despite all her best efforts, turned out to be her own worst enemy?

CHAPTER TEN

A MOVIE THEATER without the popcorn.

The thought went through Chloe's mind as Brad guided her to the first row of seats in the observation room. Angel's was a teaching hospital so it stood to reason that there would be a room like this one, but she was surprised by how big it was, the transparent glass in front of them stretching from side to side like a giant screen.

No one else was in there but them at the moment, and Chloe found herself torn between wishing others would join them and hoping they wouldn't.

"Can they hear us?"

"Only if I turn on the system. It would be distracting to the surgeon if he could hear everything that went on in this room."

The words bought things to mind that made a wave of heat wash up Chloe's neck and collect behind her cheeks. Surely he'd never—

"The glass is two-way, though. We can see out and they can see in."

Was he setting her mind at ease or giving her a subtle warning not to get any ideas about practicing her flirting?

No fear of that. Her soul still showed the scorch

marks from the last episode. Brad was way out of her league. While he could brush off that kiss and never think about it again, she was having some serious problems putting that chapter behind her.

What had she been thinking to suggest it in the first place? All Brad had to do was look at her sideways, and her heart started thumping like a jackrabbit's back leg when danger was near.

Like it was doing this very moment.

Cade entered the surgical area, where the patient and anesthesiologist were already waiting. He glanced up and nodded towards them. Chloe felt a strange kind of detachment looking down at the scene, almost as if she were having an out-of-body experience and was actually standing on the surgical floor.

But she wasn't. She was here with Brad.

If only she could detach from him as easily.

"Does the patient know other people could be watching this?"

He nodded. "It's disclosed in the admissions paperwork."

"I can't help feeling like a peeping Tom sitting here, though."

Brad leaned closer and their shoulders bumped. "It's the best way for surgical residents to hear and see exactly what goes on during surgery. They can observe how the team works together, learn new techniques or how to manage any complications should they arise."

It made sense, and it wasn't like the patient saw a crowd of people staring down at her. It just seemed intrusive somehow.

But so much less so now as Brad's shoulder was still touching hers. A steady stream of warmth seemed to be flowing from that connection, traveling down the length of her arm, settling in her belly.

Cade's voice came through the speakers, causing her to jump. "Are we ready?" He glanced at each person in turn and received an affirmation.

Soon caught up in what was happening, Chloe kept her eyes glued to the monitor to her left as it provided a better view than actually looking down at the floor. "Ablation of the shared blood vessels is done laproscopically?"

"It's safer that way. No reason to make a large incision in the uterus in this case."

It was almost like watching a movie with a running commentary. She just hoped there were no twists involved in this particular storyline, and that things ran smoothly.

Cade introduced the fetoscope into the opening, feeding it through the hollow tube until he reached the blood vessels in question. She could now see the rich red vessels that were starving one twin and oversupplying the other. "Getting ready to close the vessels."

A couple of quick bursts later, Cade proclaimed the ablation a success. The only thing left to do was drain some of the excess amniotic fluid from the recipient twin's sac. Then they'd close the small incisions. Chloe only realized she'd grabbed Brad's hand and squeezed hard when she felt his other one cover their joined fingers.

"Sorry." Her words came out on a half-laugh. "I guess I got caught up in what was happening."

She let go, and Brad gave his hand a shake or two. "It's okay. I don't use it much anyway."

"Surely you've had worse things done to you?"

"Surely." He was still smiling, but his tone wasn't quite as light as it had been a minute ago.

She glanced back down at the room below to avoid looking at him. "Will both twins survive?"

"That's the hope. We should know within the next couple of days."

Minutes later, Cade exited the room, snapping off his gloves as he pushed through the door. "The hospital's lucky to have him on staff."

Brad's mouth tightened. "That's what they tell me."

"Don't you like him?"

"He's good at his job. I don't have to like him." He glanced at her. "And what about you? Do you like him?"

Chloe shrugged. "I don't really know him. The other nurses seem to think he's attractive, though."

There was a pause then Brad stared through the viewing window at the people still working around the patient, cleaning up the site and getting ready to transport her to a recovery room. "I'll bet they do."

She couldn't tell if the words were sarcastic or if he was merely agreeing with her. "I think you two are a lot alike."

That got his attention. "You think so?"

"I do."

His eyes searched hers. "And what about your ex? Am I a lot like him as well?"

A few seconds went by before she answered him.

"No. You're nothing like him."

His fingers came out and stroked her jaw and he decided her skin felt just as soft and silky as it had the day of the picnic. "Don't be too sure of that."

He saw her swallow then her gaze went back to the floor. "Believe me, you're not. He cheated on me. More than once."

He cheated on me. Brad's eyes closed as myriad emotions churned to life in his gut—outrage, anger, along with a sudden realization. "You found him with someone else the night you showed up at my apartment."

"Yes." The tip of her tongue moistened her lips, and she opened her mouth like she wanted to say something else but clamped it shut again.

However bad he might be, Brad thought, he'd never cheated on anyone he was with. He kept his relationships clean and simple. Only one woman at a time. One short-lived fling after another. "What else did he do?"

Chloe's eyes skipped away again. "Besides cheat? Isn't that enough?"

"More than enough." He studied her face, trying to see past the pink cheeks and averted eyes. "But there's something else. Something to do with this whole flirting business. Did he say you were unattractive?"

Her teeth came down on her lower lip. "No."

He waited, sensing there was something inside her fighting to come out.

"He said I was…frigid."

Brad wasn't sure what he'd expected her to say but that hadn't been it. He kept his voice very even, trying to push past the growing fury in his chest. "Excuse me?"

"W-well, *he* didn't say it. The woman he was with did. Said he was right about me…that I even looked frigid." She took a gulping breath and for a second he was afraid she might burst into tears. "I wanted to talk to someone about it, but it's just so…so…" her eyes went back to the floor "…humiliating."

He damned the man, putting his fingers under her chin and forcing her to watch him say the words. "It's not true, Chloe."

"It is true. I was standing right there when she said it." Her blue eyes flashed at him.

"I didn't mean they didn't say it. I meant that whatever that man said about you is a lie." He remembered the sexy way her body had arched in an effort to capture his mouth as they'd kissed. What had made it even hotter had been that she'd seemed totally unaware of how crazy she'd driven him, doing that. How close he'd been to giving in to his baser urges.

There had been an eager innocence about her that he'd never encountered before. It had taken him by surprise at the time, but now he understood. If he had been furious at Travis before, that emotion now paled beside what he was currently feeling. Whatever had gone wrong between them in the bedroom had been Travis's fault, and not Chloe's. He would bet his life on it.

His fingers tightened their hold. "Listen to me. You are a sexy, beautiful, desirable woman."

And he didn't trust himself not to throw her down on the floor and show her exactly how desirable she was.

"Then why didn't he want me?" Her chin trembled. "And why did I dread being with him?"

Because the man you saved yourself for was a bastard who stole everything from his beautiful wife and gave nothing in return.

"Travis cheated you in more ways than one. If I could, Chloe, I'd…"

Show you just how good it could be.

He wanted to say the words. They were on the tip of his tongue, fighting to get out. And it was true. He wanted to take her home tonight and lay her down on his bed and tease her mouth open. Taste her. Fill her. Take her to heights she'd never dreamed of.

But Jason's words clanged in his head, stopping his

thoughts in their tracks with a warning that Brad had better not hurt her.

As if sensing the war going on inside him, Chloe's lips parted. "You'd what, Brad?"

CHAPTER ELEVEN

YOU'D WHAT?

She repeated the question silently as she finished up Melanie Roberts's discharge instructions, glad that the woman—and her unborn baby—had recovered well from the surgery to repair the neural tube defect. Sending up a quick prayer that Cade's fingers had worked their magic, she stood up and made her way over to the patient's room.

More problematic had been the way her heart had leapt into her throat yesterday as she'd asked Brad what he meant. She could have sworn he'd been about to say something else entirely. Instead, he'd muttered something about kicking someone's ass, and then he'd gotten up from his seat, saying he needed to get back to work.

And that had been that. They'd both gone their separate ways and then had ridden back to the apartment on his bike. Only instead of his low, rich voice filling her head and her senses through the helmet speaker, she'd been met by silence.

She'd finally spoken directly with Jason, though, and had let him know that she was filing for divorce. She gave him the name of the attorney, and Jason had said their father would give the office a call and make sure all Chloe's bases were covered.

Entering the hospital room with her clipboard, she smiled at Melanie. "Are you ready to get out of here?"

"Absolutely." She laughed. "No offense to the chef."

"Believe me, we all feel the same way about that particular chef. He does make an excellent strawberry gelatin, though. Have you tried it?"

Melanie smiled. "Only for breakfast, lunch, and dinner."

"It never gets old, does it?" Chloe said, her hands going to her chest as she swayed back and forth as if in love. She smiled again and handed the clipboard to the other woman, showing her where to sign and going over some care instructions with her.

"I really have to stay in bed for that long?"

"Really. Your little one has to heal, and so do you." She squeezed Melanie's shoulder. "It'll all be worth it. You'll see."

"I know." Melanie scribbled her name just as a wheelchair manned by a cheerful hospital volunteer rolled through the door.

Taking the paperwork, Chloe helped her patient get into the wheelchair. "I think your husband is bringing the car round."

"He is. Thanks again for everything."

On impulse, Chloe bent down and gave the woman's shoulders a quick hug. "I want to see pictures when he's born, okay?" As she said it, she realized she might not even be here in three months' time. A pang went through her. After only a week she was already getting attached to the hospital and its patients.

And maybe a little too attached to her boss?

As long as he didn't notice, and she took care not to let things get too cozy, her secret should be safe. Although when they had been in that observation room, she could have sworn he'd been about to say something about men and women, and how he wanted to…

The huge expanse of mirrors over his bed came to mind just as the elevator doors opened, allowing Melanie and the volunteer to get in. As the wheelchair turned to face the front, her patient gave a happy wave. Chloe waved back, mortified to even be thinking about things like mirrors and Brad's naked muscular back.

Her eyes strayed longingly to the patient's abdomen just as the doors swished closed, cutting it off from view. Maybe someday *she* would be that pregnant lady. When she found someone who would love her as she was.

Even if she wasn't a firecracker in the bedroom.

Brad's words about her being desirable had given her a jolt of hope that maybe all was not lost. If she could find someone patient enough to show her the way, she'd make sure she held onto that person and never let go.

Or, if for ever was too much to ask, maybe he could at least teach her what love—real love—was.

Something smelled delicious.

Brad closed the front door to the apartment, trying to erase the image of a desperate father on his knees in the hospital chapel, begging God to spare his wife. God had. But the couple had lost their unborn baby— and with it the possibility of ever having another one. When the man's red eyes had met his in the doorway, he'd known without Brad saying a word.

"My wife?"

"She's in Recovery. She sent me to find you. I promised I would."

Brad had taken that promise to heart and had gone

searching for the man in person. He'd known instinctively where he'd find him.

He'd lost patients before, wasn't sure why this was so different. Maybe because of the way that husband had looked at his wife, as if no love had ever been greater. He hadn't left her side until she'd been wheeled away for the surgery that would change both their lives.

"Chloe?" he called, shaking free of the memories.

The scent of cooking grew stronger as he tossed his keys and wallet onto the table in the foyer of the apartment and headed for the kitchen. Relief and irritation warred for first place. Relief that she was here, and irritation that she hadn't waited for him before hopping on the subway and heading home. He'd gone looking for her once his patient had been stabilized, and had been told she'd already left for the day.

Without saying a word to him.

He needed to get over this nagging worry that Travis would come looking for her. She was an adult, she didn't need him to be a babysitter. Besides, he'd already seen what could happen between them if he got too close. Chloe needed someone who would handle her with kid gloves. That someone was not him. Maybe he'd make a visit to Katrina's to get whatever was going on with him out of his system.

The idea filled him with distaste, which in turn made his frustration grow.

"Chloe." He allowed his irritation to come to the fore as he called her again.

She popped her head around the arched doorway that led to the kitchen. "In here. I'm making us something to eat."

"Why?" The last thing he wanted was to have her

cooking for him. When it was time for her to go, he wanted it to be a quick, clean break.

Her brow puckered. "I know you've had a hard day. I thought it was the least I could do, especially as you're letting me stay in your apartment. Consider it part of my rent."

"I already told you, you're helping me out of a jam at the hospital."

"I know." She hesitated, looking into his eyes. "I heard about your patient, Brad. I'm really sorry. Are you okay?"

His jaws clamped shut as he fought to stem the unwanted tide of emotion that rose inside him. He fought hard to give his unborn patients the best possible start in life. Something he hadn't had when he'd been a kid. And when things went wrong with any of his cases, it ate away at him.

He could rail at fate as much as he liked. But just like with the padlocks on the doors of his childhood home, he'd learned that begging and screaming didn't change a thing. Those locks had taught him at least one important survival skill, however. He was an expert at bolting the doors of his heart and keeping any unwanted emotion locked out of sight, and it got the job done. He'd learned to make choices based on what he knew about the world. Just like Chloe would have to do.

She disappeared again. He stood there wondering if he should just go to his room and try to shut out the day. It's what he wanted to do, but knew he'd end up feeling like a jerk if he did, because Chloe had gone to all the trouble of fixing him something to eat.

So he followed her.

"I'm making shrimp garlic alfredo. Hope that's okay. I remember you liked Mom's version of it."

He did, although he hadn't had it in years. Mrs. Jenkins had always remembered he liked it, too. Actually, though, he liked just about anything she cooked. And she made sure he knew he had an open invitation to their dinner table.

He'd taken her up on it time and time again when the front door at his parents' house had been locked tight, or when they'd left him to fend for himself while they had gone on various business trips.

"What can I do to help?" His body relaxed. He was damned glad Chloe wasn't like Katrina or another of his dates—who'd be going on and on about her newest shoe purchase or eying his apartment with a speculative gleam. Little did any of them know he didn't intend to marry. Ever.

He may have grown up in a household that seemed like every kid's dream home—no fighting, no chiding about childhood tantrums or, later, about broken curfews and less than stellar grades. There had been no harsh emotions at all. But beneath the surface things had not been how they'd appeared. The snick of a lock had preceded hours of unbroken silence. A silence that had been more menacing than anything he'd ever known.

The Jenkinses, on the other hand, had been open with their emotions and vocal as hell when someone had done something wrong. Ben Jenkins had chewed his butt up one side and down the other after his motorcycle accident. Threatened to take his bike to the junkyard if he ever pulled another stunt like that.

Wonder what the man would think about him taking his daughter for a ride on the back of that very same bike?

Chloe broke into his thoughts. "I think I've got it covered if you want to take a shower. Besides, this is the only apron I could find in the house." It took him a second to realize what she was talking about.

The apron had been in his house? A couple of women had cooked for him over the years, but it was normally breakfast. One of them had evidently expected to stick around.

A pang went through him. Had he hurt someone the way Chloe's ex had hurt her?

No, because he never made any promises. If anything, he cut relationships shorter for just that reason. Before that claustrophobic sensation of being trapped had time to set in. He didn't want anyone to get the wrong idea.

He took a step back, wondering what was with all his melancholy thoughts tonight. It had to be because of his patient. Something about the look on her husband's face when he'd realized his wife was still alive…was going to survive her ruptured uterus. He'd seemed to take on a glow that had transcended the sorrow of losing his unborn child. The man had taken one last look at the stained-glass cross then had closed his eyes as if sending up a quick thank-you prayer before he hurried from the room, leaving Brad alone.

He'd wandered over to one of the chairs and sat down, hands draped over the pew in front of him, realizing he'd never really visited the chapel before. But there was something peaceful about it, whether it was because of the décor or because of some spiritual presence, he didn't know. What he did know was that it had made him want to find Chloe.

Only she hadn't been there.

Instead, she was here, fixing him dinner.

He relaxed a little bit more. "I'll get changed."

"Good. I'll uncork the wine." She motioned to the

bottle on the counter. One of his better bottles from the look of it, but what the hell?

He smiled for the first time that day. "I'll be back in a few minutes, then. Don't start without me."

"Absolutely not."

Evidently ten minutes was all the man needed to look and smell heavenly, because when she turned to check the cabinets for a tureen or something to put the pasta sauce in he was propped against the door frame, watching her. She let out a little squeak before she could stop it. "How long have you been standing there?"

"About a minute and a half."

Heat rushed up her face when she realized her gaze was trailing down his chest and had landed just below his belt buckle. "I, um…was just looking for a couple of bowls for the pasta and sauce."

His lips quirked as if he realized exactly what she'd been doing. "Well, by all means, let me help."

Without saying anything else, he opened cabinet doors until he found a couple of good-sized bowls.

His scent filled her head, making her feel slightly dizzy. She shook it in an effort to clear it. "I like your china pattern. I wouldn't have thought you were much for flowers, though."

The delicate gold rimming the plates and the pink roses were definitely not what she would have thought he'd pick out for himself. When he frowned, her thoughts froze. Had some past or present lover bought him dishes?

She swallowed. Not that it was any of her business but she'd already set the table with them as she hadn't been able to find any other plates in his cupboards.

He tilted one of the bowls as if seeing it for the first time. "My mother sent them as a house-warming gift."

"That was nice."

He gave a hard laugh. "You would think so, wouldn't you? My mom always knows just the right thing to say or do. She's a master at managing and meeting expectations—and instilling that trait in others. It's all about doing what's expected of you."

CHAPTER TWELVE

DID BRAD KNOW how bitter those words sounded?

Probably not. Her heart ached for him. Her own parents were so involved in their kids' lives—sometimes too involved—that she couldn't imagine what it would be like to have parents as detached at his parents had always seemed to be.

"People can change," she said. "Maybe your mom really was trying to be nice."

"I'm sure she was." The tight-lipped response told her he didn't buy her theory.

Maybe Brad was right. Chloe knew from experience that some people never did change.

Once everything was on the table, they ate in silence. Brad complimented the food but didn't seem to be in a hurry to start any kind of conversation. The silence eventually got to her. She cleared her throat. "How's the hunt for a new nurse coming? Have you had any applicants?"

"I had several interviews today, as a matter of fact."

"That's great."

So soon? Her heart plummeted, landing somewhere around her knees. She knew he was going to look for someone else. Knew she was due back at her old job in less than a week, but it wasn't easy hearing how pain-less it would be to replace her.

Why wouldn't it be? Travis had replaced her before she'd even officially left the marriage.

Besides, the sooner Brad got her out of the hospital and out of his hair, the sooner he could go back to his old, free-wheeling lifestyle. Who knew? Katrina might even stroll back into the picture as soon as the coast was clear.

She swallowed, trying to blot out the wave of self-pity that sloshed through her stomach. Chloe Jenkins: invisible and most certainly expendable.

Getting up from the table, she picked up her plate and headed for the safety of the kitchen, thanking the dinner gods that she'd finished eating because there was no way she'd be able to force down one more bite. The cheesecake in the refrigerator was going to have to wait.

She heard the scrape of Brad's chair and tensed in front of the sink. He came in and laid his hands on her shoulders. "You okay?"

"Just fine. There's cheesecake in the fridge if you want dessert."

"I'm good." He turned her to face him. "What's wrong?"

"Nothing." She was so desperate to avoid his gaze that she threw out the first thing she could think of. "Do you want another glass of wine?"

He searched her face. "Let's take the bottle into the living room and sit for a while. You can tell me about your day."

Uh…he already knew everything about her day be-cause they worked together. She saw almost exactly the same patients as he did. But right now she was more than grateful for an excuse to slide away from him. And one more glass of wine wouldn't do her in.

Whiskey, however… Yeah, she didn't want a repeat of her first night at the apartment. She'd drink a second glass and then retreat to her room or the kitchen. She could always say she needed to do the dishes.

"I'll get the table and the dishes later on. Just leave everything where it is."

Had the man read her mind? She sure hoped not, because there were things inside her head she did *not* want him to find.

Picking up her glass as Brad retrieved the bottle of wine along with his own wineglass, they made their way to the living room. Chloe was reminded of that fateful first time she'd sat here—how horrified she'd been at what she'd been wearing beneath her coat.

That seemed like a lifetime ago. Maybe it was. What had seemed like the closing of a chapter was more like the final page of a book. The new one, full of crisp white pages, was just waiting for the right opening line. Only she had no idea what that sentence would be.

Chloe sat on the brown leather sofa, glad when he didn't choose to sit in front of her on the ottoman again. Instead, he settled in the space beside her and lifted the bottle of wine to fill her glass. She dutifully held it out and watched the clear liquid trickle until it hit the halfway point. He did the same with his own then set the bottle on a side table.

As there was no way he simply wanted to talk about her day, she wondered if he was trying to find a tactful way to get her out of his apartment. She decided to take the bull by the horns.

"Did you have any luck with the interviews?"

He leaned back against the cushions, his right arm

sliding along the top of it. She swore she felt the tip of her ponytail move in the process. "None. So I've been doing some thinking."

"You have?"

He gave a soft laugh. "As surprising as that may seem to you, I do think from time to time."

This time the bobbing of her ponytail was not her imagination. What was he doing back there?

The continued subtle tugging on her hair was beginning to give her that weird quivery feeling in her stomach again. She cleared her throat in an attempt to take her mind off it, hoping he'd start talking again. "And what have you been thinking about?"

In a casual move he propped his left ankle on his right knee and shifted his body to face her. "How attached are you to your current job?"

Oh, God. He *was* trying to get rid of her. Wanted to make sure she wasn't going to cause a scene when he found her replacement. "Don't worry, I'm not desperate for a job. I already have one, remember?"

"So you wouldn't be interested in staying at Angel's on a more permanent basis?"

"I'm not sure what you mean." She thought she'd just made it clear that she wasn't angling for the position.

"Aren't you?"

Bewildered, she shook her head.

The subtle brush of something soft across the nape of her neck made her swallow. The warmth in her stomach increased. He was trailing the tip of her ponytail across her skin, and her gaze somehow landed on his mouth before she yanked it back up to his eyes. Was he trying to drive her crazy?

"Would you stay at Angel's, if I asked you to?"

Her thoughts moved slowly, as if slogging their way through thick molasses. "You want me to stay?"

"I thought I'd made that obvious at the beginning of the conversation."

"No—I thought. I thought you were trying to tell me not to get too comfortable." She licked her lips. "Are you offering me the position?"

His mouth curved in that slow, devastating smile that wreaked havoc on her senses. "That depends. Would you say yes?"

She wanted to, heaven knew. But something about the way he said it—along with that damned sweep of hair across her neck—made alarm bells go off in her head.

"Did Jason put you up to this?"

"Jason? No, of course not." His smile faded.

She gulped. She could only think of one other possibility. "Are you doing it because you think it's expected?"

The sudden darkening of his eyes told her she'd made a serious gaffe. The prickly sensation on her nape halted. He'd just talked about his mother giving him a set of dishes because it was the expected thing to do. Equating his actions with hers was not a good thing.

"Is that what you think of me, Chloe?"

"No, of course not. I didn't mean— I know you're actually…"

"Actually what?"

"A nice person." Something else she'd said about his mother's gift. Wow, she was really hitting them out of the park this evening.

He laughed, the hand in her hair tightening, forcing her to look at him. "I'm really not, Chloe. Just ask your brother. I think he might know me better than I know myself."

The pounding in her chest couldn't be her heart, could it? Because she could barely believe he was offering her the perfect way to leave her old life behind. And although she wanted to grab it before he changed his mind, she had to be sure he really wanted her to stay.

"Why do you want me here?" She touched his hand. "And please don't tell me it's because you feel sorry for me. I—I couldn't bear it."

Swish. Her hair brushed the side of her neck this time, sliding under her chin, along her jaw. Her breath caught in her throat.

"You're good at your job. The patients and the staff all like you. And I know I can work with you." Another tug on her hair. "So please don't compare me with my mother."

"Sorry about that." She smiled. "Jason told me what you had to deal with."

His head tilted. "And what was that?"

Uh-oh. "He didn't gossip about you, Brad. He just came home so angry one day I thought he was going to explode."

"Angry at me?"

"No. At your parents." She paused. "I pulled him into the backyard and pestered him until he finally let it slip."

"Let what slip?"

"That your parents had padlocks on…" She swallowed. "That they used to lock you out of the house sometimes." The words sounded horrific when said out loud, and Chloe immediately wished she could call them back.

She wasn't about to admit what else she knew. That

a teenage Brad—as tough and cynical as the best of them—had fought back tears as he'd told Jason what he'd endured. His parents hadn't merely locked him out of the house—that had been during his later years. But when he'd been younger, his mother had routinely locked him in a closet in his bedroom whenever he'd done something she hadn't liked. Jason had seen one of the locks and asked about them.

Brad hadn't understood why his parents hadn't loved him the way Chloe and Jason's parents loved their kids. The way they loved *him*.

His motorcycle accident had happened a mere week after his confession. Chloe was pretty sure it hadn't been a coincidence. She could remember her terror when she'd seen the damage to his face, his shredded T-shirt…bleeding arm.

Brad had gone very still at her words. Well, most of him, anyway. One small muscle in his cheek was tensing and releasing in a slow, methodical movement that held her captive. Made her mouth go dry.

For a second she thought he was going to withdraw his offer and get up and leave, but he didn't. He sat there, without saying a word, until that muscle finally went still. "I don't want to talk about my parents."

"Okay." She pulled in a breath, relief going through her. She was just as desperate to change the subject as he was. "What do you want to talk about?"

Her ponytail, which had gone slack over the last couple of minutes, went taut again with a couple of quick bumps, and she realized he'd wrapped it around his hand. He used it to tip her head back an inch or two.

"I don't want to talk at all."

The pupils in his eyes grew, turning black. With anger?

Maybe. But Brad wouldn't hurt her. She knew that without a doubt. "What do you want to do, then?"

"Something your brother warned me not to."

Panic started to skitter up her spine, coming face to face with a warm, lethargic wave of need that was traveling down it. The two battled for control of her central nervous system while her vocal cords acted of their own accord. "And what is that?"

"This." Brad's pupils swam before her eyes, until they came so close she could no longer see them. Then his mouth covered hers in a searing kiss.

CHAPTER THIRTEEN

SHE EXPECTED TO feel fear. There was none.

A man was using her hair to hold her prisoner—the way Travis used to do. Was devouring her mouth like he couldn't get enough of her, and all she felt was elation.

That couldn't be right.

Neither could the way her lips were pressing closer, parting to actually invite him in of their own accord instead of clamping shut to prevent the unwanted invasions of the past.

Because this was different.

Brad may have kissed her to shut her up, but she hadn't realized until now how desperately she'd wanted to repeat that day at the park.

There was no mistaking this for flirtation, though. This kiss was all business. And she couldn't get enough of it.

A small sound exited her throat. Her eyelids slammed shut as the whirling emotions caught her up in a funnel cloud, sweeping her along some unknown path. He let go of her ponytail, his hands going to either side of her face, thumbs lining the hollows beneath her cheekbones.

His tongue took her up on her invitation and she tensed for a second as it slid past her lips, but despite the desperation she sensed in his kiss he didn't hurt her.

Didn't force his way in and cut the tender insides of her mouth with his teeth.

This was exploratory. Feeling his way. Brushing along her tongue. Licking the roof of her mouth. The backs of her teeth.

Some instinct had her tightening around him, forming a channel that guided him, squeezed him. Coaxed him to stroke her.

A low groan met her ears as he did just that.

He liked it.

Brad hadn't said a word. Hadn't given her a blow-by-blow list of instructions on what he wanted her to do. And yet—as his hand moved to cup the back of her neck and the friction of his tongue across hers set her on fire—she knew.

Her arms wound around his neck, grateful just to let herself feel for once—not have to do something someone else wanted.

Yet somehow she was. The confusion of it all tangled up inside her, but she let it. She could try to unravel it later. But right now…

Umm…

His lips left hers and trailed along her cheek, kissing each of her eyelids. She wanted him back where he'd been. Hadn't finished kissing him yet. But even as she lifted her head to find his mouth again, he stayed on track with whatever he was doing. Kissing the tip of her nose. Her chin. Nudging it up so he could slide beneath it.

Okay, so she could kiss him again later. Because what he was doing right now was…was…

Fantastic.

The heat of his mouth continued down her throat

then roamed back up the side of it until he reached her ear. And bit it gently.

A shiver went over her, the air rushing from her lungs in an audible sigh.

She wanted him everywhere at once. As soon as he left one place, she missed him. But, then, so did the next place he visited. Until she was a squirming mass of need, her whole body crying out for more.

Her nipples tightened, and instead of recoiling at the thought of his touch they were seething with anticipation.

She moved closer, frustrated at the angles that kept her from pressing fully against him.

As if he'd read her mind, he eased her down onto the wide couch until her head sank into the softness of the overstuffed arm.

Then they were body to body, one of his legs between hers, the hard ridge against her right thigh unmistakable.

She waited for the fear to finally make its way into the pit of her stomach, but his mouth was back at her ear. Whispering this time.

"You okay?"

The words took her by surprise. Made tears spring to her eyes.

Not once had Travis ever asked her that. Not even afterwards.

She nodded, her lips touching his face, then following the same path he'd taken on hers. But before she could complete the trip, he'd captured them with his own, his hand on the side of her neck, thumb stroking her throat as he kissed her.

These kisses were more familiar. The same light brushes she'd experienced at the park.

That wasn't enough this time. She wanted more. Wanted that same hard kiss he'd given her a few minutes ago. But when she tried to increase the pressure, he pulled back with a soft laugh. "Your husband was a fool."

She stiffened, coming back to herself all at once. All the reasons why this was a bad idea flooded her. But when she tried to scoot away, he held her in place. She opened her eyes and found him watching her in a way that made her squirm.

He brushed a strand of hair from her forehead. "I want you, Chloe, but I don't want you to do something you're going to regret."

Regret? The only thing she regretted was that she was going to have to tell him the truth. That *he* was the one who'd end up with a pile of regrets if this went any further, not her.

"I'm not very…" Her throat closed up, and she had to fight to get the words out. "I can't…. I don't want you to be…"

Disappointed.

He cupped her face. "I won't be. Even if it goes no further than this."

Surely that wasn't the truth. But as she continued to look at him, she saw nothing but raw sincerity reflected back at her. How could that be? He was still hard against her leg. His breathing not quite steady. Would he really be okay if she called a halt to it right here?

Something inside her said he would.

She took a deep breath. "I want it to."

His fingertips brushed her cheek. "You want it to what?"

"Go further than this."

His eyes darkened. "Are you sure?"

"If you promise not to…" How could she put it into words? She didn't honestly think he'd make fun of her afterwards, but she didn't want him to get part way into it and then realize she was so not what he was hoping for. "I want to try. But I don't know if I can."

"Chloe, look at me."

She thought she had been. But she found the center of his pupil and focused.

There was an intensity swirling inside it she hadn't noticed before.

"The second you start to feel differently, I want you to tell me, and we'll stop."

She wouldn't tell him. She never did.

His fingers tightened on her shoulder. "Promise me."

And admit she was a failure? Again? She shook her head.

To her surprise, Brad sat up, dragging a hand through his hair and swearing softly under his breath.

She caught his hand before he could get up and walk away. "Please don't go."

"I don't want to hurt you."

"You won't." Did she really believe that? That the act itself wouldn't hurt? No. But even if there was some kind of physical discomfort, she knew that he would never wound her deep down inside, where it really mattered.

"Then promise me."

"I—I… It's too embarrassing." She averted her eyes.

"You don't have to use words. If you don't like something I'm doing, hold onto me like this…" he gripped her arms "…and push. That'll be my signal to back off. It's that easy. And I'll be okay with it. I promise."

"Are you sure?"

"Have I ever broken a promise to you?"

"No."

He leaned down and kissed her lips. "Okay. Your turn. Promise me."

She waited long seconds before she got up the nerve to say it. "I promise."

At her words Brad released the tension that had been steadily building in his jaw. He wanted this woman more than he'd ever wanted anyone in his life. And he'd just promised to stop the second she gave his arms a little squeeze. He hoped to hell he actually could. It had taken almost every ounce of his strength to sit up when she'd shaken her head and refused to agree to his terms. But he'd found the willpower then, and he would find it again if it came down to it. But right now all he wanted to do was kiss that beautiful mouth all over again.

The second his lips lingered on hers, a sigh rippled through her chest as if she'd been waiting her whole life for this. The thought inflamed him, made him want to take her in a rush, but he pushed the need aside and instead savored the way she returned his kisses, reveled in the tiny sounds she made when he lifted his head to move somewhere else. How could any man in his right mind call her frigid?

Chloe was anything but.

Instead, there was an untapped innocence about her that he'd never thought he'd find sexy—until now. *Virgins need not apply* had always been his motto.

He didn't need the headaches or the complications. But this was something very different. And he found himself wanting to break all his self-made rules to have her.

Just this once.

Chloe wasn't looking for another husband. And he certainly wasn't looking for anything lasting either.

Maybe he was as untouched as Chloe was, in some ways. And that thought made him tighten all over again.

Her hands on his shoulders pulled him back to her, until they were breast to chest. He eased away just long enough to recline beside her again, then wrapped his arms around her, burying his face in her neck and breathing her scent deep into his lungs. When her head shifted slightly once or twice, he leaned back and frowned, then realized her ponytail was pressing against the cushions.

That couldn't be comfortable. "Let me get that."

He tilted her head to the side, finding the elastic and sliding the loops—one at a time—over the length of hair. His fingers pushed into the thick, glossy strands and set them free. "Better?"

"Yes." She licked her lips. "Do you want to go into the bedroom?"

He did. Wanted to see her sprawled on that huge bed for a reason other than sleep, wanted to watch as she straddled him and took him deep inside. But something made him hesitate. That refusal to promise to make him stop.

Had she done that before? Let Travis do things she didn't want to do without attempting to stop him?

He nuzzled her cheek, his decision made. "Let's stay here for a while."

He was going to make this all about Chloe. Show her that all men were not created equal. Some really did care about their partner's enjoyment. Show her how much it enhanced his own pleasure to know she was responding to his touch. To his murmured words.

He could wait. For ever, if necessary. But he had a feeling Chloe had already been kept waiting far too long.

CHAPTER FOURTEEN

IT BURNED.

His touch. His lips. His body—even through his clothes. And Chloe was slowly going up in flames.

She'd never gotten this far before without tensing, without dreading what she knew was coming next. But Brad's fingers had edged beneath the hem of her shirt with care, sliding over the bare skin of her stomach until she found herself arching toward him rather than cringing away inside. He'd spent what had seemed like hours just getting to this point. As if there were nowhere else he'd rather be.

Lips touched her. Skated over her collarbone just as his hand covered her left breast, using the barest amount of friction. She pushed into his palm, asking silently for more. He responded with an equal amount of pressure in return.

He was right. She didn't need words.

And neither did he, evidently. His actions spoke volumes.

He cared about how she felt. About what she wanted. Something about that was freeing. Made her realize that Travis had been all wrong about her. She *was* able to respond. Just not to him.

Chloe pulled in a deep breath to increase the contact,

wanting something but not sure what it was. When he kissed the corner of her mouth and stayed there while he trapped her nipple between his fingertips, a whimper erupted from her throat.

That's what she'd wanted. He'd known.

His breath released on a shaky note. "You're driving me crazy, you know."

She was driving him crazy? He didn't know the half of it. She was so far over the edge she wasn't sure she'd ever be able to make it back in one piece.

Turning her head, she captured his mouth, letting him know the feeling was mutual. He deepened the kiss, his tongue finding hers and coaxing it to follow his, until she found herself where she'd never thought she'd be. He tasted of wine and all things male, and she slid her tongue in a little bit further. He rewarded her by stroking the pad of his thumb across her imprisoned nipple.

The pleasure intensified, along with her desire to take things to the next level. She'd never craved the male and female joining the way she did now. It reminded her of the expectations she'd had when she'd been young and naïve. Before they'd been shattered by reality.

But Brad was making her hope all over again.

Even through her bra the pleasure had been intense, but the second he pushed the fabric aside and the contact was flesh against flesh, she grabbed hold of his arms, hanging on for dear life.

Brad froze, and she wasn't sure what was wrong for a second then remembered their signal. He really would stop.

The second she asked.

Instead of pushing him away, she pulled him closer, her arms going around his back, one hand brave enough to slide over the curve of his butt and press her thigh against the bulge of flesh.

"Slow, Chloe."

His words said one thing but his body said something else. She hadn't had to touch him to get him hard. In fact, it seemed to be the other way around. The more he stroked and kissed her, the more aroused he seemed to get.

And suddenly she didn't want slow.

To illustrate that point, she allowed her hand to trail around to the front of his body, her fingers tracing his length, only to have him stop her.

Heat crawled up her face as remembered humiliation curled around her throat, strangling her. She never seemed to get it right.

"What's wrong?" His whispered words just made it worse.

"I don't know what you want."

"Don't you? I want you."

The words were simple enough, but if he did, why didn't he want her to…?

"If you touch me, Chloe. I'm done for." He paused. "Just let me love you."

The pained smile told her exactly what he meant, and it had nothing to do with her being inept but the opposite. He wanted her so badly that one wrong move on her part could make him come unglued.

For the next fifteen minutes he proceeded to show her with his lips, with his tongue what she'd never realized she'd been missing out on over the years. By the time his fingers finally tunneled beneath the elastic waistband of her scrubs, and then beneath that of her panties, she was shaking with anticipation. Would he rip them off her and take her in a rush?

She wanted him to. Badly.

But he didn't. Instead, his fingers found her. She wasn't even horrified to realize she was slick. All she felt was wonder when he lazily explored every inch of her, moistening his fingers and sliding them over the most sensitive spot on her body.

The world stopped turning as the focus narrowed, zooming in over and over again until everything centered over that one point in the universe. His thumb continued to stroke over her while his middle finger slid inside her without the slightest hint of resistance.

Amazing.

That word was a blip on a radar screen that appeared for less than a second before it was joined by other, crazier words, all heading for the center. *Want. Need. Take.*

Between the rhythmic stroking, both inside and outside her body, the fire that had been growing steadily higher suddenly flared out of control.

Things melded into a single point of focus: Brad's ragged breathing at her ear, the rise and fall of her hips as she asked for—then demanded—more from him, the way he increased the tempo and pressure in response.

She strained upwards as everything came together at once. And the inferno suddenly reached for her and consumed her alive.

Some distant part of her consciousness heard his murmured "It's okay. I've got you. I've got you" as she came undone all around him.

Several seconds went by before those blue eyes focused on him again, and she drew a deep shuddery breath and let it out again. "Whew. I, uh…I'm not sure I've… Is it always like this?"

As hard as it was for him to concentrate on her words

right now, he leaned down to nuzzle the bottom of her chin and tried. "Always like what?"

"I've never done *that* with a man."

His head came back up. *That?* Since she was married he was pretty sure she'd had sex before, unless Travis was crazier than he'd thought. So that meant… "You've never had an orgasm with a man?"

Her cheeks flamed, and she shook her head.

He swore under his breath. She'd said Travis had cheated, that he'd called her frigid, but surely he'd tried to warm her up before he'd entered her. If not… Sudden anger flared in his chest. That was his signal to stop right here.

"I think you've had enough for one night." He forced a smile to take the sting out of the words, thankful they both still had their clothes on.

"No! I mean, what about you?" Her thigh brushed against his still aching flesh, causing him to grit his teeth. "You haven't…"

"No." And it looked like tonight was going to be a very long night.

"Please, Brad. I want to. I *need* to." Her throat moved. "Just to know once and for all."

He wasn't sure what she meant, but he was going to have to move away from her. Soon. "Know what?"

"If there really is something wrong with me."

He said I was frigid.

His fingers tightened their hold on her. Travis Maroni deserved to have a couple of important items lopped off.

He smoothed the hair back from her face and kissed her mouth. "There's absolutely nothing wrong with you. I think we just proved that."

"But you don't want to finish it."

If she only knew. "I *do* want to." He nudged his flesh

against her to prove his point. "I'm just not geared towards…" He had been about to say "being gentle" and then hesitated. The women he'd been with were as sexually aggressive as he was, for the most part. He'd never felt the need for anything else.

But having this conversation was doing crazy things to his body—he found himself wanting what he'd never wanted before. And it was contrary to what his body was clamoring for him to do: bury himself inside her as hard and as fast as he could, and to hell with the consequences.

She leaned up and kissed his chin, her fingers touching his face. "Then take me to bed. Please."

He was damned if he did…and damned if he didn't. Because if he refused, she'd see that as proof that Travis was right. But if he carried her off, there was no guarantee he was going to be able to hold off long enough to prove her biggest fear was baseless.

"Please."

That whispered plea was his undoing. He rose to his feet and scooped her up, pausing to place a long, hard kiss on her lips. Her response was instantaneous, her arms going around his neck, opening to let him in.

You're going to live to regret this, Davis.

Since when had that ever stopped him? Striding to his bedroom, bypassing the switch to the overhead light, he laid her down on the bed and then flicked on the bedside lamp. He sat down beside her and helped her take off her shirt and then shimmy out of her scrubs, leaving her panties and bra in place.

"You're sure?" he asked.

"Yes."

He slid his fingers into her hair and kissed her again, then stood, staring at her as he unbuttoned his shirt and shrugged out of it. Her lips were still soft and swollen from his earlier kisses, her clothing askew, hair wild and untamed as it spilled over his pillow.

His pillow. All the thoughts that had spun through his head the night of her wedding came back as if it had been only yesterday.

She blinked up at him, her gaze sliding over his chest, before moving to where his fingers were undoing the buckle to his belt.

"If you don't like something, same rules apply," he said. "I want to know."

He shoved down his pants and his briefs, then kicked them to the side, watching as she assessed him, heard the quick huff of air as she breathed.

"What?" he asked.

Her eyes came up to meet his, and he saw the first hint of panic. "You're bigger than he is."

And exactly why did he get the feeling that was a bad thing?

Obviously, not only had Travis not waited for her fulfillment before taking his own, he'd evidently hurt her as well.

He moved to the end table and took out a packet, throwing it on the bed. "It'll be okay, Chloe. Trust me."

"I do." She lay back. "Tell me what you want me to do."

He smiled and hooked his fingers beneath her panties and yanked them down her legs. "Nothing. Absolutely nothing."

When he'd said "nothing", he hadn't been kidding. Brad kept her breathless with a steady stream of kisses. His tongue mimicked the sex act, varying the rate and timing of his thrusts until she was moaning into his mouth, her hands trying to force his head even closer.

Then his warm hand slid over her belly and teased her thighs apart, one finger sliding effortlessly inside her before she had time to tense up. It moved deeper, taking up the same rhythm as his tongue.

Oh!

His palm hit the most sensitive place on her body at the exact moment his tongue and finger were at their deepest. It repeated with each and every stroke. Her body went wild with want. Climbing rapidly.

Oh, God, she was going to lose it all over again. Before he'd had a chance to…

But, no, he was moving over her body, his weight settling heavily between her legs, so she couldn't clamp them shut. This time she did tense.

"Shh." His voice was at her ear, the low rumble coming out almost pained. "Relax. I won't hurt you. Promise."

Promise.

She could still grab his arms, and he'd stop. He'd promised he would.

They wrapped around his back instead. He wouldn't hurt her.

His teeth nibbled across her jaw just as she felt him pause outside her entrance. She gulped as he dipped just inside then withdrew. Nice and easy. He repeated the action and her body seemed to draw him in a bit further, her hips rising to meet him this time.

It didn't hurt. He hadn't slammed into her like she'd expected—like she was used to. And instead of burning friction, she felt the smooth, steady glide of his body against hers.

She licked her lips and used the pressure of her hands on his back to ask for a little more. He gave it.

Further this time.

Two more strokes and he was all the way inside her, and the sensation was…

Heavenly. Stretching, full, but in a good way. Such a good way.

She lifted her hips again, and Brad matched her movement for movement. His hand slid between their bodies and found her again, coaxing her with his touch.

"Watch me, Chloe," he whispered, his teeth nipping the joint between her shoulder and her neck, wringing another moan from her throat.

Her lids parted, and she realized they'd been screwed shut since the moment he'd lain beside her on the bed. And since his lips were still against her neck, still torturing her with slow sensual love bites, her eyes were drawn to the expanse of mirrors above her head and the breath whooshed from her lungs.

What she felt, she could now see. The room was dim enough that their bodies didn't stand out in stark relief. Instead the play of light and shadow held her captive.

Brad's muscular haunches were tensing and releasing with each thrust, his elbows resting on either side of her shoulders. The double dose of sight and sensation was intoxicating. She saw everything. The teeth digging into her bottom lip, the arch of her neck as his mouth dragged inch by inch along her shoulder, punctuating each kiss with a bite.

Thrust…release. Thrust…release.

She lifted her hips faster, harder, still watching the ghostly reflections above her. Brad's fingers, which had been gently stroking the sensitized flesh between her legs, suddenly moved, trapping the nub between his thumb and forefinger, his head lifting to stare at her with an intensity that was frightening as his fingers echoed the pumping going on in other places. Her body went wild, and she bucked against him, desperation pouring over her in waves.

Hurry. Hurry. Hurry. Hurr—

Chloe screamed as it hit her.

"Yes!" The word hissed across her cheek as Brad went impossibly deep and planted himself there, the contractions inside her intensifying until she wondered if she could ever make it back from such a place.

The only coherent thought she could capture was that he had been right. It didn't hurt.

CHAPTER FIFTEEN

JASON WAS GOING to skin him alive.

Glancing at the ceiling, the evidence of all he'd done was right next to him curled in a ball, her hip pressed against his side, his arm stretched along her thigh. The tattoo on his shoulder tingled, remembering her lips trailing over it the previous night. He brought his hand up to scrub away the sensation.

A thin sheet was all that covered her nakedness, much like the coat she'd worn that first night.

That sheet hadn't been anywhere around when he'd finally carried her to his bed. It was as if he'd unleashed something wild and elemental in Chloe, her second orgasm creating an explosion that had engulfed them both within seconds.

Is it always like this? Her words had gutted him. Made him take her when he should have simply given her release and then set her free.

If Jason was out for blood, Brad knew exactly whose he should start with.

Against his will, he stroked her leg as he continued to stare at her in the overhead mirror. Soft hair, mussed and tangled from his fingers. Warm body that had welcomed him home not once but twice last night.

He swallowed as his flesh tightened all over again

at the memory of what they'd done together. Chloe had straddled him, just like in his earlier fantasies, but not at his insistence. She'd taken the lead that second time, hesitating only a second or two when he'd winced, his struggle to hang on becoming a physical effort that had rivaled anything he'd ever done.

When she'd frowned and asked him if he was okay, he had only been able to groan an affirmation at the gorgeous creature who'd become a siren of the worst sort, leading him to his doom as surely as those ancient sailors had been.

The question was, what did he do about her?

He couldn't bring himself to regret what they'd done because Chloe had needed to discover the truth about good sex. And it had been good. Too good. The temptation was there to keep taking what she offered. To drink his fill and then move on, just like he always did.

Just as he always would.

He shifted his body to the side and wrapped his arm around her, drawing her against him. For now he would just enjoy the feel of her body, the scent of her skin. And then he'd try to forget any of this had ever happened.

"Chloe, that's abuse." The concern in Layla's eyes was evident even beneath the shadowy canopy of trees in the park. "Tell me you're not going back to him."

Chloe wondered if she'd made a mistake telling her new friend about Travis, but she'd had to talk to someone. And when Layla had mentioned wanting to get out of the hospital for a while, carrying their coffee cups to Central Park had seemed like the obvious solution.

Layla motioned to the park bench, and Chloe gladly parked herself on it.

She took a careful sip of her coffee. "I'm not going back. But it's a little more complicated than that."

"More complicated than your husband humiliating you in bed, and then…cheating on you?" There was a strange hesitation in those last three words, as if Layla had had to push them out from somewhere deep inside her.

Should she tell her friend the extent of it? May as well. She'd already told her the worst part.

Because it was.

The night with Brad had been fabulous, wrenching a reaction from deep within her soul. One she'd never dreamed possible.

It made her realize Layla's words were true. Not only had Travis been all about taking everything for himself during their encounters, he'd done things during the act that had hurt her physically—nothing overt but subtle things that she now wondered if he'd done on purpose. Maybe punishing her for not doing exactly what he wanted.

Brad, on the other hand… She closed her eyes and sighed. Was she setting herself up for heartache of a different sort?

"I slept with Brad last night."

"Brad?" Layla's mouth popped open. "Brad Davis? *Our* Brad Davis?"

Okay, so hearing it put in those terms wasn't the most reassuring thing in the world.

Chloe nodded. "So technically *I've* cheated on Travis as well."

A hand covered hers. "Oh, honey. You're talking apples and oranges here. You've filed for divorce, right?"

"I've talked to a lawyer. He's drawing up the paperwork. The sooner this is over, the better."

"Good." A jogger went past, and they both waited until he was some distance away before either spoke. "Is it awkward, seeing Brad at work?"

"You have no idea."

He'd already been up and out of bed when she'd awoken this morning. Neither of them had said anything about what had happened, and Chloe had been glad. She'd wolfed down the bacon and eggs Brad had made, surprised by how hungry she was. And also by how energized her body felt. She was sore, but it was a good soreness. Brad had brought her to completion each time before giving in to his own needs. Were all men except Travis like that?

"Oh, I think I do." Layla's soft words pulled her from her thoughts. For a panicky moment she thought her friend was saying that she'd slept with Brad as well, but there'd been no hint of anything between them when he'd asked Layla to show her around the hospital.

"I don't understand?"

Layla leaned back and crossed her legs, brushing an imaginary speck of dust from her navy pants. "Alex Rodriguez."

"What about him?"

When the other woman turned toward her, her nose crinkling, Chloe got the message. "Oh. You two…"

"A long time ago." There was a long pause. "I was married to someone else at the time."

So she hadn't just pretended to know what Chloe was going through. She'd been through something similar.

"So are you and Alex still together?" Chloe had never seen the legendary neurosurgeon in person, but there was a kind of awe that hung in the air whenever his name was mentioned.

"No. After I left LA, I never thought I'd see him

again. I didn't even realize he was at Angel's until the day of my interview."

"How awful." She put her arm around Layla's shoulders and gave her a quick squeeze.

"It has been." Layla smiled. "It feels so good to be able to tell someone about it."

Chloe thought for a minute. The last thing she wanted to do was go home and face Brad after what had happened the night before. And it sounded like Layla could use some downtime as well. "Why don't we go out tonight after work? Just us girls? There's a tapas bar in the meatpacking district that's supposed to be great. We can grab a bite to eat and drown our sorrows."

As long as she stuck to frozen daiquiris, rather than straight whiskey, she should be fine.

"I'd love that. What time do you get off?"

"Six."

"Great. Do you want to meet in the lobby?"

"Sounds good."

Layla took one last sip of her coffee then crumpled her cup. "So…how was it?"

"How was what?"

Her friend's brows went up, and she gave her a pointed smile. "The sex. With Brad."

Draining her own coffee cup, Chloe climbed to her feet, her cheeks heating. "It was…amazing."

CHAPTER SIXTEEN

CHLOE CRACKED OPEN another peanut and popped it into her mouth.

The noise in the tapas bar was unbelievable, especially for a Thursday night. She and Layla had to almost yell to be heard. But it was just as well. Her own churning thoughts seemed to leach away into the chaos that surrounded them. It did feel good to get away for a while, which brought up another point. If she was going to stay in New York, she was going to need to get her own place.

That was, if Brad still wanted her to stay.

Why wouldn't he? He'd been with Katrina after all and had still expected to work with the woman afterwards. Was this any different?

No. She could be just as much of a grown-up as Brad. No more of this idealistic naivety she'd carried around with her for the last six years. Travis may not have knocked it completely out of her, but the reality of the way Brad lived his life sure had. He seemed to have everything together and was perfectly happy. No wonder he'd laughed at her for wanting to hang onto her virginity until marriage. And he was right. What had it gotten her?

No, it was time to make some changes, starting now.

Layla's hand suddenly went to her wrist and squeezed. Blinking at her, Chloe saw her friend mouth, "Oh, God."

She followed Layla's gaze, and her own eyes widened. Brad had just walked through the door with another man.

Oh, no! She'd left a note on his desk, saying she was going out to dinner with a friend. She'd assumed he'd head home, although she had no idea why.

Her head suddenly pounded. What if he was here to pick up a woman? Ugh! Maybe she could crawl beneath a table and hide.

But if Chloe was horrified, Layla looked positively stricken, her face as pale as a ghost's. Looking back at the men, she realized why.

That had to be Alex.

The men were almost the same height with wide shoulders and powerful frames, but whereas Brad's hair was an inky black, the other man's was a shade or two lighter. Female heads followed their progress as they made their way deeper into the place, and just when Chloe hoped they'd head to the bar without noticing them, Brad's eyes swept the interior and found hers.

Oh, hell.

He bumped the other man's shoulder and nodded their way.

"Please, no." Even through sounds of clinking glasses and noisy conversations Layla's quiet plea came through loud and clear. But there was nothing to do but sit there and watch the nightmare unfold.

Of course the only available table when they'd first arrived had been one with four chairs. And the place was still packed. Any hope of scrambling away or slipping out the door was long gone. Even now, the two men headed toward them.

Brad stood behind one of the empty chairs. "I got your note and assumed you were headed for O'Malley's. I guess I assumed wrong."

O'Malley's was the hospital staff's go-to place for drinks after work. Was that why Brad had come here instead? Hoping to avoid her? Her heart contracted even more as Alex nodded towards Layla and said hello. Knowing what she did now, this had to be unbearably awkward for Layla. But she displayed none of the panic from a few minutes ago. Instead, her face was as cool as her smile, and she motioned to one of the chairs. "Do you want to sit?"

Brad glanced at her, one brow lifted in challenge. She gave a quick shrug. If he wanted to sit, who was she to stop him? He drew the chair a little closer, crowding her a bit. When his elbow touched her arm as he reached for the peanut bowl, she froze, a quick shiver running through her.

The other man sat as well but, unlike Brad, he kept his distance from Layla. A waitress came over to take their order.

"I'll have a whiskey. Neat." Brad smiled at Chloe's frozen daiquiri. "I see you're going for the lighter stuff nowadays. Smart girl. Especially if you end up being our designated driver."

Was he making a reference to her behavior the last time she'd tried drinking straight whiskey?

"Drive your bike?" she said. "No thanks."

A slow smile went across his face. "But you don't mind taking a ride every once in a while."

Her face heated as Layla and Alex both turned to

look at her. The question on Layla's face was as plain as day.

She ignored it and shifted her glance to the neurosurgeon, taking in his brooding eyes, wide shoulders, long fingers drumming on the table's Formica surface. The man was freaking gorgeous. No wonder Layla had fallen hard and fast for him all those years ago.

"So how did you two wind up in the meatpacking district?" Layla asked.

"We were trying to get away from the crowds," Alex said.

Layla's brows went up, and her lips twitched. "So were we."

Instead, Brad and Alex had found the two people who were trying to avoid this very meeting. And while she and Layla were having to work to be heard, the men's voices seemed to carry with ease, seemingly unaffected by the room's noise.

"Have you ordered dinner?" Brad's arm went to the back of her chair in a strangely proprietorial move that would have made her laugh under different circumstances. But now it just made her nervous. Did he think she was going to practice her flirting skills on Alex or something? And there was no way she would, even if she were tempted. Not after what Layla had told her.

"We ordered appetizers." She licked her lips. "We can share if you'd like."

Something touched the back of her blouse and she almost jumped out of her skin before she realized it was his thumb, stroking back and forth from its perch on the chair. She stared straight ahead, afraid that if she looked at him he'd flash that lazy smile at her that turned her words to gibberish and her insides to mush.

"I might share," he said. "Or I might want more of the same. It depends on what you're having."

More of the same?

Good heavens. Was he talking about food or their time under those mirrors? This man was out of her league in so many ways.

"I'm having sh-shrimp cocktail." Yep, even without looking at him she was having trouble getting her words out.

Layla spoke up. "I'm having nachos."

"Sounds good to me." Alex's eyes fastened on Layla's and the other woman went pink. If Chloe hadn't known better, she'd think there was still something between these two.

Thankfully, once the men's drinks arrived and the extra appetizers had been ordered, Alex and Brad proceeded to talk shop, trying to see who'd had the oddest cases over the years. Some of them made everyone at the table laugh, and some were just plain bizarre. When Cade's name came up later in the conversation Brad's mouth thinned as he asked how he'd come to be in New York.

Alex paused for a moment, before shaking his head. "I'll tell you about it later."

Layla caught her eye, the pediatrician's released breath puffing out her cheeks before she mouthed, *"Can you believe this?"*

Her thoughts exactly. Chloe's laugh changed to a cough when both men stopped to look at her.

"Something funny?" Brad asked.

"Oh, um, no." She glanced at her watch. Almost eleven. "I'm probably going to need to get back to the apartment, actually. I'm wiped."

Yeah, last night had been long. Followed by a day

that had had her emotions swinging from high to low. She really was tired.

"Me too," said Layla.

Alex leaned back in his chair. "I'm going through your part of town. Can I give you a lift?"

Chloe saw the other woman's teeth come down on her lip, and she looked torn. Finally she shook her head. "No, I'm good. I'm going to catch a cab and head right to bed."

Alex's jaw tightened but he didn't argue. "Okay." He glanced at Chloe and Brad. "How about you two?"

"I've got my bike."

"Right." He tossed a couple of bills on the table and stood. "See you tomorrow?"

The words were directed at Layla, who nodded. "Tomorrow."

Giving Brad and Chloe a stiff nod, he headed out the door.

Layla's eyes followed his exit, making Chloe's heart ache for her friend. She reached over and caught her hand. "Are you sure you don't want me to go with you? I could even sleep over if you want."

Brad's mouth murmured close to her ear, "Scared?"

His words may have been lost in the din around them but she heard it loud and clear. And the answer was a great big yes.

"I'll be fine." Layla squeezed her hand. "Thanks, though. And for tonight. I had a good time."

So had Chloe, even after Brad and Alex's unexpected appearance. Or maybe it was because of it. Something she didn't want to spend too much time thinking about in case the answer wasn't one she wanted to face.

Because despite what had happened between them last night, her days of living with Brad would soon come to an end, as would his part in her life—just like it had when she'd gotten married. It wouldn't be any different just because they'd had sex. Brad had slept with lots of women and had walked away from all of them without a problem. She was just a face in a crowd.

Why, then, did the thought of becoming another discarded woman turn her soul to ice and her heart to lead?

CHAPTER SEVENTEEN

"YOU WANT ME to what?" Brad couldn't have heard her correctly.

Two days had passed since their fateful encounter. Followed by two nights of lying in bed. Alone. Knowing that the only thing separating them was a wall.

And a locked door. He hadn't forgotten about her asking for the key. He'd noted the one she'd left in the bathroom door as well.

Surely sleep deprivation had affected his eardrums, along with his mind. And hers. Because this morning she was standing in his hallway, already dressed in her work scrubs, asking if he would teach her about sex.

She shrugged, not quite meeting his eyes. "I— It's not a big deal, really. You *know* things."

The way she spoke said it *was* a big deal. At least to her.

"Things." Just having this discussion in calm rational tones seemed ludicrous somehow. Of course, Cade's smirking image chose that very moment to waltz across his thoughts, reminding him of the whole flirting incident. Exactly how far would Chloe go to learn about these so-called "things"? Or who would she ask if he refused?

Hell, what was he going to do? Jason had called him

yesterday to check on Chloe, and Brad had been short with him on the phone. It was none of his damn business what his sister did, but he didn't want the wrath of the whole Jenkins clan coming down on his head either. "It's not for ever. Just until I find my own place."

He propped his shoulder against the door frame of his bedroom. "And just what kind of knowledge would this entail? Instructional or practical?"

Are you actually thinking about doing this, Davis? You've got to be out of your damned mind.

"Is there a difference?"

He crossed over to her, toying with the idea of scaring the living daylights out of her and making her see how dumb an idea this really was.

Only she'd planted the thought in his mind, and he couldn't seem to banish it. He could have her in his bed, whenever and however he wanted. No guilt. No worrying about going through the romantic little formalities like dating.

Better yet, he could hear those sexy little whimpers she made when he stroked down her throat, kissed the shadow of her breast.

And that, my dear Chloe, is how you make a man hard without even touching him.

"There's a big difference." He planted his hands on the wall on either side of her head and stared down at her. "Instructional involves this…" He touched a finger to her temple and drew tiny circles. "Head knowledge."

He moved in closer and slid his hands behind her until they'd curved over her delectable butt, pulling her tight against him. "Practical knowledge involves doing. Repeatedly."

"Oh." Wide blue eyes blinked up at him.

"Which will it be, Chloe?"

"P-practical."

He leaned his head down until his lips grazed her cheek, drawing them across until he reached her ear. "Good answer."

Hell, so much for scaring her. He'd just sealed the deal. Well, almost. There was just one more thing.

"We need some ground rules," he whispered, the scent of her filling him with something that had to be pure lust.

"Ground rules?" She seemed dazed, tilting her head closer to his mouth. Good. That's just how he wanted her. Off balance. Willing.

He gave a soft laugh. "Surely you don't think I'm going to agree to your crazy plan without thinking this through?"

"I suppose not. If you don't want to…"

"Oh, I want to. Make no mistake about that." One hand released her butt and found her ponytail and used it to tilt her head up. "And if I didn't have to be at work in less than half an hour. I'd show you exactly how much."

"Oh."

"Yeah. 'Oh.'" He bent down and planted a hard kiss on her mouth, which quickly spun out of control. The scent of the jasmine soap she'd put in his shower filled his lungs, and he sucked it down greedily. Yes, he was crazy. Was a fool for going along with this, but what the hell? He'd done all kinds of stupid things during his life and had lived to tell the tale.

Still kissing her, he pulled her closer, letting his body's reaction speak for itself. He needed her to know exactly what this meant. He was going to have her. Tonight.

And she'd see exactly the kind of practical knowledge he had in mind.

When he came up for air and looked down at her, he relished the way her clear blue eyes had darkened, the outer ring no longer distinguishable from the lighter center. It seemed she was serious about wanting this.

And he was shocked to find that he wanted it just as much as she did. He'd toyed with the idea of extending their time together, and she'd just given him all the ammunition he needed—had made it easy. Too easy. And that set a little warning bell off in the back of his mind. But for now he would ignore it. Chloe had come to him for help. And he wasn't about to turn her away.

"Are there still going to be ground rules?" Her voice had gone all breathy and feminine and hell if it didn't make him want her that much more.

"Definitely."

"Like what?"

"You'll sleep in my bed."

"Every night? Even when we're not…"

He nipped her lips. "Even then."

Why had he just made that a condition of their arrangement? *Practicality.* When he wanted her, he could just roll over and have her.

"What else?"

"No other men between lessons."

This time she frowned. "Of course not." She leaned her head back. "Were you planning on having other women?"

His brows contracted. Did she really think he would? "No."

His fingers closed over her hips, feeling a possessiveness that startled him. No, not possessiveness. It was protectiveness. It had to be. He didn't want her to wind up with another bastard like Travis.

Right. And that's exactly what he'd tell Jason: he was sleeping with his sister to protect her.

That was sure to get him a fist to the face…maybe two.

And would Jason be wrong? Probably not.

He let her go and took a step back, dragging a hand through his hair. Time to get real. "Are you sure about this?"

Chloe blinked at him then gave him a slow smile that made his stomach flip, made him want to reach for her all over again. "More than sure. I want you to teach me everything you know."

Teach me everything you know.

Chloe rolled her eyes as she adjusted the blood-pressure cuff on her next patient. Had she really said that to him?

That wasn't what she wanted. Not really. She'd had a husband who'd tried to teach her everything he knew, and it had been the worst six years of her life.

No, what she wanted was for Brad to teach her about her own body. Teach her how it felt to be loved. Really loved. Teach her how to ask for what she wanted.

She smiled as the blood-pressure cuff deflated on their twin-to-twin transfusion patient. "One twenty over seventy. That's ideal."

Sitting on a stool, she noted the woman's weight and other vital information. "So how are the babies doing?" Cade's nimble fingers seemed to have worked a miracle.

"My obstetrician thinks both twins have stabilized but wants me to meet with the surgeon to make sure everything's progressing well."

The words *"progressing well"* struck a nerve. Her own situation with Brad seemed to have turned some kind of corner, and she wasn't sure how she felt about it any more.

Immersing herself in her work seemed to be the only thing keeping her sane at the moment. The more patients she saw, the less chance she had to think about tonight. About what was going to happen. Brad had made it clear he wanted her. The sooner, the better.

It's what she wanted as well, right? Somehow, though, she'd expected him to balk at the idea. Or at least put up some kind of token argument. Instead, he'd dragged her against him with the talk of ground rules and wanting to start immediately.

He could have any number of women who were infinitely more experienced than she was. And yet he was agreeing to sleep with her in what she'd come to see as a cold-blooded arrangement that she'd been stupid to even suggest.

So why did he seem so eager?

She wasn't that beautiful. Men didn't swoon at the sight of her. So what was he getting out of it?

Maybe he pitied her. Was trying to help out the next poor sucker who got involved with her.

That explanation didn't seem to fit either, although that could just be because she was too mortified to think it might be true.

Swiveling her attention back to her patient, she nodded at the gown on the end of the bed. "Our fashion designer is dying for you to try out her latest creation. While you're getting dressed, I'll page Dr. Coleman and let him know you're here." She squeezed the woman's shoulder. "We're all pulling for those little ones."

"Thank you. They've got a lot of family and friends praying for them too."

"I'm glad." She picked up the chart and headed for the door. "See you in a few minutes."

Chloe went to the nurses' station to call Cade. Before she could do that, he appeared in the flesh. "Clara Serrano is here." She handed him the chart.

"Everything look okay with her?"

"Her vitals are all normal. She's feeling movement from at least one of the fetuses. Dr. Morris wants to see if the size ratio has changed at all."

"Sounds good. I'll take a look." He tapped the counter with the chart. "Have you seen Dr. Davis, by any chance?"

She had. Quite well, actually. But that's not what Cade was asking. "I haven't seen him since this morning." Not since he'd dropped her off at the hospital entrance and then revved up his bike and rounded the corner on his way to the parking garage. He hadn't touched her as she'd unsnapped her helmet and shaken her hair loose, but his smoldering look had spoken volumes. She was getting some tonight.

The thought made the corners of her lips curve much higher than they should have.

Cade evidently thought so too, because his brows went up and he leaned his elbows on the desk, bringing him a little closer. "Very nice. Is that smile for me?"

"That's what I'd like to know." The low voice came from beside them, making Chloe jerk to attention and spin to face it.

Brad. And although his tone was calm and reasonable, his expression was anything but. Narrow-eyed, with lips in a tight hard line, he studied her face—from which her smile was now gone.

Cade, on the other hand, straightened. "Is it against hospital policy to comment on someone's pretty smile?"

"I'd prefer that you both do your jobs instead."

A thread of anger ran up her spine, replacing the warm anticipation of a few seconds ago. "I think we both were. If you'll excuse me, I'll go and check on one of my other patients."

She stalked toward the nearest room, having no idea which patient it belonged to. All she knew was that her irritation was out of proportion to the situation. But if Brad thought he could use their little agreement to his advantage at work, he was going to find out he was dead wrong.

A hand on her arm stopped her before she made it halfway to the door. She came to a halt, already knowing who it was but unable to bring herself to look at him. Not with the way her chin and everything inside her was trembling.

"Hey, hold up a second." He turned her round. "Sorry to step on your toes, but I don't trust the guy. Something's going on with him."

"He was just trying to be nice."

His gaze trailed over her face, stopping at her lips. "Maybe I'm afraid he'll make a move on you."

"And if he did? I'd think you'd be glad."

His palms slid down her arms, creases forming between his brows. "And why would you think that?"

"It's obvious, isn't it?" Her voice dropped to a whisper, not wanting anyone to hear what she was about to say. "Poor little Chloe needs a tutor. Who wants to be stuck with that kind of duty?"

Certainly not her ex, who'd made his exasperation plain.

The corners of Brad's eyes crinkled as he continued to look at her. "You make it sound like a death sentence."

Chloe shrugged. "You said it, not me."

There was a pause, then his fingertips stroked across her cheek. "You're a beautiful, sexy woman. Any red-blooded man would give his right arm to be in my position. Even Coleman. It's why I don't want him hanging around you."

"He's not hanging around me."

"Maybe he'd like to."

Chloe tried to decipher his meaning. "And that would bother you."

His eyes darkened, his smile fading. "Oh, yeah. It would bother me a whole lot. Because you're all mine. At least for now."

CHAPTER EIGHTEEN

THE BATHROOM DOOR wasn't locked.

As strange as she found his aversion to keys, in this instance it suited her purposes. Brad had said he was going to take a shower, and Chloe had stood there undecided. Her irritation about the scene at the hospital had faded, and anticipation had wormed its way back into her head.

Should she wait for him to get the ball rolling or try to hurry things along? Their last time together had been all about her—he'd seen to her every need. Maybe this time she could return the favor. After all, she knew the mechanics of it. And instead of waiting for Brad to ask for what he wanted—something she'd never had to worry about with Travis, because he *always* had—she could beat him to the punch.

Maybe this way she wouldn't feel like a receptacle—there to be used at someone else's convenience—like she had during her marriage.

She eased the door opened and slid inside, the dense moist fog from the shower enveloping her. The clean scent of shampoo filled her senses, and she relaxed, a smile working its way up from her chest.

Things were about to get interesting.

Pulling a towel off the rack beside the door, she

padded over to the shower on bare feet and set the towel down on a nearby stool. She paused at the curved entryway that led to the interior of the stall and tried to plan her first move. Before she had a chance to do anything, a hand reached round the corner and snagged her wrist, hauling her through jets of water—which came at her from all angles—until she smacked into a bare, muscular chest.

She screeched as the warm spray continued to pelt her hair and her scrubs, plastering them to her body.

"What are you doing?" she spluttered. "How did you even know I was out there?"

"I have my ways." He reached around her and adjusted the spray until it was less cyclonic and more mist-like.

"You do? That sounds a little scary." She laughed to cover up the fact that she was only half kidding.

"Does it?" He leaned against the tiled wall and pulled her between his splayed legs, his already stiffening flesh pressing into her belly. He seemed unfazed by the fact that she still had all her clothes on. She, on the other hand, was aware of every inch of his nakedness.

"Yes," she whispered.

"It should." His hand slid into the wet locks of her hair and held her in place as he kissed her, before going to the bottom of her shirt, hauling it over her head and dropping it onto the black marble floor next to him.

She swallowed. Here it was, the test of her mettle. It was one thing to get carried away like they had on the couch a few nights ago and let things go further than she'd meant them to. It was another thing entirely to sneak into a bathroom intent on doing unto him as he had done unto her.

Only he'd turned the tables on her. Again.

Time to turn them back her way.

She took a step backwards, forcing herself to maintain eye contact as her fingers found her bra clasp and released it, feigning nonchalance as she tossed the garment on top of her shirt. She was rewarded by the darkening of his pupils as they slid over what she'd revealed.

So far, so good.

The best part was that he wasn't directing her every move. She was free to go in whatever direction she chose.

And she chose this. Her thumbs hooked in the waistband of her scrubs and pushed them over her hips, then she stepped out of them. One corner of his mouth tilted, and when she chanced a glance down, she saw the spark of interest was holding steady. Okay, so it was more than a spark. Much, much more. The sight gave her a shot of confidence.

She could do this.

Measuring out another dose, her fingers plucked at the elastic band of her satin panties and she raised her eyebrows.

"Definitely." His voice had dropped to a low growl.

Her cheeks heated, but she slid the underwear down, his eyes following her progress. Once off, her toes curled around the garment and nudged it towards the growing stack of clothes.

Now they were both naked. Both equal.

His arms opened up. "Come here."

She moved back into the circle of his embrace and pressed her lips to his collarbone, adding a little bite like he'd done to her shoulder the last time they'd been together. A groan erupted from his chest when she moved over an inch and repeated the act, her tongue lapping over each spot. He tasted wonderful.

Brad's hands went to her shoulders, kneading and stroking, his eyes closed as she made her way down his chest, licking beads of water from a masculine nipple as she went. His breath hissed through his teeth, fingers tightening on her for an instant or two before relaxing their grip, thumbs stroking the sides of her neck.

Lord, her body was already pulsing down below, and he hadn't even touched her in any of those places yet. When he did…

She was going to go up in smoke.

Reaching his other nipple, she changed tactics, tightening her lips, her mouth tugging on it with slow, steady strokes.

"Hell, woman," he ground out, one hand moving to fist in her hair, though whether to urge her to continue or pull her away she wasn't sure…and didn't really care. Because she was already on the move. Down his abdomen, following a thin, fascinating trail of hair.

The muscles of her stomach turned inside out, clenching and releasing, a terrible excitement building deep inside her.

The moment of truth.

She went down on her knees, the water on the floor of the shower warm and wet. Just like his skin. Just like between her legs. Closing her eyes, she kissed his thigh, his arousal brushing intimately along the side of her cheek as she drew her tongue in a slow arc up to his hip.

The hand in her hair tightened fractionally, drawing her back toward the middle.

"I want your mouth," he whispered.

Chloe froze, familiar pressure crowding her chest, obstructing her throat.

She'd been planning to. And she wanted it. More than anything. She parted her lips and started to lean forward, but the past wouldn't release its grip on her airway. Her breath came in terrifying gusts, her lungs sucking down every drop of oxygen they could find. Fear began to paralyze her body, shutting down one muscle group after another.

Her lids squeezed together. "I can't." A half-sob came out. "I can't. I can't."

The second he let go of her hair, she lurched to her feet, forcing her legs to move.

Move, move, move.

She ran, her feet slipping once, before she regained her balance, her only goal: escape.

Brad caught her before she reached the door, damning himself to hell for his mistake. The second his arms wrapped around her waist, she broke into wrenching sobs that gutted him, branded him the worst kind of fiend. He'd been so caught up in the moment, in the exotic sensation of her lips brushing across his skin, that he'd forgotten she wasn't like the women he normally went after. And Chloe had paid the price.

"Shh." Still holding her, he lowered himself to the floor, ignoring the chill of the marble, until he had her cradled in his lap, her head pressed into his shoulder as she continued to cry. "It's okay. God, Chloe, I'm sorry. I never should have…" He closed his eyes, his throat working against the flow of emotions.

What had he been thinking? He'd known all along he was not the right man for this job. He'd just proved himself right.

He kissed the top of her head as her sobs slowed, tightening his grip to make sure she didn't try to run again, his hand stroking up and down her back. "Talk to me. Please."

"I wanted to…but Travis…" Her voice cracked between words.

Something from one of their earlier conversations came to mind. The whole talk of being frigid, the affairs with other women. "What did he do, Chloe?"

She shook her head, avoiding his gaze.

"Tell me." He forced his voice to remain soft, trying to coax it out of her.

"He m-made me do things."

He blinked then, as her meaning took hold, raw fury rose in his chest filling his head. "He forced you?"

Her head tilted back and watery eyes met his. "No, he didn't rape me. But he would tell me what he wanted, and then when I tried to do them…it hurt. Or…" she licked her lips "…I couldn't breathe."

Which explained exactly what had happened in the shower. What kind of bastard got his kicks from hurting someone like Chloe? "Why didn't you tell someone or leave him?"

Her shoulders rose and fell. "I was convinced it was me. And our marriage was good in most other areas." Her eyes closed. "At least, I thought it was. And I felt trapped, like there was no escape."

Trapped. Just like he'd felt when locked in that closet as a child. Just like he felt now when any relationship started to go on for too long. And like Chloe, he'd never told anyone about what had happened…until Jason had asked about the padlock hanging open on the back door of his house. Locked doors still made him edgy, even today. Would it be the same for Chloe with sex?

He looked down into her eyes. "You don't have to do anything you don't want to do. Ever. Do you understand me?"

"I wanted to. That's just it. I wanted it to be good for you. I just…couldn't."

"Me being with you makes it good, Chloe. I get pleasure out of *your* pleasure."

He watched as she digested that piece of information. When her brows puckered, and she appeared doubtful, he leaned back against the wall with a sigh, carrying her with him. "When I do something that makes you whimper, when you return my kisses—when my touch makes you fall apart. *That's* what gives me pleasure."

"Really?"

"Really."

She scrubbed the back of her arm over her eyes. "I'm sorry. For taking off like that."

He gave a soft laugh. "You scared me."

She touched his face. "Can we try again?"

Was she serious? He'd already screwed up once. Didn't trust himself not to do so again in the heat of the moment.

She reached up, her thumb brushing across his lower lip. "Please, Brad. I need to erase the bad memories and replace them with good ones."

"Are you sure?"

"Yes."

He hesitated. He'd already told himself this was the end—that he was all wrong for this kind of thing—but her heartfelt words and the fact that his body was responding to her touch in a way that was impossible to hide made him rethink his decision. If he said he didn't want to, she'd know he was lying, and the rejection might damage her more than she already was.

Helping her up, he went and switched off the shower then picked up two towels. Slinging one around his waist, he used the second one to dry Chloe off, patting every inch of her body then sliding the soft towel under and over her right breast, the nipple tightening as he did so. He repeated the act on the other side and lingered there until she leaned into the friction, her eyes fluttering closed.

His body responded instantly, and he put his mouth to her ear. "*That's* what gets my motor running." He dropped the towel to the floor and scooped her up in his arms and carried her off to bed.

Chloe rolled over, her breathing ragged, while his senses were still firing like crazy.

Brad followed her, leaning on one elbow as he stared down at her flushed cheeks, the faint sheen of perspiration on her brow. He'd allowed her to find her own way this time, although it had nearly killed him, his body straining under the pressure of keeping still. The result had been well worth it.

He might never recover, in fact.

Experienced or not, she set him off the second she touched him.

And that mouth. Lord. He'd tried to draw her away before she got too close, but she'd brushed his hands aside, insisting. The heat of it as it had closed over his flesh…

He shuddered. It was like nothing he'd ever felt in his life.

The graphic image flashed through his skull, and he swallowed hard as a part of his anatomy defied gravity and stirred back to life. So soon.

What the hell was she doing to him?

"You're a witch," he whispered, reaching to brush her hair from her forehead, needing the contact, wishing he could roll her on her back and start all over again. But he didn't want to scare her.

Not the way he was scaring himself.

He'd never minded the mirrors the former occupants had left over his bed. Until today. Seeing their entwined images reflected back at him had taken his normally icy control and shaved it down to nothing. He'd barely lasted until she'd climaxed.

Her lips curved and she caught his hand, carrying it to her chest where her heart beat strong and firm against his palm. "So it was okay?"

"More than okay. Much more."

That was another problem. The sex had been good. Really good. Which could create problems down the road. As a doctor, he was used to patients—pregnant though they might be—getting a little case of hero-worship when the team helped them right a troubled pregnancy.

Chloe had been stuck in a terrible marriage, with a man who'd selfishly used her and given nothing back. Hell, anyone would look better than what she'd had. And she'd had her first *man*-made orgasm less than a week ago. The last thing he needed was for her to become infatuated with him. Because he couldn't be locked into a relationship. He'd feel as trapped as she had with Travis—as trapped as he'd felt as a kid. Things could turn ugly really quickly if he wasn't careful.

He dropped onto his back and put his hands behind his head, not bothering to cover himself. His reflection stared back at him, his need still very much in evidence. Disgusted, he flicked his glance over a couple of inches and found Chloe's eyes on him as well. Great.

Those mirrors were being ripped down from that damned ceiling the first chance he got.

As if realizing something was wrong, Chloe's brow puckered. "You okay?"

"Peachy."

Her head twisted sideways, looking at the real him, rather than the image above them. "Brad?"

Her voice had gone from purring contentment to uncertainty.

He was damned if he did. Damned if he didn't.

Well, then, he might as well make sure he was as damned as possible.

He reached for her and hauled her on top of him. "I'm fine. Just wondering if you've had enough lessons for one night?"

As if he'd actually taught her anything. She had been the one who'd taught *him* a thing or two.

"Can you? I mean, aren't you…done?"

He slowly ground against her. "Does it feel like I'm done?"

She gave a soft laugh. "I had no idea it was even possible."

"Yeah, well, neither did I." He nuzzled the fragrant skin just below her chin. "Which is why I've decided you're a witch."

Chloe wiggled her body until she was positioned at just the right spot, then slowly took him inside her, the air hissing from his lungs as the impossible became entirely probable. And any argument he might have made vanished in a puff of smoke, leaving only him and Chloe…and the fiery need that threatened to consume him.

CHAPTER NINETEEN

THE SOUND OF a buzzer awoke her, along with Brad's muffled curse.

"What is it?" she asked, cracking her eyelids and trying to focus on the glowing numbers of the clock. Eight o'clock. On Saturday. Wow, it was hard to imagine a week had gone by since that fiasco in the shower. A week of sharing Brad's bed. If she squinted her eyes just right, she could almost pretend they were in a normal relationship.

"It's the interphone. It must be the doorman. I'll see what he wants."

Levering himself out of bed, he walked to the door, his naked butt the best kind of eye candy there was. Chloe propped herself up on her elbow to watch, all thoughts of sleep gone. A second or two out of the room, she heard a thump and then a strangled curse.

She smiled. Not quite as cheerful this morning as she'd thought he'd be. Well, she was in a happy mood today. She'd gotten word yesterday that her paperwork at the hospital had gone through. She was officially part of the Angel's team. She and Brad had gone out last night to celebrate. Then had come back to the apartment and had another celebration. A much more private one.

She felt like a child who's just gotten her first taste of chocolate and couldn't stop gobbling it up, even though she knew she was eventually going to pay for her greed. But Brad was an intensely passionate—and pretty much insatiable—lover. Which served her purposes to a T. She'd never thought she'd see soreness as a good thing. But this was a different kind of discomfort, one that served as a reminder of all the pleasure that had gone on before.

Brad appeared in the doorway. "Get dressed."

The barked order took her by surprise. "What?"

He was already rummaging in his dresser for some clean briefs and dragging them over his hips. "Your brother is on his way up."

"Jason?" Her mind went blank for an instant before she realized exactly what Brad was saying. "Oh, my God," she shrieked, leaping out of bed.

Scurrying around, trying to round up her clothes, she yanked on the nearest article she could find, her shirt. Then found her jeans.

"Chloe."

"What?" Her voice was sharp with panic as she shimmied into the garment.

His hands circled her upper arms as he looked down at her, his eyes dark. "You might want to rethink your top. Unless you want me to drag you back to bed while your brother waits in the living room."

"My…" She glanced down and realized that not only was her white T-shirt on backwards but her nipples were clearly visible through the thin fabric. A very unlady-like word exited her mouth followed by more panicked flailing as she tore apart the bedclothes in search of her errant bra.

"Looking for this?"

She cut a glance his way and found the item dangling from a lean index finger, his lips curved in amusement. Worse, he was already dressed, looking immaculately groomed except for the dark stubble lining his face.

He also looked perfectly edible.

Snatching her undergarment with a glare meant to cut him in two, she ripped her T-shirt back over her head and jabbed her arms through the bra straps. Her hands were shaking and she couldn't get the thing hooked at the back. Brad came to the rescue, snapping it, then his hands curved around to cup her breasts.

"Stop it." The man really was overwhelming some-times. How could he be so blasé?

He did as she asked, but his raised brows said he was just as cool as he seemed.

And that doorbell was going to ring at any second. She turned her shirt right side out and yanked it on.

What were they going to tell Jason?

Nothing. She was a big girl, she didn't owe him an explanation. But he and Brad were best friends. She didn't want to jeopardize that.

She dragged her hands through her hair. "How do I look?"

"You want the truth?"

Her glance went back to her chest. Nothing was sticking out that she could see. Both girls were belted in place. "Yes, I want the truth."

"You look like you spent all night in my bed."

Her eyes widened. "Oh, God. That's not good."

He put his hands on either side of her face and planted a hard kiss on her lips. "I disagree. It was very good."

"But my brother…"

"Isn't going to know what happened unless you tell

him." He skimmed a finger across her cheek. "Or unless you keep blushing every time I look at you."

She closed her eyes and sucked down a few quick breaths.

The bell at the front door went off, and she grabbed Brad's arm to keep herself upright.

"Relax," he said. "It's going to be fine."

The trip to the front door felt like she was marching to her own funeral. "No blushing. No blushing. No blushing."

Brad gave her a quick look as he put his hand on the doorknob then he pulled open the door. There stood Jason, a bouquet of daisies propped in the crook of his arm.

"Sorry for the short notice. I had some business in the city and thought I'd check and see how Chloe is doing."

Chloe was *doing just fine. Until now.*

Brad glanced her way, and her cheeks tingled, a sure sign that blood was about to be pumped into them. Time for damage control.

"I'm fine." The tingle turned to warmth, and Jason's eyes narrowed.

"Has Travis been bothering you? Because Mom and Dad warned him there would be repercussions—"

"No, he hasn't." *Let's just change this subject, shall we?* "But I am thinking about staying in the city on a permanent basis."

"What? The folks think you should come home. Stay with them for a while."

Brad spoke up for the first time, his voice smooth and sure. "The hospital has offered her a job. I think she's old enough to decide what she wants to do."

She was certainly old enough to share Brad's bed. Something she prayed Jason didn't figure out.

Her brother looked from one to the other before his gaze settled back on Chloe. "Where are you going to live?"

You mean once my lessons end and I'm declared frost-free?

"She can stay with me until she finds a place. I have a guest room."

Heat bloomed in her cheeks. That guest bed hadn't been used in a week.

Brad caught her eye, and one corner of his mouth lifted. Yep. Her face was as red as the business end of a branding iron. And her handsome host had marked her for life.

"Let me just find something to put the flowers in. Thank you for bringing them."

"You're welcome."

Taking the flowers and feeling guilty for abandoning Brad, she hurried away to the kitchen.

Jason's voice, low as it might be, followed her into the room. "I'm holding you to that promise."

What promise? He had to be talking to Brad, not her.

"I haven't forgotten."

"Good. Because she's already been hurt by one asshole. Don't make it two." Her brother gave a quick laugh that was halfway between jest and warning. "Because I'll be coming for you if you do."

Jason had underestimated his sister.

Brad was rapidly discovering just how strong Chloe was. She was a great nurse, compassionate, efficient and capable as hell. Even if he hadn't had an ulterior motive in hiring her, she'd be a great catch for any hospital. Or for any man.

Anyone except for him.

As if summoned, she came out of one of the exam rooms, a file folder in her hand. She gave him a little wave and a smile.

Was it his imagination, or was there a little bounce to her step that hadn't been there two weeks ago?

Maybe there was. But that sexy little blush was still there, as strong as ever. All she had to do was look at him and her face lit up like a set of red Christmas lights.

He was almost sure that Layla had figured something out. And maybe even Cade.

That, on the other hand, gave him no pleasure at all. He'd made a huge mistake with Katrina and had paid dearly for it. He thought he'd learned his lesson, but maybe not.

But this wasn't a real affair, right? Emotions weren't involved. Not that they'd been involved with Katrina either. At least, not on his side. Sex was sex, and nothing more.

There were times he wondered if his parents had messed him up for good. Left him with a hole where his heart should be. Deprive a kid of love for long enough, lock him away where he can't be seen or get into trouble, and maybe that organ shriveled down to a useless hunk of flesh, good for nothing except pumping blood from one place to the next.

Chloe plunked the file into a holder outside one of the rooms and made her way over to him, bumping her shoulder against his arm. "How's it going?"

The playful tone seemed to heighten his recent misgivings. His lips tightened. "Let's keep our personal and professional lives separate, shall we?"

He knew he'd hurt her the second she took a step back, her teeth nibbling on her lower lip. "Sorry. No one's around, and I just thought…" She squared her shoulders. "It won't happen again."

Jason's words came back to haunt him: *She's already been hurt by one asshole. Don't make it two.*

"Hey." He reached for her hand, only to have her take another step back.

"I have to get back to my patient, Dr. Davis." The cool tone and her use of his title drilled home the fact that he couldn't hold her to one standard while holding himself to another. In other words, hands off while at the hospital. It seemed to have worked a little too well, because her cheeks weren't pink at the moment, they were as pale as ivory. She wasn't thinking about the way they'd passed their morning before coming to work.

And he doubted he'd be passing his evening that way either.

Aware of Brad's eyes following her progress, she headed for the exam room. She knew he wanted to keep things quiet at work, so why had she gone and done something so stupid? Because it was hard for her to compartmentalize things the way Brad evidently could. He could make love to her by night and then coolly go about his day as if nothing had happened.

And really it hadn't. Not for him anyway.

Just as she touched the door, the phone at the nurses' station buzzed.

Damn. So much for a quick exit. Ignoring him and moving back to the central desk, she picked up the phone. "Prenatal, this is Chloe."

"Hey, Chloe. Guess who?"

The blood drained from her face at the sound of the voice on the other end of the line. "Travis?"

Out of the corner of her eye she saw Brad's head swivel her way. She put her head down and stared at an open chart, hoping he'd just go away. Why did the men in her life have to end up being jerks? Although somehow Brad's words had wounded her much more than Travis's ever had. Something she didn't want to dissect at the moment. "Why are you calling me?"

"Why do you think? I made a mistake. I want you to come home."

This time, rather than the show of tears he'd put on the last time he'd gotten caught, there was an almost sneering quality to his voice that made her skin crawl. As if he knew something she didn't. "You can talk to my lawyer. We're through."

Hopefully Brad had already gone off to see a patient or something.

"Not quite. Did you know your parents pulled their accounts last week?"

What did that have to do with her? "Does that surprise you? It would be kind of a conflict of interest to manage your ex's parents' investment funds, don't you think?"

"No, because we're going to kiss and make up."

She couldn't believe he'd actually said that. "That's not going to happen."

"No? I'm sure they…and your lawyer would be interested in knowing that you're now shacking up with your boss. Along with other more interesting things."

Was he threatening her? How did he even know about Brad? She glanced up to find the man in question standing in front of the desk, brows lifted in question. She shook her head and motioned for him to go away. He stayed right where he was.

"Good luck with that," she said. "If you think my parents are going to be railroaded into letting you handle their financial affairs, you're sadly mistaken."

"It might be fun to try. How's that working out, by the way? Is he tired of playing doctor with a terminal patient yet?"

Meaning her. Oh, God. And she'd thought he couldn't hurt her any more. She should have hung up the second she'd heard his voice. Why hadn't she? Because she'd wanted to make sure he didn't hurt anyone else she cared about.

Tears formed in her eyes and she averted her glance, terrified she might break down in front of Brad. He'd already witnessed one freak-out session, she didn't want to make it two. "He...he isn't playing doctor—"

Fingers prised hers from the receiver, making her realize just how hard she'd been gripping it. Putting the phone to his ear for a second or two, Brad listened before dropping it back onto the handset.

"I'll have his calls blocked."

She twined her hands together, bile rising in her throat. "He threatened to tell my parents about us."

"Let him."

She blinked back her surprise. How could he be so calm about it after he'd lectured her earlier for teasing him? It brought to mind what she'd heard her brother say the other morning. "Did you promise Jason you wouldn't sleep with me?"

"I did." He didn't bat an eye.

"Then why did you?"

"I didn't want you sleeping with someone else to get what you need."

She nodded. Her voice small, she had to ask the question that had hovered since their first time together. "Did you want me at all?"

He reached over to finger a strand of hair that had come loose from her ponytail. "I think I've already answered that question as well. Do you want me to prove it right here?"

Something in her relaxed. Travis knew exactly where to hit her, but Brad knew exactly how to calm her fears. She was almost ready to forgive him for his earlier words. "What about keeping the private and professional lives separate?"

"I shouldn't have said that, Chloe. I know you're not going to broadcast it over the hospital loudspeaker."

She thought about Travis's call. "I don't need to, evidently."

"You want to know what I think?"

Did she? Maybe he thought they should call a halt to things.

"Yes."

"He was fishing. He doesn't know anything."

He paused, his hands dropping to his sides before he continued. "That man damaged something very precious, and I'll never forgive him for that."

Chloe swallowed back a wave of emotion. This coming from Brad—a man who, as a boy, had been dealt a hand just as bad as hers. Worse really, because she'd made a conscious decision to marry Travis, whereas Brad hadn't had a say in who had raised him. "I feel the same way about your parents. I hate what they did to you."

He stiffened, his face clearing of all emotion. Before he could respond, though, Ginny came round the corner and sat at the desk. Brad nodded at the other nurse and then asked for updates on a couple of patients, casually thumbing through the files in question.

How could he flip the switch on his emotions like that?

A few seconds later he said he had a meeting to attend and walked away. As he waited for an elevator, Chloe got this weird sinking feeling in the pit of her stomach that grew as he stepped into one, the doors sliding shut and hiding him from view.

Someday they would be doing this for the very last time. Either Brad would move on or she would, and this part of their relationship would be over for ever. And as much as she hoped otherwise, she didn't think they'd ever be able to go back to being just friends.

Because she loved him. And she had for a very long time.

CHAPTER TWENTY

"I JUST GOT word that your twin-to-twin transfusion patient is in labor." Layla's concerned voice met her as she came into the lobby.

"What?" Chloe's heart sank. Two weeks had gone by since the woman's surgery and things had looked so promising.

"They're trying to stop it, but it looks like they may be too late. They're giving her steroids, just in case."

To help the babies' lungs develop. At thirty weeks, the twins could survive, but not without some major intervention. And one or both babies could have deficits to overcome, especially the donor twin.

"Where is she?"

Layla put her arm around her shoulders. "She's up in Labor and Delivery."

That meant they didn't really expect to stop labor altogether, just delay the inevitable.

"Is Cade there with her?"

"I'm sure he must have been called in, as he did the surgery."

"Thanks. I think I'll go up and see how she's doing."

Layla gave her shoulders one more squeeze then let her go. "There's a team standing by to take over if she delivers."

"Where's Brad?"

"I haven't seen him in a while."

Neither had she. They'd gone their separate ways that morning after arriving. He said he'd see her back at the apartment, hinting that she'd need to take the subway home.

They'd made love last night, but had there been something a little more reserved about him than usual?

Probably her imagination. Not in her imagination was the horrifying realization that her teenage infatuation hadn't dried up after all. It had lain dormant in her subconscious—like a seed—waiting for a drop of water to make it spring back to life.

Well, it had gotten not just a drop, not just a trickle, but a whole waterfall over the last couple of weeks and, like the beanstalk from the fairy tale, had grown to terrifying proportions.

Only it wasn't infatuation. It was love. And although she couldn't exactly pinpoint when it had started, she remembered the deep fear she'd felt when Brad had walked through the door to her family home after his motorcycle accident. Limping. Bleeding. Hopelessness in his eyes that had shocked and frightened her.

Jason's words about the locks in Brad's house had sprung to mind. About how cruel someone would have to be to do that to a young, vulnerable child. And she'd hated his parents with a fury that had never completely died.

And neither had her feelings for him, evidently. She'd felt the warning signs when she'd danced with him at the wedding…and when he'd asked her to go for a ride on his bike after he'd graduated from medical school, but she'd refused.

What if he'd suddenly realized how she felt and was

upset about it? She'd been careful to keep her emotions in check last night as he'd brought her to fulfillment, biting her lips to avoid saying or doing anything that might tip him off.

But maybe he'd seen through her act and was trying to figure out a way to let her down easily.

Well, that was impossible. If she'd thought her heart had been broken over Travis, she had no idea how it was going to survive the tidal wave of hurt now bearing down on it.

And Brad didn't have to do anything to make it happen. This time, it was all her.

Brad had cured her of one problem, only to be the cause of another. Much in the way that radiation could cure one type of cancer while causing another type to develop further down the road.

She sighed. And how was that for an insensitive comparison? Her problems were mild compared to what her twin-to-twin patient was going through right now. Better to focus her energies on praying for those babies' survival rather than rail at the fates over something inconsequential. Because, ultimately, she would survive this.

The maternity wing was a beehive of activity with groups of doctors and nurses discussing cases, while behind one of those doors lay Clara Serrano, fighting for her children's lives.

Surprisingly, she spied Brad in one of the clusters—the same one that Cade was in. She didn't think he'd be here, and the fact that he'd not even tried to find her to tell her about Clara made her insides cramp.

She'd come up to see what was going on, but hesitated, feeling very much like an outsider all of a sudden. Brad glanced up from his discussion and saw her, and motioned her over. Again she hesitated. If he'd wanted her here, he would have called her like he had the day Clara had had her surgery. Instead, her cellphone had remained silent as she'd drunk her coffee alone in the park.

Alone. Maybe that's what she was meant to be.

When she started to back toward the elevators, Brad broke away from his group and came towards her. "Were you looking for me?"

She shook her head. "I heard Clara had been admitted and came to see how she was doing." Another flare of hurt erupted. "Why didn't you call me?"

"I didn't realize you'd want me to." There was a cool edge to his voice she didn't like.

"She was one of my patients."

He glanced away for a second before looking at her again. "There was nothing you could do. I didn't want to worry you."

There was more to it than that but, other than call him a liar, what could she do?

The urge to spin away and get back into the elevator was almost overwhelming, but she forced her feet to remain where they were. Her chin went up. "I thought we'd already established that I'm a big girl. I can take care of myself."

He studied her face before nodding. "Come back over with me, then. You can get caught up on what's happening."

Chloe stood in the group and listened as various updates came from Clara's room.

"Contractions are still progressing, unfortunately. There's no going back now." The latest doctor to exit the room broke the news everyone had been dreading. "Let's get ready."

Clusters of people broke apart hurrying in various directions to do their parts in making sure mother and newborns had the best possible shot at a good outcome.

"Did the ablation procedure benefit the smaller twin at all?" she asked Brad.

"It's only been a couple of weeks so theoretically it had an effect, but it's hard to tell just how much of one at this point."

She nodded. "I have to get back to work. Will you let me know how it goes?"

"Sure."

He tweaked her ponytail as she turned to go, and when she glanced back over her shoulder, he was smiling. She sucked down a lungful of air, feeling the tension drain from her body. Maybe those weird vibes she'd been feeling had been the result of an overactive imagination. It wouldn't be the first time she'd driven herself crazy coming up with the worst possible scenario and then worrying it to death. Except in the case of her ex it had been all that and more.

She could only hope that this time she was wrong.

The next few hours passed in a whirlwind of activity for Brad. Word had gotten around the hospital about Clara Serrano's condition, and he'd been fielding all kinds of questions. He could only imagine what the phones were like in other parts of the hospital. The administrators must be buried under an avalanche. Laws prevented them giving out specifics on the patient, but because the syndrome was relatively rare, other facilities would soon be asking questions to help them deal with their own cases.

Clara still hadn't given birth, but they were expecting the babies to make an appearance at any time.

He hadn't seen Chloe again since their encounter on the floor of Labor and Delivery, but he hadn't gone out of his way to see her either. She'd acted differently last night, and although he couldn't put his finger on what it was, there'd been a sense of detachment that hadn't been there on previous nights.

Oh, she'd been just as sensual as always, but he couldn't shake the feeling that she'd been holding something back. That had bothered him. But what had stunned him even more had been his reaction to it. In his previous relationships, when one or both parties had begun to cool, he'd been fine with it. Had had no qualms about walking away. Anything was better than being locked into something with no way out.

This was different. He'd held onto Chloe just a little bit tighter, almost as if trying to pull her closer, even as he felt her emotional withdrawal. Why did he care so much? This was supposed to be a temporary arrangement. It *would* be a temporary arrangement.

He just had to convince his heart of that.

That was the tricky part. He'd been programmed from childhood that withdrawal was normal. That the more you cared about someone, the further away they would pull. And if you fought against it, tried to do something that got you noticed…the locks began clicking shut.

That was just the way it was. He'd learned his childhood lessons well and had the routine down to a science. Either he pulled back or the woman did. Either way, the result was the same. A relatively painless separation. And he remained free to move on.

Just because that wasn't how things worked in the Jenkins family it didn't mean that he should start smothering those around him or trying to hang onto something that was obviously not meant to be.

Like him and Chloe?

Exactly like that.

So why had she acted so wounded when he hadn't called her about Clara Serrano? He was just saving them both some heartache. If she wanted to fling open that door and walk away, he was going to let her—it wasn't locked. His gut churned at the thought.

Maybe it was harder for her to pull back because she'd been wired differently. Her childhood had been spent in the bosom of her family, protected and cared for. Was that why she'd been so quick to believe the rubbish Travis had dished out about a love that lasted for ever?

In his experience, it didn't. And if it did, he sure hadn't experienced it.

His gut twinged again, and he reached for a nearby bottle of antacids with a frown. All he needed right now was an ulcer.

No, all you need is Chloe.

Popping the pill into his mouth, he crunched down on it, focusing on the sounds of his jaw pulverizing the pill, hoping it would obliterate that last thought as well.

He didn't need anyone.

The phone rang again. He swallowed and glanced at his watch as he picked up. Four-thirty. He'd be officially off duty in another hour. "Davis here."

"Bradley? This is your mother."

His eyes closed. Not today.

He couldn't remember her ever calling him at work before. Personal lives and professional lives had to be kept strictly apart.

Shock roiled through him as he realized he'd used

almost those exact same words with Chloe the other day, explaining why she shouldn't tease him at work. The hurt on her face could have mirrored his own hurt each time his mother had aimed a well-manicured finger at the closet in his room.

Oh, hell, no!

"Bradley." His mother's voice was a little sharper this time.

"Yeah, I'm here."

"Aren't you going to ask me how I am?"

Was he? He should. It was social convention, and if nothing else, she followed that to a T. She expected him to follow suit. That's why he had a useless set of fancy dishes in his kitchen cabinets.

But it was easier to comply than to argue. "Of course. How are you, Mother?"

"I'm fine." Even though she'd been the one to demand he ask the question, she brushed it away just like she always did. He felt the muscles of his jaw stiffening, and he glowered at the bottle of antacids.

Before he could reach for them, she went on in her proper little voice, "Your father has received some distressing news."

His father. A nice enough man but one who'd never stood up for his son, who'd let his wife discipline him however she saw fit.

"I'm sorry to hear that. Anything serious?"

"He has pancreatic cancer."

The words slipped by him almost without him noticing...until he pulled them back and paid attention. "Dad has cancer?"

"Yes. He found out a month ago." There was a slight pause. "He wants to see you."

A month ago. His father had cancer and no one had

seen fit to call him until now. The acid levels in his stomach grew deeper, the antacid he'd just taken swept away in the onslaught. "Why?"

He was almost proud of the cool, indifferent tone of his voice, but inside a little boy cried out for a response. Wanted to know why his father hadn't loved him enough to intervene.

"He wants another opinion."

Ah, so that was it. This was no call for a sentimental reunion. His mother had a need for him, and she wasn't afraid to let her request be known. "I'm a prenatal doctor, Mom, not an oncologist."

"He still wants to see you. He has copies of all his tests and blood work."

He fought back a sigh. "I know an excellent doctor who specializes in—"

"Bradley!" His name cracked over the line. "If we had wanted another specialist we would have called one. He wants you."

Did she honestly expect him to drop everything and run to be by his father's side? He'd thought about trying to reconcile with his parents over the years, but hadn't been sure he wanted to make the effort. And as they'd drifted further and further apart, the desire to settle things between them had drifted with it.

But if his father was already a month post-diagnosis, who knew how much time he had left? If he didn't at least make the effort, could he forgive himself?

Probably not. It wasn't like they were on the other side of the world—just the other side of the state. He could be at their house in less than an hour. "I'm at work until Saturday. Will that be soon enough?"

"I'll tell him." There was no direct response to his question, so he assumed his father wasn't on his death-bed. A click on the other end confirmed that she'd hung up without saying goodbye.

Not that he'd expected it.

As he set the phone down, he stared at it, half expecting it to start jingling again. But it remained silent for once. And in the quiet of his office he tried to absorb the reality of his mother's words. His father had cancer and was asking for him.

CHAPTER TWENTY-ONE

BRAD WENT TO bed alone.

Chloe hadn't set foot in the guest room in two weeks, other than to get her clothes for the next day, so she was torn as to what she should do.

He hadn't said anything, but had come home looking drawn and sick. Before she could ask if he was all right, he'd disappeared into his room without a word and still hadn't re-emerged.

At nine o'clock she'd finally sat down and eaten a plate of leftovers for dinner, straightening the kitchen afterwards. It was now decision time. He'd said at the beginning of their arrangement that he wanted her in his bed every night, even when they weren't intimate. Did that still hold true? If not, wasn't she letting herself be used?

She drew her knees to her chest on the couch, knowing the answer to that was no. She was the one who'd asked for help, who'd practically flung herself into his arms. If he was tired of her, she had no one else to blame but herself.

And he had apologized for the incident in Labor and Delivery. Had said he didn't want her to worry. Things had seemed to be back to normal when she'd got in the elevator this afternoon.

So what had happened to change all that?

He hadn't even stopped long enough to tell her about the twins. Luckily, Layla had kept her abreast of the news as the afternoon had worn on. They'd been born, a tiny twin and an even tinier twin. But they were fighting with all their might. The next several days would give a more accurate picture of their prognosis. But at least they'd survived their birth. Each day was one step closer to health.

The door down the hallway opened, and Brad came down in sweat shorts and a T-shirt, a black and white sports bag clutched in one hand.

"Where are you going?" The question was ludicrous, but what else could she say?

"To the gym." He snatched the keys to his bike from the foyer table. "Don't wait up."

That was all very well and good, but it still didn't answer her question. Did she go to his room or not?

Not.

In his current mood she didn't think he'd be very happy to find her there on his return.

Fine. If he was okay with it, she would be too. She knew it was a lie, but maybe if she said it often enough, she'd eventually believe it.

Taking herself off to the bedroom, she shut the door a little louder than necessary, but what the hell. There was no one home to hear it. Still, it gave her a certain sense of satisfaction.

She pulled her clothes off and changed into a nightgown. She'd gotten used to sleeping in the buff, because Brad said he liked feeling her bare skin against his, but it seemed strange to sleep naked if it was just her.

Pulling back the beige striped bedspread, she crawled under the covers and grabbed the remote to the television. She idly flipped through the channels, pausing at a nature show where the image of a lion taking down a gazelle flickered across the screen. The huge feline held its prey by the throat, cutting off its air supply and suffocating the poor creature.

Chloe gulped and switched the channel, trying not to see any similarities with her current situation. An old black and white western was the only other option, but it was better than lying in bed in the dark and brooding about what was wrong with Brad. If things didn't change, though, she was moving out. The sooner the better.

Brad frowned. He'd heard voices when he'd first come through the door to the apartment and had assumed Chloe was on the phone. But the handset was in its holder. Maybe she was on her cell. He made his way back to his room, dumping the bag on the floor as he went through the door. His frown deepened. Chloe wasn't there.

Was he surprised? He'd barely spoken a word to her when he'd come home, but he hadn't been able to. If he had, she'd have started asking all kinds of questions. Questions he hadn't been ready to answer. He'd had second thoughts about going to see his father and had decided to head to the gym and work off some of his frustration. He hadn't wanted to touch Chloe in his current state of mind. But now that he was back, he wanted to pull her close and let her sweet scent lull him to sleep.

The voices continued until a scream followed by sobs came from the guest room.

Had Travis somehow gotten into the apartment?

He went to the door and tried the knob, only to find

it locked. That damn key! Why had he ever given it to her? Sweat began to form on his upper lip. "Chloe?"

No answer, but the sobbing continued unabated. The locks weren't meant to keep intruders out—or wayward children in—just to keep someone from entering a room unannounced. He put a shoulder to the door and shoved hard. The lock gave way and the door burst open, just as he'd suspected it would.

A figure on the bed moved. Sat up. The crying continued, but it wasn't coming from that direction. He pivoted and saw the television set. Still on. A woman on the screen being held at gunpoint.

"Brad? What's wrong?"

The adrenalin still pumped through his system, his heart pounding from its effects. He dragged a shaky hand through his hair, trying to calm his chaotic thoughts as he turned back round. "I heard… I thought Travis had somehow gotten in."

She reached on the nightstand for something. One click and the television went off, throwing the room into darkness. "Sorry. I must have fallen asleep with it on."

He came over and sat on the edge of the bed. "Is there a reason you're in here rather than in there?" He nodded toward the hallway leading to his room.

"Well…you didn't seem very happy when you came home. I thought it was better this way."

"It's not. Sorry for not making that clear." He smoothed her hair off her cheeks. "I got some bad news today and wasn't sure how to deal with it."

"Anything you want to talk about?"

"Maybe tomorrow." His arm went round her back and held her against him, needing the contact more than he should. "Come to bed with me."

"Are you sure?"

He nodded. "I want you next to me."

"Crawl in here with me, then." Chloe pushed the covers down her legs.

Brad stood and stripped off his street clothes, glad he'd chosen to shower at the gym. But when he got in and slid his hands down her back, they were met with some kind of flocked fabric. "Do you have to wear this?" he whispered. "I want your skin under my hands."

She sat up. "Help me, then."

He helped her shed her nightclothes and then folded her close, pulling the bedding up around them. Chloe snuggled against him and a few seconds later kissed the base of his throat, her fingers coming up to touch his face.

Although he knew she'd found the moisture there—wasn't sure exactly when his vision had blurred—she didn't ask about it or try to talk. She just wrapped her arms around him and squeezed. He squeezed back, the roller-coaster of emotions he'd experienced during the day quieting before sliding to a halt.

Chloe had somehow made everything all right. And she'd done it without uttering a single word.

They didn't need a second opinion. His father was dying.

He slid the last report back in its folder. "I don't understand."

His father reclined on the bed, and although he'd always had the body of a runner, wiry with ropy muscles, his cheeks were more angular than Brad had ever seen them. His skin was sallow, the yellow signifying liver involvement.

Brad's mother wasn't in the house: his father had sent her out to get something.

"I needed to talk to you alone. Tell you how…sorry I am. For the things that went on when you were younger. I didn't stand up to your mother when I should have." He paused and then cleared his throat. "I know if I don't say it now, I might never get another chance. I'm proud of you, Brad. You've become a fine man."

A fine man. One who didn't like locked doors and who couldn't be in a relationship for longer than a couple of months.

Brad waited for the anger to rise up and swallow him, but it wasn't there. All he felt was regret. "I appreciate you saying that."

What else was there to say?

"You'll be around for your mother after I'm gone? Despite everything that happened, I know she loves you."

Was he serious? Brad was the last person his mother had ever wanted around. He swallowed, not sure how to answer. "She'll be fine. She's a strong woman."

His father shook his head. "I know it seems that way, but we married right out of high school. She was pregnant with you at the time. She's never been alone—really alone—in her entire life. She needs to know someone will be there once I'm gone, even if she won't come out and say it herself."

Why was his father telling him all this?

Because he was the fall-back plan.

Even as the thought went through his head, he dismissed it as ridiculous. But was it? His mother and his father had always presented a united front to the world—she was the brick and he was the mortar. His mother would be lost without him, despite her garden parties and all her social acquaintances.

She'd be as lost as he had been as a child.

"She'll need you," his father repeated.

Chloe came to mind. She'd needed him too. Things hadn't worked out with Travis, and she'd come running to him. Had asked for his help when it came to flirting and the bedroom.

Had he been her fall-back plan as well?

Bile rose in his throat even as he swallowed in one hard movement, trying to make the ugly thoughts disappear.

"She doesn't want me, Dad. She never has." Brad wasn't sure if he was talking about his mother or about Chloe. But maybe it was one and the same. And this was a hell of a time to realize he loved the woman who was currently sharing his bed.

Damn her. Damn his mother.

His father reached out and grasped his hand. "It might not seem like she wants you right now, but she will."

"And you expect me to just…"

He couldn't bring himself to say the words. *And you expect me to just drop everything…to forget how she treated me—how you treated me—as a child?* Because, despite his apology, his dad didn't realize what a huge impact those things had had on him… All his dad knew was that they'd provided him with every material thing he could possibly want or need. And more. They'd given him everything.

Except love. And a childhood free of fear.

He'd had to go elsewhere to find that. And he had, in the Jenkins family. And most recently in Chloe Jenkins's arms—Chloe, who had her own issues with fear.

His whole life was one big circle of irony, which now seemed to be closing in on him as surely as that

closet from long ago. His parents hadn't wanted him.
Until now.

And Chloe hadn't wanted him either—had ignored
him from the second she'd said "I do" to Travis.

Until now.

CHAPTER TWENTY-TWO

WHEN WAS MAKING love *not* making love?

When it was sex.

Chloe lay curled on her side in a tight ball, her breathing still heavy and uneven, while Brad stared at the ceiling. She'd been lying right beside him, still caught up in the afterglow, when her eyes had happened to meet his in the mirror and had been shocked by the cold emptiness she saw there.

She'd had to roll over to block out the sight.

She might love him, but he did not return the sentiment.

God, she was such a fool.

He'd shocked her tonight by coming through the door and grabbing her off the sofa. Pressing her against the nearest wall, he'd propped his elbows on either side of her head and stared down at her for a long time. Just as suddenly he'd lowered his head and kissed her. The second they'd touched, it had been as if a bomb had gone off. He'd devoured her, using his lips, his tongue…his teeth, his body telling her in no uncertain terms that he'd wanted her. Badly. Couldn't wait to have her. She'd never seen him like that before.

She'd been thrilled. Ecstatic. Surely he felt the same way about her that she did about him.

There'd been none of the slow build-up that had always gone on between them. He'd shoved her scrubs and panties down and off and had lifted her onto his hips, burying himself inside her within seconds. Had carried her to bed like that. Still kissing. One hand under her butt, the other buried deep in her hair, holding her to him as he'd groaned into her mouth and surged inside her with each step.

Then she'd free-fallen onto the bed, with Brad still on top of her, still inside her. All around her.

She hadn't known what had been going on in his head, but whatever it was she'd been right there with him. Had been ready for him the second he'd touched her. She'd scratched and bitten and moaned out her need, her hips rising to meet each thrust. She'd tasted blood, but didn't know whose it was. His? Hers?

God!

She'd gone up in flames. Had held onto him as she'd come crashing back down to earth.

Until she'd realized he had no longer been holding her. Tension had radiated off him as he'd pulled out of her without a word, rolling onto his back. She'd frowned, glancing into the mirror above her.

And she'd seen it.

Lord, she'd almost told him she loved him, had gritted her teeth at the last second and let the words sing through her head instead. What a disaster that would have been, if she'd said them out loud.

He'd have laughed in her face.

Or worse.

She pulled in a careful breath as she lay there. Then another one, before she got up the courage to say the words. "Do you want me to leave?"

Chloe didn't know exactly what she meant by the

question. Wasn't sure if she was talking about his bedroom or about his life.

The silence was deafening. Her heart gave a few painful thumps. But when she braced herself to get up, his hand was on her hip, gripping tight. "No. Don't go."

"Are you sure?"

Brad rolled on his side and put his arm around her. "Yes." He pulled her back against him. "I'm sorry. Did I hurt you?"

She swallowed, tears burning at the back of her eyes as she realized what was wrong with him. That's why he'd looked that way. Why he'd been so stiff and unyielding. He thought their lovemaking had been too rough, that he'd hurt her like Travis had done.

"No. Couldn't you tell?"

His arm tightened. "I wasn't paying attention to anyone but…" a beat went by "…myself."

She turned her head and kissed his upper arm, where his tattoo was. "I got a little carried away too. I think I might have bitten your lip."

There was a pause as if he was testing out that admission. "I didn't even feel it."

Her cheek rubbed where her lips had kissed. "Didn't you feel anything?"

"I felt everything. Except that." His chest rose and fell in a sigh. "I don't want to hurt you, Chloe."

She stiffened. Was he still talking about the sex? "I already told you, you didn't. I'm fine."

"Are you?"

What was with the enigmatic questions? Just when she'd thought she had him figured out, he changed direction and confused her all over again.

She shifted in his arms, until she was facing him. She swept the hair off his forehead, like she'd done in the park. That day seemed like ages ago. "What's wrong, Brad?"

His throat moved. "My father has cancer."

Chloe stared at him. "My God. When did you find out?"

"A couple of days ago. I went to see him today."

And then he'd come home and taken her to bed. The desperation she'd sensed in him hadn't been because of her at all but because of the devastating news he'd gotten. It also explained the emotional withdrawal she'd sensed in him over the last couple of days.

"Is it serious?"

He nodded. "Terminal."

She grabbed his hand. "I'm so sorry. It's good that he wanted to see you, though."

"He wants me to take care of my mother."

Chloe searched his eyes, but they were devoid of emotion. "Take care of her how?"

A quick shrug. "He wants me to be there for her."

Now she understood. His father wanted him to be there for a mother who'd never been there for Brad. Not really. Her heart ached. "Will you?"

"I don't know. I'll have to give it some thought."

The coolness in his voice sent a chill over her, but she hadn't walked where Brad had walked. Hadn't been on the receiving end of abuse that drove you to despair, drove you to take chances you knew you shouldn't. She thought about Travis. Well, maybe she had walked a mile or two in his shoes.

Maybe more than that. Hadn't her experience with Travis caused her to look up an old friend and ask him to have sex with her? And then gone and stupidly fallen in love with him?

Oh, yeah. She'd taken some chances that she'd known she shouldn't. And had taken them anyway.

She pushed the thought away. It wasn't the same thing at all.

Wasn't it?

Clearing her throat, she cast around for something to say. "How long does he have?"

"Three months. Maybe four."

Sadness washed over her. She would probably be out of Brad's apartment by that time. Would he even tell her what was happening with his father?

Maybe. The lovemaking they'd just shared said he might.

And as much as she wanted to close her eyes and ignore it, a little kernel of hope was lodged firmly in her heart. Like a blood clot that preceded a heart attack?

God, she hoped not.

Maybe there was the equivalent of a clot-busting drug she could take that would get rid of the thing once and for all.

Or maybe she could just ignore whatever it was and pray she had the symptoms all wrong. That what she'd thought was love was actually just a bad case of indigestion that would soon wash through her system, never to be seen again.

Yeah. Right.

Because lying in bed with him right now, she knew there was no place she'd rather be. Now, if she could only convince Brad to give them a chance...

CHAPTER TWENTY-THREE

"Mom, how are you?"

Chloe opened the door to the apartment and gave her mother a hug. Her mother was earlier than she'd expected. Thank heavens Brad had already left for work and she was up and dressed. First Jason and now her mother. But at least her mother had called last night to make sure it was okay to drive over. No rushing around to cover up her and Brad's nocturnal activities.

"I know you said you were fine, but I wanted to come by and see for myself." She cupped her daughter's face and studied her. "You look good. Happy."

"I am. I feel like I've been given a new lease of life." She tugged her mother inside. "I have some coffee made if you want some. Can you stay? Oh, I have so much I want to tell you."

Her mom laughed. "There's a new-fangled device called the telephone, you know." Her smile faded. "I kept hoping you'd call. Jason said you were doing okay, but I was worried."

Chloe led the way into the kitchen and pulled down two tea cups. Brad's mother's china pattern. The woman he was supposed to take care of. "I'm doing better than I expected. I really like working at the hospital."

"And how's Brad?"

"Fine." She concentrated on pouring the hot liquid into the cups, hoping her cheeks weren't steaming as much as the coffee. "He wants me to stay in the city." She clarified, in case her mom got the wrong idea. "At the hospital."

"And what do you want to do?"

Chloe desperately wanted to believe in happy endings. Wanted to stay here. With Brad. And be a part of his world. But she didn't know if it was possible. He hadn't spoken about feelings per se or hinted that he wanted to deepen their relationship. "I think I need some time to figure things out."

"That makes sense." Her mom spooned some sugar into her cup and stirred. "It was good of him to let you stay."

"Yes." She poured milk into her own cup. "Let's go into the living room."

Chloe put a tray on the center ottoman and set her cup and saucer down. "How's Daddy?"

"He's helping put a new roof on the community center."

"In this heat?"

Her mom took a sip of her coffee. "You know him. Thinks he's still in his thirties."

"Yes, he does." How could one father be in the prime of his life at fifty and another father be dying? It didn't make sense. She couldn't imagine losing one of her parents…would be devastated when it happened.

But not Brad. Or maybe he'd just buried his feelings so deep no one could get to them. Not even the man himself.

Could she blame him? After the way his childhood had been?

But it wasn't just his parents he seemed to be apathetic about. He'd had dozens of women over the years, probably more. And yet none of them had made a dent in that armor he wrapped around himself. He'd never mentioned Katrina again. It was as if the woman had never existed.

As much as Brad disliked locks, that hadn't stopped him from boarding up his heart and padlocking it shut. Who knew if the right key even existed? Or if it did, if she could find it. She had no idea where to start looking.

Her mom was saying something, looking at her quizzically.

"I'm sorry, what?"

"I asked how you like the city so far."

That was an easy question. "I love it."

"I was kind of hoping you might want to come home. We miss you."

Chloe wrapped her hands around the delicate china cup, the expensive porcelain feeling brittle all of a sudden beneath her palms. "I miss you too. I just don't think I can go back right now."

"Maybe after the divorce goes through?"

"Maybe."

"Do you need me to stop by the house and pick up your clothes? Or I could ask Travis to send them."

The thought made her cringe. "No, I don't want anything that's there." Clothes and shoes were replaceable, and she'd rather not have any reminders of that time.

Her mom was silent for a moment or two. "What happened, Chloe?"

Lord, she didn't want to go through any of the sordid tale. "He hurt me."

"Physically?"

"He didn't hit me, no." She was going to leave it at that. No need to tell her family that what had started out as verbal ridicule had escalated into a form of abuse. Layla's words had convinced her it really had been. How far would he have gone if she hadn't found out about his affairs? Maybe he'd even wanted her to discover the truth just to hurt her more.

"I'm sorry, honey. Why didn't you come to your father or me?"

"I just couldn't." Maybe for the same reasons Brad had never told anyone about his own abuse.

"Chloe, look at me."

Her eyes came up and found blue eyes so like her own probing, trying to find a way to help, just like she always had. Tears pricked and she blinked to keep them at bay.

Her mom took the cup from her hands and placed it on the tray, then she pulled Chloe close and wrapped her arms around her. Chloe rested her head on her shoulder, just like she had when she'd been a little girl, and let her mom's love wash over her. "Don't let anyone do that to you again." Another pause. "Not even Brad."

She tensed. Had her mom figured out what they were doing? Had she realized the depth of Chloe's feelings for him? Maybe. She was a smart woman. "I won't, Mom. I promise."

He missed her.

The thought kept pricking at him all day long at work, like a splinter he felt constantly but couldn't find and pull out. She was off duty, spending time with her mother. He didn't like the way her absence left a hole in him, but wasn't sure how to deal with it. Ever since he'd left his father's house he'd been feeling more and more uneasy about the way things were headed. Sooner or later the whole situation would start closing in on him, just like it always did. And by delaying the inevitable, they were both going to pay the price. Soon.

He might not be the smartest guy in the world, but he knew deep down he couldn't give her what she wanted—what she deserved—any more than Travis had. Maybe he could in the bedroom but not emotionally. He might love her, but he was smart enough to know he didn't do those kinds of feelings well. Chloe, on the other hand, embraced those soul-searing emotions, maybe a little too well. It's why she'd been so damaged at Travis's hand after their marriage. She'd trusted him and he'd betrayed that trust—in more ways than one.

Wasn't she leaving herself open to more hurt by getting involved with him? He dragged a hand through his hair as the splinter inside him pushed deeper, poking at places he'd rather not examine.

He and Chloe might be able to come together for a period of time, but there was no way it could last long term. He didn't do relationships like the one Mr. and Mrs. Jenkins had. One that seemed to flourish for decades. Chloe's family had had room not only for their own children but for a lost soul who'd appeared on their doorstep beside Jason.

How did someone open their hearts like that? He had never been able to get to that point. He was really good at superficial relationships that didn't require anything more than a couple of nights a week. But every day? For the rest of his life? He didn't think he had it in him.

He suddenly understood the shaky panic that had closed in on Chloe as she'd knelt in the shower stall that day. The one that had caused her to wheel away and run. Because that's exactly what he wanted to do right now: run.

Chloe had claimed their time together would help prepare her for the future. Teach her how things worked in the bedroom. How men and women flirted and interacted in normal relationships.

Normal.

As if he could teach her anything about that. *Damn it!*

He should have left her to Coleman. No doubt the surgeon would do a hell of a lot better job than he could. Maybe he could even give her the kind of future she was looking for. Had this all been some kind of ego trip for himself? Some weird control thing…not wanting Chloe to be attracted to anyone but him?

The thought made his stomach turn over. Maybe he *was* as much of a destroyer as Travis had been.

Was it time to start backing off?

Maybe. Before things got too messy. Before Chloe got in over her head.

Like he was.

Chloe deserved the best that life could give her. And if she had to choose between him and Cade Coleman, using the eeny, meeny, miny, mo method, Brad was *not* it.

CHAPTER TWENTY-FOUR

"CLARA SERRANO'S TWINS are still hanging in there." Happiness bubbled through Chloe as she caught at Brad's hand in the empty elevator.

She'd stepped into it at the last second after she'd seen him round the corner and press the button. She hadn't seen him since that morning, and she wanted to talk to him. To see if that kernel of hope had any soil to cling to.

"I heard." He answered her statement by crossing his arms over his chest in a way that forced her to let go of his hand. He stared straight ahead.

She frowned. "Is something wrong?"

"No." His voice was calm, but even so…

Was he going back to the whole not mixing personal and professional stuff? She'd thought they'd already worked through that. "There's no one else in the elevator."

Brad nodded at the small camera mounted in the corner.

So he was worried. It wasn't like that image was broadcast to the whole hospital or anything.

They reached the ground floor, and the elevator doors opened. Brad waited for her to get out then followed her. "I'm going to be working late for the next several nights, so don't wait up."

The words sent a warning through her head that she chose to ignore. "Anything I can help with?"

"No, I just have to catch up on some things."

She blinked. Not much of an explanation. Something came to her. "Is it your father?"

"No. Just hospital business." He glanced to the left as if impatient to get away.

Chloe swallowed, trying not to see things that weren't there. Brad was not Travis. Working late did not mean the same thing it had in her marriage.

Except she and Brad weren't married. They'd never made any vows, hadn't promised to be faithful to each other for ever. Only for as long as their time together lasted. Maybe he was ready for it to be over and was hoping she could take a hint.

"I've got a meeting in a few minutes. Can you make it back to the apartment on your own?"

Her lungs burned as she tried to draw a slow, careful breath. "Yes. I'll be fine."

As he nodded and walked quickly down the nearest corridor, Chloe wondered if she really would be.

Over the next several days a troubling pattern emerged. Brad came home late at night and left before she got up in the mornings. She suspected he might even be sleeping on the sofa in his office and coming home just to shower and change clothes. She saw him in passing on the fourth floor, but he always seemed to be headed in the opposite direction.

A chill went through her, and it didn't take a brain surgeon to figure out he was avoiding her. She was back to sleeping in the guest room, and this time there was never a knock on the door. Never a hint that he wanted that to change. Thinking back to the last time they'd made love, despite the urgency she'd sensed in him, she couldn't help but wonder if he'd planned on that being their last time together. Her treatment had run its course, and he was ready to move on to the next patient.

Shuffling some papers at the nurses' station, she jumped when Ginny's voice came from her left. "You okay, honey? You're looking a little pale today."

The nurse sat in the seat next to hers. Chloe wasn't sure what to say. Talking to her about Brad was out of the question. But she was going to have to make a decision because she couldn't go on like this.

"I'm fine." Chloe closed her eyes for a second or two. "No, I'm not, actually. I need to get some fresh air. Can you cover for a few minutes?"

Ginny glanced at her watch. "You're only a half-hour away from finishing your shift. Why don't you go on home?"

"Thanks. I think I will." Impulsively, she leaned over and gave the other woman a hug. "You've been incredibly nice to me. Thank you."

"Hey, it's not like you're going away for ever. Are you working tomorrow?"

"No, it's my day off." Her mind tried not to look more deeply at Ginny's words. *It's not like you're going away for ever.*

"Go home and get some rest, then. I'll let Brad know."

As if he'd care. She should probably hunt him down and demand to know what was wrong, but deep in her heart she already knew. Asking for verification—or, worse, begging him to change his mind—would just make her seem needy and desperate. Just like she'd been when she'd gone to Travis's hotel room.

She rode the elevator to the ground floor and made her way into the heat of the afternoon. The park across the street beckoned to her and she headed for it, glancing at the bench where she'd drunk coffee several times. The air was warm and muggy but she needed to think before getting on that subway and riding home to Brad's empty apartment.

As she wandered down the nearest path, trying to figure out what was going on with her…and with Brad, her mother's words came back to her, whispering a plea that she couldn't ignore. *"Don't let anyone do that to you again. Not even Brad."*

That wasn't what forced her to a decision, though, it was her response to her mother's statement that did. "I won't. I promise."

If she stayed here one more day, she'd be breaking that promise.

Her eyes filled with tears but she stood up straighter and pulled in a long deep breath. She may have been like an ostrich for the last few days, but she'd just lifted her head and taken a good look around. She was finally ready to take the hint. And as much as she didn't want to go back to Connecticut, that's where her family was. Not here in New York.

She'd allowed one man to pummel her heart into the ground. That was not a mistake she was going to repeat with anyone else.

Not even Brad.

Sitting on a nearby bench, she rummaged around in her purse for a pen and a piece of paper. Then with a sick heart and dry eyes she began to write.

Brad dropped into his office chair and scrubbed an exhausted hand across his face. He couldn't go on like this for ever without it eventually affecting his patients. He was going to have to face the music and do the deed. He'd broken things off with women before and, though it was never fun, it was always followed by a sense of relief. Certainty that he'd done the right thing.

So why couldn't he dredge up that certainty now?

Because he'd never loved any of the other women he'd dated.

Dragging in a breath, he decided to go home early. Chloe could stay with him until she found another place to live. He had some contacts in the city…so why hadn't he used them before now?

Because deep down he didn't want her to leave. But he knew that was what was best for both of them.

Reaching for his phone, he stopped short when he spied an envelope lying in the center of his desk…addressed to him. It was a hospital billing envelope so it wouldn't ordinarily raise an alarm, except for the neat, dainty letters printed in blue ink on the front of it. A stream of foreboding slid up his spine.

He planted his hand on the offending object and dragged it towards him.

Don't open it.

Ignoring his subconscious, he turned the envelope over and started to reach for his letter opener before he saw there was no need. The flap wasn't sealed. It was loose, allowing a peek at the sheet of paper inside. Pink. Feminine.

The foreboding grew.

Katrina had left an envelope very much like this one. But all he'd felt then had been irritation that she'd left him in the lurch.

The urge to pick up his phone and get hold of his doorman was strong—he could ask him to make sure

Chloe didn't leave the building before he got home. But he didn't. Instead, he sat there for several moments, staring at that sheet of paper, the slight ticking of his black office clock keeping time with his thudding heart.

Well, hell. Sitting here wasn't going to change anything. He slid the paper from the envelope and opened it. When he'd finished reading, his hand slowly turned into a fist, crushing the paper, along with all his hopes and dreams.

She'd beaten him to the punch. He should be glad she'd let him off the hook. No hard talks. No trying to let her down easily.

But way down inside him was a deep-seated emptiness that no one would ever be able to fill again.

Because Chloe was gone.

CHAPTER TWENTY-FIVE

"I WARNED YOU not to hurt her."

Almost before Brad could register Jason's presence in his doorway, a fist connected with his jaw hard enough to send stars shooting across his field of vision.

When he could focus again, he saw his friend shaking his hand, swearing a blue streak. "Damn you, Davis. What the hell is wrong with you?"

Brad's jaw throbbed, pain coming and going in waves, but it didn't hold a candle to the agony he'd endured over the last couple of days. "Is that all you've got, Jason? Because I've beaten myself up a whole lot harder than that."

Pushing past him, his friend headed for the freezer and laid his hand across the nearest frozen item he could find. "I think I broke my damn hand."

"There are worse things to break."

Jason sent him a glare and then frowned. "You look like hell."

"Yeah? Well, a right hook'll do that to you."

"That's not what I mean and you know it."

Brad tested his jaw and winced, before walking over to his friend. "Let me take a look at that hand."

The door to the freezer slammed shut with enough

force to send a gust of cold air rushing past his cheek, but Jason obediently held out his hand.

The purpling metacarpal of the middle finger caught Brad's attention, and when he pressed near the neck of the bone, his friend hissed a breath in. "God, what the hell did you do to my hand?"

"What did *I* do to it?" He tried a smile and then stopped as pain radiated through his jaw. "You're not going to be using this for a while."

"Too bad, because I'd planned on flipping you off on my way out of town."

His friend had every reason to be angry. Brad knew he should have called a halt long before things had gone as far as they had, but old habits died hard. He set Jason's hand on the bar and grabbed a bag of frozen peas from the freezer. Peas that Chloe must have bought because his freezer had been empty before she'd arrived. Just like his heart.

"Here. Hold this on it while I get my keys and take you to the hospital."

By the time Brad came back, Jason had parked his butt on the bar stool. "I can't ride on your bike with my hand like this. Besides, we're not going anywhere until you tell me what's going on. My sister won't talk to anyone, but we all know something's wrong. Something to do with you."

She hadn't told them? Not that he'd expected her to blurt out every unpleasant detail but he'd figured she'd tell her parents he'd treated her badly and that she'd had enough. He'd never actually expected her to leave the city, though. She'd talked about not wanting to go back to Connecticut until the divorce was final. The fact that she'd gone anyway made him wonder how deeply he'd hurt her. Jason's arrival added to that worry, driving salt into an already open wound.

He wasn't about to stand here and tell his friend he'd been sleeping with his sister, although Jason had probably already figured it out. Why else would he have let fly with his fists the second he had opened the door? "I wasn't trying to hurt her. I was trying to keep her from getting hurt."

"Yeah? Well, you didn't do a very good job. She's barely eating, just stares out the window. Dad thinks it's because of Travis." Jason adjusted the impromptu icepack, swearing again. "But I know the real reason."

Brad swallowed. Yep. Jason knew. "And what's that?"

"She's in love. With you. Although I have no idea why."

Hell. God, no.

This was what he'd been hoping to avoid. Why he'd pulled away. He tried to say something but the words caught in his throat. Stuck there.

Jason frowned, his eyes narrowing as he took a closer look at Brad's face. "Oh, man. It's not just her, is it? You love her back, don't you?"

"No, I…" This was his friend. Someone he trusted. He owed it to him to play it straight. "Yes. But I don't do long-term relationships, you know that. My folks—"

"Give that garbage a rest, Davis. How long have we been friends?"

"What does that have to do with anything?"

"Just answer the question."

Brad thought back. "I don't know. Twenty years. Maybe more."

"Exactly. That's pretty 'long term,' if you ask me." His friend smirked. "How many meals have you eaten at our house? How many ugly pairs of socks has my mom knitted you for Christmas?"

A smile came to his lips. "A lot. I still have most of those socks stuffed in a drawer somewhere."

"Bingo."

Something akin to hope blossomed in his chest. Was Jason right? They'd been friends for most of their lives. Jason knew him almost as well as he knew himself.

Could he be right about Chloe?

His history with her went back just about as far. When he'd graduated from medical school, she'd been the one he'd come home to celebrate with. But that wasn't all. The look of horror on her face the day he'd wrecked his bike had changed something inside him. His chest went tight as comprehension washed through him.

She saved you. Kept you from attempting anything else.

Memory after memory swirled through his head. Chloe in her wedding dress, blushing as she'd danced with him. On the back of his bike as they'd ridden to the hospital, her arms around his waist. Lying on a blanket in the park, her lips parting as she welcomed his kiss. Her gentle touch as she'd traced the lines of his tattoo. Gasping out his name as they'd made love.

He put the pieces of the puzzle together one by one. And the realization that came with it almost brought him to his knees.

He may not have learned how to love from his folks, but he had from his friends.

From Chloe.

He looked across the bar at Jason. "You're right. I love her."

"Now you're talking"

"Let's take you to get some X-rays. Then I'm going home." When Jason's brows drew together, he clarified. "Home to Connecticut."

"Come out of there, you little bastard."

Chloe wasn't sure if she was talking to the weed in front of her or the persistent pain in her heart, but she grabbed the plant with two hands anyway and tugged. It still wouldn't budge. With her headphones blaring a country tune in her ears, she grunted and repeated the act, only to have the plant slip from her grasp, sending her right onto her backside.

She swore again. Time to pull out the big guns. Reaching behind her, she felt for her gardening shovel. If she couldn't pull the sucker out, she'd dig it up by the roots. Just like she was going to do with her wayward emotions. Her fingers closed over the handle of the shovel just as something shiny dropped onto the ground next to her hip.

She blinked, letting go of the shovel to push up the brim of her ball cap so she could see what it was.

It was a gold-colored key that looked like it came out of…

Her heart started tripping over itself as she turned and found a pair of boots standing behind her. Black leather. Attached was a familiar set of legs, narrow waist…leather motorcycle jacket.

"Brad." His name came out as a whisper of sound, the music in her ears all but forgotten. Until his lips moved and she realized she couldn't hear him.

He frowned, tilted his head and then squatted next to her, plucking one earbud from her ear and then the other. The music fell away.

Picking up the key, he reached for her hand then placed the object in her palm. She stared at it.

"I need your help opening something," he said.

She pushed air across her vocal cords, but nothing came out. She licked her lips and tried again. "Opening what?"

He rolled his fingers into a fist and pressed it against the left side of his chest.

Surely he couldn't mean...

"I don't understand. You wanted me to leave. You all but screamed it."

She noticed a dark smudge on the left side of his jaw.

"I know it seemed that way, Chloe, and I'm sorry. I had some stuff to work through."

"About your father?"

"No. About you and me." He touched the metal object in her palm. "I know I've done some stupid things and I'm not sure how to make them right. But no one else will ever hold that key. Only you. I'm asking you to use it."

She had to know for sure. No more guessing. "Use it on what?"

"Me."

Something in his voice made her take a closer look at him. "What happened to your face?"

A slow smile curved his mouth. "Would you believe that Cupid uses his fist nowadays instead of arrows?"

Cupid? Did that mean...?

As if he'd read her thoughts, he nodded. "I love you. I wasn't convinced I had what it takes to make you happy. I'm hoping I'm wrong about that."

Her fingers closed around the key. "You love me?"

"Yes."

One word. So very simple. And yet she heard Brad's heart and soul in it.

"I love you too."

His hand slid to the back of her neck and drew her toward him, resting his forehead against hers. "God. I didn't dare hope…"

She put her knees on the ground and twined her arms around his neck. "Neither did I." She breathed in the musky scent of rich leather and all things Brad.

He leaned down and kissed her, the lightest touch, just like he'd done at the park. It didn't stay that way for long, though. Soon it had grown and bloomed into something that couldn't be contained.

When it ended, she was gasping for breath and wanting him to do it all over again. Instead, he stood up and held out his hand. "I asked you to take a victory lap with me once upon a time, and you refused. I'm hoping this time you'll say yes."

"Yes," she breathed. Glancing at the curb, where his motorcycle stood waiting—*her* helmet resting on the seat—she started to stand up and then paused and held out the key to him. "Could you hold this for a second? I need to do one last thing."

Turning back to the weed that she'd struggled to pull out, she wrapped her gloved hands around it one last time and pulled with all her might. She felt the root shift and then break free from whatever had been holding it back. Then it was gone. Just like the junk in both of their lives.

She tossed it to the ground then stood with a smile and took the key from him. "I'm ready for that victory lap now, and I'm hoping it will carry us all the way home."

EPILOGUE

"Surprise!"

The lights came on as soon as Chloe and Brad entered the house. He smiled, glancing at Chloe to see how she'd react. The whole Jenkins clan was gathered behind the long farm-style table he'd eaten many a meal at as a troubled teenager. Ben and Jan were smiling, arms around each other's waists. Jason—sans arm brace after six weeks—wiggled his middle finger to show it was all healed and ready for business.

A shaft of pride went through Brad's chest. This family had opened its arms to him long ago. He now knew they'd be open whenever he needed them.

"What is this?" Chloe asked, glancing up at him.

"I kind of spilled the beans about what I was going to do tonight. I'd have been in big trouble if you'd said no."

She looked at the glittering diamond he'd placed on her third finger. He'd forced himself to wait until her divorce was almost final before asking her to start a whole new life.

With him.

She wrapped her arms around him and held him tight. "No chance of my saying no."

Chloe's mother came over and kissed her daughter's cheek, whispering something that made her smile.

Jan then stood on tiptoe and kissed his cheek as well. "Chloe's a very lucky woman."

"I'm the lucky one, Mrs. Jenkins."

Chloe burrowed closer with a sigh. He could hardly believe this smart, passionate woman had agreed to be his wife.

Ben clapped him on the back and held out his hand. "Welcome home, son."

A mist rose in front of Brad's eyes, and he blinked a time or two before shaking the elder Jenkins's hand. "I appreciate that, sir."

Brad's real father was still holding his own, his illness seeming to be the wake-up call he'd needed to continue working on his relationship with his son. There was still a way to go. His mother was another story, but Chloe's sweet spirit was making inroads there as well, surprisingly.

"Come on, people. This is supposed to be an engagement party." Jason plucked a strawberry from a platter of sliced fruit and dipped it into a fluffy white concoction. "Besides, you guys are over an hour late and I'm starving. Dad has ribs outside on the grill." He popped the fruit in his mouth and then picked up another piece.

Chloe's cheeks turned a delicious shade of pink, and Brad knew she was thinking about exactly why they'd been late. She mouthed, *"I love you."*

He slung an arm around her shoulders and pulled her close, catching sight of the gold key she wore on a slender chain around her neck—the same one he'd placed in her palm all those weeks ago. He picked it up and fingered it, his eyes meeting hers as a silent promise passed between them. A reminder that love was strong enough to unlock any door, as long as they did it together.

* * * * *

NYC ANGELS: TEMPTING NURSE SCARLET

WENDY S. MARCUS

This book is dedicated to men and women around the world who have found room in their hearts to love and nurture someone else's child, and in the process, make them their own – like my parents did.

With special thanks: To my wonderfully supportive editor, Flo Nicoll. I don't know how I'd make it from the beginning to The End without your guidance and encouragement. You are an absolute gem!

And to my loving family for making me food, for making me laugh, and for making me proud. And in case you're wondering, yes, my husband does read my books!

CHAPTER ONE

SCARLET MILLER, head nurse of the NICU—Neonatal Intensive Care Unit—at Angel Mendez Children's Hospital, lovingly referred to as Angel's by the staff, walked onto the brand new, now fully functioning unit she'd played a key role in designing and creating, feeling more at home than she did anywhere else. Feeling proud of all she and her wonderful colleagues had accomplished, during her four years as a manager—national recognition for providing the highest level of care available for sick and premature newborns with one of the lowest mortality rates in the U.S. A high tech yet caring, state of the art yet warm and welcoming sixty-two bed unit that the residents of New York City and its surrounding areas kept at or near full capacity on a regular basis.

"Looks like someone finally had herself a hot weekend," Linda, one of her older nurses said, walking up beside her. At least she wasn't complaining about the switch from the open floor plan of their old setup to the mostly private rooms of their new wing.

"If by someone you're referring to me." Scarlet stopped at the nurses' station, took the pink message slips held up by one of the unit secretaries and gave the young woman a smile of thanks before turning back to

Linda. "And if by hot you're referring to my oppressive, sweat-drenched, Saturday night of misery, the hottest eleventh day of May ever recorded in Weehawken, New Jersey, during which I spent more than sixteen hours without power ergo without air conditioning, then yes. I did indeed have a hot weekend."

"Uh oh." Linda glanced toward a huge vase filled with at least two dozen long-stemmed red roses and accenting ferns perched on the counter to their left.

"Uh oh what?" Scarlet asked.

"I told you we shouldn't do it," Ashley, the young secretary said, shaking her head.

Scarlet looked at her. "Do what?"

Cindy, one of her newest nurses, who'd been observing patient monitors and video feeds as part of her orientation, looked up over the counter and pointed to a rectangular golden box of chocolates, the cover askew.

"Would someone please tell me what's going on?" Scarlet didn't have time to play around, she needed to get back to work after a morning of meetings and greet the family of their newest micro-preemie, baby girl Gupta, born at twenty-six weeks, one pound, thirteen ounces, thirteen inches long, who'd arrived during her absence.

"We thought they were yours," Cindy said.

"What—?"

"The flowers. And the chocolates," she clarified.

"Why…" would they think someone had sent her red roses, the floral symbol of love and passion, typically given by men to their wives, girlfriends, and lovers, when she practically lived at the hospital, and hadn't had a man in her life since… Hmmm. Since…

She gave up rather than belabor the pitiful fact it'd been so long she'd require a quick browse of her calendar, from last year, or Lord help her, maybe the year before, to spark her memory. Not that she'd humiliate herself by actually looking. But in her defense, no woman could have achieved the level of success she'd managed—which benefited the hospital, its tiniest patients and their families as much as it did her—without putting in long hours on the job.

"Because the card that accompanied them is made out to you." Linda pointed to the mini mint green envelope sticking out of the beautiful, fragrant, partially opened blooms which did in fact have her name on it. Spelled with one t unlike the famous Scarlett she'd been named after—only her mother hadn't taken the time to get the spelling right.

Scarlet plucked the card from its plastic holder and opened it.

Dear Scarlet,
I realize you never told me your last name. I hope
these get to you. Saturday night was better than
I'd ever imagined a night with a woman could be.

Right there Scarlet knew the card wasn't meant for her. But she read on…not to snoop, mind you, but to search out any identifying information on the intended recipient.

Let's do it again soon.
Good luck at your new job.
Call me,
Brandon

Beneath his name he'd listed his home telephone number, his work number, cell number, and e-mail address. Scarlet's namesake must be pretty darn good in the sack. "Call down to Human Resources," she told Ashley. "Ask if there's a new hire named Scarlet and where she works."

While Ashley did as instructed, Cindy grabbed the card from Scarlet's hand and read it. "Yowza." She used the card to fan herself then handed it to Linda.

"Mercy me," Linda said. "You girls today." She shook her head in disapproval.

Ashley put down the phone and looked up apologetically. "A Scarlett, with two 't's, Ryan began work as a unit secretary in the pediatric ER today."

"And you all," Scarlet pointed to each of the chocolate eating culprits while squinting her eyes in playful accusation, "ate the poor girl's hard-earned chocolates."

"We had help," Linda said. "It's an unwritten rule that chocolates at a nursing station are fair game. Dig in or don't complain when you miss out. No invitation needed."

"Nursing is a stressful occupation," Cindy added. "Nurses need chocolate to help us cope and keep us happy so we can be at our caring and competent best." She snapped her fingers. "If you give me a few minutes I bet I can find a research study to support that."

Scarlet smiled. "What's the damage?" She lifted the lid. One lone milk chocolate remained in the upper right corner surrounded by approximately thirty empty little square partitions. And it'd been squeezed to reveal its dark pink center.

"I told them to save you one," Ashley said.

"We think it's raspberry," Cindy added.

"You like raspberry," Linda chimed in.

Since it wasn't in good enough shape to offer up as an 'at least I managed to save you one' peace offering,

Scarlet popped the partially mutilated chocolate into her mouth. Yup. Raspberry. Surrounded by creamy, rich, delicious chocolate. She held off swallowing to draw out the experience. Then fought the urge to inhale and let her eyes drift closed to savor the pleasure. Pathetic. "Back to work. All of you," she said with a few shoos of her hands.

"What are you going to do about the chocolates?" Ashley asked.

You. Not we. Because Scarlet always stood up for her staff. No matter what. She replaced the cover and flung the box into the garbage can. "What chocolates?" she asked with an innocent smile.

Her staff smiled back.

"What about the flowers?" Ashley asked.

Scarlet carefully placed the card back in the envelope, tucked in the flap, and inserted it back into its plastic pronged holder. "I'll bring them down to the ER after I check in on little Miss Gupta."

As far as bad days went—and Dr. Lewis Jackson, head of the Pediatric Emergency Room at Angel's, had experienced some pretty hellacious ones over the past nine months, since finding out he was the father and new primary caregiver to his demon of a now thirteen-year-old daughter—today was shaping up to be one of the worst. Two nurses out sick. A new unit secretary, who, while nice to look at, had clearly overstated her abilities, and Jessie, taken into police custody for shoplifting at a drug store and truancy.

The one bright spot in his afternoon, whether because of his scrubs and hospital ID, or Angel's excellent reputation, or Jessie's difficult past year, the police officer in charge had convinced the store manager to let her off with a warning.

Lewis stood on the curb outside the police station and raised his arm up high to hail a cab. "This is by far the stupidest and most inconsiderate stunt you've pulled since you've gotten here." And that was saying something. A yellow minivan taxi pulled to a stop. Lewis slid open the rear door, grabbed Jessie by her arms and pushed her in ahead of him.

"Angel Mendez Children's Hospital," he told the driver then closed the door. "Pediatric Emergency Room entrance. And if you can get us there in under fifteen minutes I'll give you an extra twenty."

At the added incentive, the driver swerved back into traffic, cutting off another taxi. And a bus. And almost taking out a bike-riding delivery man. Horns honked. Drivers yelled out their open windows. Middle fingers flew. A typical taxi ride in New York City.

Lewis turned his attention back to Jessie. "What were you thinking?" Leaving school. Wandering the streets of Manhattan. Unaccompanied. Unsupervised. Unprotected. At the thought of all the terrible things that could have happened to her fear knotted his gut.

Per usual Jessie didn't look at him. She just sat there in her baggy black clothes, mad at the world, and ignored him. But this time when she reached into her pocket for the beloved ear buds she used to effectively drown him out with vile music, which would likely be responsible for permanent damage to her eardrums, he yanked the white cords from her hands. "I'm talking to you, young lady. And this time you are going to listen."

She glared at him in response.

"Your behavior is unacceptable, and I have had enough. I'm sorry your mother passed away. I'm sorry

she never told me about you." And even sorrier she'd
spent so much of her time bad-mouthing him to the
point Jessie had hated him at first sight without ever
giving him a chance. "I'm sorry your life was uprooted
from Maryland to the heart of New York City. I'm sorry
I work such long hours. But I'm all you have. And I'm
trying."

He'd given up his privacy, his freedom, and a very
active and satisfying sex life to spend quality time with
and be a good role model for his daughter. He'd hired
nannies to watch her after school when he had to work,
while she'd achieved new heights of belligerent teenage
obnoxiousness to the point none stayed longer than a
month. He'd hired a car service to take her to and from
school on days he couldn't, while she didn't show up to
meet them at the designated times and locations, leaving them to wait, and charge him for every minute. He
brought home pizza, thinking all kids loved pizza. Jessie
wanted Chinese food. He brought home Chinese food,
she wanted Italian. He'd gotten her a fancy cellphone
so they could keep in touch while he was working. To
date, she hadn't responded to one of his calls or text
messages. And the only time she'd used it to contact
him was today, to ask him to come down to the police
station.

He was trying, dammit. Was it too much to expect
her to try, too?

"You left me at that police station for two hours."
Her words oozed accusation and anger.

"Because I was at work when you pulled your little
caper, and I don't have the type of job where I can run
out at a moment's notice. I have a responsibility to my
patients. I had to call in another doctor, on his day off,

pay him overtime, and wait for him to come in and cover for me before I could leave."

Jessie crossed her arms over her chest and said, "I hate you."

No surprise there. "Well I've got news for you." Lewis crossed his arms over his chest, just like his stubborn, moody daughter, and glared right back at her. "Right now I hate you, too."

The second the words left his mouth he hated himself more. Lewis Jackson, the over-achiever who never failed at anything was failing at single parenthood. Even worse, he was failing his troubled young daughter.

The taxi screeched to a halt at their destination with one minute to spare. Jessie was out of the cab and heading to the electric doors before Lewis had even paid. After practically throwing the fare, plus tip and a crisp twenty dollar bill, at the driver, he slid out and ran to catch up. "Jessie. Wait."

She didn't.

He ran into the ER. "Don't you dare—"

Jessie broke into a run, heading toward the back hallway.

Lewis took off after her. Not again. He rounded the corner in time to see the door to the unisex disabled bathroom slam shut. He reached it just in time to hear the lock click into place. Again. He banged on the door. "Dammit, Jessie, get out here." So he could apologize. So he could try to make her understand. So he could drag her into his office and barricade her inside so, for the next few hours at least, he'd know she was safe.

He paced. Flexed and extended his fingers. Felt wound too tight. And realized maybe it was best she didn't come out. Because she had him vacillating between wanting to hit her and wanting to hug her, between yelling at her and throwing himself to the ground at her feet and begging her for mercy, between letting her continue to stay with him and researching strict European boarding schools that allow only supervised visitation—once a year.

Never in his adult life had he felt this indecisive and ineffective and totally, overwhelmingly, embarrassingly inept.

"Jessie," he said through the door, trying the knob just in case. Locked. "Please come out." He used his calm voice. "I need to get back to work." And he didn't want to leave her when she was so upset.

When *he* was so upset.

She didn't respond which didn't come as a surprise since she hadn't responded to any of the other dozen/thirty/hundred times he'd called to her through a locked door. He pictured her smiling on the other side deriving some perverse sense of satisfaction from him standing in the hallway, frustrated, enraged, and in danger of losing what little control he had left.

Well enough of that.

"Fine." He stormed back to the nurses' station. "Call Maintenance," he snapped at the new unit secretary who seemed to be paying more attention to a huge glass vase filled with roses than doing her job.

He waited for her to return to her phone where she belonged.

"Tell them I need the door to the bathroom in the rear corridor opened again. And this time I want them to bring me a copy of the key."

As soon as she confirmed someone would be up in a few minutes, he hurried back to the bathroom, hoping Jessie hadn't taken the opportunity of his absence to escape and disappear until it was time to go home.

After the initial shock of finding out he was the father of a pre-teen girl, Lewis had actually gotten kind of excited at the prospect of sharing the city he loved with his daughter, taking her on bike rides in Central Park and to museums and shows, the ballet and opera, of immersing her in culture and introducing her to new experiences, teaching and nurturing her, and guiding her into adulthood.

At least until he'd met her.

Lewis rounded the corner and stopped short at the sight of Jessie standing in the hallway, facing away from him, talking to a brown-haired female hospital employee he didn't recognize. But she wore light blue hospital scrubs covered by a short white lab coat typically worn by staff in management or supervisory positions.

"Now he won't make me go to stupid Lake George," Jessie said. "I'm too bad. His parents won't be able to handle me."

Rage like he'd never before experienced forced him forward. "That's why you broke the law?" he bellowed as he stormed toward Jessie. "That's why you risked getting arrested and going in front of a judge and having to do hours of community service or some other punishment? To get out of a fun Memorial Day weekend trip with your grandparents and cousins? Of all the stupid—"

Jessie crossed her arms, locked her left leg, and jutted out her left hip, taking on her defiant pose. "I told you I don't want to go."

"Well I've got news for you, young lady. My mind is made up and my decision is final. You *are* going to Lake George." In eleven days. Because Lewis needed a break and sex and a few days to re-visit his old, relaxed, likable self, to clear his head and come up with a new approach to handling his daughter, calmly and rationally.

"He wants to get rid of me." Jessie threw herself at the stranger who barely managed to get her arms up in time to catch her.

Not permanently. Just for a brief respite. "I—"

"He doesn't want me," she cried. "He never wanted me. My mom told me so. Now that she's gone I have no one."

Lewis's chest tightened at the devastation in her voice. No, children were not part of his life plan. But since the paternity test had proved Jessie to be his biological daughter, even though she'd gotten her pretty face and unpleasant temperament from her mother, he was determined to do the best job he could raising her. A task that'd turned out to be much more difficult than he'd ever imagined.

"Jessie—" He reached for her, wanting to be the one to hold her and comfort her.

But Jessie held up her hand as she sucked in a few choppy breaths and cried out,

"He says I have to stay there. No matter what. And I can't come home early."

"Because I have to work," Lewis lied. But it sounded better than, "Because I need some time away from you to regain my sanity."

"You work all the time," she accused, scowling at him over the stranger's shoulder.

"And why should it matter if I do?" Lewis shot back. "It's not like I can get you to go anywhere or do anything with me when I'm not working."

"See how he talks to me?" Jessie said. "He hates me."

"You're laying it on a bit thick, don't you think?" the woman asked, peeling Jessie's arms off of her and stepping away, giving Lewis his first view of her name tag. Scarlet Miller, RN, BSN, MSN, CCRN. Head Nurse NICU.

"I'm totally serious," Jessie said, wiping her eyes with the backs of her hands. "He told me so." She glared at him. "In the taxi on the way here."

Scarlet turned her assessing gaze on him. "Wow," she said, shaking her head. "And all this time I've been telling Jessie you couldn't possibly be as big a jerk as she was making you out to be. I stand corrected."

Her keen blue eyes locked with his in challenge. Her face—an attractive mix of natural beauty and intelligence—in full view for the first time, Lewis lost track of the conversation for a few seconds, moving his focus to her chocolate brown hair and pleasingly trim figure. Her confident stance as she berated him. Her statement of "all this time" registered bringing him full circle to wonder why a professional adult female, who looked to be closer to his age than his daughter's, would befriend a little girl.

"If he makes me go I'll run away," Jessie said to Scarlet as if Lewis wasn't standing right there.

"No you won't," Scarlet said firmly.

Good. Another adult on his side.

"You did," Jessie accused.

What kind of nut job shared that information with a confused little girl?

"Did you not listen when I told you what a dangerous and stupid move it was?" She took Jessie by the shoulders and turned her. "Look at me, Jess."

Jess. So familiar. So caring.

The vulnerable expression on his daughter's face as she obeyed, gave him his first opportunity to see beneath her tough-teen anger and defiance to the scared little girl she'd hidden away so effectively, from him, but not this stranger. Why?

"You have what I didn't. You have me." The woman dug into the pocket of her lab coat, pulled out a business card, and wrote something on the back. Then she held it out to Jessie. "On the front is my work number and on the back is my cell phone number. You can call me anytime for any reason. I didn't offer earlier because I didn't want to interfere between you and your dad."

As it should be.

"You are not all alone, Jess. You have your father and you have me." Scarlet glanced at him before continuing. "And if, while you're on vacation, someone tries to make you do something you don't want to do or in any way makes you feel uncomfortable and your dad won't come up to bring you home, I promise I will."

Oh no she would not. "My daughter will be driven to and from Lake George by her grandparents. And she doesn't need your telephone numbers because if she needs to talk to someone anytime for any reason, she can talk to me." Lewis grabbed for the card.

Jessie thrust it behind her back.

"This entire situation is getting out of hand, Jess," Scarlet said. "You need to tell him."

Lewis stopped and looked at her. "Tell me what?"

"What's said between us stays between us," Jessie yelled at Scarlet. "You promised."

"That was before you got yourself picked up by the police and threatened to run away."

"You mean you know—?" Lewis started only to be cut off when an urgent voice came through the overhead speakers. "Scarlet Miller to the emergency room. Stat. Scarlet Miller to the emergency room."

"Saved by the hospital operator," Scarlet said with a wink to Jessie. "Talk to your father," she added before turning her back on him and walking away.

CHAPTER TWO

SCARLET JOGGED THE short distance to the large nurses' station in the center of the busy emergency room. "I'm Scarlet Miller," she said to the Scarlett she'd given the flowers to a few minutes earlier. Dr. Jackson and Jessie came to stand beside her.

"They need you in trauma room three," a nurse replied. "Pregnant teen. Walked in alone already crowning. No identification. No prenatal care. Unsure of gestation but estimated to be around thirty-three weeks. Dr. Gibbons called for a NICU team."

"And my staff must have been called into the high risk multiple birth scheduled for this afternoon." Triplets, one in distress, being delivered by Cesarean section at twenty-nine weeks. Scarlet removed her lab coat and handed it to Jessie. "Looks like I'm it. Please call the NICU and speak with Ashley," she directed the unit clerk. "Tell her I'm here and to alert Dr. Donaldson and Mac from Respiratory Therapy that I'll have them paged if I need them. And ask her to send down an incubator."

"What can I do to help?" Dr. Jackson asked.

"Would you please have someone turn on the warming table and get me a disposable gown, gloves, and heated towels?"

"Done." He turned to Jessie. "Wait for me in my office. Do. Not. Go. Anywhere."

Scarlet entered the room and introduced herself to the staff, "I'm Scarlet from the NICU."

A young girl with short black hair maybe fifteen or sixteen years old lay on a stretcher. Two nurses held her bare pale legs bent and open. An older heavyset doctor stood between them.

The girl cried out, "It hurts."

Scarlet quickly washed her hands, hurried to the head of the bed and took the girl's hands in hers. "Breathe through the pain," she said. "Like this." She demonstrated.

The girl looked up, her eyes wet with tears, her face red, her expression a mix of pain and fear. "I can't do this," she said.

"You can, and you will," Scarlet answered. "Squeeze my hands as hard as you can. You won't hurt me."

"Here comes another one," she cried out.

And as she squeezed Scarlet's hands, the memory of experiencing this very same situation when she was around this girl's age squeezed Scarlet's heart.

"Bear down and push," the doctor instructed.

"Push, push, push," Scarlet encouraged. "Just like that. You're doing great."

When the contraction ended Scarlet introduced herself, "My name is Scarlet and I'm the nurse who will be taking care of your baby when it's born." She used the corner of the sheet to blot the sweat from the girl's forehead and upper lip. "What's your name?"

The girl hesitated but answered, "Holly."

"Why are you here all alone, Holly?" Scarlet asked, fearing the answer. "Tell me who to call. A family member? A friend?"

A panicked look overtook her face. "They don't know," she said. "No one can know." Scarlet recalled her own seventeen-year-old desperation, hiding her growing pregnant belly from her high school classmates and family, dealing with the overwhelming, all-consuming fear of someone finding out, of giving birth, and of where she'd go afterwards and how she'd care and provide for her baby. Without a job. Without a high school diploma. Without the help and support of anyone.

How naïve she'd been, actually looking forward to running away, to finally having someone she could love who would love her back.

But that dream had been ripped away when she'd gone into labor months earlier than she'd expected, when her irate, powerful, and medically connected father had accompanied her to one of the many hospitals he worked with, when she'd awoken three days later with little recollection of what'd occurred after her baby had been whisked away other than her weak cry echoing in Scarlet's ears, only to be told her infant had died. According to one of the nurses—who'd had trouble looking her in the eye—she'd been so distraught when she'd been told about her baby's death she'd required sedation, and so as not to upset her further, her father had arranged for private burial. Without allowing Scarlet to see or hold the baby she'd carried inside her body for months, to say goodbye or gain closure.

And her father had never revealed the location of the grave, a secret he and her mother had taken with them to the hereafter eight years ago, leaving Scarlet to always wonder—

"Oh, God. Here comes another one," Holly cried.

"Just like before," Scarlet said, wishing it was possible to bolster this child's strength with some of her own.

"You're doing great," the doctor said at the end of the contraction. Holly flopped back onto the stretcher. "I think one more push should do it."

Holly turned her head to Scarlet, exhausted, her eyes pleading. "Promise me you'll take good care of my baby. Promise me she'll be okay."

A wound so big and so catastrophic it'd taken years to heal broke open deep inside of Scarlet at the memory of her own desperate pleas to the nurses caring for her during delivery, pleas that had fallen on deaf ears. *'I don't want my father in here.' 'I want to see my baby.' 'Please, bring me my baby.'*

"Promise me you'll find her a good home."

Why not Holly's home? *Her*. Wait a minute. "You know it's a girl?" She could only know that if she'd had a prenatal ultrasound. "Who told you it's a girl?" A medical facility would have documentation and contact information.

"I want her named Joey." She ignored Scarlet's question. "I want her to grow up happy, with a family who loves her." She stiffened. "Oh, God. Another one. I'm not ready."

"Yes, you are, Holly. Come on. It's time to have your little girl."

"Let me take over here," Dr. Jackson said, holding up the same type of light blue disposable gown he now wore.

"I've got to get ready to take care of your baby, Holly."

She didn't release Scarlet's hands. "Promise me she'll be okay." Tears streamed down her cheeks. "Promise me."

She couldn't promise that. "I'll do my best," she said.

And with a small smile she added, "I'm going to need my hands." Holly loosened her grip.

Scarlet stepped away from the bed to slip into the gown and turn so Dr. Jackson could tie the back. While she donned a mask and gloves, Dr. Jackson did indeed take over for her, talking quietly and supportively while offering direction and praise. Why didn't he show that care with his daughter?

"Don't push," the doctor delivering the baby said.

"What's wrong?" Holly asked, frantic. "I have to push. Get her out."

"The cord is wrapped around the baby's neck," the doctor answered. "Don't. Push."

Dr. Jackson held Holly's hands and instructed her to breathe. "Perfect. You are doing perfect."

After a few tense minutes the doctor delivering the baby said, "Okay, we are good to go, on the next contraction push out your baby."

In no time baby Joey entered the world with a tiny cry of displeasure, her cord was cut, and she'd been handed into Scarlet's waiting towel draped arms. She did a quick assessment and determined it'd be okay to show her to her mom before taking her into the next room. "Do you want to see your baby?" she asked walking up to the head of the bed, knowing sometimes a woman planning to give her baby up for adoption did not.

"Chest...hurts," Holly said, struggling for breath. "Can't...breathe."

"What's happening?" Scarlet asked, holding Joey close.

"Don't know," Dr. Jackson said. "But whatever it is, Dr. Gibbons will handle it. We need to stabilize the baby." He set a large strong hand at her back to guide her toward a side door leading into another room. "The warming table is this way."

"No pulse," the nurse standing by the head of Holly's bed said. "Initiating CPR." She clasped her hands together and began chest compressions.

Scarlet stopped and stared. Please, God. Don't let her die.

"Come." Dr. Jackson urged her forward, pushing open the door. "We need to focus on the baby," he reminded her.

"I know." But that didn't mean she could completely turn off concern for the mother, a young woman she'd connected with for a brief few minutes. Luckily when they reached the warming table Scarlet clicked into auto-nurse, wiping down the too quiet newborn to stimulate her as much as to clean her. "I'm going to need her weight."

"The baby scale was in use," Dr. Jackson said. "Let me go grab it."

When he left the room, Scarlet listened to Joey's chest to count her heart and respiratory rates. Then she found the equipment she needed and fastened a pulse oximeter to her tiny hand to evaluate her blood oxygen level.

The baby lay on the warmer with her arms and legs flexed, her color pale. Not good.

When Dr. Jackson returned with the scale he placed a disposable cloth over it and Scarlet carefully lifted the naked baby and set her down. "Four point one pounds." Scarlet jotted the number down on a notepad by the warmer and reported the other findings she'd noted there. "Pulse ox ninety. Heart rate one hundred and eighty. Increased respiratory effort. Color pale. Initial

Apgar score a five." All of which were abnormal for an infant.

"Let's get a line in to give a bolus of normal saline and get her hooked up to some supplemental oxygen."

While Dr. Jackson inserted a tiny nasal cannula in Joey's nostrils, taped the tubing to her cheeks, and set the flow meter to provide the appropriate level of oxygen, Scarlet started an intravenous in Joey's left arm—noting she didn't flinch or cry.

While she taped it down and immobilized the appendage in an extended position, Dr. Jackson did a quick heel stick to evaluate Joey's blood sugar level.

They worked quickly, quietly and efficiently like they'd been working together for years.

"Blood glucose twenty-five," he reported and began rummaging around a drawer in the warmer until he found the reference card for the recommended dosages for premature infants by weight. "Add a bolus of dextrose." He called out his orders and Scarlet filled the syringes and administered their contents via the newly inserted IV line.

"Come on, Joey," she said, rubbing her thighs in an attempt to perk her up.

The door slammed open and in rolled an incubator being pushed by Cindy. "You okay down here?" she asked.

"Better than expected," Scarlet replied, considering who she'd had to work with. Luckily, Dr. Jackson's reputation as an excellent physician came well-deserved.

"Good." Cindy turned to leave. "The NICU is nuts. I talked to Admissions. Baby Doe," a placeholder name since Holly hadn't shared her last name, "will be going into room forty-two."

"Call Admissions and tell them it's Joey Doe. Holly

told me she wanted her baby to be named Joey." And following through on that was the least she could do.

"Roger that." She saluted then walked over to take a look at their soon-to-be new patient. "Too bad about her mom."

"She's…?" Scarlet couldn't continue.

Cindy looked between her and Dr. Jackson and slowly nodded. "I'm sorry. I thought you knew."

Scarlet turned away, held herself tightly, fearing for the first time in years she might cry. For Holly who'd died too young. For Joey now alone in the world. For her own infant and not knowing if she'd suffered, if anyone had cuddled her close before she'd died, or if she'd been ruthlessly given away to strangers while Scarlet lay in a drug-induced slumber.

"You okay?" Dr. Jackson asked quietly.

Of course she was. Scarlet wasn't new to nursing. Holly wasn't the first of her patients to die. But there was something about her…"What do you think happened?"

He shrugged and shook his head. "Some congenital heart defect that couldn't withstand labor and delivery. A pulmonary embolism. Any number of pre-existing conditions that could have worsened or arisen during her pregnancy that we didn't know about. Dr. Gibbons is an excellent doctor. I have total confidence he did all he could do."

"It wasn't enough."

As if to share her agreement, little Joey Doe let out a little cry and they both looked down at their tiny patient. "Her color is improving," Scarlet noted. "And she's more alert."

With skilled, gentle hands, Dr. Jackson examined the increasingly active baby. "Heart rate down to one hundred and twenty. I'd give her a second Apgar score of seven."

Not a perfect ten, but improved. Scarlet documented it in her notes.

"She's stable enough for transport up to the NICU," Dr. Jackson said. Then he helped her get Joey situated in the incubator.

"After I get her settled in I'll access her ER file and enter my documentation."

"If you run into any trouble, let me know." He held out his hand and she shook it. "Thanks for the help."

"Anytime." She went to remove her hand from his grip but he held it there.

"We need to talk about Jessie," Dr. Jackson said. So serious. Did the man ever smile? According to Jessie, no he did not.

Scarlet took a moment to admire his tall, athletic build and short brown hair mixed with a hint of grey at his temples. He had a look of confidence and prestige she would have found very attractive on someone else. "No," Scarlet said, looking to where he held her hand. "*You* need to talk to *your* daughter." She looked up at him. "And here's a helpful hint to improving communication between the two of you." She yanked her hand back. "Stop comparing her to the perfect little boy you used to be. Just because you loved swimming and boating and all things water when you were a child, doesn't mean she does."

Later that night Lewis stood in his designer kitchen, eyeing the modern stainless steel handle on the high-end black cabinet that contained the bottles of wine he'd kept at the ready in case any of his dates wanted a glass, and considered uncorking one. Although he wasn't in the habit of drinking alone, it'd been the kind of day followed by the kind of night that warranted a little alcohol consumption to facilitate a return to his pre-Jessie level of calm.

But Lewis Jackson had never turned to alcohol to drown his problems before, and he refused to start now. He was a problem solver, a thinker and a fixer. And to do those things he required a clear head.

Since his daughter had taken up permanent residence in the loft guestroom, he tended to avoid the living area below after she went to sleep. So he walked down the hall to his bedroom, the smooth hardwood floors cool beneath his bare feet, the central air maintaining the perfect air temperature, his two bedroom luxury condo decorated to his exact specifications for style, comfort and function. And yet his home no longer brought him the welcoming serenity it once had.

Jessie hadn't said more than a handful of words—all of them monosyllabic—to him since they'd left the hospital, even after he'd insisted they eat their takeout grilled chicken Caesar salads together in the kitchen for a change. What an uncomfortable meal that'd been. Jessie, staring down at her plate, moving the chicken around with her fork. Lewis, trying to engage her in conversation, to offer reassurance about her trip to Lake George, to find out more about her relationship with Scarlet Miller, and, for the hundredth time, to gain some insight into the functioning of the pre-pubescent female mind. A booby-trapped labyrinth of erratic and illogical thought processes he could not seem to navigate through, despite successful completion of several child psychology classes and licensure as a pediatrician.

After nine arduous months of trying, and failing his

daughter at every crisis, Lewis gave in to the cold, hard fact: He could not do it alone.

And yet again, an image of Scarlet Miller popped into his head. A pretty yet unfriendly woman and a skilled professional, who, he'd found out on further inquiry, received high praise and much respect from her peers and upper management. But at the moment, all that mattered to him was her relationship with his daughter.

He reached into his pocket, pulled out the slip of paper he'd stashed there earlier, and glanced at his watch. A few minutes after eleven o'clock.

It was too late to call, but his need to talk to her, to get answers and beg for her assistance overrode common phone etiquette. After hours and hours spent considering his options, Lewis had come to the conclusion Scarlet Miller was his key to deciphering Jessie's passive-aggressive behavior and learning her secrets, to understanding her and starting a productive dialogue between them, so he could help her, so he could, please God, find something about her to love.

Lewis picked up his phone and dialed.

After a few rings a groggy female voice answered, "Hello?"

Great, he'd woke her up. And the last thing he wanted to do was anger his best hope for achieving a healthy, positive relationship with his daughter. He cleared his throat. "Hi. It's Lewis."

"I'm sorry. You have the wrong number."

"Wait. Is this Scarlet Miller?" he rushed to ask before she disconnected the call, and before it registered that if she hung up, she'd never know he was the inconsiderate louse who'd woken her. Well…unless she had caller ID. Then he'd no doubt come off looking even worse.

"Yes," she answered.

"It's me. Lewis Jackson. Jessie's dad."

"Is she okay?" Scarlet sounded instantly awake. "Did something happen?"

Lewis liked and appreciated her concern for his daughter. "No, she's fine. Upstairs asleep." At least as far as he knew. And since he'd learned the hard way never to assume Jessie was where she was supposed to be, Lewis walked to the doorway, poked his head into the hallway to confirm it was indeed eavesdropper-free, then closed and locked his bedroom door, just in case it didn't stay that way.

"How did you get this number?" Scarlet asked. "I'm sure I didn't give it to you. And I doubt Jessie would have shared it."

Okay, time for some fast talking. "I just happened to come across the card you'd given to Jessie," after searching for it in her backpack and pocketbook while she was in the shower—bad, reprehensible father—"while checking her plethora of pockets before putting her pants in the wash," he lied. "I took it as a sign I should call you."

Silence.

"Hello?" he asked.

She let out a decidedly feminine, sultry sounding moan which made him question, "Am I interrupting something?"

"No." She did it again. "I don't typically talk on the phone when I'm in bed. I'm trying to find a comfortable position."

And just like that, with the mere mention she was in bed, without-sex-for-nine-long-months-brain overtook concerned-father-brain with an enticing visual of her luscious body. A comfortable position came to mind. Scarlet spread out on top of satin sheets. Naked. Waiting.

His sex-starved body went hard.

"Soooo, *you* called me," she said. "What can I do for you?"

A loaded question if ever there was one. Because right this instant he wanted her to talk dirty, to touch herself and tell him all about it, to describe her aroused nipples and slick... Lord help him. Prolonged abstinence had effectively eradicated his ability to engage in casual nighttime conversation with a woman. From bedroom to bedroom. And if he took a few small steps, from bed to bed. And from out of nowhere, the idea of phone sex popped into his head.

"Hello. Everything okay over there?"

Totally disgusted with himself, Lewis rubbed his hand over his face and let out a breath. "A bad day followed by a bad night combined with a non-existent sex life since my daughter came to live with me and I am conjuring up totally inappropriate visuals of you, a woman I have known for less than twenty-four hours, at the simple mention of you getting comfortable in bed. In my defense, you were making some very sexy noises a moment ago, so I hold you partly responsible. But I assure you, when I picked up the phone to make this call my intentions were purely G-rated."

"And now what are they?" she teased.

"Let's just say, the next time you see me you owe me a slap across the face, because I totally deserve it."

Turned out she had a sexy laugh, too.

He shifted in the recliner to relieve some of the pressure in his pants. Not good. Scarlet Miller was not the woman to slake his lust. He needed her to fix things between him and Jessie and would not risk anything interfering with his top priority. "Please accept my sincerest apologies."

"Accepted, but not necessary," she said. "For the record, you could pass for sexy on the phone, too."

"You are not helping."

"Do you want to know what I'm wearing?" she taunted him.

"Absolutely not," he lied.

"I could—"

"Stop it."

"Fine," she said. "But you started it."

"And I'm going to finish it." Only because someone had to. "I called to talk about Jessie. To try to sweet talk you into sharing some more helpful hints on improving communication between us, because the direct approach is not working."

"Too bad. That's the closest I've ever come to having phone sex."

Did he detect a hint of disappointment? "Oddly enough, me, too," he admitted. And why did he feel so comfortable sharing that tidbit with a woman he hardly knew?

"You know you're putting me in a tough spot," Scarlet said, her voice serious. "I can't betray things Jessie has told me in confidence. She really needs a friend to talk to, and right now I'm it. It took me a long time to get her to open up."

He wanted to ask how she'd managed that, but decided to start with, "Would you at least tell me how you met?"

She took so long to answer Lewis had started to worry she wouldn't.

"That I can do." It sounded like she repositioned herself in bed. Again. "I work late on Tuesdays and Thursdays to spend some time with my night staff. So I take a break at three."

"Right around when I send Jessie down to get a snack after school."

"The cafeteria isn't usually busy at that time so I noticed her, always sitting there by herself with that 'don't talk to me' look."

Lewis hated that look.

"I saw a lot of my thirteen-year-old self in Jessie. Mad at the world. Too much time alone and unsupervised. Do you honestly think she's safe wandering around alone in a city hospital for hours waiting for you to get off work?"

Lewis did not appreciate the censure in her tone. She had no idea how hard he'd tried. "That was her doing not mine. I told her what would happen if she made one more babysitter quit. And she's not supposed to be wandering around alone," he pointed out maybe a little too forcefully. *Calm it down.* "She's supposed to be in my office doing her homework." Except his little Houdini always managed to sneak out without anyone seeing then show up hours later when it was time to go home. "What do you suggest I do? Let her stay at my condo all alone until I get home, like she'd prefer? Maybe some thirteen-year-olds are ready for that. But in my opinion Jessie isn't." And his opinion was the one that mattered.

"I agree," Scarlet said, surprising him. "But it's a moot point since I've got her spending her afternoons up in the NICU wing now."

"Where?" Why?

"We have a family lounge. It's geared towards the siblings of our babies who are often overlooked while their parents focus their attention on their sick infant. So we made them a special place with video games, toys, computers to do their homework, a television and a kid-friendly library that holds everything from picture books to young adult novels. Jessie comes up to read every afternoon."

Jessie liked to read? They actually had something in common? Yet in the nine months she'd been living with him he'd never seen her with a book.

"I'm sorry. I assumed she told you."

"Aside from mostly no's and the occasional yes, she hardly speaks to me. I do get a lot of shrugs, exasperated breaths and eye rolls, though. And when she does surprise me with a full sentence, it's usually to tell me how much she hates me, that she knows I don't want her, or that she wishes I'd died instead of her mother." Then he'd rather she'd just stayed quiet.

"She has a lot of anger."

Rightly so. But, "It's been nine months. Shouldn't it be dissipating a bit by now?"

"If only time was all she needed."

"Tell me what she needs. I'll do anything."

Silence.

"Please," Lewis said. "If you want me to beg, I will." He slid to the edge of the recliner, fully prepared to drop to his knees. "I am that desperate."

Silence.

Lewis started to lose hope that Scarlet would be the panacea he needed.

Then she spoke. "If you can slip up to the NICU family lounge around four o'clock tomorrow you'll see a different side of Jessie. One that I'm sure will make you proud."

An opportunity he would not miss. "I'll be there."

"She can't know I told you. Say you came up to check on baby Joey, and my staff told you where to find me."

"Will do."

"I'm giving you an opportunity for a positive interaction with your daughter, Lewis. Don't screw it up."

CHAPTER THREE

AT THREE-THIRTY on Wednesday afternoon, washed up
and gowned, Scarlet opened Joey's incubator. The baby
refused to suck so Dr. Donaldson had placed a naso-gas-
tric tube for feeding. "Hey there, you sweet little girl,"
she said softly so as not to startle her. Joey blinked her
eyes and stretched in response to Scarlet's voice.

Good.

Scarlet pressed her index finger against the baby's
tiny palm so she could grab onto it. "I promised your
mommy I'd take good care of you." A promise she intended to keep. She repositioned her many tubes and
carefully wrapped her in a baby blanket. "We need to
get you drinking from a bottle so you can grow up big
and strong." She lifted her and slowly moved to the
rocker two steps away, careful not to pull on the many
lines connected to her.

Once situated, she began to rock. Joey made a contented little moan and cuddled into her. "Don't get too
comfortable," she warned and picked up the little bottle
beside her. "We've got some work to do."

Since taking on a management role, Scarlet missed
providing direct care to the NICU's tiny patients. "Open
up." She rubbed the special nipple along Joey's bottom
lip and squeezed out a drop of formula.

So far the NICU social worker hadn't been able to come up with any information on Holly. Police were reviewing missing persons reports and Holly's post mortem picture had been faxed to OB/GYN offices, prenatal clinics and schools within a thirty mile radius of the hospital. Scarlet couldn't help wondering why Holly didn't want her family to know about the baby. For fear of their reaction to her pregnancy? Shame? Scarlet could relate. But what if there was more? What if her home environment wasn't safe for her baby? If her parents were unfit to raise a child, like Scarlet's had been? Or if someone abusive would have access to the baby?

And what if Holly was never identified and her family never found? What then? Joey would wind up in an over-burdened, flawed child welfare system. Helpless and vulnerable.

Promise me she'll be okay. Promise me you'll find her a good home. A dead mother's final plea to Scarlet, who had absolutely no control over Joey's placement.

Unless she sought to adopt her.

An absurd notion, considering Scarlet didn't spend enough time at home to keep a pet alive. How could she work the hours she did and effectively care for an infant? The question that'd been weighing on her mind for months as her biological clock beat out the second by second withering of her reproductive organs.

Baby Joey fell asleep in her arms and Scarlet savored a few minutes of peace in the darkened quiet room, loving the feel of Joey in her arms. Like she did every time she held a NICU patient, she tried to convince herself. But no, it was different with Joey, maybe because Joey's mom had entrusted her daughter to Scarlet. Maybe because Holly reminded her so much of herself, and Joey, now all alone in the world, had wound up like Scarlet's baby when she'd been purposely chemically incapacitated.

Regardless, Scarlet had a vested interest in Joey and would do whatever she could to assure the child a bright, happy and safe future.

Grandma Sadie, one of their volunteer cuddlers, came in to Joey's room and whispered, "Linda told me to come relieve you."

Grandma Sadie had been in Scarlet's first volunteer cuddler orientation class, back when she'd implemented the program four years ago. Research showed preemies benefited from human touch and interaction. And cuddlers filled the gap when exhausted parents needed a break, or when babies, like Joey, had no family to love them.

She glanced at her watch. "Perfect timing." Since she had to get over to the family lounge before Lewis arrived.

Scarlet busied herself by re-shelving books and putting away toys. Then she spoke with a few moms sitting at a table in the back of the room, enjoying a rest and some coffee while Jessie held 'story time' to occupy their five little girls who ranged in age from two to five. They sat in a circle on the floor, each taking a turn in Jessie's lap while she read their selection.

When Lewis entered the room, Scarlet motioned for him to be quiet and come to stand beside her.

So engrossed in her task, Jessie didn't notice his arrival as she made an exaggerated honking noise that sent the little girls into a pile of gigglers.

Lewis watched his daughter, his face a mix of awe and disbelief.

"Jessie holds 'story time' around four o'clock every afternoon," she whispered. "The moms meet up for a few precious minutes of adult conversation, while your daughter gives each of their children some special attention." Scarlet looked up at him. "She's really something special."

Jessie finished one book and, with a big smile on her face, accepted a kiss on the cheek from the girl in her lap. Then the circle shifted, the next little girl climbed in her lap and she began to read again.

"I can't believe it," Lewis whispered, his eyes locked on Jessie. "She's actually smiling."

"She has a beautiful smile," Scarlet pointed out.

Lewis turned to her. "This is the first time I've ever seen it."

"Dad," Jessie walked up beside them. "What are you doing here?"

"I'm sorry. I didn't mean to interrupt," Lewis said. "I came up to check on the baby born in the ER yesterday, and the secretary at the desk told me I'd find Scarlet in here."

Good man, very convincing.

Jessie stood defiant, ready to do battle. "If you're going to yell at me please do it outside. I don't want to upset the girls." Who sat watching Jessie, still in a circle, awaiting her return.

Lewis went rigid. "Why do you think I'm going to yell?"

"Because you always yell."

Lewis looked close to lashing out so Scarlet touched his arm to stop him. "Always is one of those words you need to use carefully," Scarlet cautioned Jessie. "It's rare someone *always* does something."

"You don't know my dad," Jessie replied with an eye roll, and Scarlet couldn't keep from smiling.

"If I was going to say anything," Lewis said. "It'd be how nice it was to see you smiling for a change, and how proud I am to know you're spending your time helping out here."

Jessie looked stunned.

One of the moms came over. "Is this your dad?" she asked Jessie who nodded hesitantly as if embarrassed.

The woman put her arm around Jessie's shoulders. "You have a gem of a daughter." She looked in the direction of Lewis's name badge and added, "Dr. Jackson. You've done a wonderful job with her."

Lewis answered, "Thank you." Then he turned to look at Jessie. "I wish I could take the credit, but it was all her mother."

Jessie ran from the room.

Lewis and Scarlet caught up with her by the elevators and she turned on her father. "Why are you being so nice?" Jessie asked her voice full of accusation. "You hated my mom, and you hate me."

A couple exited the elevator, avoiding eye contact as they passed by.

"Honey, I have never hated your mother, and I don't hate you," Lewis said, impressing Scarlet with his calm. "I let my anger and disappointment at having to pick you up at the police station get the better of me yesterday, and I am deeply sorry for what I said."

Jessie stood there, her arms crossed tightly over her mid-section, looking down at the ground.

"Now that I know where you're spending your afternoons, I can stop worrying," Lewis said quietly.

"I'm sorry I didn't tell you," Jessie offered, still not looking up.

It was a start. But with the Memorial Day weekend of doom fast approaching, was it enough to get Lewis and Jessie talking about what they needed to talk about? Probably not. Which meant Scarlet had to figure out a way to intercede without Jessie finding out.

Later that night, after spending more time thinking about Lewis and his daughter than sleeping, Scarlet settled on what she'd do. Of course it'd taken until well after midnight to finally make up her mind—the reason she sat in the far corner of the mostly deserted hospital cafeteria hours before her lunch break, waiting for Lewis.

He walked in and went directly to the coffee dispensers, giving Scarlet time to play voyeur, watching from afar, admiring his long legs, short hair, and good looks. The man made basic green scrubs look like upscale attire. Clean and neatly pressed. And dare she add, pleasingly filled out.

No wonder she'd heard his name bandied about by so many of her single co-workers.

She skimmed up his legs, to his narrow waist and wide chest, to his smiling face, to his eyes staring straight at her.

Busted.

She smiled back and waved.

He paid the cashier and headed toward her. "You like what you see?" he asked with the cocky smile of a man who knew he looked good, pulling out the chair across from her at the small, two-person table along the wall.

"Actually," she took a sip of coffee, playing it cool. "Just pondering the age old question of boxers or briefs."

He leaned in close.

She added straight white teeth, clean shaven, and a

hint of expensive cologne to his growing list of unsettlingly pleasing attributes.

"Use your imagination," he whispered.

Oh he did not want her to go there. Too late. She closed her eyes and pretended to imagine his naked form with various undergarments. Okay. So she didn't totally pretend. When she opened her eyes to find him studying her, she flashed her sweetest smile and said, "Commando it is."

He laughed out loud.

"Suffice it to say, I no longer owe you a slap across the face." She blew out a breath and fanned herself. "We are now even." Come to find out he had a beautiful smile, so much like Jessie's.

"You make me forget I'm the father of an impressionable teenage girl."

"You know being a parent does not sentence you to a life of celibacy. Why don't you pull up your date book and call one of your five star babes to take the edge off. It'll calm you down. I'm happy to take Jess to dinner and a movie." She smiled back. "Your treat, of course."

He rested his elbows on the table and leaned in close. "Why is it we never met *before* Jessie came into my life?"

Oh that was easy. "Probably because I don't dress to attract male attention, my boobs don't enter a room before I do, and I've never gone to O'Malley's after work intent on finding a sexy doctor to go home with." And she had a brain and self-respect and stayed away from men who didn't put any effort into getting to know a woman before making a play to get her into bed.

His smile grew even bigger. "You think I'm sexy?"

And full of himself. "Based on your reputation, I think it's safe to say certain women find you sexy. Or else they simply put up with you in a desperate attempt to snag themselves a doctor husband." She shrugged. "It's a discussion for another day." She looked at her watch. "Unless you'd like to continue rather than talk about Jessie, who is the reason I asked you to meet me here. Your choice. I've got rounds with the neonatologist in fifteen minutes."

That knocked the cocky grin from his lips.

Good.

"What can you tell me about Jessie's mom?" she asked, hoping to get him to figure out Jessie's issues on his own, so she could avoid having to come right out and tell him.

He took a sip of coffee before answering. "There's not much to tell. She was a barista at a coffee shop around the corner from my medical school. We dated a few times, and by dated," he looked at her pointedly without apology or regret, "I really mean got together for sex. When she put pressure on me to spend more time with her, we fought. She became a distraction so I broke it off," he said matter-of-factly. "I needed to focus on my studies. So I found another coffee shop and she, according to a ranting message left on my answering machine, found a man who appreciated her—likely one more easily manipulated by her histrionics. After that I never saw, spoke with, or to be honest, thought about her again until I received a call from her attorney nine months ago informing me she'd died and I had a twelve-year-old daughter."

The news of his situation had spread through the hospital like pink eye in a room full of toddlers. "That must have come as quite a shock."

"You have no idea."

At age sixteen she'd found out she was pregnant and

had no recollection of having sex. At seventeen she'd given birth only to wake up to find her baby gone. She had some idea.

"Well this entire Lake George vacation mess could have been avoided if you'd taken the time to get to know Jessie's mother before you slept with her."

"Trust me," he said. "If I'd have taken the time to get to know her, I would not have slept with her."

For some reason that struck her as funny.

"Enjoying this are you?"

"No." She shook her head. "Okay. Maybe a little. But moving on." Since plan A didn't work, time to move on to plan B. "Let's play doctor."

He looked around then leaned in and whispered. "To do the game justice we'll need some privacy."

"You are unbelievable," Scarlet reprimanded him. "I am trying to clue you in to Jessie's fears about Lake George. But maybe it's not as important to you as I'd thought. And since there are plenty of more important things I could be doing." She pushed back her chair.

"Wait." He grabbed her hand to stop her from standing. "I'm sorry," he said, sounding sincere. "I can't help it. There's something about you." He studied her as if trying to figure out what. "I'll behave. I promise." He held up his right hand, as if that made his words more believable.

"Okay, then." Scarlet slid her chair back under the table. "You're the doctor. I'm going to tell you a hypothetical situation and you're going to tell me what you think."

"Hypothetical," he clarified with a tilt of his head and one raised eyebrow.

"Yes." She nodded. "Purely hypothetical."

"Got it."

"A woman has a near-death drowning experience as a little girl and grows up with a crippling fear of the water. She has a daughter. The daughter grows up under the mother's watchful eye, never allowed in the ocean, a lake or a swimming pool, and therefore never given the opportunity to learn how to swim. Do you think it's reasonable to assume the daughter may also develop a fear of water?"

He smacked his forehead with the heel of his hand. "And all this time I've been playing up how much fun she'd have at the lake, jumping off the dock in the backyard," he said. "Boating. Tubing. Riding wave runners. I've no doubt traumatized her. Why didn't she tell me?" He looked at Scarlet for the answer.

"It's been seventeen years since I've spent any time in a thirteen-year-old's mixed up mind, but maybe she's embarrassed. Or she doesn't want you to blame her mom. Or she somehow thinks you'll belittle her fear or force her to deal with it. I honestly don't know."

Lewis sat there, staring at the table.

"What are you going to do now that you've taken the time to really put some thought into why Jessie doesn't want to go to Lake George and you've come up with the possibility she may be scared of the water," Scarlet asked. "And might I say good job of coming up with it totally on your own and without the help of anyone else."

Determined eyes met hers. "When we get home tonight I'm going to sit Jessie down and we're going to discuss her exact reasons for not wanting to go to Lake George. And if she doesn't bring up a fear of water or an inability to swim, I will find a way to work it into the conversation."

Finally. "I think that's a wonderful idea."

The words weren't fully out of her mouth when someone came to stand beside their table. Scarlet looked up to see Linda from the NICU, looking down at where Lewis still held her hand in his.

"Well what have we here?" Linda asked with a gleam in her gossip-mongering, match-making eyes.

Not good.

"Must I spend my Saturday afternoon in this touristy hell that is Times Square?" Scarlet complained as they maneuvered along the crowded sidewalk. Lewis kept an eye on Jessie who stopped to look at scarves laid out on a street vendor's table.

"Stop being a cynical New Yorker," he chided delighted to be away from the hospital and his condo, to be outside on a beautiful sun-shiny spring day on his first fun New York City excursion with his daughter. And having Scarlet along upped the enjoyment factor significantly.

"Technically I'm a Jersey girl."

Maybe so, but she looked the part of a chic New York City woman in her wedge-heeled open toed sandals, which displayed some perfectly manicured bright red toe nails, a pair of trendy knee-length cargo shorts that sat low on her hips, and a clingy red tank that accentuated her flat abdomen and small—although not too small—breasts. An over-sized red leather bag slung over her shoulder, a sleek ponytail fastened with a fancy silver clip, and silver hoop earrings finished off her very fashionable, very appealing look.

"Remind me again why I'm here?" she asked.

Jessie didn't buy a scarf, but she did purchase a pretzel. He watched her count her change like he'd told her and put the money into her front pocket. "Because you told Jessie she could call you anytime for any reason."

Scarlet snapped her fingers. "Right. And she wanted *me* to take her shopping for a bathing suit and some new vacation clothes."

After his conversation with Scarlet, Lewis had carefully, patiently and tactfully worked to pry the truth out of Jessie. And once she'd opened up to him, months of accumulated fears, concerns and tears had come pouring out. They'd talked for hours, and before bed Jessie had actually said, "Thanks, dad." His first amiable 'dad' followed by his very first hug and kiss good night from his daughter. A moment he would never forget. And though he'd never admit it to anyone, he'd teared up after she'd left the room, overwhelmed with relief. And hope.

"Yet somehow *we* wound up in Times Square. If *I'm* the one taking her to lunch and shopping," Scarlet peered up at him from the corners of her eyes, "Why are *you* here again?"

"Because I'm financing this little clothes shopping expedition, so I get the right of final approval."

Scarlet's smile did something tingly to his insides. "Oh you think so?" she asked.

He was the father. He knew so.

In an attempt to avoid a very persistent man trying to hand her a leaflet of some sort, Scarlet bumped into him and tripped. Lewis caught her around her narrow waste. "We're not interested," he said firmly and the man retreated.

"Why's that guy out in public in his underwear?" Jessie went up on her tiptoes and strained her neck to see around a group that'd gathered on the sidewalk. "And a cowboy hat and boots? And why are people taking their picture with him?"

"Let's keep walking," Lewis said, steering Jessie and Scarlet away.

"He does it to attract attention to himself so he can make some money by charging people who want to take a picture with him," Scarlet explained. "Tourists spend money on the craziest things."

Lewis watched the huge jumbotron on the side of a building to find the spot where the cameras were aimed. "Hold on." He turned Jessie. "Look up."

She did. "Hey." She waved both arms over her head and jumped up and down. "That's me."

"And me," Scarlet said with a big smile as she jumped and waved, too.

Lewis bent to talk into Scarlet's ear, noticing she smelled as good as she looked. "How touristy of you."

She stuck out her tongue at him then looped her arm through Jessie's. "Come on. This store has some great clothes."

As much as Lewis hated Jessie's baggie black garb—that'd turned to be hand-me-downs from a neighbor since her mom had been too sick to work and couldn't afford new clothes—Lewis was not at all a fan of Jessie's revealing, burgeoning-figure-hugging choices. "No," he said again and Jessie stormed back to the dressing room. Unfortunately it seemed last night's parental epiphany did not mean smooth sailing from then on.

"You know you're going to have to give a little," Scarlet said, remaining by his side instead of following Jessie.

"That shirt was too tight." He swallowed. "Do you think she needs a…" God he hated this. Daughters should not have breasts for boys who will soon be men to look at. Suddenly baggie black attire didn't seem all that bad.

Scarlet smiled, enjoying his angst a little too much. "Bra?" she asked. "Do I think your daughter needs a bra?" she teased.

"Ssshhh," he said. "Keep your voice down."

She didn't. "Tell you what I'm gonna do," she said like some cheesy salesman trying to sweeten the deal. "If you let Jessie get three outfits and two bathing suits of her choice, I will accompany her to Macy's." She cupped her hands at the sides of her mouth and whispered, "For some bras."

"No V-neck shirts and no bikinis," Lewis clarified.

"If you get stipulations then so do I. I'm thinking I'll suggest she get padded bras to double her bust size."

Witch. "Okay. She can pick from the last batch of stuff she tried on." Which thankfully didn't contain any of the hideously trampy items of clothing Jessie had tried to convince him to consider at the onset of this shopping nightmare.

"Deal." She held out her hand.

He shook it.

"You'll get through this," she said. "Tight shirts and bras are nothing." She waved a flippant hand. "Just wait until she gets her period."

Lewis thought he might throw up right there by the girls denim shorts rack. As a pediatrician he didn't hesitate to discuss breast development, menstruation, and birth control with his patients and/or their nervous parents. But the role of father caring for a developing teenage daughter had taken him into new territory. Had Jessie already gotten her period? Doubtful since he didn't have any feminine supplies in the house and she hadn't asked him to buy any. Had anyone had 'the talk' with her? Did she know what to expect? And what about safe sex? And sexually transmitted diseases?

He now had a vividly clear understanding of parental apprehension and avoidance when discussing reproductive matters with their children.

Pain typical of an ulcer started to burn through the lining in his stomach.

His doctor self knew what had to be done.

His father self would rather preach the pros of maintaining virginity until marriage.

"He looks pale," Jessie said, standing in front of him with her arms full of clothes.

"Men often do when shopping for clothes with women." Scarlet looked up at him with deceptively innocent eyes and smiled. "You feeling okay, papa bear?"

"You are a mean woman," he said so only she'd hear.

"Nah," she said. "If you're nice to me, maybe I'll handle 'the talk'" she made air quotations around 'the talk', "for you."

A total father copout, but thank you! "Lunch is on me," Lewis said, his vigor returning. "Then we'll go to Macy's to buy Scarlet a nice little gift for accompanying us today," he said to Jessie.

They found a little Italian bistro on 46th Street whose posted menu appealed to them all and squeezed into the last available corner booth, Jessie and all her bags on one side, Scarlet and Lewis on the other. When the waiter came to take their drink order Lewis asked Scarlet, "Would you like to share a bottle of wine?" Maybe bra shopping wouldn't be so bad with a nice relaxing buzz.

"No thank you," she said to him. Then she turned to the waiter. "Just water for me, please."

After ordering a soda Jessie said, "Scarlet doesn't drink alcohol, Dad."

"But don't let me stop you from having," Scarlet added quickly.

Lewis decided on an iced tea.

"You don't have to tell him why," Jessie said very serious. "What we say between us stays between us."

"It's not something I share with everyone I meet," Scarlet said. "But it's not a secret, either."

Jessie jumped at the chance to share the reason. "When Scarlet was sixteen she went to a party where the kids were drinking alcohol," Jessie said in horror. "She drank too and got so drunk she passed out."

"I hope you have a good reason for discussing your drunken teenage exploits with my daughter," Lewis said.

Scarlet turned to face him, her eyes met his. "Obviously alcohol impaired my ability to make good decisions because a few weeks later I found out I was pregnant."

She watched him, so Lewis was careful to maintain a neutral expression. He knew he should say something, but what? I'm sorry? How horrible? What happened to the baby?

"That's why kids shouldn't drink alcohol," Jessie said, taking the pressure off of him by filling the silence. "Because it makes them do stupid things they don't remember doing. I'm never drinking alcohol even after I turn twenty-one." She took her soda from the waiter and pulled the paper tip off of the straw.

"Good girl," he said, knowing a thirteen-year-old's declaration of long-term sobriety could be recanted without his knowledge at any time as she moved toward adulthood.

Jessie took a sip of soda then said, "Scarlet's baby is the reason the two of us met."

Very interesting.

Scarlet stared at her water glass, sliding her fingers through the droplets of condensation on the outside. If he wasn't mistaken, a hint of a blush stained her cheeks.

"Jessie, I don't think Scarlet is comfortable with you telling me all this." Even though he wanted to hear more.

"No," Scarlet looked at Jessie. "It's okay. Go on." She glanced at him. "Might as well get it all out." She turned back to Jessie. "It's not good to keep things from your dad."

Later, he'd thank her for that.

"The nurses told Scarlet her baby had died."

Scarlet jumped in to add, "Which is why I decided when I grew up I'd become a nurse who specializes in caring for premature infants."

And from what Lewis had heard and witnessed first-hand, she did a phenomenal job of it.

"But since her father was totally evil and wouldn't let her see her baby and refused to tell her where he'd had the baby buried, she started to wonder what if the baby had really survived?"

If the topic of conversation had been fiction rather than fact, Lewis would have smiled at Jessie's story-telling, wide-eyed and full of intrigue.

"I know it sounds ridiculous." Scarlet picked up the story. "But what if my dad had my baby transferred to another hospital and arranged for her to be adopted? Which, if you knew my dad, you'd know was something he was fully capable of pulling off, considering he also managed to make all documentation from my hospital stay, including any record of the birth, death, or transfer of my daughter, mysteriously disappear. And he did it without any remorse at all to save himself the embarrassment of having an unwed teenage mother for a daughter." Anger seeped into her voice and Lewis felt her stiffen beside him.

How horrible to have endured so much trauma at such a young age. He moved his knee to touch hers in a show of support that seemed to relax her.

"Anyway," Scarlet went on. "If my daughter is in fact alive, she'd be about Jessie's age. And when we met I told Jessie I'd hope if someone saw *my* daughter looking as sad and lonely as she did, they'd take the time to talk to her, and try to cheer her up, and see if there was anything they could do to help her."

"Which is what Scarlet did for me," Jessie said.

"And I am so glad she did," Lewis said, turning to Scarlet. "I'm sorry about your daughter, but words cannot express how thankful I am for the kindness you've shown to mine." Scarlet Miller had a true compassionate soul beneath her tough, joking exterior.

"No biggie." She shrugged off his heartfelt thanks, seeming uncomfortable with the attention. "What do you think happened to our waiter?" She looked down at her menu. "I'm starving."

He allowed the change of topic, but someday soon, when Jessie wasn't around, they'd talk more about his appreciation for all she'd done for Jessie and for him. And he kind of looked forward to getting her alone. Scarlet Miller was fast becoming a woman he wanted to get to know much better.

In Macy's Scarlet said, "If you'll excuse me and Jessie, I have some shopping to do up in the lingerie department." She shooed him away. "Go shop for man things. We'll meet you by women's shoes in half an hour."

If there were any way he could have done it without Jessie seeing, and without getting slapped, he would have kissed Scarlet right then and there.

Forty-five minutes later they appeared, Scarlet carrying a Macy's bag, Jessie empty-handed.

"Did you find what you needed?" he asked. *Please say yes.*

"Yup," she held up a bag he hoped contained Jessie's new undergarments.

"This is for you." He handed her the biggest box of chocolates he could find in the store. "Thank you for coming with us today."

"Wow." Scarlet took the box. "The fat cells in my thighs are vibrating with excitement in anticipation of room to expand."

"I heard how much you and your staff like chocolate," he said, referring to the box they'd devoured before it could be redirected to his new clerk.

"That we do." She smiled. He liked making her smile, liked the way her smiles made him feel. "Thank you, from all of us. But in the future, you don't need to buy me things to spend time with you and Jess. I had fun today."

"Me, too." Jessie hugged Scarlet.

Lewis did, too. In fact today had been the most fun he'd had in months. Even with talk of periods and bras.

When they exited Macy's Lewis asked Scarlet, "Where are you headed from here? You want to share a cab?"

"Nah." She held up her Metro card. "I'm going to hop a bus to the hospital. I want to stop by to visit Joey before I head home."

"Is there a problem?"

She shook her head. "No."

As Lewis watched Scarlet's appealing form walk away, he realized he was sorry to see her go. And as he raised his hand to hail a cab his mind went to work on creating a reason to see her again soon.

CHAPTER FOUR

"FANCY MEETING YOU here," Lewis greeted Scarlet with a big handsome smile as she exited the elevator on her way to the cafeteria.

"A big coincidence indeed on account of it's Tuesday and you now know I meet Jessie in the cafeteria on Tuesdays and Thursdays around three," she replied, not letting her happiness at seeing him show. In an unexpected turn of events, she'd been looking forward to the next time their paths would cross. And hoping it'd be sooner rather than later.

"I walked her over." He held up a cup of coffee. "Then I waited, hoping to see you."

How sweet.

"I need a favor," he said.

Not so sweet after all. She tried to walk around him.

He stepped in front of her. "For Jessie. One more and I'm done," he promised. "Then I won't bother you again."

Well forget about the fun they'd had on Saturday, and the signs of a friendship forming between them—that she'd obviously misinterpreted, and the unwanted stirrings of attraction that were totally his fault. All Lewis Jackson wanted from her was help with his daughter. "Lucky me," she said. "One more favor and you'll be done with me. I will have exhausted my usefulness to you, and I didn't even have to take off my clothes."

She pushed past him.

"Oh no you don't." He draped his arm around her shoulders, guiding her, rather firmly, to the quiet back hallway before releasing her. "What's wrong?"

Scarlet adjusted her lab coat. "This must be a whopper for you to manhandle me into listening."

"Why are you mad at me?" he asked, looking truly confused.

Because maybe it'd be nice for a man, one man, any man, to see her as more than a neighbor to get his mail while he's out of town, or a competent professional nurse managing the NICU, or a resource for parenting his teenage daughter. Maybe it'd be nice to be noticed and appreciated as a woman, someone nice to spend time with and not bad to look at, maybe even a little sexy in the right outfit and dim lighting.

"What did I do?"

"Nothing," she said. "Stressful day. Overreaction. Let's move on. What's the favor?"

"Did you *want* to take your clothes off?" he asked seriously. "Tell me where and when and I will happily and enthusiastically join you."

Two weeks ago she'd have fired off a sarcastic comeback meant to shut him down. No, she did not want to earn a place on his long list of meaningless one-night-stands or have her name tossed into the hospital's gossip channels as his latest conquest. But now, things weren't so clear. He was different than she'd first thought. A caring doctor. A nice guy. A father trying to be a better parent. Maybe—

Loud male voices interrupted her thoughts seconds before two men turned the corner into the back hallway.

"Damn you, Cade," the older of the two men said, pushing the other man up against the wall. "Do you hear what's being said about me? People are questioning my integrity and my skill as a surgeon." Both tall and handsome with dark hair, they could have passed for brothers. "I give you a job and this is how you repay me by trying to ruin my reputation?"

Before they noticed them, Lewis pulled her into an alcove outside a closed janitorial closet door. "This has been brewing for weeks," he whispered. "Let's give them a few minutes to work it out."

"Who are they?" Scarlet whispered back, trying to ignore his close proximity and oh so yummy scent, and the feel of his big, solid, warm body touching hers in so many places.

"The older one is Dr. Alex Rodriguez, the somewhat new head of pediatric neurosurgery," he said quietly, his mouth right next to her ear, his hot breath making it difficult to concentrate. "The other one is his half-brother, Dr. Cade Coleman, a prenatal surgeon."

Scarlet peered around the corner.

"Get your hands off of me," the younger one—Cade—yelled, twisting out of his brother's grasp. "I didn't know it was a secret. What's the big deal? You were cleared of the charges. Nothing sticks to you."

She turned back to Lewis. "What charges?" she asked quietly.

"From what I've heard, Alex was named in a malpractice suit a few years ago after one of his patients died."

A voice she now recognized as Alex's yelled, "What's that supposed to mean?"

"You always come out on the plus side of things," Cade replied. "Something bad happens, things get tough you walk away clean and leave others to deal with the mess."

"So that's what this is about? Me leaving? You still haven't forgiven me?"

Scarlet leaned in toward Lewis and whispered, "I don't think we should be listening to this."

"If we leave now we'll interrupt." Did he have to breathe so hot and heavy with every response? She tried to ignore the warm flush spreading along the right side of her face, down her neck to her chest. "And they'll know we're here."

Alex said, "I couldn't take it anymore, the verbal and physical abuse. You were so young and your dad loved you so much. If I'd had any idea he would turn on you after I left, I would have stayed. I promise you that."

"A lot of good that did me then," Cade said, sounding worn out. "And it means little to me now."

"There's nothing I can do to change what happened other than to apologize. I know it doesn't change anything, but from the bottom of my heart, I'm sorry. For leaving. For everything you had to endure because I wasn't there to protect you or help you."

Scarlet whispered, "How horrible for both of them."

Lewis nodded. "Now you understand why I didn't want to interrupt?"

She nodded. When no one spoke Scarlet peeked around the corner. Both men stood there not looking at each other. Then Alex said, "Can we get past it?" He held out his hand.

Cade looked at it.

Scarlet wanted to scream, "Take it. He's your brother for heaven's sake." Oh how she'd wished for a sibling growing up.

Eventually Cade shook his brother's hand, and Alex

took the opportunity to pull him into a hug. "I love you," he said.

Cade didn't reply, but he did pat Alex on the back.

When the men broke apart, they turned and started to walk in her direction. Scarlet ducked back into their hiding spot, sucked in a breath, and tried to blend in with the wall. "They're coming this way."

Lewis jumped to action, moving her into the corner, pressing her back into the wall with the front of his body flush against hers.

Okay. Not a bad plan. She'd be well hidden. But what about—?

Her brain ceased to function when he lifted her chin, lowered his head, and set his soft, moist lips on hers.

Just for show, she rationalized, to create a plausible reason for them to be there. In an effort to up the realism of their fictitious interlude she slid her hands up and clasped her fingers behind his neck.

Just playing her part.

His lips separated and his tongue ventured out to explore the seam of her mouth. Looking for entry? Only one way to know for sure, Scarlet created a slim smidgeon of an opening, purely for investigative purposes to see what he'd do.

And *hello*, Lewis thrust his tongue into her mouth, over and over. Something about the taste made her mouth water, made her body ready, made her want—

He closed his arms around her, deepened the kiss and thrust his hips.

Whoa. Holy hard-on. This was realism run amok. At work.

Scarlet forced her head to the side, breaking the kiss. "We can't."

He released her instantly but didn't move. The sound

of their heavy breathing filled the quiet. "I'm sorry," he said. "I guess I got a little carried away."

"You guess?" She placed her hands on his chest and pushed him back, needing air, but not feeling steady enough to move away from the support of the wall.

He looked down at her and ran a thumb along her lower lip. "You look like you've been thoroughly kissed," he said with the small smile of a man re-living the experience in his mind.

"Perfect," she snapped, losing patience. "When I'm on my way to meet up with your daughter. What were you thinking?" Scarlet took a tissue from the pack in her pocket and tried to wipe away the remnants of their kiss.

"Well at first I was thinking about hiding you and giving us an excuse to be tucked away in our little nook." He reached out to touch her cheek. "But you felt so good. And I've wanted to kiss you for so long."

She swatted his hand away. "We've known each other for all of eight days and every interaction we've had has revolved around your daughter or work. Exactly how long could you possibly have wanted to kiss me?"

"Day three," he answered without hesitation. "In the cafeteria, when you closed your eyes to imagine me in my underwear."

"I was pretending," she lied.

"No you weren't." He grinned.

So sure of himself and his appeal. The haze of arousal cleared. Beneath his respected physician, nice guy, good father façade the fire of his womanizing sex-seeker still burned at his core. "Waiting five whole days to kiss a woman you've only recently met must have required quite a bit of restraint for someone like you."

"Someone like me?" he asked, raising his eyebrows. Amused.

"Yes." She took out her hairband and started to redo her ponytail. "Someone used to having sex with a woman within hours of meeting her."

He laughed. "If only it were that easy."

It *was* easy. For him. His good looks, charm, and a smooth confidence combined to form a lethal concoction that wreaked havoc on a woman's good sense. On *her* good sense. "You disgust me." She lunged back into the hallway.

"Stop." He said, holding on to her arm. "I'm sorry. I got carried away. But don't go getting all holier-than-thou. You enjoyed my kiss." He leaned in. "Don't try to deny it."

No one was that good a liar.

He let out a breath. "Did I blow any chance of you helping me with one more thing for Jessie?" he asked seriously. "Of us maybe being friends?"

"Of course I will do what I can to help you with Jessie," she said. "She's a good kid and doesn't deserve to suffer for the transgressions of her father."

He smiled, not at all offended by her remark. "Thank you for that," he said.

"I'll defer decision on the friends issue until I see how you do at keeping your lips to yourself when we're together." Because as each day passed with no progress in locating Holly's family, Scarlet became more determined to keep baby Joey out of the hands of strangers and more excited about the idea of raising the tiny girl as her own. And as a single woman it would be hard enough to get approval to foster and hopefully adopt Joey. She couldn't chance rumors of an illicit association with a known hospital player, tarnishing her stellar reputation.

"Deal." He held out his hand.

But she kind of didn't want to touch him since her body was just starting to return to normal.

"Don't be a coward." His smile was all dare.

She shook his hand.

His skin smooth and warm. His grip powerful.

Stop it!

"During our long talk the other night," he said, seeming unaware of how the simple act of him touching her hand affected her. "Jessie told me she's not happy sleeping in the loft."

She'd mentioned that to Scarlet, too. "It has no door. And it's the *guest*room." Jess had shared that it felt like he was keeping her there temporarily until he figured out what to do with her.

"It *was* the guestroom before Jessie came to live with me. I put her up there because the loft has a bed in it."

Made perfect sense.

"But I want her to know she has a permanent place in my home with her very own bedroom and her very own door. I was hoping you'd help me make it happen while she's away. As a surprise for when she comes home."

"I think that's a great idea," Scarlet said.

"If you'd discreetly find out what colors she likes and what her ideal bedroom would look like, maybe, if you have some time over the weekend, we could go shopping and you could come back to my place and help me put it all together."

"Right," she said with as much sarcasm as she could muster. And to add to her overall 'don't for one minute think I'm going to fall for your scheme' body language, she crossed her arms over her chest, cocked her head and gave him 'the look'. "Like I'm going to go over to your condo when Jessie isn't there." Not. Especially after that kiss. Only an insane woman would do that.

"I'd treat you to lunch." His eyes met hers. "And a nice dinner."

"So I'd feel indebted to you," she said, shaking her head. "Not gonna work."

"I will be the perfect gentleman." He held up his right hand, again, as if that somehow made his words more believable. "Absolutely no kissing. I promise."

"You know I think that holding up your right hand thing only works in court. And only when your left hand is resting on a bible."

He smiled.

"And aren't you supposed to be working all weekend?" she asked. "Isn't that the reason you're sending Jess on vacation without you?"

He turned away and let out a breath. "Call me a bad person, a bad parent. But I'm smart enough to know when I've reached my limit. I need a break from parenting so bad I lied, to my parents *and* my daughter." His eyes met hers. "I will not apologize for taking a few much needed days for myself."

"All parents deserve a break, Lewis," Scarlet said, touching his arm to let him know she understood.

He covered her hand with his. "Please," he said. "Will you help me?"

Scarlet was tempted to say she had to work all weekend.

"Perfect gentleman. I promise," he said. Then he snapped his fingers. "Let's go to the chapel. I'm sure I can find a bible in there."

Scarlet smiled.

"Say you'll help me." Lewis tilted his head and made an innocent face. "For Jessie, who should not suffer for my transgressions."

And Scarlet understood how he'd so successfully

charmed so many women out of their panties. But after the year Jessie had endured, she deserved a beautiful bedroom in her father's house. Scarlet was a grown woman, she could handle him for a few hours. "Fine. Call me after she leaves," Scarlet said. "And we'll set up a time to meet."

"Thank you," he said.

She looked at her watch. "If I don't get back to my unit soon they'll send out a search party." Who would find her alone with a handsome doctor, in a quiet, cozy corridor, with a pair of swollen, red, thoroughly kissed lips.

She smoothed her hair, stepped back and spread her arms wide. "Presentable?"

He looked her up and down. "Perfect." He did the same. "Me?"

Scarlet scanned his person, making sure to spend a little extra time on the most noticeably aroused part of him to enjoy a moment of satisfaction from her role in that arousal. "Button your lab coat."

He did then he bent to pick up his now cold cup of coffee that he must have set down in the corner of their hiding spot at some point.

"I'll pump Jessie for decorating ideas," she said.

With a nod and a wave Lewis turned toward the ER and Scarlet headed in the opposite direction to see if Jessie was still waiting for her in the cafeteria.

Lewis walked back to the emergency department feeling out of sorts. In forty-eight hours he'd be dropping Jessie off at his parents' house up in Westchester County, leaving him with four full nights and three full days to himself. To do whatever he wanted with whoever he wanted. Yet he hadn't made one phone call or sent one text message or one e-mail to any of the two dozen or so women he knew for a fact would jump at the chance to spend time with him—in and out of bed.

Because he wanted to fix up Jessie's room.

Because he wanted to spend time with Scarlet, the woman who'd been occupying his mind way too often of late, the woman he'd just promised to be a perfect gentleman with. What the heck had he been thinking?

That kiss.

He adjusted his scrub pants. In his present state, one size did not fit all.

Okay, so Scarlet Miller had the good looks and trim figure he preferred. But he liked his women easy— emotionally and sexually. Did that make him shallow? Yes. But it also made him honest. With his schedule and work responsibilities, he hadn't been looking for anything long term or challenging. And he had no doubt smart, quick, feisty Scarlet would be a challenge.

Lewis returned the flirty smile of a cute blonde woman he recognized from Respiratory Therapy as she walked toward him on the opposite side of the hallway. He considered a wink, decided against it, but glanced at her fingers anyway. No wedding ring. No engagement ring. It'd be so easy to ask her out, to do all the right things and to say what needed to be said to get her into bed.

He was, after all, a master of seduction.

Yet the idea of slipping into that role, of spouting insincere flattery, and having to tolerate uninspired, unwanted conversation for the sole purpose of getting laid no longer held an appeal. Lord help him, he'd lost his desire to play the game.

He took out his cell phone and pretended to read a message until he passed her by.

Scarlet pushed her way back into his thoughts. Her soft, plump lips. Her scent. Her taste. Her barely audible moan of surrender as she'd softened against him. He may have lost his desire to play the game, but he had not lost his desire for the opposite sex, more specifically, his desire for Scarlet Miller.

He turned the corner, getting closer to the familiar sounds of his busy department, looking forward to immersing himself in his work, of focusing his mind on something other than his daughter's friend and confidante, a woman he could not have.

"Dr. Jackson," one of his more experienced nurses called out when she saw him. "Your timing is excellent. The consult you requested for exam room four is being done as we speak. Dr. Griffin was able to come after all."

Though quiet and a bit gruff with the nursing staff, Dr. John Griffin had an excellent rapport with children and was one of the finest orthopedic surgeons Lewis had ever worked with.

"And two ambulances are on the way," she continued. "Three-year-old male fell from a subway platform. Numerous scrapes and bruises. A notable laceration above his left eyebrow. Alert and responsive."

"What do we have open?" he asked, shifting back into work mode.

"Exam room two, bed three?"

"That works." At the sound of sirens he hastened his pace. "And the second one?"

"Thirteen-month-old female. Possible drowning in the bathtub. Mom is inconsolable, says she got distracted by an important phone call."

More important than her toddler? But Lewis had worked as a pediatrician long enough to know better than to make snap judgments about parents based on limited information. "Do we have a trauma bed available?"

She looked at the white board—which looked more like a red, green, and black board with all the writing it had on it—and said, "Trauma three, bed one."

The electric doors opened. An EMT walked beside a fast-moving stretcher squeezing an ambu bag, manually ventilating his small patient. "Unable to intubate en route," he reported.

"Trauma three, bed one," Lewis told the female EMT pushing the stretcher, and he set his full cup of now cold coffee on the counter at the nurses' station and got back to work.

Two hours later, finished for the day, he took the elevator to the NICU to pick up Jessie.

"Hi, Dad," she greeted him and actually sounded glad to see him. Lewis wanted to run up and hug her and cement the moment in his memory. Luckily rational thought prevailed. "Is it okay if I stick around for a little while? Scarlet asked if I could watch Nikki for a few minutes."

"Sure," Lewis said, setting down his backpack and dropping onto the soft couch. "Who's Nikki?"

The door opened and a little girl with red pigtails, a face full of freckles, wearing a pair of eyeglasses ran to hug Jessie. She really had a way with young children. Watching her, Lewis entertained the first inkling of a hope that maybe she'd follow in his footsteps and become a pediatrician.

"This is Nikki," Jessie said.

"I'm four." Nikki held up four fingers on her right hand.

She looked to be closer to three. "Nice to meet you, Nikki," Lewis said. "I'm Dr. Jackson, Jessie's dad."

"She's a NICU graduate," Jessie explained. "That means she got big enough and healthy enough to go home with her parents."

"And two," Nikki held up two fingers, "big brothers."

A woman with red hair similar to Nikki's joined them. "Would you mind telling Scarlet that Erica Cole is waiting for her in the lounge? I don't mind talking with new parents out here, but I can't handle seeing all the sick babies." She shuddered. "Brings back so many memories."

"Of course." Lewis stood. "Keep an eye on my bag, Jessie." She nodded from where she knelt on the floor, setting out a bunch of dolls.

Lewis entered the darkened, quiet NICU, so unlike his bustling ER, and walked to the first of two nurses' stations. "I'm looking for Scarlet Miller," he said to a young secretary, keeping his voice low. An older nurse he recognized from the cafeteria when he and Scarlet had met to discuss Jessie walked up beside him. "May I ask what for?" the nurse, he looked at her name badge, Linda, asked.

"Erica Cole asked me to relay the message she's waiting for Scarlet in the family lounge," he said.

"She's in with Joey Doe," Linda said with a shake of her head. "If you ask me she is getting way too attached to that baby."

"No one asked you," a younger, nurse said to Linda. "Room forty-two," she said to Lewis. "Come. I'll show you the way."

Lewis followed her. "It's so quiet in here."

"Not always." The nurse smiled. "But we try to maintain a calm, soothing environment as premature infants are hypersensitive to their surroundings." She stopped and pointed. "There she is."

Through the half glass outer wall he saw Scarlet sitting in a rocker beside Joey's incubator, feeding her from a special bottle, staring down at the tiny baby girl with a loving smile, looking very much like a mother caring for her own newborn. He walked to the doorway and cleared his throat to get her attention.

She looked up guiltily.

"How's she doing?" he whispered.

"Still not taking the bottle, but we keep trying." She lifted Joey to her shoulder and rubbed her back.

"Any news on her family?"

"No," Scarlet answered. "Are you here about Joey or did something else bring you up?"

"I came to get Jessie and she said you asked her to watch Nikki."

"Shoot." She glanced up at the clock on the wall. "I lost track of time."

"Erica Cole asked me to tell you she's here."

Scarlet stood.

"I'll take over," the nurse offered.

"Thank you." She handed Joey into the other nurse's care. "I changed one wet diaper. She's taken next to nothing from the bottle." Scarlet removed a disposable gown, balled it up, and pushed it into a waste bin.

"I have a couple in crisis," Scarlet shared quietly as she exited the room. "Erica Cole is a member of a group I formed for moms of NICU graduates. There are about fifty of them who are willing to come in with their children to talk to new parents who are having difficulty adjusting to the NICU and bonding with their babies." She looked up at him. "It gives new parents whose infants are struggling to survive a little hope. Sometimes it makes all the difference."

"Yes it does," he said from experience. Because Scarlet had given him that little hope that'd made all the difference with Jessie. She was a truly extraordinary woman.

He stood at the desk and watched her through the glass of a small private room as she spoke with a couple. Although he couldn't hear her words, her small smile conveyed understanding and compassion, her gentle touch conveyed support and caring. The couple watched her as she spoke, trust evident in their eyes. The woman started to cry and Scarlet took her into her arms and hugged her while the man turned his head as if trying to hide his emotions.

"Our Scarlet is something special," Linda said, coming to stand beside him. With such a big unit, did she have nothing better to do than hover?

"Yes she is," Lewis said, not taking his eyes off of Scarlet as she handed the woman a box of tissues and led her out of the room.

"She deserves a good man who will appreciate all she has to offer and treat her right."

Linda's tone implied a better man than him.

"No argument there."

But after eighteen years of riding the manic-depressive, passive-aggressive maternal roller coaster of emotions, Lewis had used up his lifetime supply of energy earmarked for understanding, appeasing, and striving to meet the ever-changing expectations of women. He preferred the ups of flirty banter, new acquaintances, and satisfying sex to the downs of compromise, arguments, and frustrating disappointments inherent in long term relationships.

After a childhood spent catering to the whims of a mentally ill mother, Lewis would not regress to allowing another woman any degree of control over his life. Ever.

He was his own man. He did what he wanted when he wanted and didn't have to get approval from or justify his actions to anyone. At least that'd been his pre-Jessie modus operandi.

Now the waters of his life had gotten unrecognizably muddy.

He couldn't bring various women home night after night, not with an impressionable young daughter watching his every move. Most unsettling, with four days of freedom ahead, was the fact he seemed to have lost the anticipatory thrill of the chase, catch, and release. Random, meaningless hookups with generic, unmemorable women no longer appealed to him. But neither did monogamy or marriage. So where did that leave him?

Lewis left the NICU without another word to Linda, entered the lounge to get his backpack, and told Jessie to meet him in his office when she was done. He needed time to think.

It'd taken a near successful suicide attempt for his mother to get his father to lift his head out of his prestigious surgical practice long enough to acknowledge the toxic level of dysfunction in their family. With renewed attention, love and support from her husband and some long-overdue treatment his mom's condition had stabilized.

Unfortunately for Lewis, the damage to his ability to form lasting, trusting, positive relationships with women was done.

Instead of waiting for the elevator, he took the stairs down, needing to burn off some energy.

Supportive evidence of his lack of interpersonal finesse: The past nine months of torture with Jessie.

Although things were finally turning around thanks to Scarlet, his daughter's friend and confidante, a woman who deserved more than a man like him, a woman whose appeal extended beyond good looks. A woman he could not have, who made him want with an intensity he'd never before experienced.

A problem not easily solved.

He exited the stairwell.

One thing was for certain, having her in his condo, with the two of them alone and hot for each other, would only complicate matters. After their kiss, he no longer trusted himself, despite his promise of perfect gentlemanly behavior, which meant he needed to figure out a way to get her help in designing Jessie's new room without her actually stepping foot into his condo.

CHAPTER FIVE

On Thursday morning Scarlet fought the urge to fling her arms out to the side and twirl. She tamped down the desire to skip through the halls of the hospital shouting, "I did it!" A manager needed to maintain some degree of decorum. But nothing could wipe the grin from her face as she walked toward the employee changing rooms to wash up and change into a pair of hospital scrubs—her standard work attire.

After months of ups and downs riding the 'I want a baby' 'I don't have time for a baby' teeter-totter, compounded by hours spent obsessing over her finances, living situation, and work schedule, Scarlet had done it. She'd taken action, the first step. True, frequent sex until she got pregnant would have been significantly more enjoyable than page after page of paperwork, but hopefully her early morning meeting with Joey's social worker would lead to the same outcome. Motherhood.

Granted her chances of becoming a foster parent and later adopting Joey would be better if she were part of a married couple, but Joey needed a mom and Scarlet wanted a daughter, and if she didn't try she'd have no chance at all.

Scarlet reached up to push on the door to the changing area at the same time someone from inside must have yanked it open because her hands met air. Forward momentum sent her stumbling into a hard male chest.

How embarrassing. She'd been so preoccupied she'd tried to enter the men's changing area.

Wait a minute. She glanced at the sign on the door: Women Only.

Whew.

"I'm sorry," a male voice said. She looked up to see a man she now recognized as Dr. Alex Rodriguez. "I shouldn't have…" he mumbled, releasing her without looking at her. "I didn't plan to… Damn it." He hurried off.

Scarlet entered cautiously, not sure what she'd find. A beautiful blonde woman, her fashionable attire covered by a white lab coat, sat on a bench, staring at a locker, looking dazed, running two fingers back and forth across her lips.

This was none of Scarlet's business. She walked to her locker and worked the combination lock, already running late.

The woman sniffled and Scarlet couldn't ignore her. "Are you okay?" she asked, walking over to where the woman sat.

The woman must not have noticed Scarlet's presence because she jumped.

"I'm sorry," Scarlet said. "I didn't mean to startle you."

"I shouldn't be in here," the woman said with a sweet southern twang, looking sad.

"It's not like your presence is disturbing anyone." Scarlet scanned the otherwise empty room. "I'm Scarlet Miller." She held out her hand. "I work in the NICU."

The woman looked up and with a small smile she

shook Scarlet's hand. "I'm Layla Woods, new head of pediatrics."

"I've heard about you," Scarlet said.

Layla gasped and brought her hand to her heart. "Already?" She looked about to cry.

"Good things. All good things," Scarlet hurried to add. "From Dr. Donaldson, a neonatologist who works on my unit. He said he was on your interview committee."

Layla seemed to relax.

"He thinks you're perfect for the position."

"I wanted it so badly." Layla's blue eyes locked on hers. "It was supposed to be my chance for a new start. But I had no idea…" She stopped.

"This is about Dr. Rodriguez."

Layla let out a breath. "It's already spread around the hospital. I can't do this." She stood and reached for her purse. "Not again. I have to—"

"Wait." Scarlet stepped in front of her. "I mentioned Dr. Rodriguez because he nearly knocked me to the ground in his hurry to leave the locker room. The *women's* locker room, might I add."

"We had an argument," Layla said quietly, sitting back down. "He followed me in." She touched her lips again. "Five years," she whispered. "And nothing has changed."

This was like piecing together a puzzle on a game show. Scarlet sat down beside Layla. "I've got a few minutes if you want to talk about it," she lied. Because she didn't have a few minutes, she needed to get up to her unit to evaluate two new overnight admissions, a critically ill newborn with congenital diaphragmatic hernia and a struggling little boy born at twenty-nine weeks to a heroine addicted mother, now suffering from neonatal abstinence syndrome.

Luckily her staff, comprised of some of the highest skilled clinicians in the country, functioned competently and independently. And they knew how to reach her if they needed her. "Maybe it'd help me to understand if you started from the beginning."

Layla nodded. "Alex and I used to work together. We had a…thing." She looked away as if embarrassed.

"It happens," Scarlet said. Not to her, but to plenty of her co-workers, working long hours in stressful situations, experiencing instances of wretched loss and sorrow interspersed with jubilant miracles of recovery, men and woman needing to share solace and unadulterated joy in the arms of others who understood the constant demands of the medical profession.

"A little boy died," Layla said. "He was our patient. His parents sued the hospital and Alex." She looked down at the ground. "My name got dragged into the case since I was the one who requested Alex as consult. Our relationship got called into question and now people at this hospital have found out. I can't escape it."

"I'm guessing you both were cleared of any wrongdoing if you and Dr. Rodriguez both made it through the rigorous hiring process here at Angels'."

"Innocence doesn't matter to the gossips," Layla insisted. "Being found guilty in the court of public opinion can be just as damaging to one's professional reputation as an actual 'guilty of malpractice' verdict in the courts."

"Not here," Scarlet told her. "The residents of New York City and the surrounding areas trust this hospital and its administration to employ top quality medical personnel. Hundreds of physicians apply for jobs here every year. Only a very small percentage of them make it past the first stage of the interview process."

"But—"

Scarlet didn't let her finish. "People are going to talk. Don't let a bunch of gossipers determine your future. Administration would not have chosen you if you weren't the best person available to head up Pediatrics. If this is your fresh start, if this is the job you want, don't be so quick to give it up."

Layla reached out to take her hand. "Thank you."

They sat there in silence until Layla said, "He kissed me." She ran her fingers over her bottom lip, again, mindlessly. "We had a bad break." She looked at Scarlet. "How is it possible that one kiss can erase five years apart like they never happened? How can one kiss make me want a man who is totally wrong for me?"

Scarlet had spent the night pondering the exact same thing. "You still care for him."

"I don't want to," Layla said quietly.

Scarlet's cell phone rang. She stood, "I've got to get back to work," and held out her hand. "It was nice to meet you, Dr. Layla Woods." When Layla shook her hand Scarlet added. "On behalf of the NICU staff, welcome to Angel's. We're happy to have you here."

Layla smiled. "Thank you."

Finally up on the NICU Scarlet retrieved her stack of messages and found her charge nurse, Deb, at the rear nurses' station. "I'm here," she said, pulling out a chair to sit beside her. "What can I do?"

"Our transport team is en route to St. Vincent's Hospital to pick up a twenty-six weeker. Estimated return at ten o'clock. Labor and delivery reported a mom at thirty-three weeks with severe pre-eclampsia is on her way to the OR for an emergency C-section. And we have another pre-term multiple birth scheduled for eleven o'clock. That's five new admissions and we only have three incubators available."

"Contact discharge planning and find out where they're at with the coordination of home care nursing visits and durable medical equipment for Simms in twenty-two and Berg in twelve," Scarlet said. "We have two more scheduled for discharge today. I'll see what I can do to move things along. Anything else I need to know?"

Deb smiled. "I took care of baby Joey's morning feeding, like you asked, and she took a few sucks on the nipple. She's getting there."

Scarlet's day brightened considerably.

Deb looked around then leaned in and whispered, "Did you do it?"

Scarlet nodded. So far, Deb and the social worker assigned to Joey's case were the only people to know about Scarlet's application to become a foster/adoptive parent.

"She's a lucky little girl," Deb said.

"If things work out, I'll be the lucky one." To finally have a daughter to take care of and love, after all these years of wanting, a chance to be a mom, and she'd help an abandoned infant in the process. God willing, someone had done the same for her daughter.

"What are your chances?" Deb asked.

"They'd be better if there was a Mr. Miller and I didn't work such long hours," Scarlet scanned through her messages to see if any were urgent. "But Joey will likely go home requiring some level of specialized care that I am more than qualified to provide. I put down I'd take a six week maternity leave, like any new mom would get, to stay at home to care for her. So if nothing else, they may give her to me for the six weeks during which time I will figure out a doable work schedule to convince the decision-makers that permanent placement with me is what's in Joey's best interest." Exactly what Holly would have wanted. What Scarlet wanted.

Deb shook her head.

"What?"

"Six weeks," she said quietly. "I don't know how we'll survive without you."

"I've budgeted for an assistant head nurse but never filled the position because up until now I haven't needed to." She looked at Deb pointedly, hoping to relay the message she was the only person Scarlet would accept for the job. "Maybe it's time I started taking applications."

Deb, quick on the uptake as usual, asked, "You think I'm ready?"

More than ready. "Yes. Let's see how things work out with Joey. Promise me you'll think about it."

"Oh I will," Deb said.

With a "Thanks for holding things together until I got here," Scarlet left to say a quick good morning to her precious baby girl, before she got to work.

Hours passed like minutes, but Scarlet found the time to feed and cuddle Joey once and rush down to the cafeteria to meet Jessie for their standing three o'clock cafeteria date.

"Hey," Scarlet said, placing her orange tray down on the table opposite Jessie's. "You all ready for your trip?" She pulled out a chair and sat down.

Jessie picked up her apple and wiped it with a napkin. "Yup."

"You feeling better about the lake and the swimming

and boating?" Scarlet felt terrible that she'd missed meeting up with Jess on Tuesday so they hadn't done much girl-talking since their Saturday outing.

Jessie chewed her bite of apple. "Grandpa Richard said everyone on the boat has to wear a life jacket—they keep you afloat if you should wind up in the water—even him and grandma." She took a sip of milk. "And Grandma's going to take the girls to the craft store so he can teach me to swim without interruption."

Scarlet loved how Jessie now spoke excitedly about the trip she'd been dreading for months.

"Grandpa thinks I'm big and strong and smart enough that I should be swimming by myself by the end of the trip."

"That's great."

"Then I won't ever have to be scared of the water again."

Scarlet hoped Grandpa Richard came through as promised.

After another bite of apple Jess turned serious. "Will you do something for me?"

Scarlet swallowed down a spoonful of yogurt. "Of course."

"I'm worried about my dad."

Who Scarlet hadn't seen or heard from since their kiss.

"He's been real quiet. And he hasn't been eating much. I think maybe he's getting sick." She slid a key and a piece of paper across the table. "I'm going to call him every day. But if he doesn't answer I'll need someone to make sure he's okay."

"Jess." Scarlet reached out to touch her hand. "I'm sure your dad will be fine. Maybe he's sad about you leaving."

"He's all I have now," she said. "What if something happens to him while I'm gone?"

Jessie didn't say it but Scarlet heard, "What will happen to me?"

"I promise, if you need me to check on your dad, I will," Scarlet said.

"I wrote down his telephone number so you could call him, too." She shrugged. "If you want. And our address." She pointed to the piece of paper under the key. "I told the man at the desk in our building that you have permission to go right up because you're my friend."

Scarlet smiled. "I'm glad we're friends."

Jessie smiled back. "Me, too."

"I don't want you to worry about your dad. Go on your trip and have fun. I'll call him every day, so if you get busy and forget it's no big deal."

Jessie lunged out of her seat, around the table, and into Scarlet's arms. "Thank you," she said, squeezing Scarlet tight. "I'm going to miss you."

"You're most welcome," Scarlet said, squeezing her back. "You'll only be gone for four days, but I'm going to miss you, too."

In the slightly more than twenty-four hours since Jessie had given her the key to Lewis's condo, Scarlet hadn't spent one second thinking she'd actually have to use it. Well…except for the dream where she'd snuck into his home late at night…under cover of darkness…into his bedroom…into his bed…naked.

Whoa. She shifted her bags and fanned herself, the motion futile in the stuffy elevator taking her up to the twenty-first floor of Lewis's posh upper-east-side building. That'd been a hot one.

But since it had nothing to do with a well-being check, it didn't count.

The elevator pinged its arrival and the doors opened to a décor of opulent elegance that mimicked the lobby. Two antique chairs upholstered in a floral maroon fabric with magnificently carved, dark-stained wooden arms and legs sat at an angle on either side of a small matching table and below a large ornate gold-trimmed mirror. Quiet and the smell of wealth greeted her.

It reminded Scarlet of her youth. The memories were not pleasant ones.

Each door she passed looked the same. Pristine. Just like the bland textured walls that surrounded them.

The hallway, the lobby, the entire building, while lovely, lacked personality. Where were the signs of life, the feeling of warmth and welcome? Scarlet loved her New Jersey apartment, for her crazy boisterous neighbors and the smells of their varied meal menus, as much as its proximity to New York City.

She found Lewis's door and stopped. What if he was in there with someone? What if the reason she and Jessie couldn't reach him was he'd turned off his phone so as not to be disturbed during his four days of debauchery.

"Please, Scarlet. You have to go. What if he's lying on the floor dying and there's no one to help him?" Boy Jessie had a vivid imagination.

She lifted her hand to knock. Stopped.

What if he answered the door partially dressed and reeking of sex? She swallowed down a lump of regret-coated disappointment—which made no sense since they'd only known each other for two weeks and could barely even qualify as friends.

But that kiss.

She shook her head to dislodge the memory. Not

that it'd worked any of the other five dozen or so times she'd tried.

Best to just get it done and be gone. With a fortifying breath she knocked.

And waited.

She knocked harder.

Nothing.

She slid her hand into the front pocket of her jeans, closed her fingers around his key, and prayed she didn't have to use it.

"Lewis," she yelled, knocking even harder. "It's Scarlet. Open up." She pressed her ear to the door to listen for any sounds coming from inside.

Nothing.

Scarlet removed the key from her pocket, and trying to ignore an overwhelming feeling of dread, inserted it into the lock.

Lewis stood under the spray of hot water hoping to wash away his funk. He missed his old life, but it turned out, not as much as he missed Jessie. Talk about a totally unexpected twist. And since he'd dropped her off at his parents' house the night before, he'd spent a large chunk of his 'I'm finally free to do whatever I want' time thinking of her, wondering what she was doing, regretting not going to Lake George, wishing he could be the one to teach his daughter to swim, to help her overcome her fear of the water, bemoaning the missed opportunity to reinforce the tenuous bond that'd formed between them over the past week.

But if he suddenly barged in on her vacation Jessie would know he'd lied about having to work, to get rid of her, exactly as she'd suspected.

Tenuous bond severed.

Served him right for lying in the first place.

More than once he'd picked up the phone to call Scarlet, to fill the quiet. To cheer him up and make him smile. But at some point in their conversation she'd undoubtedly bring up his request that she help him with Jessie's room and look to make arrangements to get together. And even though it'd been three days since he'd changed his mind about having her over, he had yet to tell her. He wasn't ready to put an end to the possibility. And she'd no doubt want to know why—women always wanted to know why, and he had no idea how to answer.

"I want to have sex with you so bad I don't trust myself to be alone with you without a thirteen-year-old chaperone?"

What if the stars aligned and she admitted, "I want you, too." Because after their kiss, he could tell she did.

What then?

They'd pack a lifetime's worth of sex into the next seventy-two hours and it'd be great—Lewis would make sure of it. But she'd want more. They always wanted more, more of his time, his attention, his lifestyle, and money.

Things Lewis was not prepared to give.

And he couldn't risk hurting Scarlet's feelings or making her angry. Not with her close relationship to Jessie which she could easily use to turn his daughter against him. A woman scorned and all.

So what if Scarlet didn't seem the type?

You never could tell. His mother had managed to hide her true self from teachers and neighbors. Lewis wouldn't risk it.

But that didn't stop him from thinking about spending time with her. Doing…anything. He smiled. She could probably make a root canal enjoyable. Pleasurable. He pictured her sitting beside the exam chair, her hand on his bare leg—because he'd chosen to wear shorts that day—caressing him, moving up the sensitive skin of his inner thigh, sliding higher, the feel of her sensual touch obliterating the oral surgeon and the drill.

His body reacted the way it always did when images of him and Scarlet alone together popped into his head.

All the confirmation he needed that calling her to cancel their shopping/decorating date had to be done, and out of fairness to her and her weekend plans, soon.

Lewis turned off the shower, grabbed his towel from the hook and dried himself.

No more putting it off. He set his towel on the counter. He'd call Scarlet now. After the weekend he'd hire a professional decorator. Or he and Jessie could work on the room together, their first father-daughter project.

He opened the door leading to his bedroom, and along with a rush of cool air came a voice that sounded alarmingly similar to Scarlet's. "Please tell me you're alone."

Great. He'd progressed from conjuring up images to actually hearing her. Lunatic.

"And that you're appropriately covered up," she added.

What? He grabbed his towel, wrapped it around his waist and stepped out of the bathroom. Sure enough, Scarlet Miller, star of his nighttime/daytime/all the time fantasies, sat perched on the corner of his bed, fully dressed with her hand covering her eyes.

"What are you doing here?" he asked.

"Are you decent?" she responded.

He stared at her enticing lips as she spoke, noting a hint of shine. Residual lip gloss? Or had she run her plump tongue over those luscious lips while visualizing him in the shower?

"Why are you so quiet?" she asked.

He smiled, crossed his arms over his bare chest, and leaning his shoulder against the doorframe, stared at her. The ponytail she always wore, in the basic hairband she used for work, expensively distressed skintight jeans, open-toed trendy, strappy sandals, enticingly manicured peach-colored toenails, and a sleeveless, silky, peach-colored button-down blouse.

She created a tiny V-opening between her fingers and looked at him. Then she let out an annoyed breath, moved her hand to point toward the bathroom and whispered, "Is there someone else in there?"

Lately she was the only one he wanted in there. "What are you doing here?" he asked again. "In my bedroom? On my bed?" His body liked seeing her there for real and the part of him already hardened with interest from the mere thought of her, got even harder and started to rise up to check things out.

Scarlet eyed his crotch and jumped up like she'd seen a cobra. "Sorry." She backed toward the door to the hallway.

Lewis demonstrated a level of restraint he didn't know he possessed when he stood his ground rather than give in to the powerful urge to stop her.

"Jessie's been trying to call you," she said.

"Dammit." Lewis strode over to his nightstand and flicked on his cellphone. "I turned it off so no one from the hospital would bother me." He scrolled through his messages counting thirteen from Jessie and five from Scarlet. "What's wrong? Did something happen?"

"Newsflash, papa bear," Scarlet said, her calm confidence returned. "Fathers of scared little girls are not allowed the luxury of turning off their cell phones."

He dialed Jessie. She answered on the first ring, like she'd been sitting there waiting for his call, and immediately started to cry.

"Don't cry, honey," he said, feeling like the worst parent ever. "I'm sorry. My phone was off. I thought you'd be so busy having fun you'd forget all about me." And he'd completely failed to consider that maybe she'd want to talk to him about her day or her progress with swimming. Or that maybe she'd need reassurance or praise or an encouraging word from her father, him, the worst parent ever.

"If something…happens to…you," she said between hiccupping breaths, "where do I go next?"

Next? "Jessie, nothing is going to happen to me."

"That's what my mom thought, too," she cried.

His chest burned in response to her sobs.

"I want to have a say where I go," Jessie said.

Because she was so unhappy with where she'd wound up, so unhappy with him?

"I want to go to Scarlet."

At her mention, he remembered the current topic of their conversation was standing in his bedroom doorway, listening.

Only when he turned to see if Scarlet had overheard Jessie's demand, he saw no sign of her. Relieved, he walked over to close the door. "As much as you like Scarlet," he said quietly. "She's not family." And according to his revised will, on the off chance something did happen to him, Jessie would go to live with his sister.

"She feels like family to me," Jessie insisted. "Please ask her, Dad. Promise me you'll ask her."

Lewis sat down on the bed. "Okay," he agreed. What

else could he say to his hysterical daughter who was hours away? "I promise."

After a few moments of silence, in a voice barely louder than a whisper, Jessie shared, "I went out on the boat."

"I'm so proud of you,' Lewis said. Slowly Jessie calmed down and they had a nice conversation. At the end he had to promise to keep his cell phone charged, turned on, and with him at all times, before she'd hang up.

With Jessie taken care of Lewis pulled on a pair of briefs and jeans and left the room to find Scarlet.

"Stop with the guilt trip," she said into her cell phone, her back and shapely butt to him. "I had to do a favor for a friend uptown. It'll take me forever to get down to the South Street Seaport now. You all eat without me. I'll see you next time."

She'd changed her Friday night plans for him and Jessie.

"Right," she said sarcastically. "You have me all figured out. I'm ditching you for a night of wild sex with a hot guy, because it is so like me to do something like that. As a matter of fact he's naked and waiting for me in his bedroom as we speak."

He wasn't, but he could be in two seconds.

She listened to the person on the other end of the call then said, "It hasn't been *that* long."

How long?

"Well," she said. "I'll finally have something to talk about the next time we get together for girls night out, then. That is if he hasn't fallen asleep while I'm wasting quality sex time talking to you."

Quality sex time. Lewis wanted some quality sex time. He *needed* quality sex time. And this conversation was seriously weakening his resolve to stay away from Scarlet.

She paused then laughed. "In a closet."

A closet? Okay with him.

"Only if he asks real nice," she said.

Lewis could do real nice.

"I'm always good," she said.

Of that Lewis had no doubt.

She laughed again. The sound filled him with joy.

"Okay." He heard the smile in her voice. "Tonight I'll be bad."

Oh yeah. He liked the sound of that.

She stiffened.

Idiot. Had he actually said the 'oh yeah' out loud?

Scarlet turned her head slowly. Their eyes met. "Gotta go," she said into the phone and ended the call. "So much for giving me a little privacy like I gave you when you were on the phone," she said to him.

Without conscious thought his feet walked toward her, taking the rest of him with them.

"Whoa." She held up both hands. "Apparently you are under the mistaken impression I am here for more than a wellness check."

"I did hear mention of wild sex with a hot guy," he pointed out. "Thank you for the compliment, by the way."

She stepped back. "Well you obviously didn't listen close enough to the inflection in my tone to detect my sarcasm."

"Let's not waste anymore quality sex time with talking," he half-teased, reaching for her.

"Touch me and lose a finger," she threatened.

He stopped with his hands mid-air, mere inches from her shoulders, and waited.

She looked up at him with those beautiful eyes. "I'm serious."

He smiled. "I know. But I think I need a stronger deterrent because even though you are the absolute last woman I should be lusting after, I want to put my hands on you so bad right now I'm willing to sacrifice my phalanges to do it." Actually, he was prepared to sacrifice a lot more.

Scarlet, obviously the smarter of the two of them, turned and walked away. And he let her. "The absolute last woman you should be lusting after?" She moved a used glass from the counter to the sink. "As in you'd rather lust after Hilda from the endoscopy department before you'd lust after me?"

Lewis shivered, and not in a good way. Hilda was big and mean and she had kinky gray hairs sprouting on her chin.

"Or Morgan in Administration?" she went on.

That woman was the skinniest, coldest, stiffest female he had ever met.

"Or Gretchen from Food Service?"

Renowned for her hairnet and tan stretch pants that clung to every single pouch of cellulite as much as for her shiny gold tooth.

Scarlet looked at him from the corners of her eyes. "I'm not sure if I'm relieved or insulted."

Lewis pulled out a stool, sat down and set his elbows on the island counter in the center of his kitchen. "The absolute last woman as in your friendship with my daughter makes things…complicated."

"Yeah," Scarlet agreed. "That it does." She walked to the side of the island directly opposite him and asked, "What if I wasn't friends with Jess? If you saw me in a bar, would you try to get me to go home with you?"

In a heartbeat. To clarify, "I wouldn't *try* to get you to go home with me. I *would* get you to go home with me."

"Oh you think so?" She laughed. "Rather confident, aren't you?"

When it came to women that would be a capital Y*E*S. To both.

"How would you go about it?" She crossed her arms over her chest. "Give me your best line."

He stood. She looked up at him warily. "It's not so much what I say as how I say it," he explained as he walked toward her. "It'd be loud and crowded in the bar, so I'd have to lean in close like this." He turned her to face him, stepped forward, and leaned in, putting his mouth inches from her ear. She smelled so good. "I'd start off quiet, knowing you can't hear me." He whispered some gibberish.

"What?"

"Exactly." He uncrossed her arms. "So I'd move in closer." He did, brushing the front of his thigh against the front of hers, setting his lips close enough to touch the inner rim of her ear and, making sure to expel a hot rush of breath, as he said, "I forgot my phone number, could I borrow yours?"

She didn't laugh or criticize his corny line. Instead she closed her eyes and tilted her head to the side, ever so slightly, giving him better access.

Success.

He slid his hand up the nape of her neck and, keeping his voice soft and deep, said, "Or maybe I'd say something like, 'I love that blouse.'" He ran a gentle finger down the inside of an arm hole, caressing her delicate skin as he did. "'It'd look perfect draped over the back of the chair in my bedroom.'" Just to introduce the idea of her getting naked in his condo. He made sure his lower lip grazed along her earlobe as he moved away.

"Wow," she said on an exhaled breath. "You're good." She opened her eyes and blinked as if trying to get them back into focus. "On that admission I think I'd better be going." Without further hesitation she turned and moved away.

"No," he said, taking her hand, desperate to keep her close. "Please. Don't go." Because he didn't want to be alone, because he liked spending time with her, because, Lord help him, he craved her with a ferocity capable of significant damage to his manly assets if he didn't do something about it.

"I don't know," she said in that teasing tone of hers. "You promised to be a perfect gentleman around me." She looked down at his hand squeezing hers. "Yet the vibe I'm getting is anything but gentlemanly."

Perceptive.

"I promised not to kiss you again," he clarified, pulling her back to him. "And I won't." He nuzzled in close to her ear and whispered, "Unless you ask me real nice." He'd get *her* to make the first move, to beg him to touch her for real. Then she'd have no basis to be angry with him afterwards.

"Suppose I stay," she asked. "What did you have in mind for us to do that doesn't involve kissing?"

Caressing. Licking. Exploring. "Anything you want."

CHAPTER SIX

ANYTHING YOU WANT.

Yikes! An open invitation like that could get a girl into trouble. Or it could satisfy the increasingly distracting yearning responsible for loss of sleep, poorly-timed bouts of daydreaming, and an on-edge/wound-too-tight feeling that Scarlet felt certain a night of stellar sex would remedy.

"*Anything* I want?"

His lips formed a sexy half-smile. "In the closet or outside of it."

So he'd heard that comment. "We do girls night out once a month," she explained, trying to ignore the effects his close proximity had on her body. "My friends like to share their sexual exploits over pricey cocktails. And let me tell you, I have some adventurous friends."

"Dare I hope birds of a feather flock together?" he asked.

In her case, they did. But she wouldn't tell *him* that. "Anyway," she emphasized, moving along. "Out of all the places they've had sex, and there have been some interesting places, no one in the group has ever done it in a closet."

"I think you should be the first," he said in earnest.

Oh did he?

"I have three that can accommodate us," he added.

She looked up at him. "Us? As in you and me?" She gestured back and forth between them. "As in you and the absolute last woman you should lust after because of my friendship with your daughter?"

"So you have something to talk about the next time you go out with your girlfriends." He stared into her eyes. "It sounded like it's been a while since you had anything…adventurous to contribute."

Eighteen months to be exact. In her defense, they'd been very busy months involving long hours spent at the hospital, with her all female staff. And the majority of men she came in contact with were either married, in the midst of family crisis, or doctors. None of them viable boyfriend material, especially doctors, her professional colleagues, who were as preoccupied by their patients and worked the same insane amount of hours she did. A relationship would never work.

And yet she'd been entertaining some relationship-worthy thoughts about Dr. Lewis Jackson—in a closet.

"You're a standup guy, Dr. Jackson." She used his professional credential to remind her who she was dealing with. "Ready to stuff yourself in a closet for me and all."

"The perfect gentleman in me is willing, able, and ready to assist you in one-upping your friends. And when we're alone, please call me Lewis."

"Will you respond to Lou?"

"Only if it's preceded by 'kiss me.'"

Not gonna happen. After experiencing the good sense eradicating power of his kiss firsthand, and dreaming of it night after night since then, if Scarlet had any hope of keeping things between them platonic, she could not invite, encourage, or in any way appear to welcome another kiss, because if his lips made contact with hers, she would not be able to resist him. And resist him she must.

Scarlet liked Lewis, as a friend. A friend she happened to be crazy attracted to. Would a night of sex squelch that attraction or make it even more difficult to ignore? Would it lead to awkward interactions or ongoing secret hookups behind Jessie's back? Would it remain private or would someone find out?

Would it hurt Jessie or negatively impact Scarlet's chances of adopting Joey?

She refused to risk either.

Time to take back control.

She sidled up to Lewis, pressing her breasts to his chest, reaching up to cup the back of his neck and pull his head down so she could whisper in his ear. "I hope you were serious when you said anything," she whispered. "What I have in mind will involve strength." She caressed his biceps. "And patience. I don't like to be rushed."

"You set the pace," he said, wrapping his arms around her. Two large hands gripped her butt and pulled her bottom half flush with his. "You're in charge."

"That's what I like to hear," she said quietly, keeping her mouth close to his ear. Then she puckered up and made the loudest kissing noise she could.

When Lewis jumped back she said, "Now put on a shirt. We're going shopping."

"Shopping?" he asked, holding his ear.

"You did say anything I wanted." Scarlet walked to the bags she'd dropped at the front door when she'd arrived and bent to retrieve her backpack.

"But shopping wasn't at all what I'd had in mind," he mumbled.

Scarlet looked down so he wouldn't see her smile as she unzipped the front pouch and took out the advertisements she'd printed. "I found the perfect comforter set and accessories for Jessie's room." She carried the pictures back to the kitchen and spread the top few out on the island counter. "I ordered them and they're waiting for us to pick them up at Macy's." She looked over to him. "Of course if you hate them or they're too expensive I can cancel the order. Or I'll pay half. Or all if I have to. I want her room to be amazing." The kind of room a girl would love to spend time in. A room she'd want to invite her friends over to see.

"I can afford to pay for my daughter's bedding, thank you," he groused, reviewing the results of the hours she'd spent on the Internet.

"I thought we could paint one wall this color." She held up the color swatch she'd gotten from the paint store and pointed to the shade with red X. A dark, grape jelly purple. "Jessie told me you have hardwood floors throughout but this throw rug will offset the deep coloring of the wall perfectly." She pointed to a picture of a colorfully designed rug. "I couldn't find it in stock anywhere local, so we'll have to order it."

"Stop," he said. "The rug is fine, but there will be no purple wall. Not in my condo."

His bland, shades of cream condo. "That's your problem, Lewis," she said, prepared for this battle. "You can't think of it as a wall in *your* home. You need to think of it as a wall in *Jessie's* bedroom. A wall with personality. A wall with posters of her favorite bands." Scarlet hurried over to one of the bags and pulled out the three posters and the lavender and purple picture board she'd purchased. "It won't be a wall of solid purple. We can put the bed on that wall. And hang these.

See?" she pointed to the accent colors on the posters and picture board. "Shades of purple. Purple is her favorite color, did you know that?" Scarlet couldn't remember ever being so excited about a decorating project. "She's going to love it."

Lewis scooped up her papers. "You've put a lot of time into this," he noted.

And she'd enjoyed every minute of it. "Growing up I promised myself if I was ever lucky enough to have a daughter, I'd do a better job than my mother did with me." She shrugged. "Not that Jessie is my daughter or anything. But so far she's the closest I've come to the real thing." Hopefully that would change soon.

"Let me guess," Lewis said. "Boring bedroom."

"*Beautiful* bedroom." She emphasized the beautiful. "Very high-end. Designer everything. In floral prints and pastel colors I hated. A showroom that had to be maintained as such on the off chance one of mom's snooty friends happened by to take a peek. No shoes on the carpet. No eating on the bed. No pens or markers. No makeup. No pictures or posters or anything to reflect my style and taste." A fictional set in which she served as a decorative prop to add to the illusion of the happy, successful, fairytale family.

"I like the comforter set," he said, studying one of the advertisements. "And I'm fine with the posters and even the rug." He looked at her. "Jessie can do whatever she wants in her room," he hesitated, "within reason, of course. But there will be no purple wall."

"When I asked about her ideal bedroom, Jessie specifically said it'd have a purple wall. It's what she wants." What would make her feel settled and in her own space. And Scarlet was going to see that she got it.

"It's important for children to know they can't always get what they want."

"Considering her mother is dead and she was forced to leave the only home she'd ever known and all of her friends to live with a man she'd never met and attend a school she hates, I think Jessie has already learned that lesson," Scarlet pointed out.

"She hates her school?" he asked, looking truly puzzled.

"When she talks, don't be so quick to dismiss what she says as complaining or being difficult. Listen to her. She has some valid grievances."

Lewis opened his mouth to say something but Scarlet held up her finger to stop him. "You can discuss them with her when she gets home, *after* you present her fabulously funky new bedroom with the bright purple wall that will show her, and leave no doubt, that you have given her a permanent space of her very own."

"She'll have her very own bedroom with her very own door. She doesn't need a purple wall."

Stubborn. But so was Scarlet. "I am not giving up on this," she said. It was too important. "What do you want?"

"What do you mean what do I want?"

"What do I have to do to get you to agree to the purple wall?"

That got his attention. His lips curved into a slow, sexy, seductive smile. "Let me get this straight," he said. "You'll give me whatever I want to get me to agree to let you paint a wall in Jessie's room purple?"

"I didn't say *whatever* you want, you pervert," she clarified, instantly regretting her impulsive statement. "Like I would actually sleep with you to get you to agree to a paint color. Is that how the women you prefer get

you to do what they want? By offering you sex? Paint
the wall. Don't paint the wall. Your call. I've done what
you asked me to do. You have pictures, store names and
confirmation numbers on the advertisements. My work
here is done." She turned toward the door.

"A kiss," he called out.

She stopped.

"On the lips. With tongue."

And Jessie would get her purple wall. Scarlet turned
to face him. "You honestly expect me to compromise
my principles and use my body as a bargaining tool."

He stood there so cocky and confident, attractive,
alluring… "Only your mouth."

Seemed a minor deed for a major victory that would
mean so much to Jessie. "No other physical contact."

He pulled out a stool and sat down. Then he leaned
back, rested his elbows on the island counter behind him
and spread his thighs. "I will be a perfect gentleman."

She walked toward him. "For the record, a perfect
gentleman wouldn't coerce a woman into kissing him."

He smiled. "Okay, maybe not a perfect gentleman,
how about a close-to-perfect gentleman?"

She eyed his naked chest, which was close to perfect indeed. Smooth and muscled with minimal hair.
"Maybe you should put on a shirt first," she suggested,
because she'd been the one to specify no other physical contact during their kiss, and it would be the ultimate humiliation if she broke her own rule. And her
hands wanted to feel him so bad she had some serious
concern as to whether she'd be able to stop them. Her
palms started to tingle in anticipation. So did her lips.

"Time's running out," he said.

"You have got to be kidding me. I can't believe—"

"Five. Four."

Counting. He was actually counting.

"Three."

She would not be rushed, would not allow herself to be forced into kissing him without some serious mental girding. "Stop."

"Two."

Then again, what harm could a teeny tiny kiss do? She stepped between his thighs.

"One."

She set her lips to his, a gentle touch. He kept his lips relaxed, so full and warm with a hint of mint. And something else, something decadent and desirable, something she wanted more of. She shifted to get a better taste. He opened for her and Scarlet accepted his invitation, sliding her tongue into his mouth—only because it'd been one of his stipulations and not at all because she wanted to.

She moved in closer and, oops, had to steady herself by placing her hands on his warm, smooth, firm chest. Yum!

More. Her body erupted in a blaze of yearning.

She deepened the kiss, pressed her body to his, and noticed her fingers had found their way into his hair, which was probably a better place for them than option B—unbuttoning her blouse so she could feel his skin against hers.

Her nipples ached for attention. Her long-neglected sex throbbed with need.

Lewis sat completely still, keeping his hands to himself, being a close-to-perfect gentleman. While Scarlet's rational self lobbed idle threats at her aroused self for even considering sliding out of her jeans, straddling his crotch, and rubbing until she found release. *So close*.

"Do it," he whispered against her mouth, as if he

could read her mind. "Or tell me what you want. Anything."

Damn him.

So in control, the entire time.

Scarlet gathered every bit of mental and physical strength still at her command. It wasn't much, but it turned out to be enough to push away. Breathing heavy she glanced in his direction. Instead of the cocky expression she expected, he looked as dazed as she felt. Instead of loose limbed confidence he had his hands clamped on the counter behind him with a white-knuckled grip. So he wasn't as in control as he appeared. Good. "There," she said, wiping her mouth, turning away, hoping to hide how much his kiss had affected her. "Now that that's done, let's go buy some paint."

Let's go buy some paint? The only place Lewis wanted to go was to bed to finish what Scarlet had started, to feel the wet heat between her legs, to taste her, there. To arouse her to the point she'd agree to anything. Everything. To indulge in her passion, to indulge his passion.

"Don't look at me like that," she said. "We had a deal."

"A deal that included no other physical contact." Maybe he hadn't minded at the time, it feeling so amazingly good to have her hands on him and all, but he sure minded now, all worked up with no relief in his immediate future. He stood and adjusted his pants to make some much needed room in the groin area.

Scarlet actually blushed. "Sorry about that. I may have gotten a little carried away," she admitted.

Unfortunately, not carried away enough.

Next time. There would most certainly be a next time. And soon, or he'd burst.

In an attempt to distract himself from his body's demands, he picked up the pile of pictures she'd brought with her and sifted through the ones he hadn't yet looked at, amazed at the amount of time she'd obviously put into the task of creating the perfect teenage escape for his daughter. More than bedding and matching accessories, she'd researched page after page of jewelry display thingies, shelves, fancy hooks, and even some contraption called a Bubble Chair that hung from the ceiling.

A lighted makeup mirror. He let that one fall to the counter. Jessie was too young to wear makeup.

A purple lap desk. A funky silver floor lamp. A back-of-the-door mirror.

All in addition to the time she'd spent shopping for posters of Jessie's favorite bands and picking out paint swatches.

He didn't have the heart to tell her he'd changed his mind about her helping him after she'd already put in so much effort. And since the main reason for his change of mind was so they wouldn't be alone together, and here they were, alone together, he may as well accept all she was willing to offer.

Whoa.

He came to a picture of a crib and changing table set. He moved on to the next page, a baby bath, and the next, an infant car seat, followed by an ad for huge pink butterfly wall decals. He held them up to her. "I'm thinking these were intended for someone else?"

Scarlet hurried over and grabbed them from his hand. "They're mine."

So defensive. "Why are you carrying around pictures of baby items?" Please say because you're helping a friend. Please don't be one of those baby-obsessed women who yammer on about their nonsensical biological clock.

"We're wasting time." She carefully folded the papers in half and shoved them into her backpack. "Go get dressed. The paint store closes at seven."

Lewis looked at the clock on the microwave. Five thirty-seven. How long could it possibly take her to answer one simple question?

"I can go myself," she threatened, picking up her pocketbook and reaching for the door knob.

"Hold on," he said. "Give me a minute." He turned and headed toward his bedroom. But this conversation was not over.

At ten o'clock that night Lewis and Scarlet finally returned to his condo. Lewis dropped the cumbersome bags of bedding and miscellaneous girlie junk he'd carried for what seemed like miles as they'd trudged through at least a dozen stores.

"Having the paint and painting supplies delivered was a good call," he told Scarlet, looking at where the doorman had neatly arranged the items to the side of his entryway.

She carefully unloaded their more delicate purchases, which she'd insisted on carrying. "I can't believe we got all the shopping done in one night." She pushed some flyaway hairs away from her flushed face.

They'd done more shopping in four hours than Lewis typically did in a month. Heck, in three months. He should be cranky and exhausted and looking forward to pouring a beer then pouring himself into his recliner. And yet he felt energized. Scarlet's enthusiasm for her task, her determination to find the exact item she sought, and her excitement when she did, made every minute of their expedition fun.

So what if she was trying to re-create the bedroom of her teenage dreams. Jessie was one lucky girl to be on the receiving end of all Scarlet's creative ideas and planning.

She covered her mouth and yawned. "Sorry," she said. "I was up at six."

Lewis remembered that while he'd moped around in his bathrobe, missing Jessie, bemoaning the loss of the man he was pre-fatherhood, trying to envision his future—a vision Scarlet kept popping up in, she'd put in a full shift at work.

"Would you like a cup of coffee?" he asked.

"That'd be great." She took out her cell phone, walked across his living room, and with her back to him, made a call.

"Hey," she said to someone on the other end of the call. "Can you pick me up at the bus stop later tonight?"

Lewis set the filter in the coffeemaker and measured out enough coffee for four cups.

"No. Thanks anyway. Have fun," she said.

"Problem?" he asked.

"I live six blocks from my bus stop," she said absent-mindedly as she scrolled through information on her phone. "It's bad enough I have to navigate Penn Station and ride the bus back to Jersey with the Friday night drunks. I'd rather not have to walk home, alone, in the dark with one of them following me."

She shuddered as if it'd happened before. The thought of Scarlet, hurrying home, in fear, with some intoxicated miscreant in pursuit set off a surge of protectiveness he'd only ever felt for Jessie.

"How did you plan to get home after girls' night out?" he asked.

She looked up from her phone. "I sleep at my friend's apartment downtown, so I don't have to make the trek home late at night."

"If you'd already planned to stay in the city, you can stay here," he blurted out.

She gave him the 'yeah right' look. "Nice try." She pressed the screen on her phone, lifted it to her ear, and turned her back to him, again.

Lewis added water, replaced the carafe, and flipped on the coffeemaker.

Scarlet spoke into her phone. "Hey. It's about a quarter after ten on Friday night. If you get this message in the next few minutes and can give me a ride home from the bus stop tonight, call me back."

Lewis waited for her to end the call and said, "You're being silly. I think I've proven myself a close-to-perfect gentleman. You can sleep in Jessie's room. I'll put fresh sheets on the bed," he held up his right hand, "I give you my word—"

"Stop with the raising the right hand bit," she said. "I thought we talked about that."

"A carryover from Boy Scouts," he admitted. Then, keeping his right hand raised he bent his pinky, held it in place with his thumb to make the scout sign, and recited the oath. "On my honor I will do my best to do my duty to God and my country and to obey the Scout Law; To help other people at all times; To keep myself physically strong, mentally awake, and morally straight."

She smiled and nodded. "Very impressive."

Standing at full attention he added, "On my honor I will not step one foot on the stairway leading up to the loft while you're up there." He decided it best to keep the 'unless you invite me up' part to himself.

She seemed to mull it over. "Then we could prep for painting tonight and get started first thing tomorrow."

"Exactly." Although not his first choice of things to do during their time alone together, that'd work. "I've still got stuff I need to move out of there." Luckily he'd spent part of his afternoon, sorting junk, boxing up his books and journals, and removing the artwork and pictures from the walls.

"I can help with that," she offered.

So far today she'd cancelled plans with her friends to come check on him, only let him treat her to a slice of pizza and a bottle of water for dinner, carried almost as many bags as he had, without one complaint, and now she was offering to help him move boxes and furniture. "Except for your good looks and fantastic figure," which he took a moment to peruse, "you are not at all like the women I used to date."

She gave him a big smile. "Thank you. I'll take that as a compliment."

He'd meant it as one.

"I like my coffee light with one teaspoon of sugar if you have it." She walked to the kitchen. While he poured she said, "If I stay over tonight, and that's still a big if, I need to know you won't tell anyone at work. Or Jessie. Especially Jessie. I don't want anyone to think…"

"There's something going on between us," he finished for her as he placed her mug of coffee within reach.

She pulled out a stool and sat down. "Yeah."

Most women loved to brag about dating him. But he was fast learning Scarlet was not most women.

He held up the scout's sign again and said, "Scout's honor."

She smiled. "How long were you in the Boy Scouts?"

"Through Eagle Scout," he said. The highest, most prestigious level.

"That's quite an accomplishment."

Yes it was.

"But you don't seem the camping, outdoorsy type."

He wasn't, but his father had made Eagle Scout, and Boy Scouts had been the one father son activity his dad had made time for. "I grew up in Northern Westchester. I didn't migrate down to the city until I got accepted at NYU."

She blew on her coffee then took a sip.

With the brief lapse in conversation that followed, Lewis took the opportunity to fulfill his promise to Jessie. "When I spoke to Jessie earlier, she made it clear that if something should happen to me, she'd much rather go to live with you than with my sister. I told her you're not family and it's not your responsibility to take her in. I don't expect you to say yes, so don't feel in any way pressured. But she made me promise to ask you if you'd be willing, so I'm asking." He leaned back against the counter and lifted his coffee mug. There. He'd done what he'd promised to do. Now he waited for the backlash. He took a sip. How dare he put Scarlet in such a difficult position? How dare he expect her to take on the role of parent to a child who wasn't hers? How dare he set her up to be a bad person by saying no when Lewis, Jessie's father, should have been the one to tell her no when she'd first mentioned the idea.

But Scarlet looked up at him with an expression that was anything but angry and said, "If it doesn't cause a problem within your family, I'd love to."

What? "You'd…"

She smiled. "I'd be happy to have Jessie come live with me."

He stood there, speechless.

"She's a great kid, Lewis. Don't look so shocked."

"You'd have to change your life around." Like he had.

"If something's important, you find a way to make it work," she said. "Jessie is important to me. So I'd find a way to make it work. Not that I'll ever have to because you're young and healthy. But if Jessie needs me, I'll be there for her."

As simple as that.

Lewis walked to the counter opposite Scarlet and looked down into her eyes. "Someday you're going to be an exceptional mom to some very lucky children." And an outstanding wife to one extremely lucky man. For the first time in years, the idea of marriage, as in marriage to someone exactly like Scarlet, did not make him feel like he was buried under a ten foot high pile of cinderblocks.

She looked down into her coffee cup and quietly said, "Hopefully sooner rather than later."

Which brought to mind her pictures of baby paraphernalia and Lewis got a heavy feeling in his gut. "Sooner as in that's why you're carrying around pictures of baby furniture and supplies?" Was she already pregnant? Was she trying to get pregnant?

She looked up at him with the same excited expression she'd had when they'd found the purple lava lamp. "Since you've already agreed to keep my sleeping over a secret, can I trust you with one more?"

He nodded, no longer certain he wanted to know.

"I'm in the process of trying to adopt Joey."

CHAPTER SEVEN

LEWIS DIDN'T IMMEDIATELY respond. Understandable. Scarlet took a sip of her coffee and waited for him to process what she'd told him, figuring his reaction would likely be indicative of what she'd face when she shared the news with the rest of her colleagues.

After a minute or two of deep concentration, Lewis carried his mug around the counter, pulled out the stool beside her and sat down, immediately swiveling to look at her. In a low, calm, almost placating tone he said, "A dying mother's final plea for you to take good care of her baby and make sure to find her a good home does not make you responsible to adopt the baby."

"I know that," Scarlet snapped. Her reasons for wanting to adopt Joey had turned into so much more.

"You and Holly clicked. I get it," he said. "You saw your teenage self in her. You see the baby you lost in Joey."

Very perceptive of him, surprising since she'd thought him to be so superficial when it came to women.

"But those memories are clouding your judgment."

"They most certainly are not." She didn't appreciate him talking to her like she was an unstable patient in need of coddling.

"I'm sure you've dealt with thousands of infants

through your work at Angel's. Dozens maybe hundreds who were abandoned or taken from their drug addicted mothers. Have you ever considered adopting any of them?"

No, she hadn't.

"I see the answer in your face," he said like he'd caught her trying to hide something. "So why now? What makes Joey so special? Help me to understand."

"You know what?" Scarlet stood. "You don't have to understand. I'm doing what I want to do, what I think is the right thing to do, for reasons that are important to me." She jabbed her index finger at her chest—a little too hard. Ouch. "Maybe it's the timing, where I happen to be in my life. Maybe it's that I was close enough to Holly to hear her pleas, or that I held Joey in my arms as her mother died, or that my deciding I'd like to have a baby coincided nicely with Joey needing a mother."

"Think about it," Lewis said. "Really think about it. You don't know Holly's family or medical history. What if there's a history of mental illness? Addiction? Or autosomal dominant disease?"

"If Joey exhibits any signs or symptoms, I'll get her the best medical and/or psychological treatment available." Like any good parent would do.

He let out a frustrated breath. "Eighteen years, Scarlet. Do you really want to take responsibility for someone else's daughter for eighteen long, dramatic, exhausting years?"

"Be careful," she cautioned, with a glare. "Your pessimistic view of fatherhood is showing."

"It's not pessimistic," he insisted "It's realistic. And Jessie is my own flesh and blood. Do you honestly think you'll be able to love another woman's baby?"

His thoughtless words slapped the calm right out of

her. "I can't believe this," Scarlet yelled. "Not fifteen minutes ago you asked me to consider taking in Jessie if something were to happen to you. Did you not think, that in your absence, I would nurture her and love her and raise her as if she were my very own daughter? Newsflash, Lewis, a woman doesn't have to give birth to a baby to be a loving mother. And the responsibilities of parenthood don't magically disappear when a child turns eighteen." Well, except for her parents they did.

"I know that. I'm sorry," he said. So. Damn. Calm. "I didn't mean to upset you."

Too late. "Well you did. Giving a baby up for adoption, whether willingly or unwillingly, is not an easy thing. On the days I'm convinced my baby lived, I pray she was adopted by a woman who loves her as much as if she were her very own biological child, a woman who makes her feel special and wanted every single day of her life."

Scarlet felt tears start to gather in her eyes. "My personal experience aside, I have to believe that woman exists. With Joey I have the chance to actually be that woman for a baby who needs me, to allow Holly to rest in peace because her daughter will be well cared for, to do for Joey what I pray to God another woman has done for my baby."

Do not cry. Don't you dare cry.

"What do you mean by your personal experience aside?" he asked.

She did not want to talk about this. But the shift from lamenting to loathing worked to keep her tears from falling. "I was adopted as an infant to complete the happy family picture on the annual Miller Christmas card. Their no muss no fuss approach to gaining parenthood status. Mom didn't have to give up her daily cocktails and dad didn't have to deal with mom's less malleable nature when sober. No changes to mom's figure, no disruption to dad's work schedule. The ideal solution. Only they hadn't anticipated the imperfect daughter I turned out to be."

"I'm sorry," he said quietly.

"Don't be. I had everything a girl could wish for—as long as she didn't wish for a mom and/or dad who cared anything for her beyond maintaining appearances." She gave a flippant wave of her hand. "Blah, blah, blah. Poor little rich girl. My childhood could have been a lot worse, and I know it."

"Did you ever try to locate your birth parents?"

Hard to do when her birth was purported to be a home birth and an address that turned out to be in a strip mall was listed as the place of birth on her birth certificate. Knowing her dad's scheming nature, she couldn't even be sure the date of birth listed was correct. So why waste her time? "My purpose for sharing that I was adopted was to show that people become foster parents and adoptive parents for a variety of reasons, some of them self-serving. I can't save every baby born into a bad situation, but I can, and will, do my very best to save Joey."

She picked up her phone and brought up Joey's picture. "She's a real sweetheart, loves to cuddle." She smiled at the memory of holding her before she'd left the hospital that afternoon and the contented little noises she'd made. "When the nurses can't get her to quiet down they come get me. It's like she can sense my presence before I even open the incubator and she stops fussing and waits for me to pick her up. She knows me. She's bonded with me." And Scarlet had bonded right back.

"Can I see?" Lewis asked, motioning to the phone.

Scarlet turned the screen in his direction.

"She's a cutie that's for sure."

"My cutie," Scarlet said. Her soon to be daughter. Oh how she loved the sound of that.

"What about Holly's family?" he asked. The annoying voice of reason. "Or the father's family?"

"I talk with the NICU social worker daily. The police still have not been able to identify Holly. In the meantime, Joey's started to take the bottle, she's gaining weight, and if all continues to go well, Dr. Donaldson plans to discontinue the NG tube on Tuesday or Wednesday. She may be ready for discharge as early as a week after that, and I'm trying my hardest to make sure she'll be able to come home with me."

"So soon? I thought it takes months to adopt a baby."

"Since Joey may still require an apnea monitor and strict intake monitoring to assure she's getting adequate nutrition at home, the social worker is trying to push through approval for me to be her foster parent first. I've already had my personal interview and I have a home visit scheduled for Wednesday morning."

"What about your job?"

Scarlet leaned her hips against the island counter and reached for her mug. "I'll take some time off when she first comes home, like any new mom." She took a sip. "Then I have an old nursing friend lined up to take care of her until she's big enough and healthy enough to start at the hospital daycare. I already have her on the waiting list, just in case."

"Sounds like you have it all figured out," he said, taking her free hand into his. "I hope everything goes the way you want it to."

"It will," Scarlet said. It had to. "I can feel it in my heart." Because Joey had worked her way in there.

"Joey's a lucky little girl to have you looking out for her," Lewis said.

"No" Scarlet squeezed his hand. "I'm the lucky one." She set down her mug as a wave of tiredness crashed over her, making her yawn. She brought her hand up to cover her mouth. "Excuse me."

"You're exhausted. Go get ready for bed," Lewis suggested. "Guest bathroom is over there." He pointed to a hallway to the right of the kitchen. "I'll run upstairs to make up Jessie's bed for you."

"But I'd hoped—"

"Tomorrow," he said, walking to the front door. He picked up her backpack and her canvas overnight bag and carried them to her. "I'll do what I can do alone tonight."

Considering she was usually in bed before ten and it was fast approaching eleven, going to sleep sounded pretty good. She stood and took her things. "Thank you."

"No," he said. "Thank *you*." He stared down into her eyes. "For giving up your plans with your friends to put Jessie's mind at ease that I was okay, for going shopping with me after you'd worked a full day, and for finding the time to help me with Jessie's room, when you have so much going on."

"You're welcome," she said, appreciating his sincere appreciation. He looked about to kiss her, and since Scarlet knew where that would lead, she stepped around him and went to wash up for bed.

Scarlet opened her eyes to shadowed darkness and looked over to her clock to check the time. Only it wasn't there. The sheets smelled different. The air felt cool on her face, but the buzz of her old window a/c unit was noticeably absent. She turned to the other side and noted the time. One thirty-seven.

A dim light from the floor below lit the room enough for her to recognize Jessie's loft bedroom.

Her stomach growled.

She should have let Lewis buy her that second slice of pizza. No sense trying to sleep when her body required sustenance, so she threw off the covers, got out of bed, and quietly went in search of food. At the bottom of the stairs she heard a noise to her right and stopped. In the dark she could just make out a person on their hands and knees inside of Lewis's coat closet. With a flashlight.

Doing what?

A cold fear crept up her back, settling into a disturbing chilly tingle at the base of her skull.

Did Lewis keep a safe in there? Was he being robbed? Was she standing three feet from a gun-carrying criminal?

The person moved.

Scarlet swallowed a scream.

She looked down the dark hallway to where Lewis lay in peaceful slumber, totally unaware. She needed to wake him. She needed to get help.

A male grunt from the closet made her jump.

It was a man. He moved again, and oh my God, started a backwards crawl out of the closet.

Doing the first thing that came to mind, Scarlet set her bare foot to the burglar's backside, pushed as hard as she could, shoving him back inside the closet, and slammed the door shut behind him. "Lewis," she screamed as loud as she could over her shoulder. Please don't let him be a heavy sleeper. "Wake up. There's a man in the closet." She pushed her back against the door, straightened her legs for leverage, and used all one hundred twenty-one of her pounds to hold him off. "You're being robbed," she yelled. "Wake up, Lewis. Call 911. I need help."

Someone knocked.

From inside the closet.

"Scarlet," a muffled male voice said.

Holy cow. He knew her name.

"Scarlet, it's Lewis," the man in the closet said, oh so calm.

That's when she noticed he wasn't making any attempt at escape. "What are you doing in the closet?" she asked.

"Some crazy woman pushed me in here and closed the door."

Ah yes, the crazy woman, that would be her, but better safe than sorry.

"If you're really Lewis," and chances were good he was since there was no activity in the vicinity of Lewis's bedroom and she'd yelled loud enough that if he was in there, he'd have heard her, "what did we have for dinner?"

"Pizza," he answered correctly.

Alrighty then. Scarlet moved toward the entryway, felt around until she found the light switch and flipped it on.

The closet doorknob turned and Lewis emerged, squinting against the bright overhead light.

"Well look at that," she said, trying to lighten things up. "Dr. Lewis Jackson coming out of the closet." Dressed in nothing but a pair of skin tight black bike shorts that hugged every curve, every bulge... Oh she would definitely be re-creating this moment over and over for years to come.

"Ha. Ha," he said without humor, probably with some type of scowl on his face, but she was too busy ogling his scantily clad body, from his bare shoulders down, to notice.

He put his hands on his hips. "You like what you see?" he asked.

Oh, yes, very much.

"No need to answer," he said. "Your body's doing it for you."

She looked down at her chest and sure enough, her nipples had transformed into hard little male hormone sensors beneath the thin cotton of her tank. "Don't flatter yourself," she said, crossing her arms so the girls could react to their environment in private. "It's freezing in here." It wasn't, but she ran with that line of reasoning anyway, lowering her eyes to stare at his groin. "Which would explain the, uh," she cleared her throat, "shrinkage."

Then, right before her eyes, his member did the exact opposite of shrink. And suddenly Lewis's condo started to feel rather warm.

It'd been so long since Lewis had had a beautiful, sensual woman so close. Scarlet looked so damn good standing there in her tight little pink tank top and short pink boxer shorts, with her long, smooth legs and shapely curves exposed to him for the first time. He wanted her so much that her eyes focusing in on the part of him that wanted her the most worked as effectively as if she'd put her mouth on him.

She shifted her gaze. "So what were you doing in the closet?" she asked.

"Why are you out of bed?" he countered. Dare he hope she'd been on her way to his bedroom for a little naked companionship?

"I'm sorry," she said, not sounding sorry at all. "Is there some house rule that says overnight guests need to remain in bed until morning?"

"Only when they're in *my* bed."

She fidgeted with a gold outline of a heart dangling from a delicate chain around her neck. And if he wasn't mistaken, her skin took on a slight flushed appearance.

"Well I got hungry," she said. "Now it's your turn. What were you doing in there?" She pointed to the coat closet. "And why were you doing it by flashlight?" Based on her determined expression, she had no intention of letting the topic drop.

So he told her the truth. "With our earlier talk about closet sex I got to thinking. What if you decided you wanted to give it a go? What shape were my closets in? The walk-in in my bedroom was clean and spacious, but I got the feeling that wasn't the experience you were going for."

She shook her head in agreement.

"I had to pile up boxes in my office closet to give us room to move around and paint. Which leaves this." He gestured with both hands.

Scarlet walked to the coat closet and looked inside. "It's not too bad."

"I've spent the last hour working to clean and de-clutter it." And in doing so his bedroom walk-in was no longer as neat or accessible as it'd been two hours earlier. "By flashlight, might I add, so the living room light didn't shine into the loft and disturb you."

"How sweet." She turned to him with a smirk. "The

sleeping bag spread out covering the hardwood floor at the bottom is a nice touch."

Doing it in a closet didn't mean they had to be uncomfortable. "I found it in the back and figured it'd be a good idea to air it out."

She leaned in the closet, went down on her knees and reached for something.

An opportunity Lewis couldn't resist. He lifted his bare foot, gently set it on her beautifully rounded right butt cheek, and gave her a little shove.

"Hey," she cried out, falling forward, deeper into the closet, as planned.

He followed her in, dragging the door closed behind him, landing on his knees beside her. "Payback."

She laughed and wiggled around, her leg brushed against his, her foot came dangerously close to— "Whoa." He grabbed it. "Easy does it. We're in tight quarters here."

She clicked on his flashlight and shined the light on a strip of condoms he'd hidden in the far corner under the sleeping bag. At least he'd *thought* he'd hidden them.

"Once a Boy Scout, always a Boy Scout," he explained. "A good Boy Scout is always prepared."

"On the off chance you might wind up in a closet with a woman and need a condom," she added sarcastically.

He smiled. "On the off chance I might wind up in the closet with *you* and need a condom."

Scarlet looked at him. He looked at her. Neither spoke. The air around them grew thick with lust or maybe from a buildup of carbon dioxide.

"So here we are," she said, sounding uncharacteristically nervous.

"Yes," he shifted onto his back—because if he sat

up his head would disappear into the bottoms of the coats—and bent his legs, setting his feet on the sleeping bag. "Here we are."

She sat squeezed into the back corner, with her knees bent up to her chest and her arms clutched tightly around her shins, facing him. "Lewis, I don't think—"

"Don't think." He reached for her hand and tugged. "Just for tonight, one night, let's not think about anything or anyone. Only us. You and me." His tug progressed to a coaxing pull. "We're the only two people in our little closet world. Nothing exists outside these four walls."

He held his breath. She had to come to him willingly. Would she?

He stayed quiet. He waited. He prayed to the God of Blue Balls.

Mere seconds before he was about to break down and beg, his prayers were answered. Scarlet slid in next to him, lay down on her side and rested her head on his shoulder. The best part of all, she shimmied in so close to his side not even a molecule of dust could squeeze between them.

He curled his arm around her hip.

"Promise me one thing," she said, setting two fingers on his chest, tracing a figure-eight around his nipples, then skimming them down, all the way down, so close, almost there. She cupped him and Lewis nearly came on contact.

He dropped his knees open, as best he could, considering the left one hit the closet door, to give her room to maneuver around unimpeded. "Anything." At this moment in time he would give her any damn thing she wanted to get her to squeeze him and stroke him, to straddle him and take him inside of her hot body.

"Tomorrow." She hesitated, but while she did she kept her hand moving. Up and down. Tip to base. Lower. Amazing.

"Afterwards," she continued. "When Jessie comes home and we return to our regular lives, promise me things won't get weird between us."

The constant motion of her hand made it difficult to think clearly. But Lewis knew one thing for certain. He valued Scarlet's friendship, and would do everything in his power to see that whatever happened between them in the next forty-eight hours didn't interfere with it. "I promise."

As if his reassurance cleared away any lingering doubts, Scarlet pushed herself up and lifted her tank over her head revealing a pair of beautiful, nicely rounded, dark pink-tipped, fantasy-worthy breasts. Those flashlight batteries had better hold out until he had the chance to see every last inch of her.

"Remove your shorts," she said.

Gladly. A lift and a lift, down, off, done.

When he finished she climbed on top of him. "Hey, what about yours?" He palmed the tiny cotton shorts covering her ass and guided her right where he wanted her. The feeling transcendent, better than any other time with any other woman. Ever.

He pushed off with his feet and thrust his pelvis up to grind against her wanting, no, needing more.

"You in a hurry?"

He didn't want to be, but taking it slow would not work, not this first time, not when he was primed and ready. Oh. So. Ready.

"I'll go slow next time." He reached up to cup her shoulder blades and pulled her down, needed to have her hot naked flesh pressed to his, needed to feel her aroused nipples, the curve of her waist, the smoothness of her skin, her hair, her lips.

God help him, her lips.

Time passed in a series of deep, passion-filled kisses and desperate caresses. Lewis felt cocooned in a place he never wanted to leave. The temperature rose. Their moans grew louder, their movements more urgent.

Then it happened. In the process of rubbing along his erection she shifted at the same time he lifted and the leg opening of her shorts drifted and Lewis entered paradise.

"Condom," she cried out.

Holding perfectly still, when every cell of his body demanded he pull back and thrust into her over and over and over until he finally…finally found the release he'd been craving for so long, was a feat worthy of a gold medal in restraint.

Scarlet eased off of him, reached for something, and handed him a condom. While she rushed to finish undressing in the close confines of their tiny closet, Lewis sheathed himself. When she finished and pushed up onto her knees, Lewis thought, This is it! The moment I've been waiting for and fantasizing about. But instead of climbing onto him, she reached up into the coats and started pushing them to the side to create a space for herself .

Then she closed her hands around the thin metal rod and yanked on it. "Do you think this will hold me?"

It figured. A simple him on bottom her on top wasn't good enough for Scarlet. "So I guess I have my answer," he said with a smile. "Adventurous birds do flock together."

She smiled back. "I thought maybe if you could go up on your knees."

He did. "Given this some thought, have you?"

Her smile widened. "I may have spent a few minutes imagining what I'd like to do with you if we ever wound up in a closet together."

Not just any man, but with him. Lewis liked that.

She lowered her body until she hung in front of him. Lewis liked that even more.

"Take my legs and wrap them around your waist."

"With pleasure." Lots and lots of pleasure. He lined them up and she crossed her ankles behind him. "You ready?"

"Oh, yeah."

He thrust into her, already knowing how good it'd feel, buried himself as deep as he could possibly go and took a moment to savor the intensity of her tight heat surrounding him, gripping him.

"Hanging from a closet rod here," she reminded him. "Fast would be good."

Lewis gave her what she wanted, what he wanted, driving into her, over and over. Her breasts bobbed at eye level, an inviting treat he couldn't pass up. She cried out when he sucked her nipple into his mouth.

"That feels so good."

Lewis repositioned himself to free up one of his hands so he could caress her elongated torso, starting at her hip, up her ribs, to her other nipple. And while thrusting into her, and lavishing attention on one breast with his mouth, he fondled the other one, because he wanted to make her feel a thousand times better than good.

Scarlet moaned and rocked against him faster and more urgent.

"Faster," she said.

He met her thrust for frantic thrust. His balls tightened. Her body stiffened.

And with a loud crack the cheap peace of crap rod holding Scarlet broke and she started to fall. Lewis grabbed for her, lost his balance, but delayed her descent enough that when they both hit the ground it was on top of a pile of coats.

"Don't stop," she said, pulling him on top of her.

He couldn't straighten his legs and had his head mashed up against his leather jacket. "Are you okay?" Lewis asked, the doctor in him wanting to examine her for injuries.

"I will be in a minute." She wrapped her hand around his erection and guided him back in.

No hysterics. No complaints. A woman focused on the finish, and Lewis set out to make sure it was a grand finish indeed.

Several hot, sweaty, fantastic minutes later, he and Scarlet both breathing heavy, still joined, she said, "I can't wait for next girls' night out."

He nuzzled up close to her ear. "You're welcome."

She ran her fingernails lightly up and down his back. "Sorry I destroyed your closet."

He wasn't. Not one bit. "You can make it up to me," he offered.

"Oh I can, can I?" She contracted her vaginal muscles and squeezed him. "Supposing I agree to make it up to you." She squeezed him again. "Just how do you propose I go about it?"

She wanted ideas? He had dozens of them. "Let's move to my bed and I'll show you."

CHAPTER EIGHT

ON SATURDAY MORNING Scarlet rushed down the hallway leading to Lewis's condo and used the key Jessie had given her to unlock the door.

Lewis sat at the island counter in the kitchen, wearing nothing but a pair of navy cotton lounge pants, reading the newspaper. So much for getting back before he woke up.

"Sorry I'm late," she said, closing the door behind her.

"How's Joey?" he asked, walking over with his arms out to take the bag and carryout coffees in her hands.

"Joey is sweet and precious as always." She hung her pocket book over the back of a stool. "Another little preemie and her parents, however, are giving my staff a tough time, and I got caught up in it, one of the pitfalls of going in to visit Joey on my days off." She washed her hands and dried them with a towel while Lewis set the table.

"I'm usually the one to run out for breakfast in the morning," he said, removing the lid on one of the coffees to sniff it.

"The French vanilla one is marked with an F." *Men*. She picked up the coffee with a big black F on it and handed it to him. "And I'm perfectly capable of getting our breakfast. We independent girls don't rely on men to feed us." She opened the bag and a heavenly smell wafted into the air. She had worked up a lumberjack of an appetite in the early morning hours. "Spinach, feta, and egg white on a whole wheat wrap for you." She put the wrap on one plate. "Oatmeal and fresh fruit for me." She set both on the other plate.

Lewis pressed in close behind her, placed his hands on her hips, and lowered his mouth to her ear. "Stop," he said quietly. Then he turned her to face him. "You're not late. I'm not in a rush to get started on Jessie's room. And I refuse to let one more minute in your presence pass without a proper good morning."

He set his soft, warm, inspiring lips to hers and all the stress of the last two hours dissipated. Instant relaxation. Except, she turned her head away, "We're out of our little closet world. It's afterwards." Time for things to return to normal, if that was even possible after the night they'd shared, the effects of which still lingered in a delicious little full body hum of supreme satisfaction.

"By my calculation we have twenty-four more hours." He kissed her temple. "To do whatever we want as often as we want." He kissed her cheek. "I don't have to leave to pick up Jessie until tomorrow afternoon." He kissed her lips and the reasons she shouldn't be kissing him started to fade.

All but one. Twenty-four more hours on the receiving end of the tender, considerate, affectionate side of his nature, and Scarlet feared, for her, there'd be no going back to a casual friendship between them.

He deepened the kiss.

So. Good. Arousal started to take over. No. She forced her head away, again, adding a push to his chest.

"While you're busy getting yourself all heated up, our breakfast is getting cold."

"Lucky for us I own a microwave."

She twisted away needing some space. "We have a lot to do today." She pulled out a stool and sat down to eat her breakfast.

On a sigh of what she interpreted as disappointment, Lewis did the same.

"So what does your staff say about you showing up on your days off to visit with Joey?" he asked, then took a bite of his wrap.

"They're kind of used to seeing me." She didn't have much of a life outside of work. "If I don't have anything going on, I stop by the hospital over the weekend to catch up on paperwork and check in on my weekend-only staffers."

"But now you're going in specifically to spend time with Joey."

She blew on a spoonful of oatmeal. "Only a few people have commented."

"Like that nurse Linda?"

"Yup." Scarlet smiled. Linda may be a set in her ways nosey gossip, but she was one of the best and most reliable nurses on Scarlet's team and over the years had become a good friend. "She's voiced her concern that I'm getting too attached. If she didn't derive such pleasure from sharing the secrets of others, I would have told her why." She turned to Lewis. "What made you single out Linda?"

"We met the day I visited the NICU. She basically warned me off. I got the feeling she doesn't think I'm good enough for you, which is rather upsetting because I'm a good catch. Women want me."

After seeing and experiencing him in action, she

understood why. "Obviously not the right women, or after all the sampling you've done, you'd have found one worthy of an exclusive commitment lasting longer than a month."

Lewis choked on something.

Scarlet patted his back.

His air flow restored, he responded, "Some men," he glanced at her, "perfectly nice, hard-working, decent men just aren't cut out to commit to one woman long term."

"Is that the speech you plan to give Jessie when some jerk of a boyfriend breaks her heart?" Scarlet speared the last strawberry in her fruit bowl and ate it. "Maybe something like, 'Stop crying, honey. He's a great guy. He's just not cut out to commit to one woman long term.'" She looked up at him. "Does that sound as lame to your ears as it does to mine?"

He pushed away his half eaten wrap. "It makes me sick to think about having to have that conversation, of Jessie ever dating someone like me."

His genuine emotion surprised her. "I'm sorry. I was out of line." But saying he wasn't cut out for a long term commitment was crap. If he found the right woman and was willing to put in the time and effort necessary to maintain a relationship, he had a great many qualities that'd make him an excellent boyfriend/fiancé/husband.

"What would *you* say to Jessie?" he asked.

Scarlet swiveled her chair in his direction. "I'd tell her if that loser couldn't see how smart and special she was, if he didn't appreciate all of her wonderful, caring qualities and didn't value her enough to choose her above all the other women out there, then he didn't deserve her."

Lewis stared at her with an odd expression. A little surprise around the eyebrows. A hint of a grimace around the mouth. A definite warmth, with a possible hint of longing, or was it affection, or more likely appreciation, in his eyes. Yes, it had to be appreciation, for her help with Jessie, for providing an outlet for him to relieve nine months of pent up sexual frustration, both of which she hadn't minded at all.

"Eat up, papa bear." Scarlet reached for his plate and slid it back in front of him. "You have a couple of years before you need to worry about it, and we have a lot of work to do today." She stood, cleared her plate, and tossed her garbage in the pullout bin. "I'll meet you in the bedroom." Hold on. That didn't sound right. She turned to look at him over her shoulder. "That would be Jessie's new bedroom." In the interest of self-preservation, she would not be returning to Lewis's bedroom, regardless of Jessie's return date.

Scarlet had changed into a pair of scrub pants she'd borrowed from the hospital and an old black tank she'd had in one of her bags and was on her knees removing one of the two outlet covers on the wall they'd be painting when she sensed Lewis's presence behind her. Already, in such a short time together, her response to him had transformed. Softening. Weakening. Accepting.

And while her rational self knew he was only playing the part of seducer, she was quite effectively and thoroughly being seduced by his sweet words and loving touches. Mind and body. Heart and soul. If she wasn't careful and did not finish up work on Jessie's room and leave his condo soon, she would not escape this weekend without irreparable damage to her willpower where he was concerned...and to her heart.

"So how did a self-professed poor little rich girl get so handy?" he asked.

"I'd hardly call the ability to use a screwdriver handy." She moved on to the next outlet.

Lewis got to work taping at the seam of an abutting wall. "But you have to admit, it's not a skill typical of rich girls."

"I've been on my own since I turned eighteen." Since her birthday when she'd given her parents the ultimatum, 'Tell me the truth about what happened to my daughter or you will never see or hear from me again.' They'd seemed relieved to be rid of her, their stint as parents complete, the disruption to their lives over. "Dad paid my college tuition." Probably to ensure her ability to obtain respectable employment suitable for bragging, as much as financial independence so she'd never darken their doorstep again. "I juggled a couple of jobs and took care of everything else."

She gathered up the outlet covers and screws, carried them to the closet and set them on top of a box. "Not much money left over to pay people to do things for me. So I learned to do them for myself." She picked up the other roll of painter's tape. "And you know what? I found I liked the feeling of accomplishment when I stood back to look at a room I'd painted or a discarded chair I'd cleaned up and reupholstered or a light fixture I'd replaced. And I still do." She carried the stepladder over to the wall so she could work up by the ceiling, positioned it where she wanted it and climbed to the top step.

She'd only applied about six inches of tape when Lewis clamped his hands around her waist. She stopped and tilted her head down. "Care to explain this sudden tactile display?"

He looked up innocently. "I figured if I told you to get down and let me do the ceiling you'd probably go off telling me you're more than capable of standing on top of a ladder and doing it yourself."

"Probably."

"So I'm doing the close-to-perfect gentlemanly next best thing by making sure you don't fall."

She reached up and resumed her work. "You mean you're taking the opportunity to ogle my butt."

"And what a lovely butt it is," he said with a satisfying amount of appreciation in his tone. "But to be fair, it's right in front of my face. Otherwise I'd be much more circumspect about it."

"Cute." She spread another foot or so of tape and needed to climb down to shift the stepladder. Lewis kept his hands on her waist until she reached the floor. Once there she stepped back and held the tape out to him. "If you want to do the ceiling, go right ahead. I'm not some crazed feminist who won't accept a man's help when it's offered."

He smiled. "Upon further consideration I decided I'd rather be in charge of safety while *you* do it."

"Of course you would." She liked this flirty side of him way too much. Rather than argue and banter and have to stare at his naked chest for one minute longer, she climbed back up and finished the job as quick as she could.

When she was done, Lewis moved to tape the other side of the wall. "Jessie mentioned your parents died in a car accident a few years ago."

A topic she had no interest in discussing. "If you don't like working in quiet, maybe you could turn on a radio. I like everything but rap." But she'd happily listen to it to avoid discussing her parents.

"So you don't want to talk about it."

"What's with the sudden interest in my past?" A past she'd worked hard to put behind her and rise above.

"Just making conversation."

"How about those Mets?" she joked. "Beautiful weather we're having, don't you think?"

"Very funny," he said. "I was thinking more along the lines of meaningful conversation. You know, the type friends have when they want to learn more about each other."

None of her other friends pushed her to talk about her parents, and she had no intention of sharing how she'd found out about their accident days after it'd happened, in an FYI type of e-mail from one of the 'cousins' she used to occasionally keep in touch with, the night before the funerals. An afterthought. She slid him a sideways glance. He'd stopped working and stood there staring at her. So serious. "Fine."

She walked over to get the drop cloth to protect the floor. "You want the dirty details, here they are. My parents were both killed in a single car motor vehicle accident. They died instantly, or so I was told. I hadn't talked to them or seen them in years. It didn't affect my life one bit." Except for the sick day she'd taken to attend the double funeral—love and happiness aside, they *had* given her a place to live and provided for her basic necessities. While there, the attorney for the estate had given her the news, "They left everything to dad's brother and mom's sister. You know, to keep it in the *real* family." She ripped open the plastic wrapper with a little more force than necessary. "Which was fine with me since I didn't need or want their money." But it'd served as one last reminder that she didn't belong in their family, in any family.

* * *

While it wasn't good form to think poorly of the dead, Lewis couldn't help thinking Scarlet's parents had gotten what they'd deserved. "Wow." He found it difficult to fathom how two people could be so callous toward the daughter they'd made the conscious decision to welcome into their lives. "Hard to believe someone who turned out as good as you was raised by such a heartless couple."

Her stiff posture softened and her smile returned as she tilted her head and said, "Why, thank you."

That smile made his insides feel light and airy. "You are most welcome."

Scarlet went down on her hands and knees and began to tape the edge of the drop cloth to where the wall met the floor molding. After entertaining a brief thought of covering her, easing down her scrub pants and taking her from behind, because damn she had a beautiful body and even after all they'd done last night he still hadn't gotten his fill of her, Lewis forced himself to look away and get back to taping.

"Truth is," she said. "Getting pregnant changed my life."

"I bet it did."

"Not in the way you might think." She spread out more of the plastic sheeting by his feet, working as she spoke. "It made me a better person. Having a baby growing inside of me, while petrifying at the time, taught me to put someone else's needs ahead of my own. It gave me someone to love and hope for a happier future. It made me want to be more mature and responsible."

She tapped his foot and he stepped onto the drop cloth so she could tape it into the corner.

"My baby is the reason I decided to become a nurse. I had some great professors who taught me empathy, caring and compassion."

"Those things can't be taught," Lewis said. "Either you have them or you don't." And Scarlet most certainly had them.

"Then I must have some genetic predisposition." She tilted her head up and shouted. "Thank you birth parents wherever you are."

He couldn't imagine what it must be like to not know the parents responsible for your birth, to not know your heritage. "Your birthparents must have been pretty special people." To have created someone as special as Scarlet.

"Except for the fact they gave away their daughter." She stood. "Oops." She covered her mouth playfully. "Did I say that out loud?"

She sure had.

"My bad," she said.

"Maybe they were trying to do the right thing. Maybe they gave you up because they thought it was in your best interest to be raised by another family."

She looked over at him. "If something is important, you find a way to make it work. If I was important to them, they should have at least *tried* rather than casting me out as a newborn."

Not everyone was as strong and determined as Scarlet.

"Or a note would have been nice," she said. "To explain why. Maybe a birthday card or a holiday card to let me know they hadn't forgotten about me," she added quietly, looking so sad. Then she shook it off. "Enough about me. How about we dissect your life for a while?"

No. His life was not a topic open for discussion. He

felt that same old twinge of anger laden disappointment and resentment that accompanied even the briefest thought of his childhood. "I think I'll go get that radio now," he joked, while seriously considering running to his room to grab the one by his bed.

"I don't think so." Scarlet jabbed a paint roller in his direction. "It's your turn to contribute to our *meaningful conversation*."

Maybe so, but Lewis never shared his past, with anyone. Some memories were better left buried. "It's time to paint," he said. "I need to concentrate or I'll ruin Jessie's purple wall." On the plus side, maybe that'd mean they could repaint it another, more muted color. Like eggshell.

"Afraid you'll make me feel bad with tales of your perfectly happy, loving childhood?"

Not a chance.

"You won't." She carried over a can of paint. "But unlike you." She sent him a playful glare, at least he took it as playful. "I will respect that you don't want to talk about it and move on."

A woman who didn't push and push until she received the answers she sought was an unusual thing. He watched her, the head of one of the largest and most highly regarded NICUs in the nation, unconcerned with the flyaway hairs that'd escaped her pony tail, squatting on his floor, with a screwdriver in her hand, prying open a can of paint.

Beautiful. Confident. Smart. Helpful. Caring. Fun. Sexy. Hard-working. Dedicated. There was not one thing he didn't like about Scarlet Miller.

She caught him staring. "You like what you see?" she asked seductively.

Oh yeah. "Very much so."

"Good." She held up the top of the paint can and turned the awful lollipop purple covered side toward him. "I told you it was an amazing shade. Jessie is going to love it."

"I wasn't talking about the paint."

Without comment she turned and bent over to pour the hideous color into a roller pan, not before he'd seen her smile.

Lewis gathered up the rollers and brushes, opened both windows and they started to paint. As time dragged on, his guilt grew. Scarlet had been so open about her difficult past, and when she'd given him the opportunity to reciprocate, he'd changed the topic. And she'd let him.

She deserved more, but where to begin and how much to tell?

He continued to paint. The silence closed in around him. Pressure to share…something started to build until he couldn't stand it any longer. "My mother suffered from undiagnosed bipolar disorder throughout my childhood," he said, concentrating on each thick purple stroke. "Every day I navigated her mood swings like a soldier traversing a deadly minefield. I'd wake up each morning never knowing what to expect."

He bent to get some more paint on the roller. "Would she be manic and energized, exhibiting grandiose expressions of love? Or would she be depressed and short-tempered, impossible to please and blaming me for every little thing?" Unfortunately for him and his sister, she'd tended toward the depression more than the mania. And even though once he'd started to drive, staying away from the house could have easily been arranged, he'd refused to leave his younger sister unprotected.

"I'm assuming she stabilized with treatment or you wouldn't have sent Jessie off with her."

Per usual Scarlet's first concern was Jessie. He liked that. "From what my sister tells me, with medication, for the last fourteen years my mom has been the perfect parent, in-law, and now grandparent to my two nieces. Not that it matters to me because I rarely speak to my mom and dad." He couldn't forget years of neglect when his mom had been too depressed to shop for food or prepare meals or do laundry or clean. Nor could he forgive a dad who'd left at dawn and returned home after they'd all gone to sleep, under the mistaken impression a few twenty dollar bills tossed on the kitchen counter each night made up for his absence, made up for the verbal abuse he wasn't there to stop, for the responsibility of practically raising his sister, of existing on edge, of missing parties with his friends, missing out on his childhood.

Yet he'd accepted their offer to take Jessie away for the weekend out of total desperation.

"What prompted treatment?" she asked.

"Suicide attempt. A cry for help dad could no longer ignore. One that necessitated he stop seeking escape in his work as a surgeon and pay attention to his family for a change." The old rage and resentment started to rise. He inhaled. Exhaled. Would not let it take over.

In his peripheral vision he saw Scarlet stop painting and turn to him. "How terrible."

She didn't know the half of it since, at the young age of seventeen, Lewis had been the one to find her... naked...in a bathtub half-filled with bloody water...both wrists slit. And lying on the white tile floor, covered in his mom's blood was the Boy Scout pocket knife he'd cherished, one of the few gifts his father had given him.

His mother had known when he'd be home from school, an hour before his sister. She'd known his routine, had known he'd go straight to the hall bathroom. She'd planned for Lewis to be the one to find her. And that Lewis could not forgive, because no child should ever…ever have to experience the overwhelming helpless panic…the confused desperation…

Scarlet appeared at his side and placed her hand over his on the handle of the roller, lifting it from where he held it pressed up against the wall. "You don't have to talk about it." With a few adept strokes, she fixed the drippy mess he'd made.

But now that he'd started talking he wanted her to know, to understand. "Living with my mother was… awful." Times one million. He looked down at her. "When Jessie moved in with me, all angry and sulky and difficult, and month after month went by with no improvement in her behavior, it started to feel like history repeating itself. I had no control over my life. Confrontation after confrontation. Trying so hard but never being able to get it right. Never knowing what would set her off. Never knowing what each new day would bring. At the thought of living on that unpredictable rollercoaster again I panicked." To the point he'd actually considered sending Jessie to live with his parents. "But the more I fought to take back control, the worse things got between Jessie and me."

Scarlet set down both rollers, stepped in close and hugged his waist. "I'm sorry. I had no idea." She squeezed him tight. "It will get better," she said confidently.

Lewis wrapped his arms around her shoulders and held her tight, relieved by her confidence, wanting to believe her, needing to believe her.

"And I'll help in any way I can," she added.

She'd already done so much. It calmed him to know he didn't have to go it alone, that he could count on Scarlet to be there for him and Jessie. They stood there in each other's arms, her cheek pressed to his chest, and Lewis had never felt closer to another human being.

"We're quite the screwed up pair," she said.

To him they felt like the perfect pair. But they'd taken a sojourn from real life. Once Jessie came home everything would change.

"You want to know what's even more awful than growing up with your mother?" Scarlet asked, looking up at him, her eyes serious. Apparently that wasn't a question she wanted answered because she continued on without giving him a chance to speak. "That you haven't moved past it, that you continue to fear it and let it impact your relationship with your daughter and women in general."

Lewis opened his mouth to shout out an affronted, "That's not true." But the words wouldn't form, because as humiliating as it was to admit, after more than a decade of avoiding his parents, and in the process, suppressing unwanted destructive emotions he had no desire to re-visit, she was right. Not that he'd let her know. "You think you have me all figured out, don't you?"

"Don't worry," she said with a wink, stepping out of his embrace and picking up her roller. "Your secret's safe with me." She returned to her side of the wall.

Even though he'd much prefer holding Scarlet in his arms for a few more hours, he picked up his roller and resumed painting. "Why do women think they have all the answers?" he asked.

"Why do men think they're too complex for women to figure out?" she countered.

"Touché." Scarlet was not easy. She challenged him. And it turned out he was starting to like being challenged.

"Here's a bit of Scarlet trivia for your inquisitive mind." She stopped painting and looked over at him. "At the insistence of my parents, I trained with the School of American Ballet at Lincoln Center, the official training academy for the New York City Ballet, for seven years and performed in four productions of *The Nutcracker*."

He'd be in awe of that accomplishment later. Right now he couldn't get the image of Scarlet the ballerina out of his head. Her hair pulled back into a tight bun, a pale pink bodysuit hugging her thin frame, graceful arms, strong legs and her chin held high. And toe shoes. Spinning.

"You're imagining me in a leotard, aren't you?" she asked with a smile.

"I am not." What was a leotard anyway?

"You are so easy," she laughed.

And simple as that she'd lifted his mood. Lewis took the opportunity she'd provided to steer the conversation in the more fun, flirty, and sexy direction he preferred. "Yes I am," he walked toward her and turned her to face him. "So easy that all you have to do is blink and you can have me." He stared into her eyes. "Any way you want me."

She blinked.

"That is not fair," she protested. "Blinking is involuntary. I can't stop myself from blinking."

"A blink is a blink," he goaded her.

"Fine," she said, like he knew she would. He had yet

to see her back down from a challenge. "I want you up against a wall."

Doable. He slid his thumbs into the elastic waistband of his pants preparing to lower them.

"That wall." She pointed to the one they'd almost finished painting.

He removed his thumbs and studied the wall, weighed his options: Sex with a post coital purple staining on his back, butt and hair vs. no sex and no purple staining. A tough decision.

"Come on, Lewis." She did a little goading of her own. "A promise of any way you want me is a promise of any way you want me."

"I'm thinking."

"Time's up," she said. "And since you worry about me working on top of the stepladder, and all that's left is the top portion of the wall, I'll leave that to you to finish."

They'd completed the painting a lot quicker than he'd anticipated. Now he'd have to think of a way to convince Scarlet to stick around and go out to dinner with him. He wasn't ready to let her go, not when they could have one more night together. "I have a couple of guys coming at four o'clock to help move the furniture down from the loft."

"You don't need me here for that."

"I know we won't be able to position the bed up against the wall or hang anything on it until the paint is completely dry, but don't you want to be here to set the room up? To hang the curtains and put on the new bedding and position the wall hangings on the other walls? Don't you want to make sure the room turns out exactly as you've envisioned it?"

She didn't answer right away.

Good.

He went on, "Then I have a special evening planned, a thank you for your help."

"A simple verbal thank you will suffice. And when did you have time to plan a special evening?" she asked, full of suspicion.

"This morning while you were out."

"You expect me to believe between the hours of eight and ten on a Saturday morning you managed to make special plans for this evening?"

And his friend Clark, who owned a hot new restaurant just off Central Park, had not been at all happy about the early call. But after he stopped complaining about the hour, he'd been happy to accommodate Lewis's request for a table at seven o'clock. "I most certainly did."

"Do tell, then."

"I'll be happy to," he said. "Tonight, in the cab on the way there."

CHAPTER NINE

SCARLET ENTERED LEWIS'S condo after their Saturday night date, glad she'd decided to go. He'd promised her a fantasy evening and he'd delivered, a delicious dinner at an upscale restaurant where they were treated like royalty, a private violin serenade at their hidden table, a romantic dance to the melodic notes from a baby grand piano, a rose from a street vendor. All capped off by a horse drawn carriage ride under the stars in Central Park.

They'd walked hand in hand and whispered secret cravings, shared tender touches and sweet kisses.

"I had a wonderful time tonight," she said.

"The fantasy doesn't have to end yet." An accomplished charmer, he held out his hand palm up in invitation.

Scarlet took it and allowed herself to be led to his bedroom, a decision she'd made while in his arms during the carriage ride. Tomorrow she would return to reality and responsibility. Tonight she'd live out the rest of the fantasy, pretend he cared for her as much as she cared for him, and savor each moment they shared as if it were her last, because come next week, when she, hopefully, brought Joey home, there wouldn't be room in her life for a man for quite a while.

Without turning on the light in his room he turned to her, removed her hairclip, sending her hair falling around her neck and shoulders, and combed his fingers down to her scalp to position her head up and at a slight angle. "Do you have any idea how long I've wanted to do this?"

He crushed his mouth to hers and thrust his tongue between her lips over and over. He varied his kisses, alternating between deep and universe-altering, and gentle and loving. Scarlet's knees felt weak. "Yes," she said against his lips.

He lifted his head allowing maybe an inch of space between them. "Yes, what?" he whispered.

"Whatever you want to do next, my answer is yes."

He chuckled as he worked to unbutton her blouse. "I want to make love to you." His task complete he pushed it off of her shoulders and it dropped to the floor. "Slow." He kissed down the side of her neck while he unclasped her bra. "Passionate." He tugged it down her arms and kissed down her breast. "Unforgettable." He reached her nipple, circled it with his tongue, and drew it into his mouth, sending a spear of overwhelming sensation straight to her womb. "Love." He blew cool air on her wet skin and she trembled.

"Sounds good to me." So good. The fantasy continued. She unbuttoned his shirt, tugged it off, and reached for his belt.

"Maybe you missed the *slow* part." He pulled her into a hug, bare skin to bare skin, so warm and strong.

She grabbed his butt and ground against his growing erection. "Maybe you'd consider a slightly faster version of slow?"

He rocked into her, his breathing a little heavier, a little quicker.

Good.

She reached for his belt again, this time he let her. And while she finished undressing him, he undressed her, and neither went slow.

He led her to the bed. "Tonight I am going to acquaint myself with every inch of your body."

Every inch of her body thought that was a fantastic idea.

He did something to his bedding. "Lie down in the middle," he kept his voice low and deep. "On your back with your arms over your head and your legs spread wide for me."

She loved the dominant side of his nature that emerged in his bedroom. Yet he'd relinquished control in the closet. Once in position Scarlet waited, listening but only hearing quiet, looking but only seeing darkness, feeling the cool air blowing from the central air. Her nipples tightened, her sex throbbed, and her skin tingled with anticipation. When would he come to her? Where would he start? What would he do?

A drawer opened to her left then closed. The mattress dipped as Lewis joined her on the bed. He ran his hands along her body, opening her legs wider, moving her arms so she was spread out like a starfish.

While he didn't slide his tongue over every inch of her body, he got to most of them, saving the best for last she hoped. Yes! He set his mouth where she ached with need, and arousal surged, her hips rocked and swiveled. "That feels so good."

"Slow," he said.

"Sorry, that word isn't registering." She reached down and tried to pull him on top of her. "I need you inside me. Now. Please."

He reached for something, a wrapper tore. He went

up on his knees then settled on top of her. So. Good. She bent her knees and hugged him close, felt him at her entrance, teasing in little dips in and out.

As if he knew she was about to belt out a complaint he kissed her and thrust deep. "Yes," she moaned against his lips.

"I love being inside of you."

Love. Not love love, but she'd take it. "I love *having* you inside of me."

He began to move, in and out in slow, even strokes "You smell so good, *feel* so good." He kissed her again and moved along her cheek to her ear. "So special," he whispered, still thrusting in and out. "So... perfect."

He made her feel more cherished and more loved than all of her past boyfriends combined. Scarlet would never forget this night.

She planted her feet on the bed and raised her hips up to meet him, quickened the pace and he took over. Soon she couldn't talk, couldn't think, could only feel, Lewis's weight pressing her into the bed, his body filling hers, the heat, the intense need, rising, growing, taking over, until he sent them both flying.

The next morning, Scarlet came awake cuddled into Lewis's side, her head resting on his arm, the residual contentment from their repeated lovemaking leaving her limp. "Mmmmmm." She turned her head to kiss his shoulder. "I could get used to waking up with you all warm and toasty."

He stiffened. "It's over, Scarlet. This can't happen again."

She knew that, they'd both agreed, but, "Wow. When you're done you're done. Good bye, get out, huh?" Like nothing that'd happened between them in the last two days mattered one bit. That hurt. "How about giving me a few minutes to wake up before you toss me from your bed?" Like a mistake that needed to be rectified as soon as possible.

On that unpleasant note, she no longer wanted to remain in his bed after all so she tossed off the covers.

"Wait." He covered her back up. "I'm sorry," he said. "This isn't easy for me."

"Oh, I disagree." She kicked the covers all the way off this time. "Pushing people away is easy." She sat up. "Being an insensitive jerk is easy. Make me mad and I'll storm off so you won't have to deal with me. Would it have killed you to say something nice? To maybe lie to make me feel good by telling me you had an amazing time this weekend and you're going to miss having me around?"

"I did. I am," he said.

"Right," she snapped. "It means so much to hear you agree to it after I suggest it." Not.

"I'm sorry." He sounded miserable. Good. "I've been lying here for an hour trying to think of the right thing to say."

"Newsflash, Lewis. You just wasted an hour."

"This isn't what I want."

She shifted to face him. "And of course this is all about you, you who pursued me, you who put the moves on me, you who got what you wanted and now can't get rid of me fast enough." She stood.

"It's not like that." He sat up. "I don't want to give you up, but Jessie's my family and she needs my full attention right now. I can't risk her finding out about us and it setting her off and ruining all the progress we've made in the past two weeks."

Progress they'd made because of Scarlet's intervention, thank you very much. "I get it," she said, reaching for her panties and jamming one leg and then the other into them. "You want me in your life on your terms. Basically when you need my advice or help with your daughter." She found her bra and slipped it on. "Or when you're so desperate for sex even I'll do, as long as I disappear afterwards so I don't disrupt your family."

She found her blouse and jerked it on. "Because family comes first and I'm not, nor will I ever be your family. I get it. I understand." She worked to button her shirt. "As long as you understand that by next week I hope to have a family of my own that I don't want *you* to disrupt. So when you realize what a mistake you've made by treating me like one of your bimbo one-night-stands, and you want to apologize, don't bother, because I'll be too busy taking care of *my* daughter and worrying about what's best for *my* daughter to care."

"I'm sorry," he said.

He was the king of sorry.

"I never meant to hurt you."

"Those words mean nothing without action to back them up." Scarlet found her pants and yanked them off the back of a chair. "From where I'm standing, you put more effort into screwing me than you did into not hurting me." She grabbed her sandals and stomped out of the room.

Worrying about Lewis coming after her turned out to be wasted brain function, because he didn't. Triple jerk loser.

But just in case he changed his mind, Scarlet rushed to put on her pants, buckle her sandals, and gather up her bags. Without a backward glance she left Lewis's condo, content to never step foot in it again.

* * *

Mid-morning on Monday Scarlet received a request to come to the nurses' station to confirm that a bouquet of two dozen red roses and an obscenely large box of chocolates was in fact for her, before her eagerly awaiting staff, who'd congregated like a pack of hungry wolves surrounding a fresh kill, broke into it. She opened the card.

I'm sorry.
L

As if that would make it all better.

"They're mine," she confirmed, tearing off the cellophane wrapper and removing the lid. "Dig in."

While her staff fought each other to pick the perfect sweet treat, Linda plucked the card from Scarlet's hand. "Ooooh. L. How mysterious," she said. "Might that L belong to Dr. Lewis Jackson from the emergency room? What's he sorry for?"

"I'll never tell." Especially not Linda. She turned to get back to work.

"Hey," Linda called out. "What about your flowers?"

"You all can enjoy them, too." Scarlet didn't want Lewis's easy-way-out attempt to appease his guilt.

On Monday afternoon Scarlet ignored the flashing message light on her phone and the stack of pink message slips a secretary had hand delivered to her. Didn't people have any respect for Memorial Day? She sank into the rocker in the peaceful sanctuary of Joey's room, couldn't wait to take her six week maternity leave.

"I've got your baby furniture all picked out," she told Joey who lay contentedly swaddled in her arms. "It's on a thirty day hold. All I have to do is call and they'll deliver it within twenty-four hours." As soon as she received her foster parent approval which she hoped to get soon after her Wednesday home visit.

She jiggled the bottle to get Joey sucking. "I'm thinking a pretty butterfly theme for your room. I may have overdone the pink color scheme a bit, but I've been dreaming of having a little girl for so long. It feels like I've been waiting for you my whole life." Scarlet hugged Joey close. "I can't wait to take you home and have you all to myself."

Someone cleared their throat from the doorway.

Pam, Joey's social worker stood there with a man and woman Scarlet didn't recognize. "I'm sorry." Pam looked truly pained as she said it. "I tried to call you. I left three messages. I couldn't wait any longer."

Scarlet looked at the couple standing with Pam, the woman much shorter than the man, late thirties or early forties, both dressed conservatively, their faces bereaved, their eyes focused in on Joey, and dread squeezed her heart.

She knew what Pam was about to say before she said it.

"This is Michelle and Peter Quinnellen," Pam said quietly. "Holly's parents."

Scarlet's lungs seized. Tiny scraps of the picture perfect future she'd imagined for herself and Joey floated like snowflakes in her peripheral vision. "Are you sure?"

"The police checked and I verified," Pam said almost apologetically. "Michelle is a homemaker and Peter is a businessman in Pennsylvania." Pam made an effort to sound upbeat. "They're active in their church."

Scarlet's mother had been a homemaker, her father had been a businessman, and in their case, active in their church had meant donates a lot of money. Labels said nothing about a person's true character or why Holly had been too scared to tell her parents about her pregnancy.

Scarlet wanted to scream, "Where have you been? Why wouldn't Holly give us your contact information? What was she so scared of? And why are you here for Joey when you weren't there for your own daughter?" But she couldn't speak, couldn't move, felt weighted down and on the verge of complete collapse.

Pam looked down at the floor. "They're here for Joey."

Scarlet's world started to spin out of control. She gripped the arm of the rocker for stabilization.

Linda showed up in the doorway. "Is everything okay in here?"

No, things were not okay.

Michelle studied Scarlet. "You're the one," she said quietly. "The nurse Pam told us about." She took a tentative step into the room. "The one who was with Holly when she delivered, the one who's taken a personal interest in Joey."

Much more than a personal interest, she loved the baby sleeping in her arms, she'd hoped and planned and dreamed… The heaviness of loss and despair settled on her chest.

"Did Holly…?" Michelle brought a tissue up to her nose. "Did Holly suffer?" She let out a sob and Peter put his arm around his wife and tucked her into the side of his taller body, strong and protective.

Scarlet gave the woman points for believable concern for her daughter and the man points for believable concern for his wife. She pushed her personal hurt aside, gathered up some professionalism and answered, "It was quick. She didn't suffer." Even if she had, what would be the point of telling the girl's parents?

"Thank you for being there with her," Michelle said, looking like she was barely holding it together. Scarlet knew the feeling. "And for taking such good care of baby Joey."

Scarlet didn't want a thank you. She wanted to stand up and run and take Joey with her. She wanted to cuddle and love and raise Joey, she wanted them to be a family. They were supposed to be a family.

But Joey had her own family, one that did not include Scarlet.

"May I hold her?" Michelle asked.

No you may not!

"Holly begged me to find Joey a good home with a nice family," Scarlet said. "If you'd answer me one question, I need to understand why she didn't think that good home with a nice family was with your family?"

"We taught our daughter abstinence," Peter finally spoke. "We live in a small community. The members of our church, who comprise the majority of our closest friends, would not have looked kindly on Holly's pregnancy."

"We didn't even know she had a boyfriend," Michelle said. "But she's our daughter, our blessing, our only child. We loved her, unconditionally. Nothing would ever have changed that. Nothing," she said firmly. "She should have come to us, I wish she'd come to us. We would have understood, we would have helped her and protected her."

"That's the truth," Peter said.

"Then maybe she'd still be here." Michelle's voice cracked. "Why did she trust that woman more than her own mother?" She looked up at Peter and started to cry. "Why?"

"We'll never know," Peter said, taking his wife into his arms, trying to fight his own tears. "You need to be strong for little Joey." He rubbed Michelle's back. "She needs us to be strong."

"What woman?" Scarlet asked.

"Holly ran away thirty-four days ago," Michelle said, sounding heartbroken. "We have been looking for her around the clock since then. We never considered she'd come all the way to New York City by herself."

Pam entered the conversation. "The police made the connection during a raid on a brownstone on the lower east side, suspected baby brokers who made contact with pregnant teens online. During a search they found Holly's wallet in a box."

"May I hold her?" Michelle asked again, taking another step closer.

Scarlet stared down at Joey, fast asleep, the baby's tiny hand holding onto her index finger, totally unaware of the tumultuous feelings churning inside of Scarlet as she prepared to give up yet another daughter. So what if she hadn't yet been approved and the paperwork hadn't yet been signed. In Scarlet's heart, Joey was hers.

"Come," Linda said. "You need to wash your hands and put on disposable gowns. Do either of you have any signs of cold or illness?"

With the Quinnellens occupied, Pam walked over to Scarlet. "I'm so sorry," she whispered. "I know how much—"

"Don't," Scarlet snapped. "Not here. Not now."

Pam placed a sympathetic hand on Scarlet's shoulder and nodded in understanding.

Transferring Joey into Michelle's arms was the absolute hardest thing Scarlet had ever done. A slight joy when Joey cried out her dissatisfaction at being taken from Scarlet, because she recognized Scarlet and preferred her to all others, was quickly tamped down by Scarlet's professional responsibility to ease the transition which was in Joey's best interest.

"She likes it when you tilt her like this." At the sound of her voice, Joey went silent. Scarlet repositioned Joey to face into Michelle more. She moved away and Joey started to cry again. Michelle looked stricken. So Scarlet went down on her knees and moved in close to both grandmother and baby. "Come on, you grumpy girl. Take the bottle for your grandma."

Michelle put the nipple into Joey's mouth and the baby started to suck.

"That's a good girl." She leaned forward and placed a kiss on Joey's forehead. "Good bye, sweet baby," she whispered for only Joey to hear, the ache of loss tearing at her heart, a throbbing pressure building in her head as each bubble of hope she'd had for her and Joey's future together burst then vanished.

When Scarlet tried to stand up, praying her legs would hold her, Michelle pulled her into a one-armed hug. "Thank you," she said. "I can see how much you love baby Joey and I want to assure you we will do right by this little girl. And we'll make sure she never forgets the special nurse who took such loving good care of her and watched over her until we could find her. We'll make sure she knows she can talk to us about anything and we will always love her and be there for her, no matter what."

Scarlet couldn't hold back her tears. "Thank you for that." But she'd reached her limit, had to leave this room this instant. With her last bit of strength she stood and wiped her eyes. "I, uh…" Despair clogged her throat at the thought of leaving Joey. She cleared it, had to be strong. "…have to get back to work. Linda would you familiarize Mr. and Mrs. Quinnellen with Joey's medical status, care to date, and her treatment/discharge plan."

"Of course," Linda said quietly. "Don't you worry about a thing."

When Scarlet left the room she came face to face with many sad, concerned faces as the majority of her day shift staff stared back at her from behind the nurses' station. Thank goodness her charge nurse, Deb, was among them. "Back to work everyone," Scarlet said. "I need to speak to you in my office, Deb."

As soon as Deb followed her in and closed the door Scarlet said, "I need to head out." Her voice cracked, and Scarlet hoped she'd be able to hold herself together long enough to make it out of the hospital.

"I'm so sorry," Deb said.

Scarlet couldn't talk about it. "You're in charge," she told Deb, discarding her gown. "And I am entrusting you with the task of making sure Joey's grandparents are trained and proficient in all the care she'll require on discharge." A clean break would make it easier for everyone involved, which meant she'd just held and cuddled and kissed Joey for the last time. Tears burned her eyes. She kept her head down and pulled open the bottom drawer of her desk to retrieve her pocketbook. "If you have any concerns let me know."

"Of course," Deb said.

Someone knocked on her door.

Scarlet didn't look up. "Who is it?" she asked Deb.

"Pam and a woman I've never seen before," Deb said quietly.

"Seconds from a clean getaway," Scarlet whispered.

"What should I do?" Deb asked.

Scarlet didn't feel capable of pretending she was okay. But Pam knew how much she wanted Joey and how devastating the surprise arrival of her grandparents had been. If she were knocking on Scarlet's door it must be important, so she looked up and motioned for them enter.

"This is Polly Seymour," Pam said from the doorway. "A family friend of the Quinnellens."

"I'm a nurse and I've dreamed of working here at Angel's," Polly said way too enthusiastically for the mood in the office as she reached out to shake Scarlet's hand.

Scarlet shot a why-did-you-bring-this-woman-into-my-office look at Pam who immediately responded, "She accompanied Michelle and Peter to New York in case they needed assistance with Joey's care. I thought she could put your mind at ease about the type of people they are."

Was the concern in Pam's eyes for Scarlet or for Joey?

"They're lovely," Polly said. "Truly lovely people. We've attended the same church for years. I'd have given anything for a mother, who am I kidding, for any member of my family to be as attentive and caring as Michelle." Although Scarlet didn't know the woman, she had an impassioned sincerity in her tone that made her words believable. "Peter may look strict and in charge, but Michelle calls the shots in that family."

Scarlet got the feeling that was a good thing.

Polly chattered on about a county fair and an angry uncle and Michelle coming to her aid. But it was more information than Scarlet could handle in her present frame of mind. She glanced at Deb for help.

"Thank you so much for stopping by," Deb stood, interrupting Polly mid-perky sentence. "If Scarlet doesn't leave now she'll be late for an important meeting."

"Oh, of course," Polly said. "We can't have that now, can we?"

Deb herded Polly and Pam toward the door.

"While I'm here I'm going to apply for a job," Polly said, over her shoulder.

"Best of luck," Deb said, closing the door behind them.

"Thank you," Scarlet said.

"Why don't you head over to my place? Kev is working from home today and I'll get there as soon as I can. You shouldn't be alone."

"I'll be fine," she said with a forced smile. "I'll have my cell phone on for emergencies."

"Well turn it off and focus on you for a change," Deb said. "Tonight *I'll* have *my* cell phone on and I'm going to leave word that I'm on call for emergencies. You go home and take care of you."

Scarlet picked up her phone to turn it off. Joey's picture came up and Scarlet could take no more. She set her head down on the desk and started to cry. And what made the entire situation infinitely worse was the one person she wanted to run to and confide in and accept comfort from—Lewis—had unceremoniously kicked her out of his life.

And now she'd lost Joey, too.

Scarlet had never felt more alone.

Deb pulled up a chair, sat down beside her and rubbed Scarlet's back. "Get it all out."

Scarlet worried if she didn't get this mini-outburst under control she'd be there all night. She sniffled and grabbed for a tissue.

"When you're done," Deb continued, "we'll head down to the cafeteria for some hot fudge sundaes."

Scarlet laughed then sat up and wiped her eyes. "I will not be responsible for you cheating on your diet."

"Fine," Deb said with a pout. "Then I'll sit there and watch *you* eat one."

"Only a true friend would do that," Scarlet said, squeezing Deb's arm. "But it's not necessary." The laugh made her feel a little better so she took the opportunity to make her exit. "Will you run interference for me?"

"Sure thing your head nurseness." Deb stood and bowed. "Call me if you need me."

"I will." No she wouldn't.

Lewis followed the GPS directions to Scarlet's three story, Robin's egg blue apartment building then drove around the residential block in search of street parking, losing patience, anxious to see her and be with her. The smell of sausage and peppers greeted him as he entered her building. A child's or children's crayon drawings taped along the walls welcomed him. Each of the four doors on the first floor was painted a different color, each with its own unique decorations.

He climbed the worn wooden stairs to the second floor and stopped at the bright turquoise door with the big red Welcome sign and the small plate of wrapped chocolates hanging from an interesting wire rack, lucky number seven. Scarlet's apartment.

So warm and inviting. So Scarlet.

He knocked.

No answer.

He imagined her inside, heartbroken and distraught,

and knocked even harder. "Scarlet," he yelled. "It's Lewis, open up."

He gave her a couple of minutes but still no answer.

He pounded with the side of his fist. "I know you're in there." Actually, he didn't. "I'm not leaving until you open this door." Because he didn't know where else to look for her, but he'd beat on every door in this building if he had to. He would not leave until he found her.

The door opened about three inches. "There. I opened it. Now leave." She started to close it.

He jammed his hand in so she couldn't, but that didn't stop her from trying. Ouch! "Wait."

"I'm feeling sorry for myself," she said, sounding weary. "It's not pretty. Go away."

Pretty or not he had no intention of leaving her alone and miserable. He pushed on the door. "Let me in."

She pushed back. "No. Shouldn't you be on your way to get Jessie?"

"When I heard about Joey's grandparents showing up I called my dad and told him I had to take care of something important." *Someone* important. "He and mom offered to bring Jessie into the city after dinner." Which they were more than happy to do for the chance to see the inside of his condo for the first time.

"Great. Poor pitiful Scarlet got too attached to one of her patients. News of my breakdown is probably all over the hospital by now." She must have walked away because all of a sudden the door flew open and Lewis, who had his shoulder pressed against it, lurched forward into her apartment with its tiny sunny yellow kitchen and eclectic mix of old and modern furniture.

He walked to where she'd plopped onto the couch and wrapped herself in a colorfully striped afghan, noting all the crumpled tissues on the coffee table and floor.

"Joey was more than a patient," he acknowledged. "And I have no idea what's circulating around the hospital." He moved to the far end of the couch and sat down. "Your nurse Linda called the ER and insisted they get in touch with me immediately."

"Linda can be pretty insistent," Scarlet said.

More like relentless. To the point she'd harassed the unit secretary to tears. "I called her back and she told me what happened." At which time Lewis's heart had stopped. "She gave me your address." And told him if he wanted to prove himself worthy of Scarlet, this was his chance.

Without any further thought of his mother, or his avoidance of long term relationships with women, or how a relationship with Scarlet might affect Jessie, Lewis had grabbed his car keys and left his condo. Scarlet needed him and worthy or not, he would be there for her.

After a solid twenty-four hours considering his life, past, present, and future, and Jessie's life, past, present, and future, Lewis came the decision he could not, would not, give up Scarlet. She'd become an integral part, a special part, of his life. He could love her, he would love her. He felt certain of it.

Somewhere in the Lincoln Tunnel Lewis decided he *did* want to prove himself worthy of Scarlet, he wanted to be the type of man she deserved, the type of man she'd want to spend her time with, her life with. By going to her, putting her before Jessie, and demonstrating with his actions how much he cared, Lewis hoped to be taking the first steps toward convincing her.

Scarlet smoothed down her messy hair. "Sorry she bothered you."

"I'm not sorry, and it wasn't a bother." He *wanted*

to be the one to comfort her and take care of her, to show her how much she meant to him. "How are you doing?" A stupid question he regretted the second it left his mouth. If her puffy red eyes and her pink nose and dry lips were any indication, she'd probably been crying for hours.

"How do you think I'm doing?" she asked calmly. "Today I lost my second daughter. Today it became clear I am destined to spend the rest of my life taking care of other peoples' babies, never to have one of my own, to live alone and be alone." She grabbed a tissue from the box beside her and blotted at her eyes.

"You're not alone," he said, reaching for her hand which she moved away.

She looked up at him with red puffy eyes. "No. At this particular moment in time I am not alone. But in two minutes when you leave here to meet up with your parents and your daughter I'll be alone, and the night after that and the night after that and the night after that." She started to cry and Lewis's entire body ached to hold her.

"Come home with me," he offered. "Come be there when Jessie sees her new room for the first time." *Let me take care of you.* "It'll cheer you up."

"Jessie's *your* daughter," she said. "I don't belong there."

"Of course you do." He slid closer intending to put his arm around her and tell her how important she was to both him and Jessie.

But she pushed him away. "Don't," she snapped. "Don't think you can come in here pretending to care about me," she yelled. "You don't get to turn it on and turn it off when it suits you. It's over," she screamed.

"This can't happen again." She threw his callous words back in his face.

"I didn't mean—"

"Yes you did," she sobbed. "I can't handle this right now. I need you to leave."

"But I want—"

"Don't you get it?" she yelled. "I'm done caring about what you want. You used me—"

"I did not."

She glared at him. "You hurt me, and having you here is making me feel worse, not better. Now get out," she screamed wildly, throwing off the afghan and stomping to the door which she yanked open. "Get. Out." Tears streamed down her cheeks.

Lewis stood. "Let me make you a cup of tea." To calm her down so they could talk, so he could fix things between them.

"I don't want tea," she screamed. "And I don't want you, in my apartment or anywhere near me."

Her words slammed into his diaphragm, inhibiting his ability to draw in the air necessary to make speech possible.

"Please go," she said, leaning her back against the door, looking exhausted and completely defeated. "You shouldn't have come."

Lewis didn't agree, but rather than upset her further, he left.

CHAPTER TEN

About half past six the following Monday evening Scarlet sat in her office reviewing Joey's chart, especially Deb's notes regarding discharge readiness. Joey thrived under Michelle's constant attention and was scheduled to go home tomorrow. In the past week Scarlet had managed to put aside her sorrow enough to be happy for Joey, and for Michelle and Peter. They'd fallen in love with Joey as quickly as Scarlet had, and she felt at peace with Joey going home with her family where she belonged.

Michelle promised to send pictures, which Scarlet would proudly hang up on the wall with all the other NICU graduates.

One of the unit secretaries came to her door. "I know you said you didn't want to be bothered unless it was an emergency, but there's a girl on the phone for you. She says her name is Jessie and she sounds upset."

"Put her through," Scarlet said and disengaged her Do Not Disturb button so she could answer the call. Come on. Come on. Had something happened to Jess? To Lewis? She tapped her pen on her desk blotter while she waited.

As soon as the phone rang Scarlet snatched up the receiver. "Hey, Jess. What's wrong?"

"I got it," Jess said.

"You got what?"

"*It*," she said with emphasis. "I need stuff."

"What language are you speaking, because I'm not following."

"The cramping crimson curse."

For the first time in days Scarlet smiled. "So if I'm deciphering this correctly, you got your period and are in need of some feminine supplies. Welcome to womanhood."

"Please don't talk like that. It makes me want to vomit."

Scarlet's smile grew. "Where are you?"

"In the bathroom."

"Where's your dad?"

"Outside of the bathroom yelling that dinner will be ready in fifteen minutes. How soon can you get here?"

The last place Scarlet wanted to go was to Lewis's condo, to be reminded of what they'd shared. "You know you can talk to your dad," she said. "I'm sure he'd—"

"Do not go there," Jessie interrupted. "You told me if I ever needed you, and I need you."

Truth be told, the place she wanted to go even less than Lewis's condo was back to her apartment and the empty bedroom with pink walls and butterfly decals that'd been waiting for Joey—which is why she'd been putting off leaving the hospital tonight. Jessie needing her gave Scarlet an excuse to put it off for a little while longer. "I'll swing by the drugstore, and assuming I can catch a cab, I'll be there in twenty minutes."

"Thank you," Jessie said and disconnected the call.

Half an hour later Scarlet exited the elevator on Lewis's floor and tried to ignore the memory of them walking down this very corridor, hand in hand, so happy.

She reached his door and knocked.

Expecting Jessie to answer, she felt as shocked as Lewis looked when he opened the door.

"What are you doing here?" he asked softly.

"I'm sorry to bother you," she said, holding up the drugstore bag. "Jessie called me."

"Scarlet," he said, his voice filled with emotion. "You could never bother me. You're welcome here anytime."

Yet he didn't open the door enough to allow entry. "May I come in?"

"Yes. Of course." He moved to the side and opened the door wider. "Please. Come in."

Jessie stood in the living room.

"I got what you—"

"I lied," Jessie said. "I didn't...you know." She walked over to Scarlet and took the bag from her hand. "But when I do, now I'll be ready."

"Why?" Scarlet asked.

Jessie moved to close the door to the hallway then she positioned herself in front of it as if trying to block Scarlet's exit. "Because you two need to talk."

"Jessie," Lewis cautioned.

"I know. It was wrong, and I'm sorry." She glanced back and forth between them before stopping on Scarlet. "Dad told me you both spent a lot of time together working on my room."

Among other things. Hopefully the warmth on her face did not present itself as the bright red blush she feared.

"He really likes you as in more than a friend likes you," Jessie said.

"That was supposed to be a private father daughter conversation," Lewis interjected.

He'd told Jessie he really liked her?

Undeterred by Lewis's scowl Jessie continued, "He wanted to know how I'd feel if he asked you out on a date."

"That's enough," Lewis said.

No it wasn't, not until Scarlet heard her answer. "What did you tell him?"

Jessie rested her back against the door and clasped her fingers together over her belly. "Before my mom died, we spent a lot of time talking. She said she had to cram years of motherly wisdom and advice into a few short weeks so I'd better be prepared to listen." Jessie's lips curved into a small smile at the memory. "I am totally covered on *it*," she locked eyes with Scarlet, "dating and safe sex. So neither of you need to worry."

Yeah right.

"She also told me that she'd always be my mom and no one could replace her in my heart. But that didn't mean I shouldn't make room in my heart for another mom someday, because there was plenty of room in there, and she didn't mind sharing."

Tears welled in Scarlet's eyes. "I think I would have liked your mom."

"I *know* she would have liked you," Jessie said with tears in her eyes, too.

"We talked about this, honey," Lewis said to Jess. "Scarlet and I dating does not mean we're going to get married."

Of course it didn't, because to men like Lewis, dating equaled sex and marriage didn't fit into the equation.

"I know that," Jessie said, wiping at the corner of her eye. "Mom dated lots of guys. To be honest," she looked up at Lewis, "I kind of wondered if you even liked women anymore since you haven't gone on a date for the whole nine months I've been living here."

Scarlet had to laugh at the horrified expression on Lewis's face.

Jessie turned back to Scarlet. "He admitted he did something stupid and hurt your feelings. He's not sure if he asks you out if you'd even say yes. He says he's waiting for the right moment, but waiting is making him cranky. So would you go out with him?"

"Don't answer that," Lewis said to Scarlet. Then he turned to Jessie, "That's a conversation Scarlet and I will have in private."

"I guess that's my cue to leave. But before I go, just so we're clear," Jessie said. "Not to put pressure on the two of you or anything, but having Scarlet as my next mom would be totally awesome." She walked over to give Scarlet a hug. "If I had a say," she whispered. "You'd be my choice."

"I love you, Jess," Scarlet said, squeezing her tight. "No matter what happens between me and your dad, that will never change."

"I'm glad," Jess said. "Now," she stepped out of Scarlet's embrace. "I am going to disappear into my very own bedroom—which I love, love, love, by the way, and thank you thank you thank you for my purple wall—to let you adults talk." She walked toward her bedroom.

When she was out of sight Lewis said, "I screwed up."

Jessie called out, "He screws up a lot. But—"

"I don't need any more help," Lewis yelled to her.

"Shutting up now," Jessie called back, her words followed by the slam of her door.

"I think that's her favorite part of having a door," Lewis said.

Scarlet smiled.

After an awkward pause they both said, "I'm sorry," at the exact same time.

"You have nothing to be sorry about," Lewis quickly added.

"I was awful to you last Monday. I dumped the brunt of my anger on you and you didn't deserve it." Doing so had made her feel even worse after he'd left. And she'd spent a good part of her week trying to figure out how to apologize.

He looked at her with such concern, such caring. "You had every right to be upset. After what I did, seeing my face made you feel worse. I understand."

"But I appreciate the gesture. I really do." It'd just taken a few days.

"Come sit down." He put his hand at her low back to guide her to his black leather sofa, and Scarlet's body came alive on contact, like it always did when he touched her. She sat and he sat beside her, taking her hand in his and resting both on his thigh. "I want to tell you what I should have said Sunday morning."

"It's okay. It's over. I'd prefer to move on and not revisit it." Since she'd finally come to terms with the fact there couldn't be more than friendship between them.

"You scare me," he said.

She looked up at him. "How nice of you to share." Since she was still a little shaky on the emotional stability front, she directed the conversation to a more neutral topic, "So did Jessie have fun in Lake George?"

Apparently Lewis would not be sidetracked. "You make me feel things and want things I've never felt or wanted before, things that before meeting you I was convinced I'd never feel or want."

Could he be any vaguer? "What kind of things?" she asked.

He stared into her eyes. "Long term things."

Scarlet wasn't sure how she felt about that.

"But I'd grown to care for you so much, so deeply in such a short amount of time. I didn't believe it was real. How could it be? We've only known each other for a few weeks. It's not normal to think about spending the rest of your life with someone after only a few weeks. Heck, for someone like me it's unprecedented."

He brought her hand to his lips and kissed it.

"Yet there I was," he continued. "Lying in bed with you, picturing a long happy life of waking up with you by my side. But the longer I lay there, the more it seemed too good to be true, the more I convinced myself it had to be the circumstances that'd brought us together. I was grateful, and dare I admit maybe a little dependent on you for your help with Jessie. And it'd been so long since I'd been intimate with a woman."

"I'm not sure I like where this is headed," Scarlet admitted.

"My thoughts were all jumbled. Then you woke up and startled me and I have no idea why 'It's over. This can't happen again,' were the first words to fly out of my mouth but they did. Once they were out I couldn't take them back because I wasn't ready to commit to what asking you to stay would have meant."

"Then I got mad and stormed off."

"You had every right to. If I were you I'd have hit me."

Scarlet smiled. "I'll remember that for next time."

"There won't be a next time." He brought her hand

up and pressed it to his heart. "What I should have told you when you woke up in my arms last Sunday morning is I see how smart and special you are. I appreciate all of your wonderful, caring qualities and I value you and your friendship more than any other woman out there."

The fact that he'd remembered her speech to sooth a broken-hearted Jessie almost word for word touched Scarlet.

"You're important to me," he said. "I want to find a way to make us work, I want us to be together, but I need time," he said. "I should have told you all that, but I didn't. So now I'm asking for another chance. If we can take it slow, I promise to do my best to piss you off as little as possible, as long as you're willing to cut me some slack here and there. I'm entering into new territory here."

"New territory?"

"Exclusivity, a committed relationship, with you."

Scarlet sat there, unsure what to say in response to his sincere words.

Lewis picked up on her uncertainty. "Unless that's not what you want…" He released her hand.

"I care about you, I really do." But she'd spent a lot of time thinking about her future lately, and she'd decided not to give up on her desire to have a baby either naturally or via adoption or IVF. "I don't think we're looking for the same things in a relationship. If I'm going to date a man exclusively, at this stage in my life, it'll be with the intention of getting married and having babies and a house with a yard where I can plant flowers. I want a big family filled with love." It's what she'd dreamed of for so long and time was running out. "If those things aren't part of your plans for the future," and she was pretty sure they weren't, "I think we're better off as friends."

"For you, I'm open to anything. Everything," Lewis said. "You're the only woman I'd consider for my bride. But how about we date for a while to make sure it's the right choice for both of us. If we decide it is, you want babies, I'll give you babies. You want a house with a yard, we'll find one. You want a big family, for you I'll accept mom's standing invitation for weekly Sunday dinner."

For the first time since losing Joey, Scarlet felt a return of hope for a happy future. "I'd like that."

"Regardless of what happens, as of today you and Jessie and I are family. When you're alone in your apartment, you'll never be completely alone because we're only a phone call away. You need company, you come here, it's getting late, you sleepover."

"I don't think that's a good idea." Not with Jessie around.

"In the loft," he said. "After you help me pick out a big comfortable futon to put up there."

So sweet. "Thank you."

He leaned in and whispered, "But after Jessie goes to bed we can…" he wiggled his eyebrows.

"I'd like that, too," she whispered back.

"So where do you want to go on our first official date as a couple?" he asked. "To seal the deal, so to speak."

Scarlet thought for a moment. "How about we take Jessie to see her first Broadway play?"

He sat back and looked at her. "You want to include Jessie on our date?"

"Of course I do," she said. "We're a family." She loved the way that sounded, the way it felt. To be part of a family. Her family. She smiled and moved in close. "But afterwards I want you all to myself."

Lewis pulled her onto his lap. "And you can have me all night long." He kissed her.

Jessie picked that moment to call out. "Are you guys almost done? Can I come out now?"

Scarlet jumped to her own spot on the couch and dried her lips on her wrist. Lewis adjusted his pants and crossed one leg over the other. "Yes," they both answered together.

"Good," Jessie said, coming back into the living room. "Because I just remembered I have a question." She walked over to the coat closet, opened the door, and pointed at the coats piled on the sleeping bag on the floor topped off by the broken metal rod. "What the heck happened in there?"

Lewis leaned in, put his hand up to shield his mouth from Jessie, and whispered, "Dating with a teenager in residence is not going to be easy."

To which Scarlet whispered back, "When something's important you find a way to make it work. And you, Lewis Jackson, are very important, to me, too."

* * * * *

LET'S TALK
Romance

For exclusive extracts, competitions
and special offers, find us online:

f facebook.com/millsandboon

⊙ @millsandboonuk

𝕏 @millsandboon

Or get in touch on 0844 844 1351*

For all the latest titles coming soon, visit
millsandboon.co.uk/nextmonth